MELODY

MELODY

V.C. Andrews®

G.K. Hall & Co.
Thorndike, Maine

This Large Print edition is published by G.K. Hall & Co., USA
and by Chivers Press, England.

Published in 1996 in the U.S. by arrangement with
Pocket Books, an imprint of Simon & Schuster, Inc.

Published in 1997 in the U.K. by arrangement with
Simon & Schuster Ltd.

| U.S. Hardcover | 0-7838-1906-4 | (Core Collection Edition) |
| U.K. Hardcover | 0-7451-5404-2 | (Windsor Large Print) |

Following the death of Virginia Andrews, the Andrews family
worked with a carefully selected writer to organize and complete
Virginia Andrews' stories and to create additional novels, of which
this is one, inspired by her storytelling genius.

This book is a work of fiction. Names, characters, places and
incidents are products of the author's imagination or are used
fictitiously. Any resemblance to actual events or locales or
persons, living or dead, is entirely coincidental.

The text of this Large Print edition is unabridged.
Other aspects of the book may vary from the original edition.

Set in 16 pt. Bookman Old Style by Rick Gundberg.

Printed in the United States on permanent paper.

British Library Cataloguing in Publication Data available

Library of Congress Cataloging in Publication Data

Andrews, V.C. (Virginia C.)
    Melody / V.C. Andrews.
      p.   cm.
    ISBN 0-7838-1906-4 (lg. print : hc)
    1. Large type books. I. Title.
[PS3551.N454M45 1996]
813'.54—dc20   96-27669

MELODY

PROLOGUE

I think as soon as I was old enough to understand that Mommy and Daddy were having serious arguments, I felt like an outsider, for if I appeared while they were having one, both of them would stop immediately. It made me feel as if I lived in a house with secrets woven into the walls.

One day, I imagined, I would unravel one of those secrets and the whole house would come down around me.

Just a thought.

But that is exactly what happened.

One day.

1

The Love Trap

When I was a little girl, I believed that people could get what they wished for if they wished hard enough and long enough and were good enough, and although I'm fifteen now and long ago stopped believing in things like the Tooth Fairy, Santa Claus, and the Easter Bunny, I never completely stopped believing there was something magical in the world around us. Somewhere, there were angels watching over us, considering our wishes and dreams and occasionally, when the time was right and we were deserving, they granted us a wish.

Daddy taught me this. When I was still small enough to sit comfortably on his muscular right forearm and be carried around like a little princess, he would tell me to close my eyes really tight and wish until I saw my angel nearby, her wings fluttering like a bumble bee.

Daddy said everyone had an angel assigned to him or her at birth, and the angels did all they could to get humans to believe. He told me that when we are very little it's much easier to believe in things that grown-ups would call imagination. That's why, when we're little, angels will appear before us sometimes. I think some of us hold on a little longer or a little harder to that world of make believe. Some of us are not afraid to admit we dream even though we're older. We really do make a wish when we break a chicken bone or blow out our birthday candles or see a shooting star, and we wait and hope, even expect that it will come true.

I did so much wishing as I grew up, I was sure my angel was overworked. I couldn't help it. I always wished my daddy didn't have to go down into the coal mines miles under the earth, away from the sun in damp, dark caverns of dust. Just like every other coal miner's child, I had played in the openings of the deserted old mines, and I couldn't begin to understand what it would be like going down deep and spending a whole day below the fresh air. But poor Daddy had to do it.

As long as I could remember, I wished we lived in a real house instead of a trailer, even though right next to us, living in their trailer, were Papa George and Mama Arlene, both of whom I loved dearly. When I wished for a house, I just added a little more and wished they would live in the house next to ours.

We would both have real backyards and lawns and there would be big maple and oak trees. Papa George would help me with my fiddling. And when it rained hard, I wouldn't feel as if I were living in a tin drum. When the wind blew, I wouldn't fear being turned over and over while asleep in my bed.

My wish list went on and on. I imagined that if I ever took the time and wrote all the wishes down, the paper would stretch from one end of our trailer to the other.

I wished hard that Mommy wasn't so un-happy all the time. She complained about having to work in Francine's Salon, washing other women's hair and doing perms, even though everyone said she was an excellent hairdresser. She did enjoy the gossip and loved to listen to the wealthy women talk about their trips and the things they had bought. But she was like a little girl who could only look in the window at beautiful things, one who never got to buy any of them herself.

Even when she was sad, Mommy was beautiful. One of my most frequent wishes was that I would be as pretty as she was when I grew up. When I was younger, I would perch in her bedroom and watch her at her dressing table meticulously applying her makeup and brushing her hair. As she did so, she preached about the importance of beauty care and told me about all the women she knew who were attractive but neglected themselves and looked simply awful. She told me if you were born pretty, you had an obligation to look pretty whenever you were in public.

"That's why I spend so much time on my hair and my nails, and that's why I have to spend so much money on these special skin creams," she explained. She was always bringing home samples of shampoo and hair conditioners for me to use as well.

She brought home perfumed bath oils and would soak in our small tub for over an hour. I would wash her back or, when I was old enough to be trusted, polish her toenails while she manicured her fingernails. Occasionally, she did my toenails and styled my hair.

People said we looked more like sisters than mother and daughter. I had inherited her small facial features, especially her button nose, but my hair was a lighter shade of brown, hair the color of hay. Once, I asked her to dye my hair the same shade as hers, but she shook her head and told me to leave it be, that it was a pretty color. But I wasn't as confident about my looks as she was about hers, even though Daddy told me he rushed home from work because now he had two beautiful women at home waiting for him.

My daddy stood six foot three and weighed

nearly one hundred and ninety pounds, all muscle from working in the mines so many years. Although there were times when he returned home after a very long day in the mines aching, and moving slowly, he didn't complain. When he set eyes on me, his face always burst out with happiness. No matter how tired those strong arms of his were, I could run into them and he'd lift me with ease into the air.

When I was little, I would anxiously wait for the sight of him lumbering up the chipped and cracked macadam that led from the mines to our home in Mineral Acres trailer park. Suddenly, his six feet three inches of height would lift that shock of light brown hair over the ridge and I would see him taking strides with those long legs. His face and hands would be streaked with coal dust. He looked like a soldier home from battle. Under his right arm, clutched like a football, was his lunch basket. He made his own sandwiches early in the morning because Mommy was always still asleep when he woke and got ready for work.

Sometimes, even before he reached the Mineral Acres gate after work, Daddy would lift his head and see me waving. Our trailer was close to the entrance and our front yard faced the road from Sewell. If he saw me, Daddy would speed up, swinging his coal miner's helmet like a flag. Until I was about twelve, I had to wait close to Papa George and Mama Arlene's trailer, because Mommy was usually not home from work yet herself. Many times, she would go someplace and not make it home in time for dinner. Usually, she went to Frankie's Bar and Grill with her co-workers and friends and listened to the juke box music. But Daddy was a very good cook and I got so I could do a lot of the cooking myself, too. He and I ended up eating alone more times than not.

Daddy didn't complain about Mommy's not being there. If I did, he urged me to be more understanding. "Your mother and I got married too young, Melody," he told me.

"But weren't you terribly in love, Daddy?" I had read *Romeo and Juliet* and knew that if you were desperately in love, age didn't make a difference.

I told my best friend Alice Morgan that I would never marry anyone until I was so head-over-heels in love I couldn't breathe. She thought that was an exaggeration and I would probably fall in love many times before I was married.

Daddy's voice was wistful. "We were, but we didn't listen to older, wiser heads. We just ran off and eloped without thinking about the consequences. We were both very excited about it and didn't think hard about the future. It was easier for me. I was always more settled, but your mother soon felt she had missed out on things. She works in that beauty parlor and hears the rich ladies talking about their trips and their homes and she gets frustrated. We got to let her have some freedom so she doesn't feel trapped by all our love for her."

"How can love trap someone, Daddy?" I asked.

He smiled his wide, soft smile. When he did that, his green eyes always got a hazy, faraway glint. He'd lift his gaze from my face to a window or sometimes just a wall as if he were seeing images from the mysterious past float by. "Well . . . if you love someone as much as we love Mommy, you want her around you all the time. It's like having a beautiful bird in a cage. You're afraid to let the bird free and yet you know, it would sing a sweeter song if it were."

"Why doesn't she love us that much, too?" I demanded.

"She does, in her own way." He smiled. "Your mother's the prettiest woman in this town — for miles and miles around it too — and I know she feels wasted sometimes. That's a hard thing to live with, Melody. People are always coming up to her and telling her she should be in the movies or on television or a model. She thinks time's flying by and soon it will be too late for her to be anything else but my wife and your mother."

"I don't want her to be anything else, Daddy."

"I know. She's enough for us. We're grateful, but she's always been restless and impulsive. She still has big dreams and one thing you never want to do to someone you love is kill her dreams.

"Of course," he continued, smiling, "I have every reason to believe you're going to be the celebrity in this family. Look how well Papa George has taught you to play the fiddle! And you can sing, too. You're growing into a beautiful young woman. Some talent scout's going to snap you up."

"Oh Daddy, that's silly. No talent scouts come to the mining towns looking for stars."

"So you'll go to college in New York City or in California," he predicted. "That's my dream. So don't go dumping dirt on top of it, Melody."

I laughed. I was too afraid to have such dreams for myself yet; I was too afraid of being frustrated and trapped like Mommy thought she now was.

I wondered why Daddy didn't feel trapped. No matter how hard things were, he would grin and bear it, and he never joined the other miners to drown his sorrows at the bar. He walked to and from work alone because the other miners lived in the shanties in town.

We lived in Sewell, which was a village

16

born from the mine and built by the mining company in the lap of a small valley. Its main street had a church, a post office, a half dozen stores, two restaurants, a mortuary, and a movie theater open only on the weekends. The shanty homes were all the same pale brown color, built with board-and-batten siding and tar-paper roofs, but at least there were children my age there.

There were no other children near my age living in Mineral Acres trailer park. How I wished I had a brother or a sister to keep me company! When I told Mommy about that wish once, she grimaced and moaned that she was only a child herself when she had me.

"Barely nineteen! And it's not easy to bring children into the world. It's hard on your body and you have to worry about them getting sick and having enough to eat and having proper clothing, not to mention getting them an education. I rushed into motherhood. I should have waited."

"Then I would never have been born!" I complained.

"Of course you would have been born, but you would have been born when things were better and not so hard for us. We were right in the middle of a major change in our lives. It was very difficult."

Sometimes, she sounded as if she blamed me just for being born. It was as if she thought babies just floated around waiting to be conceived, and occasionally they got impatient and encouraged their parents to create them. That's what I had done.

I knew we had moved from Provincetown, Cape Cod, to Sewell in Monongalia County, West Virginia, before I was born, and we didn't have much at the time. Mommy did tell me that when they first arrived in Sewell as poor as they were, she was determined not to live in a shanty, so she and Daddy rented a mobile home in Mineral Acres, even though it was mostly populated by retired people like Papa George.

Papa George wasn't really my grandfather and Mama Arlene wasn't my real grand-mother, but they were still like grandparents to me. Mama Arlene had often looked after me when I was a little girl. Papa George had been a coal miner and had retired on dis-ability. He was suffering from black lung, which Daddy said was aggravated by his refusal to give up smoking. His illness made him look much older than his sixty-two years. His shoulders slumped, the lines in his pale, tired face were cut deep, and he was so thin Mama Arlene claimed she could weigh him down with a cable-knit sweater. Still, Papa George and I had the greatest of times when he helped teach me the fiddle.

He complained that it was Mama Arlene's nagging that wore him down. They always seemed to be bickering, but I didn't know any other two people as dedicated to each other as they were. Their arguments were never really mean either. They always ended up laughing.

Daddy loved talking with Papa George. On weekends especially, the two could often be found sitting in the rocking chairs on the cement patio under the metal awning, quietly discussing politics and the mining industry. Papa George was in Sewell during the violent times when the mining unions were being formed and he had lots of stories, which, according to Mama Arlene, were not fit for my ears.

"Why not?" he would protest. "She oughta know the truth about this place and the people who run it."

"She got plenty of time to learn about the ugly things in this world, George O'Neil, without you rushing her into it. Hush up!"

He did, mumbling under his breath until she turned her fiery blue eyes on him, making him swallow the rest of his angry words.

But Daddy agreed with Papa George: the miners were being exploited. This was no life for anyone.

I never understood why Daddy, who was brought up on Cape Cod in a fisherman's family, ended up working in a place where he was shut away from the sun and the sky all day. I knew he missed the ocean, yet we never returned to the Cape and we had nothing to do with Daddy's family. I didn't even know how many cousins I had, or their names, and I had never met or spoken to my grandparents. All I had ever seen was a faded black and white photograph of them with Daddy's father seated and his mother standing beside his father, both looking un-happy about being photographed. His father had a beard and looked as big as Daddy is now. His mother was wispy looking, but with hard, cold eyes.

The family in Provincetown was something Daddy didn't discuss. He would always change the subject, just saying, "We just had differences. It's better we're apart. It's easier this way."

I couldn't imagine why it was easier, but I saw it was painful for him to talk about it. Mommy never wanted to talk about it either. Just bringing up the family caused her to start crying and complaining to me that Daddy's family always thought little of her because she'd been an orphan. She told me she had been adopted by people who she said were too old to raise a child. They were both in their sixties when she was a teenager and they were very strict. She said she couldn't wait to get away from them.

I wanted to know more about them and about Daddy's family, too, but I was afraid it would start an argument between her and

Daddy, so after a while, I just stopped asking questions. But that didn't stop their arguments.

One night soon after I had gone to bed, I heard their voices rising against each other. They were in their bedroom, too. The trailer home had a small kitchen to the right of the main entrance, a little dinette and a living room. Down a narrow hallway was the bathroom. My bedroom was the first on the right and Daddy and Mommy's was at the end of the trailer.

"Don't tell me I'm imagining things," Daddy warned, his voice cross. "The people dropping hints ain't liars, Haille," he said. I sat up in bed and listened. It wasn't hard to hear normal conversation through those paper-thin trailer walls as it was, but with them yelling at each other, it was as if I were right in the room with them.

"They're not liars. They're busybodies with nothing else to do with their boring, worthless lives than manufacture tales about other people."

"If you don't give them the chance . . ."

"What am I supposed to do, Chester? The man's the bartender at Frankie's. He talks to everyone, not just me," she whined.

I knew they were arguing about Archie Marlin. I never mentioned it to Daddy, but twice that I knew of, Archie drove Mommy home. Archie had short orange-red hair and

21

skin the shade of milkweed with freckles on his chin and forehead. Everyone said he looked ten years younger than he really was, although no one knew his exact age. No one knew very much about Archie Marlin. He never gave anyone a straight answer to questions about himself. He joked or shrugged and said something silly. Supposedly, he had been brought up in Michigan or Ohio, and had spent six months in jail for forging checks. I never understood why Mommy liked him. She said he was full of good stories and had been to lots of exciting places, like Las Vegas.

She said it again now during the argument in the bedroom.

"At least he's been places. I can learn about them from him," she asserted.

"It's just talk. He hasn't been anywhere," Daddy charged.

"How would you know it's just talk, Chester? You're the one who hasn't been anywhere but the Cape and this trap called Sewell. And you brought me to it!"

"You brought yourself, Haille," he retorted, and suddenly she stopped arguing and started crying. Moments later, he was comforting her so softly I couldn't hear what he was saying and then they grew quiet.

I didn't understand what it all meant. How did Mommy bring herself here? Why would she bring herself to a place she didn't like?

I lay awake, thinking. There were always those deep silences between Mommy and Daddy, gaps they were both afraid to fill. Then the arguments would pass, just as this one did, and it would be as if nothing ever happened, nothing was ever said. It was as if they declared a truce over and over because both knew if they didn't, something terrible might happen, something terrible might be said.

Nothing was as mysterious to me as love between a man and a woman. I had crushes on boys at school and was now sort of seeing Bobby Lockwood more than any other boy. Since my best friend Alice was the smartest girl in school, I thought she might know something about love, even though she had never had a boyfriend. She was nice, but unpopular because she was about twenty-five pounds overweight and her mother made her keep her hair in pigtails. She wasn't allowed to wear any makeup, not even lipstick. Alice read more than anyone I knew, so I thought that maybe she had come across some book that explained love.

She thought a moment after I asked her. She replied it was something scientific. "That's the only way to explain it," she claimed in her usual pedantic manner.

"Don't you think it's something magical?" I asked her. On Wednesday afternoons she would come to our trailer after school and study with me for the weekly Thursday geometry test. It was more for my benefit than hers, for she ended up tutoring me.

"I don't believe in magic," she said dryly. She was not very good at pretending. I was actually her only real friend, maybe partly because she was too brutally honest with her opinions when it came to the other girls at school.

"Well then why is it," I demanded, "that a man will look at one woman specially and a woman will do the same, look at one man specially? Something's got to happen between them, doesn't it?" I insisted.

Alice pressed down on her thick lower lip. Her big, brown round eyes moved from side to side as if she were reading words printed in the air. She had a habit of chewing on the inside of her left cheek, too, when she was deep in thought. The girls in school would giggle and say, "Alice is eating herself again."

"Well," she said after a long pause, "we know we're all made of protoplasm."

"Ugh."

"And chemical things happen between cells," she continued, nodding.

"Stop it."

"So maybe a certain man's protoplasm has a chemical reaction to a certain woman's protoplasm. Something magnetic. It's just positive and negative atoms reacting, but people make it seem like more," she concluded.

"It *is* more," I insisted. "It has to be! Don't your parents think it's more?"

Alice shrugged. "They never forget each other's birthdays or their anniversary," she said, making it sound as if that was all there was to being in love and married.

Alice's father, William, was Sewell's dentist. Her mother was his receptionist, so they did spend a great deal of time together. But whenever I went to have my teeth checked, I noticed she called her husband Doctor Morgan, as if she weren't his wife, but merely his employee.

Alice had two brothers, both older. Her brother Neal had already graduated and gone off to college and her brother Tommy was a senior and sure to be the class valedictorian.

"Do they ever have arguments?" I asked her. "Bad arguments?" I wondered if it was just something my mommy and daddy did.

"Not terribly bad and very rarely in front of anyone," she said. "Usually, it's about politics."

"Politics?" I couldn't imagine Mommy caring about politics. She always walked away when Daddy and Papa George got into one of their discussions.

"Yes."

"I hope when I get married," I said, "I never

have an argument with my husband."

"That's an unrealistic hope. People who live together must have some conflicts. It's natural."

"But if they do, and they're in love, they always make up and feel terrible about hurting each other."

"I suppose," Alice relented. "But that might be just to keep the peace. Once, my parents didn't talk to each other for nearly a week. I think it was when they argued about the last presidential election."

"A week!" I thought for a moment. Even though Mommy and Daddy had their arguments, they always spoke to each other soon afterward and acted as if nothing had happened. "Didn't they kiss each other good night?"

"I don't know. I don't think they do that."

"They don't ever kiss good night?"

Alice shrugged. "Maybe. Of course, they kissed and they must have had sex because my brothers and I were born," she said matter-of-factly.

"Well that means they are in love."

"Why?" Alice asked, her brown eyes narrowing into skeptical slits.

I told her why. "You can't have sex without being in love."

"Sex doesn't have anything to do with love per se," she lectured. "Sexual reproduction is a natural process performed by all living things. It's built into the species."

"Ugh."

"Stop saying *ugh* after everything I say. You sound like Thelma Cross," she said and then she smiled. "Ask her about sex."

"Why?"

"I was in the bathroom yesterday and over-heard her talking to Paula Temple about —"

"What?"

"You know."

I widened my eyes.

"Who was she with?"

"Tommy Getz. I can't repeat the things she said," Alice added, blushing.

"Sometimes I wonder," I said sitting back on my pillow, "if you and I aren't the only virgins left in our class."

"So? I'm not ashamed of it if it's true."

"I'm not ashamed. I'm just . . ."

"What?"

"Curious."

"And curiosity killed the cat," Alice warned. She narrowed her round eyes. "How far have you gone with Bobby Lockwood?"

"Not far," I said. She was suddenly staring at me so hard I had to look away.

"Remember Beverly Marks," she warned.

Beverly Marks was infamous, the girl in our eighth-grade class who had gotten pregnant and was sent away. To this day no one knew where she went.

"Don't worry about me," I said. "I will not

have sex with anyone I don't love."

Alice shrugged skeptically. She was annoying me. I sometimes wondered why I stayed friends with her.

"Let's get back to work." She opened the textbook and ran her forefinger down the page. "Okay, the main part of tomorrow's test will probably be —"

Suddenly, we both looked up and listened. Car doors were being slammed and someone was crying hard and loudly.

"What's that?" I went to the window in my bedroom. It looked out to the entrance of Mineral Acres. A few of Mommy's co-workers got out of Lois Norton's car. Lois was the manager of the beauty parlor. The rear door was opened and Lois helped Mommy out. Mommy was crying uncontrollably and being supported by two other women as they helped her toward the front door of our trailer. Another car pulled up behind Lois Norton's with two other women in it.

Mommy suddenly let out a piercing scream. My heart raced. I felt my legs turn to stone; my feet seemed nailed to the floor. Mama Arlene and Papa George came out of their trailer to see what was happening. I recognized Martha Supple talking to them. Papa George and Mama Arlene suddenly embraced each other tightly, Mama Arlene's hand going to her mouth. Then Mama Arlene rushed toward Mommy, who was now nearly up to our steps. Tears streamed down my cheeks, mostly from fear.

Alice stood like stone herself, anticipating. "What happened?" she whispered.

I shook my head. I somehow managed to walk out of my room just as the front door opened.

Mommy took a deep breath when she saw me. "Oh Melody," she cried.

"Mommy!" I started to cry. "What's the matter?" I asked through my sobs.

"There's been a terrible accident. Daddy and two other miners . . . are dead."

A long sigh escaped from Mommy's choked throat. She swayed and would have fallen if Mama Arlene hadn't been holding on to her. However, her eyes went bleak, dark, haunted. Despair had drained her face of its radiance.

I shook my head. It couldn't be true. Yet there was Mommy clutching Mama Arlene, her friends beside and around her, all with horribly tragic faces.

"Nooo!" I screamed and plowed through everyone, down the stairs, outside and away, with my hands over my ears. I was running, unaware of which direction I had taken or that I had left the house without a coat and it was in the middle of one of our coldest Februaries.

I had run all the way to the Monongalia River bend before Alice caught up with me.

I was standing there on the hill, embracing myself, gasping and crying at the same time, just gazing dumbly at the beach and the hickory and white oak trees on the other side of the river. A white-tailed deer appeared and gazed curiously at the sound of my sobs.

I shook my head until I felt it might snap off my neck, but I somehow already knew all the *No*'s in the world wouldn't change things. I felt the world horribly altered. I cried until my insides ached. I heard Alice calling and turned to see her gasping for breath as she chugged her way up the hill to where I was standing. She tried to hug and comfort me. I pulled away.

"They're lying," I screamed hysterically. "They're lying. Tell me they're lying."

Alice shook her head. "They said the walls caved in and by the time they got to your father and the others —"

"Daddy," I moaned. "Poor Daddy."

Alice bit her lower lip and waited for me to stop sobbing. "Aren't you cold?" she asked.

"What difference does it make?" I snapped angrily. "What difference does anything make?"

She nodded. Her eyes were red, too, and she shivered, more from her sadness than the wintry day.

"Let's go back," I said, speaking with the voice of the dead myself.

She walked beside me silently. I don't know how I got my legs to take those steps, but we returned to the trailer park. The women who had brought Mommy home were gone. Alice followed me into the trailer.

Mommy was on the sofa with a wet wash-cloth on her forehead, and Mama Arlene beside her. Mommy reached up to take my hand and I fell to the floor beside the sofa, my head on her stomach. I thought I was going to heave up everything I had eaten that day. A few moments later, when I looked up, Mommy was asleep. Somewhere deep inside herself she was still crying, I thought, crying and screaming.

"Let me make you a cup of tea," Mama Arlene said quietly. "Your nose is beet red."

I didn't reply. I just sat there on the floor beside the sofa, still holding on to Mommy's hand. Alice stood by the doorway awk-wardly.

"I'd better go home," she said, "and tell my parents."

I think I nodded, but I wasn't sure. Everything around me seemed distant. Alice got her books and paused at the doorway.

"I'll come back later," she said. "Okay?"

After she left, I lowered my head and cried softly until I heard Mama Arlene call to me and then touch my arm.

"Come sit with me, child. Let your mother sleep."

I rose and joined her at the table. She poured two cups of tea and sat. "Go on. Drink it."

I blew on the hot water and took a sip.

"When Papa George was down in the mines, I always worried about something like this happening. There were always accidents of one sort or another. We oughta leave that coal alone, find another source of energy," she said bitterly.

"He can't really be dead, Mama Arlene. Not Daddy." I smiled at her and tilted my head. "He'll be coming home soon, won't he? It's a mistake. Soon he'll be coming over the hill, swinging his lunch basket."

"Child —"

"No, Mama Arlene. You don't understand. Daddy has an angel looking over him. His angel wouldn't let such a terrible thing happen. It's all a mistake. They'll dig out the mine and find Daddy."

"They already found him and the other poor souls, honey." She reached across the table to take my hand. "You've got to be strong for your mother, Melody. She's not a very strong person, you know. There's a lot of hardship to endure these next few days. The whole town is in mourning."

I gazed at Mommy, her eyes shut, her mouth slightly open. She's so pretty, I thought. Even now, she's so pretty. She's too young to be a widow.

I drank some more tea and then I got up and put on my coat. I went out to stand near the front entrance and gaze down the road. As I stood there, I closed my eyes and wished and wished as hard as I could that this wasn't true, that Daddy would soon call out to me.

Please, I begged my angel, I don't care if you don't grant me another wish but this one. I took a deep breath and then opened my eyes.

The road was empty. It was twilight. Long shadows crept over the macadam. The sky had turned an angry gray and tiny particles of snow began to appear. The wind picked up. I heard a door slam and turned to see Papa George emerge from their trailer. He looked over at me and then he sat in his rocker and lit his cigarette. He rocked and stared at the ground.

I gazed once more at the hill.

Daddy wasn't there.

He was gone forever.

2

A Coal Miner's Grave

It was snowing the day we buried Daddy, but I didn't feel the cold flakes on my face or the wind blowing my hair when we walked to the church or afterward, when we walked behind the hearses to the cemetery.

Daddy's and the two other miners' caskets were side by side at the front of the church, one casket really indistinguishable from another, even though I knew Daddy was the tallest of the three and the youngest. The church was filled with miners and their families, store owners and Mommy's friends and co-workers at Francine's Salon, as well as some of my school friends. Bobby Lockwood looked very uncomfortable. He didn't know whether or not to smile at me or just look sad. He shifted in his seat as if sitting on an ant hill. I gave him a tiny smile, for which he looked grateful.

I heard lots of sobbing and noses being blown. Way in the rear of the church, someone's baby cried. She cried throughout the service. It seemed fitting.

Papa George said there should have been more representatives from the mining company there and that the mine should have been shut down for a few days in honor of the dead. He and Mama Arlene walked beside Mommy and me when we followed the hearses to the cemetery. Except for the crunchy sound of everyone's footsteps on the snow and the far-off wail of a train carrying away the coal, it was terribly quiet. I actually welcomed Papa George's stream of complaints.

He said that if there hadn't been an oil embargo to put pressure on the coal miners, my daddy wouldn't have been killed.

"Company saw the dollar signs," he charged, "and pushed them miners too far. But it ain't the first time, and I'm sure it ain't gonna be the last." We passed under the granite archway to the cemetery. Angels were carved in the stone.

Mommy kept her hood over her head, her eyes down. Every once in a while she released a deep sigh and intoned, "I wish this was over. What am I going to do? Where do we go now? What am I going to say to all these people?"

Mama Arlene had her arm through Mommy's and patted her hand gently and muttered back, "There, there, be strong, Haille. Be strong."

Papa George remained close to me when we reached the grave site. His flecked brown eyes filled with tears before he lowered his head, still thick with hair and as white as the flakes that flew into our faces. The other two miners who had been with Daddy when the walls caved in were being buried on the north end of the same cemetery in Sewell. We could hear the mourners singing hymns, their voices carried by the same cold February wind that tossed the flakes over the West Virginia hills and the shanties under the gray sky.

We raised our heads when the minister finished his prayer. He hurried off to say another prayer over the other two miners. Although Mommy wore black and no makeup, she still looked pretty. Sadness simply lit a different candle in her eyes. Her rich maple-brown hair was pinned back. She had bought the plain black dress just for the funeral and wore a hooded cape. The hem of the dress reached only a few inches below her knees, but she didn't appear cold, even though the wind whipped her skirt around her legs. She was in a daze even deeper than mine. I grasped her hand much more tightly than she held mine.

I imagined that if Mama Arlene and I were to let go of Mommy's arms she would just float away in the wind, like a kite whose string had snapped. I knew how much

Mommy would rather be anywhere but here. She hated sadness. If anything happened to make her unhappy, she would pour herself a gin and tonic and play her music louder, drowning out the melancholy.

I gazed at Daddy's coffin a final time, still finding it hard to believe he was really shut up inside. Soon, any moment, the lid would pop open and Daddy would sit up laughing, telling us this was all his little joke. I almost laughed imagining it, hoping for it. But the lid remained shut tight, the snowflakes dancing over its shiny surface, some sticking and melting into tears.

The mourners filed past, some hugging Mommy and me, some just pausing to touch our hands and shake their heads. Everyone said the same thing, "Sorry for your trouble." Mommy kept her head down most of the time, so I had to greet people and thank them. When Bobby took my hand, I gave him a small hug. He looked embarrassed, mumbled something, and hurried off with his friends. I couldn't blame him, but it made me feel like a leper. I noticed that most people were awkward and distant around us, as if tragedy was something you could catch like a cold.

Afterward, we all walked back from the cemetery more quickly than we had walked to it, especially Mommy. The snow fell faster and harder, and now that the funeral was over, I felt the cold cut right through to my bones.

The other two miners' families and friends were getting together to eat and comfort each other. Mama Arlene had made a pot roast thinking we would all be there, but as we left the cemetery, Mommy told her she wasn't going. She couldn't get away from the sadness fast enough.

"I can't stand any more sad faces around me," she wailed and shook her head.

"Folks need each other at times like this," Mama Arlene explained.

Mommy just shook her head again and quickened her pace. Suddenly, Archie Marlin caught up with us in his imitation patent leather shoes and his shiny gray suit, with his glossy red hair parted in the middle.

"Be glad to drive you home, Haille," he offered.

Mommy's eyes brightened and more color returned to her face. Nothing could cheer her up as quickly as a man's attention. "Why thank you, Archie. That's very kind."

"Ain't much. I wish I could do more," he remarked, flashing me a smile.

Behind us I saw Alice widen her round eyes even more.

"Come on, honey." Mommy reached for my hand, but I stepped back.

"I'll walk home with Alice," I told her.

"That's silly, Melody. It's cold."

"I'm not cold," I said, even though my teeth wanted to chatter.

"Suit yourself," Mommy said and got into Archie's car. Two large cotton dice hung from the rearview mirror and his seats were upholstered with an imitation white wool that shed on your clothes. The wiry threads were sure to get all over Mommy's black dress, but she didn't care. Before we had left for church, she told me she expected to throw the dress in the garbage the moment she took it off anyway.

"I don't intend to spend weeks mourning and wearing black," she declared. "Sadness ages you and it doesn't bring back the dead. Besides, I can't wear this black thing to work, can I?"

"When are you going back to work, Mommy?" I asked, surprised. With Daddy's death, I thought the world would stop turning. How could our lives go on?

"Tomorrow," she said. "I don't have much choice. We don't have anyone supporting us anymore, do we? Not that it was much support anyway," she mumbled.

"Should I go right back to school?" I asked more out of anger than a desire to return.

"Of course. What are you going to do around here all day? You'll go crazy looking at these four walls."

She wasn't wrong, but somehow it didn't

39

seem right to simply go on with our lives as if Daddy hadn't died. I would never hear his laughter or see him smile again. How could the sky ever be blue or anything taste sweet or feel good? I would never again care about getting hundreds on tests or parading my newfound knowledge. Daddy was the only one who cared, who was proud of me anyway. Mommy gave me the feeling she felt education was frivolous for a girl. She believed once a girl was old enough to catch a man, nothing else mattered.

Walking home from the cemetery with Alice, I felt my heart had turned into one of those large chunks of coal Daddy used to hack out of the walls hundreds of feet below the earth: the coal that had killed him. Alice and I barely spoke while we hurried toward the trailer park. We had to keep our heads bowed because the snowflakes were streaming down from the gray sky and into our eyes.

"Are you all right?" Alice asked. I nodded. "Maybe we should have gone in Archie Marlin's car, too," she added mournfully. The wind howled. It screamed.

"I'd rather walk in a storm ten times worse than get in his car," I said vehemently.

When we entered Mineral Acres, we saw Archie Marlin's car parked at our trailer. And then, as we drew closer, we heard the sound of my mother's laughter.

Alice looked embarrassed. "Maybe I should go home."

"I wish you wouldn't," I said. "We'll go into my room and close the door."

"Okay."

When I opened the door, we found Mommy sitting at the dinette with Archie. A bottle of gin sat on the table with some mixers and ice.

"Happy now that you froze your feet walking?" Mommy asked. She had already taken off the black dress and wore a blue silk robe. Her hair was down around her shoulders. She had put on more lipstick.

"I needed the walk," I said. Archie looked at Alice and me with a grin.

"There's water on the stove if you want some tea or hot chocolate," Mommy said.

"I don't want anything right now, thank you."

"Maybe Alice wants something."

"No thanks, Mrs. Logan."

"You can tell your mother everything's clean in my house," Mommy snapped. Alice was nonplussed.

"She didn't say it wasn't, Mommy."

"No, really, Mrs. Logan, I —"

"It's okay," Mommy said with a tiny ripple of nervous laughter. Archie smiled and poured two more drinks.

"We're going to my room," I said.

"Maybe you should have gone to the wake,

Melody. I don't have anything for dinner, you know."

"I'm not hungry," I said. I marched down the short corridor to my room, Alice trailing behind. After I closed the door, I threw myself on the bed and buried my face in the pillow to smother the anger building in my chest as much as my sobs.

Alice sat on the bed, too frightened and amazed to speak. A moment later we heard Mommy turn on the radio and find a station with lively music.

"She's just doing that because she can't stand crying anymore," I explained. Alice nodded, but I saw she was uncomfortable. "She says I should go right back to school."

"Are you? You should," she added, nodding.

"It's easy for you to say. Your daddy's not dead." I regretted saying it immediately. "I'm sorry. I didn't mean that."

"It's all right."

"I know if I live like nothing happened, I won't feel so sick inside. Only, what will I do when it's time for Daddy to be coming home from the mine? I know I'll just stand out there watching the road every day, expecting him to come walking over the hill as usual."

Alice's eyes filled with tears.

"I keep thinking if I stand there long enough and concentrate and hope hard enough, all this will never have happened.

It will just seem to be a bad dream."

"Nothing will bring him back, Melody," Alice said sadly. "His soul has gone to heaven."

"Why did God put him in heaven?" I demanded, pounding my small fists on my thighs. "Why was I even born if I can't have a Daddy when I need him the most? I'm never going back to that church!" I vowed.

"It's silly to think you can hurt God back," Alice said.

"I don't care."

The look on her face said she didn't think I meant what I was saying.

But I did mean it, as much as I could mean anything. I took a deep breath, the futility of my outbursts and anger washing over me. "I don't know how we will go on without him. I'll have to quit school maybe and go to work."

"You can't do that!"

"I might have to. Mommy doesn't make very much money working in the beauty parlor."

Alice thought a moment.

"There's the miner's pension and social security, too."

"Mommy said it won't be enough."

We heard a loud outburst of laughter come from both Mommy and Archie Marlin.

Alice grimaced. "My father doesn't know how Archie Marlin keeps out of jail. Daddy says he waters the whiskey in the bar."

"Mommy's just trying not to be sad," I said. "She'd entertain anyone right now. He just happens to be around."

Alice nodded, unconvinced.

I picked up my fiddle and plucked at the strings.

"Daddy loved to hear me play," I said smiling, remembering.

"You play better than anyone I know," Alice declared.

"Well I'll never play again." I threw the fiddle on the bed.

"Of course you will. Your daddy wouldn't want you to give it up, would he?"

I thought about it. She was right, but I wasn't in the mood to agree with anything anyone said right now.

Another peal of laughter from Archie Marlin reached our ears.

"The walls of this trailer are made of cardboard," I said. I put my hands over my ears.

"You're welcome to come to my house," Alice said. "My brother's the only one home."

Alice lived in one of the nicest homes in Sewell. Ordinarily, I loved going there, but right now I felt it was a sin to do anything enjoyable.

Suddenly we heard Mommy and Archie singing along with a song on the radio, followed by their laughter again.

44

I stood up and reached for my coat. "Okay. Let's get out of here."

Alice nodded and followed me out of my room and down the short corridor. Mommy was sprawled on the sofa now and Archie was standing at her feet, holding his drink in his hand. They didn't speak, then Archie reached to turn down the volume on the radio.

"I'm going to Alice's house."

"Good idea, honey. Daddy wouldn't want you moping around the trailer."

I wanted to say he wouldn't want you laughing and singing and drinking with Archie Marlin either, but I swallowed my words and pounded my feet over the thin rug to the front door.

"Don't be late," Mommy called after me.

I didn't reply. Alice and I walked away from the trailer, the radio music turned up behind us again. Neither of us spoke until we rounded the turn toward Hickory Hill. The Morgans lived at the top and from their living room and dining room windows could look down on the valley and Sewell proper.

Alice's mother was very proud of their home, which she told me on more than one occasion was a colonial revival, a house with historical architecture. It had two stories and a front porch. They had an attached garage. The house had twelve rooms. The living room looked as big as our entire trailer. Alice's room was certainly twice the size of mine, and her brother Tommy's room was even bigger. The one time I looked in at the master bedroom with its own bathroom, I thought I had entered a palace.

Tommy was in the kitchen when we entered the house. He sat on a stool, smearing peanut butter on a piece of bread and holding the phone receiver between his ear and shoulder. The moment he saw me, his eyes widened and his eyebrows lifted.

"I'll call you back, Tina," he said and cradled the receiver. "I'm sorry about what happened to your father. He was a really nice guy."

"Thank you."

He looked at Alice for an explanation of what we were doing, why she had brought me to their house. Everyone was making me feel as though I carried a disease. No one wanted to be directly confronted with sorrow as deep as mine.

"We're going up to my room," Alice told him.

He nodded. "Would you like something to eat? I'm just having a snack."

I hadn't really had anything substantial to eat for days and my stomach bubbled at the suggestion.

"Maybe I should eat something."

"I'll make us some sandwiches and bring them up to my room," Alice said.

"Mother doesn't like you to have food in

your room, Alice," Tommy reminded her.

"She'll make an exception this time," Alice retorted. Her older brother retreated from the fury of her eyes and her stern expression.

"I don't want to make any trouble," I said softly.

"I guess it will be all right as long as you don't make a mess," Tommy relented. "How's your mother doing?"

"She's doing fine," I said hesitantly. He nodded, gazed at Alice who continued to glare at him defiantly, and then he took a bite of his sandwich.

"Let's go up to my room, first," Alice suggested, pivoting and taking my hand. I followed.

We went quickly up the carpeted, winding stairway to her room.

"Sorry my brother is such a dork," she said. "We're always fighting because he's so bossy. You can lie down if you want," she said nodding at her fluffy pillows and comforter on her queen size bed. It had pink posts and a frilly light pink canopy. The headboard was shaped like a Valentine heart. I dreamed of having a bed like this instead of the simple mattress and box springs I had now.

I took off my coat and sat on the bed.

"I thought Bobby Lockwood was going to come to your house," Alice said.

"I knew he wouldn't. He looked terrified at church and at the cemetery," I said.

"I know you like him, but I don't think he's that mature," Alice remarked.

"No one's very mature when it comes to this sort of thing. I don't blame him for running away from me."

"If he really liked you, he would want to be with you, to help you."

I knew Alice hated whenever I had a boyfriend because it took me away from her.

"Right now, I don't care very much about boys," I said.

She nodded, pleased.

"I'll run down and make us some sandwiches and bring them up with milk, okay?"

"Don't get in trouble on my account."

"I won't. Just rest or read something or turn on the television set, if you want. Do anything you want," she offered.

"Thanks."

After she left, I did lie back and close my eyes. I should be with Mommy now and she should want to be with me, not Archie Marlin. She'll be sorry when he leaves and she's all alone in the trailer, I thought, and then I decided I wouldn't stay away that long. I kept hearing Daddy explaining her actions, cajoling me to understand her weaknesses. He always felt more sorry for her than he felt for himself. I was sure he was doing the same thing right now, even though it was he and not she who was shut up in a coffin.

I wondered how long it would be before my friends would stop looking at me strangely. It would be so hard to return to school, I thought: all those pitying eyes aimed at me. I imagined even my teachers would gaze at me sorrowfully and speak to me in softer, sadder tones.

Maybe Mommy was right: maybe it was better to pretend nothing had happened. That way other people weren't so uncomfortable in your presence. But wasn't that like slapping Daddy's memory in the face? Somehow, I had to find a way to keep my sorrow private and go on with my life, as empty as it now seemed to be.

If I had a brother like Alice had, I wouldn't be fighting with him all the time, I thought. Right now, a brother would come in pretty handy. He would help with Mommy and we would have each other to comfort. If he were older than I was, I was sure he would be like Daddy. I resented Mommy for being too weak and too selfish to have another baby. She didn't have to have a litter, but she might have considered my need for a companion.

I must have been a lot more tired than I realized, for I didn't hear Alice return. She placed the sandwiches and the milk on the night table beside the bed and sat reading our history assignment while she waited for me to open my eyes. It was twilight by the time I did. The lamp was on.

"What happened?" I asked, scrubbing my cheeks with my palms and sitting up.

"You fell asleep and I didn't want to wake you. The milk's a little warm, but the sandwich is all right."

"Oh. I'm sorry."

"Go ahead. Eat something. You need it, Melody."

I saw from the empty plate beside her and the empty glass, she had already eaten her snack. I took a deep breath and bit into the sandwich. I was afraid what my stomach might do once solid food dropped into it again. It bubbled and churned, but the sandwich tasted good, and I finished quickly.

"You were hungry."

"I guess so. Thanks. What time is it?" I gazed at the small grandfather clock on her dresser. "Oh. I better get home."

"You don't have to go. If you want, you could even sleep here tonight."

"No. I should go home," I insisted. "My mother needs me. I'm sorry I wasn't much company."

"That's okay. Are you going to school tomorrow?"

"No. I'm not. I'm staying home at least one day," I said firmly.

"I'll bring you all the homework and tell you what we did."

"Thanks." I paused and smiled at her. "Thanks for being my best friend, Alice."

It brought tears to her eyes and she flashed a smile back at me. Then she followed me down the stairs. Her house was so quiet.

"My parents are showering and getting dressed for dinner," she explained. "They always do that after they come home from work. Dinner is very formal in my house."

"That's nice," I said pausing at the front door to gaze back at her beautiful home. "It's nice to sit at the table like a family and all be together. You're lucky."

"No, I'm not," she said sharply and I opened my eyes wide. "We're rich, maybe, and I get the best marks in school, but you're the lucky one."

"What?" I almost laughed. Of all days, to say such a thing, I thought.

"You're the prettiest girl in school and everyone likes you and someday, you'll be happier than anyone."

I shook my head as if she had just said the dumbest thing, but she didn't soften her determined expression.

"You will."

"Alice," we heard coming from upstairs. It was her mother. "Did you bring food upstairs?"

"I'd better go," I said quickly. "Thanks."

"See you tomorrow," she mumbled, and closed the door. Somehow, I don't know how, I left feeling more sorry for her than I did for myself.

When I returned to the trailer, Archie Marlin's car was gone. It was dark inside with only a small lamp on in the living room. The glasses and nearly empty bottle of gin were still on the coffee table. I gazed around, listened, and then walked softly down the corridor to Mommy's bedroom. The door was slightly ajar so I peeked through the opening and saw her sprawled on her stomach. Her robe was up around the backs of her knees and her arm dangled over the side of the bed.

I walked in and gazed at her face. She was breathing heavily through her mouth and was in a deep sleep. I covered her with the blanket and then left to clean up the trailer. Just before I was about to go to bed myself, there was a gentle knock on the door. It was Mama Arlene.

"How are you, honey?" she asked, coming in.

"I'm all right," I said. "Mommy's asleep."

"Good. I brought some of the food back from the wake for you to have." She put the covered plates in our refrigerator. "No sense letting this go to waste."

"Thank you."

She came over to me and took both my

hands in hers. Mama Arlene was a small woman, an inch shorter than I, but according to Papa George, she had a backbone tempered with steel. Although diminutive, she still seemed able to hold everyone else's troubles on her shoulders.

"Times will be hard for a while, but just remember, we're right next door anytime you need us, Melody."

"Thank you," I said, my voice cracking, the tears burning under my eyelids.

"Get some sleep, sweetheart." She hugged me and I hugged her right back. It broke the dam of tears and I started to sob again.

"Sleep," she said softly. "That's the cure. That, and time."

I took a deep breath and went to my room. I heard her leave and then all was quiet. Off in the distance, the wail of a train whistle echoed through the valley. Some of the coal in those cars, I thought, might have been dug out by Daddy before he . . . before he . . .

Some place up north, someone would shovel the coal into a stove and for a while, be warm. I shivered and wondered if I would ever be warm again.

I wondered if Mama Arlene was right about the power of time. In the days and weeks that passed, the ache in my heart became a numbness. But that ache was always resurrected when my mind went to Daddy or when I heard someone who sounded like him. Once, I even thought I saw him walking along the road. I hated going by the mine or looking at the other miners. The sight of them made my stomach tighten and sent pins into my heart.

Mommy never returned to the cemetery, but I did — almost every day for the first few weeks and then every other day or so after that. Everyone treated me differently at school for the first few days after I returned, but soon, my teachers spoke to me just the way they spoke to everyone else, and my friends began to stay at my side longer, talking to me more, and laughing around me.

Bobby Lockwood drifted away, however, and seemed interested in Helen Christopher, a ninth grader who looked more like an eleventh grader. Alice, who somehow managed to eavesdrop on conversations all day long, told me Helen was even more promiscuous than the infamous Beverly Marks. Alice predicted it was only a matter of time before she would be pregnant, too.

None of this mattered. I didn't shed a tear over Bobby's betrayal. Things that used to mean a lot now seemed small and petty. Daddy's death had jerked me headlong into maturity. On the other hand, with Daddy gone, Mommy became flightier than ever.

The biggest effect Daddy's death seemed to have on her was to make her even more terrified of becoming old. She spent a great deal more time primping at her vanity table, fixing her hair, debating over her makeup. She continually reviewed her wardrobe, complaining about how old and out of style all her clothes were. Her talk was always about herself: the length and shade of her hair, a puffiness in her cheeks or eyes, the firmness leaving her legs, what this bra did for her figure as opposed to what another could do.

She never asked about my school work, and between what I made for dinner and what Mama Arlene did for us, she never cooked a meal. In fact, she seldom even came home for dinner with me, claiming she'd get fat.

"I can't eat as much fatty food as you can, Melody," she told me. "Don't wait for me. If I'm not home by six, start eating without me," she ordered. It got so she was only home for dinner once or twice a week. Mostly, I ate with Mama Arlene and Papa George.

Even though Mommy was worried about her complexion and her figure, she continued to drink gin and smoke. When I asked her about that, she got very angry and told me it was her only vice and everyone need a little vice.

"Perfect people end up in monasteries or nunneries and eventually go mad," she explained. "I have a lot of tension now with your father gone. I need to relax, so don't make any new problems for me," she ordered. Which I knew simply meant, "Leave me alone."

I did.

I wanted to complain too: about how often she saw Archie Marlin and how often he was at our house. But I buttoned my lips and swallowed my words. It took so little to set Mommy off these days, and after she went on a rampage — shouting and flailing about — she would break down and cry and make me feel just terrible. It got so I began to feel as if I was her mother and she was my daughter.

Our bills piled up, some simply because she just never got to them. Twice, the phone company threatened to shut off our service and once the electric company came by and put a warning on our door. Mommy was always making mistakes with our checking account. I had to take over the bookkeeping, do our grocery shopping, and look after the trailer. Papa George helped me with that, but Daddy's death had had a big impact on him, too. He looked older, sicker, and much more tired these days. Mama Arlene was always after him to take better care of himself, however he wouldn't stop smoking and he even began drinking a little whiskey in the late afternoon.

There were nights when I was wakened by the sound of Mommy's laughter and then heard Archie Marlin's voice. Soon, that laughter was coming from Mommy's bedroom. I pressed my hands over my ears, but I couldn't shut out the sounds that I knew were sounds of lovemaking.

The first time I heard that, I got so sick to my stomach and I had to run to the bathroom to vomit. Mommy didn't even hear me and never asked what had happened. Usually, Archie was gone before I rose in the morning, and if I heard him moving about in the kitchen or living room, I'd wait as long as I could before rising.

All of this had happened too quickly — far too quickly for most people in Sewell. I knew there was a lot of gossip about us. One night Mommy returned from work enraged. She had gotten into an argument with Mrs. Sampler, who had always been one of her best customers. They fought because Mrs. Sampler had made a remark about Mommy's not spending enough time in respectful mourning. From what I heard afterward, Mommy had become so shrill and wild, Francine had asked her to leave.

She was fuming, and started to drink as she recited the argument. "Who is she to tell me how to act? Does she know how hard my life is? How much I suffered? She lives in her fine house and looks down on me, judging me. Who told her she could be judge and jury?"

Mommy paused now and then to make sure I was on her side. I knew it was better not to get her any more furious than she already was, so every time she looked at me with her narrowed eyes I nodded enthusiastically and acted as outraged as I could about someone openly criticizing her.

"I hate these people. They think just because they have money, they can lord it over us. They're so small-minded. They're so —" She struggled for the right word and looked to me for a suggestion.

"Provincial?"

"Yes. What's that mean?" she asked.

"They just haven't been to enough other places to get a wider point of view," I said. She liked that.

"You are smart. Good. And you're right, too. Archie's always saying the same thing. He hates this town as much as I do. And you do," she added.

"I don't hate it, Mommy."

"Of course you hate it. What's here for you?" She gulped her cocktail and then went to the phone to call Archie and tell him what had happened.

I didn't realize how serious the incident at the beauty salon had been until days later when I came home early from school and found Mommy lying on the sofa watching a soap opera. She had obviously not even gotten dressed that day. I didn't even have to ask. She saw the look on my face and told me before I could utter a question.

"I'm not working for Francine anymore," she said.

"What! Why?"

"We had an argument. After all these years, you'd think she would be more loyal to me. I broke my back for her, did her all sorts of favors. The ingrate. That's what she is. That's what they all are."

"What are you going to do?"

"I'm not thinking about it right now. I'm too angry," she said, pouting. "What are we going to have for dinner?"

"There's the chicken from yesterday to warm up and I can make some potatoes and some green beans."

She smirked.

"If that's all we have, I guess that's what it will be," she said and closed her eyes.

My hands shook as I prepared our dinner. What would we do now? Who was going to give Mommy a job? What sort of a job could she manage? There was only one beauty salon in Sewell. Maybe, what I had told Alice would come true: I would have to quit school and find a job myself.

Daddy hadn't had enough life insurance

and what we were getting from social security wasn't enough. Besides, Mommy had spent a lot of that money on new clothes.

But she didn't appear worried. After I had the meal prepared, she changed her mind about not liking it. She ate and drank and talked a blue streak about this new outfit she was getting, with matching shoes. After dinner, she went to her bedroom while I cleaned up, and she suddenly appeared in a new skirt and blouse with new earrings. She modeled it all for me and I had to admit, she looked beautiful. Maybe she could become a professional model, I thought, and made the mistake of saying so. Unfortunately, it started her on one of her favorite rampages.

"That's what I should have been. Only I didn't have the right advice or someone who was sophisticated enough to take me to the right places. And what did I know? You have to have someone who has been places, who knows things and will help you, who will guide you. That's why the choice of a man to marry and love is so important. You can't just let your heart tell you what to do. But it still might not be too late for me," she added, happily gazing in the mirror.

The possibility cheered her.

"I just have to go to the right places and see the right people," she told me. She clapped her hands together and nodded.

"Yes, that's what I have to do." Her face beamed. She rushed back to her bedroom as if the right person were waiting there.

I felt my heart flutter. A feather of fear tickled the inside of my chest. It was one thing to dream and to wish for things once in a while. Daddy had taught me to hope for things and look forward to another tomorrow, but it was different if you lived in a world of wishes and never saw the reality of today and never cared about responsibilities. Mommy was getting more and more like that.

After I did the dishes, I went to do my homework. A short time later, I heard a knock on my door and Mommy peeked in, still dressed in her new skirt and blouse.

"I'm going to town," she said. "Leave the door unlocked."

A car horn honked and she was off. I didn't need to take two guesses whom she was with.

What will become of us? I wondered.

Two days later, I got my answer. It was more shocking than anything I expected.

3

Sad, Beautiful Dreamer

I returned from school that afternoon with an emptiness that made my chest feel hollow. One foot followed the other mechanically, the soles of my shoes barely leaving the road. A group of grade school children ran past. Their laughter had the tinkling sound of china, crisp and musical in the clear, sharp air. Children, I realized, don't really have to contend with deep sadness. They are wooed out of it with the presentation of a toy or a promise. But being mature means realizing life is filled with dark days, too. Tragedy had sent me headlong into reality. All the things I had seen before now looked different, even nature.

The snow had melted. The white oaks, with their powerful broad branches, the beech trees and poplar trees, all had leaves turning a rich shade of green. I was vaguely aware of the birds flitting from branch to branch around me. Above me, the lazy, milk-white clouds seemed pasted against the soft blue sky, but they looked like nothing more than blobs of white. Their shapes no longer resembled camels or whales. My imagination was imprisoned in some dark closet.

Usually, the first warm kiss of sunshine filled me with excitement. Things that normally made me depressed or unhappy looked small and insignificant against the promise of budding flowers or the laughter of young children rippling through the air.

But all the spring glory in the world wouldn't bring my daddy back. I missed his voice and his laughter more every passing day. Mama Arlene was wrong: time wasn't healing the wound. It made the emptiness wider, longer, deeper.

As I plodded along, I carried my school books in the dark blue cloth bag Daddy had bought me long ago. I had two tests to study for and lots of homework, so the bag was full and heavy. Alice had remained after school for Current Events Club. There was also a rehearsal for the school talent show, and I was supposed to play my fiddle in it. I had volunteered months ago, but since Daddy's death, I hadn't picked up my fiddle once. I no longer had the desire or the confidence.

Everyone else seemed to have something to do, friends to be with, activities to join. Once or twice I tried to muster some enthusiasm about something I had done before Daddy's death, but an important part of me had died with Daddy. I knew my friends at school, even Alice, were losing patience with me. After a while, they stopped pleading, begging, and encouraging me to do things with them, and I began to feel like a shadow of myself. Even my teachers had begun to treat me like a window pane, gazing through me at someone else, hardly calling on me in class, whether I raised my hand or not.

My smiles were few and far between. I couldn't recall the sound of my own laughter. Even before she had lost her job, Mommy had been complaining about my moods. Now, it was a constant grievance.

"If I can let go, you can," she lectured. Then she declared, "Maybe, he's happier where he is. At least he doesn't have to fight getting old. You won't remember him as anything but young. And where he is, he doesn't have to worry about money."

I told her that was a horrible thing to say, but she just laughed. "Suit yourself. If you want to walk around with a sad-sack face all the time, do it. You won't have any friends and you certainly won't attract any handsome boys."

"I don't care!" I shouted back. Boys and parties, long conversations on the telephone, scribbling some boy's name in my notebook — none of that mattered to me anymore. Why couldn't Mommy realize that?

I didn't want to have an argument with her today, but since she had lost her job at Francine's and not found another yet, I expected she would be home when I arrived. She said I was so depressing to be around, I made her lose her appetite. It always sounded like just another excuse to go off with Archie Marlin. Today would be no different. I braced myself for another lecture.

But when I opened the trailer's front door, I wasn't greeted with her criticisms. Instead, I saw suitcases spread open on the floor. Mommy rushed about, folding clothes and dropping them into the luggage.

"Good!" she said when she saw me. "You're home early. I was afraid the one time I wanted you here, you'd find something silly to do."

"What are you doing, Mommy? Why are you packing these suitcases?"

"We're leaving," she said smiling. "Now, these two suitcases are yours," she instructed, pointing to the smaller ones near the sofa. "I'm sorry that's all you can take, but that's all that we'll have room for in the car right now. Pick out your most important things and pack them."

My mouth dropped open. "Leaving? Where are we going? I don't understand."

"I don't have a lot of time to explain, Melody." She put her hands together and looked up at the ceiling as if giving thanks. "The opportunity has come and we're taking it," she declared. "Hurry! Get your best things packed, and remember, we don't have room for anything else right now."

"I don't understand." I stood in the doorway and shook my head.

"What's to understand? We're leaving," she cried. "Finally leaving Mineral Acres! Be thankful. Be gloriously thankful, sweetheart," she pleaded.

"But why are we leaving?"

She held out her arms, turning her eyes from her right hand to her left, as if the answer were right before us. "Why?" She laughed thinly. "Why would I want to leave this Godforsaken place, this town of busybodies, of people who have no imagination, no dreams? Why would I want to leave a two-by-four trailer in a retirement park filled with people inches away from their own graves? Why?" She laughed again, then lost her smile.

"You're supposed to be a smart student. You get all those hundreds on your school tests and you ask why?"

"But Mommy, where will we go?"

"Any place else," she said. She stared at me for a moment and then her eyes grew small. "We're going to explore, look for a nice place to live where I can have an opportunity to do something more with my life and not be smothered and stifled. Now that your father is dead, we have no reason to continue living in a coal mining town, do we?"

She smiled again, but something about that smile seemed false.

"We've always lived in Mineral Acres," I said weakly.

"Because your father was working in the mines! Really, Melody. Besides," she went on, "I've spent more money than we have in the bank trying to cheer myself up after your father's death. The life insurance is gone and you know what our bills are, how close we are to not paying them every month. You're always warning me. I can't even pay for this trailer without a job and I'm not going to beg for my job back at Francine's. There just aren't any other jobs here for me. I'm not going to become a waitress. Look at me!" she said throwing wide her arms. "Do I look like I can make a living for us in this town? I can't type and if I could, I would hate to be caged in some mine company office. We have no choice. I have to get to where there are opportunities before it's too late!"

"But how are we going?"

"Archie will be here in twenty minutes," she replied. "So we don't have much time to jabber about it."

"Archie?"

"He's leaving, too. Actually, it was his idea," she added with a happy smile. "We'll go off in his car and —"

"Archie? We're going away with Archie Marlin?" I asked, incredulously.

"It's more like he's going away with us," she said and followed it with her nervous little laugh. "But he's going to be a big help. He has friends in the entertainment business. He says I can be a model."

"Oh Mommy, he's lying! He's telling you these things just so you'll stay with him."

"What? How dare you." She wagged her forefinger at me. "Archie is a sensitive person. He cares about us. As it turns out, he has no one either. It makes sense for us to all go off together. Please," she pleaded, rolling her eyes. "Get busy packing."

"But what about my school and —"

"You'll make up the work in a different school — a better school! Oh honey," she said, clapping her hands together, "isn't this exciting? What could possibly be wrong with our trying to find a new place to live? I know you're not happy here anymore, right?"

"That's because of what happened to Daddy."

"Exactly. And nothing is going to change that, so why stay? A new beginning — a fresh start — is what we all need. But we have to do it before it's too late, Melody. Do you want me to wait until I'm too old to have another chance? That's what happened to a lot of the people who are stuck here. Well, it's not going to happen to me," she said with determination.

She smiled again. "I have another surprise. I was going to save it until we actually left, until we were on the road with nothing ahead of us but a better future," she said.

I stared at her dumbly, wondering what additional surprise she could possibly have.

"Don't you even want to know what it is?" she asked when I didn't speak.

I shook my head and gazed around. It was overwhelming. The suitcases on the floor, the house in a mess, clothes thrown everywhere . . .

"What?" I finally asked.

"Our first stop is going to be Provincetown, Cape Cod. You're going to see your father's family, finally. Well?" she said when I didn't reply. "Aren't you excited? You were always asking about them. Now, you'll get all the answers."

"Provincetown? Daddy's family?"

"Yes. Isn't it a good idea?"

"I don't know," I said. She was right: she had surprised me, something wasn't ringing true. I took a deep breath. My heart pounded. With everything happening so fast, I couldn't think straight.

"Shouldn't we plan this better, Mommy? Can't we sit and talk about it first and get organized?"

"No, because that usually means we won't

do it," she whined. "As Archie says, if you don't do something when you have the urge, you probably never will."

"Why do we have to go with him?" I pursued.

She tightened her face and narrowed her eyes. "I like Archie, Melody. He makes me laugh and I'm tired of crying and complaining. I'm tired of people looking at me as if I were some sort of freak because my husband was killed in a mining accident.

"But not Archie." She sat down on the sofa and motioned for me to join her. I sat down next to her, but I was cautious. Then she pulled me into her arms for the first time since Daddy had died. She held me tightly and began to stroke my hair and slowly I began to relax. It felt so good to have my Mommy back. I'd missed her so much. "You'll like Archie once you get to know him. He's just the medicine I need and you need, honey." She paused, but kept caressing my hair. I hoped she would never stop. "The only thing," she added softly, "is after we leave Sewell, I don't want you to call him Archie anymore."

"Why not?"

"His real name is Richard. Archie is just a nickname."

"How come he can leave so quickly? He has a job," I said, hoping she wouldn't get mad and stop holding me. Perhaps he had been caught watering the whiskey as Alice's father thought.

"It's not the sort of a job a man like Arch . . . Richard wants for the rest of his life. So we made a decision. Now, Pumpkin, I want you to go pack, and remember, only two suitcases."

"But I'll have to leave so much behind," I protested.

"George and Arlene will look after it," she said. "And after we're settled somewhere nice, we'll have everything shipped to us."

"Mama Arlene," I muttered, realizing this meant I wouldn't see her anymore. "Did you tell her about this?"

"I was just going to do that," Mommy said, "but forcing me to stand here and talk, talk, talk, has cut down on my time. I have things to pack, too."

"But don't I have to tell the school and don't —"

"Will you stop all this chatter, Melody, and get packed! Everything will be just fine. We're not the first people to move, you know. Although, I bet you can count on one hand how many escaped this rat-trap."

She smiled again and rushed off to her bedroom.

I just stood there, gazing around, still finding it hard to believe we were going to leave Sewell for good! What about going to Daddy's grave to say good-bye? And what about Alice and my other friends? I had to turn in my library books! What about our mail? And the bills we still owed — surely, we had to go to the bank. There was so much to do.

I put down my book bag and walked slowly down the short corridor. Mommy had her closet open and her clothes thrown on the bed. She stood in the center of the room, pondering.

"I hate to leave so much behind, but I'll get new things, won't I?" she decided.

"Mommy, *please.* Let's wait and do this right."

"Aren't you packing?" She turned to me angrily. "I'm warning you, Melody. When Archie arrives, we're going out that door," she threatened. "What you have packed, goes. What you haven't, stays. Understand?"

I swallowed down the lump in my throat and thought a moment. A suggestion born of desperation came to my mind.

"Maybe I should stay and live with Mama Arlene and Papa George until you find a new home for us, Mommy."

She shook her head. "I thought of that, but Papa George is sicker than ever and Mama Arlene has her hands full with him as it is. Besides, they are not really your family and can't be your legal guardians. It's too much responsibility for old, decrepit people to bear."

"They're not old and decrepit," I insisted.

"Melody, get your things into those suitcases!" Then her voice softened. "Don't make things harder than they have to be, honey. I'm depending on you to be a big girl. I'm a little frightened, too. Everyone's afraid when they start a new life. I need your support, Melody." She paused when I didn't move. "Besides, you know Daddy would want you to do what I ask," she said. "Wouldn't he?" She smiled. "Wouldn't he?"

"Yes," I reluctantly admitted.

I lowered my head and turned away. When I stepped into my small room and gazed about, I found myself confronted with an impossibility. There were so many precious mementos, especially things Daddy had bought me, like my first doll, and all the pictures. Those suitcases Mommy had set out for me were barely big enough to hold a tenth of my clothes, much less stuffed animals. And what about my fiddle?

"Ten minutes!" Mommy cried from her room.

I had ten minutes to decide what I would leave behind, maybe forever. I couldn't do it. I started to cry.

"Melody! I don't hear you putting things into your suitcases," she called.

Slowly, I opened the dresser drawers and took out what I knew were necessities, my underthings, socks, some shoes and sneakers. Then I went to the closet and chose my skirts and blouses, two pairs of jeans, and some sweaters.

The suitcases filled up quickly, but I gathered as many of my photographs as I could and stuffed them under the clothes. Then I tried to squeeze in my first doll, my stuffed cat and Teddy bear, and some gifts from Daddy. Mommy came out and saw how full my suitcases were and how it was impossible to close them properly.

"You can't take all that," she said.

"Can't I have another suitcase?"

"No. Arch . . . Richard has his things, too, and I have to take four suitcases myself. I need my good clothes so I can look nice when I go for job interviews and auditions," she claimed. "I told you, we'll send for the rest."

"But I don't need much more. Maybe a small carton and —"

"Melody, if you can't decide what to leave here, I'll decide for you," she said and reached down to pluck the stuffed cat out of the suitcase.

"*No!*" I cried. "That was the last thing Daddy gave me!"

"Well, it's obviously either this or that Teddy bear or some of your clothes. Decide. You're a big girl now. You don't need toys," she snapped and threw the cat back onto the clothes in the suitcase.

I pressed the stuffed animals down and

then I sat on the suitcase so it would close and managed to get the snaps to hold. The sides of the suitcases bulged and they were heavy, but I had gotten in the things I would positively not leave behind.

"You only need the one coat," Mommy instructed, "and the boots you're wearing. Don't forget your gloves."

"I'm taking my fiddle," I said.

"Your fiddle? Melody, please. That's a backwoods, mountain person's instrument."

"Daddy loved to hear me play."

"Well, he can't hear you now. You're not going to play it much where you'll be going, I'm sure. Maybe you'll learn how to play the guitar or —"

"I won't go if I have to leave the fiddle, Mommy." I folded my arms under my breasts and planted my back firmly against the wall. "I won't. I swear."

She sighed.

"I guess it will take time to get the shanty town out of you. Suit yourself." She marched down the corridor to finish packing up her cosmetics. I had forgotten my own toiletries and had to open one of the suitcases to get them in. I was still struggling to close it when Archie Marlin arrived.

He wore a brown sports jacket, a shirt and tie, and brown slacks. He looked a little better dressed than usual.

"Hi," he said, entering my room without knocking. "Almost ready?"

"No," I said mournfully.

It only made him smile. "I bet you're excited, huh?"

"No," I said, firmly this time.

"Scared, huh? Well, there's no need to be scared. I've been down this road before and there's nothing to fear." His voice was full of bravado.

"I'm not scared. I'm upset we're leaving so quickly."

"Best way to go is to just get up and go." He snapped his fingers. "Either you're a man of action or you're just a talker." He straightened his shoulders and pumped out his chest. I turned away so he wouldn't see the tears glistening in my eyes. "Haille!" he called.

"Oh, you're here, good." Mommy came into my room. "I'm just about packed. You can start loading the car, Richard."

He widened his eyes.

"She knows it's your real name and Archie's just a nickname," Mommy explained.

"Oh? Good. Never liked that nickname." Archie-Richard winked at me and went to get Mommy's bags.

"Are you packed?" she asked me.

"The bags are full. I just have to get this one closed."

"No problem." Archie paused as he

76

dragged Mommy's two largest bags over the floor. He left them a moment to sit on my suitcase, pressing the fasteners in and snapping them shut. "You need anything, Melody, you just ask," he told me. I snorted, hating the idea of asking him for anything.

"While we pack the car, why don't you go say good-bye to Mama Arlene?" Mommy said.

I lowered my head and put on my coat. Then I took my fiddle in its case and started for the door. Archie complained about how heavy Mommy's bags were. He struggled to get them down the steps behind me.

"Careful!" Mommy screamed. "Some of my nicest things are in those bags."

Daddy could have picked them up with just a couple of fingers, I thought.

I knocked on Mama Arlene's trailer door.

"Melody, honey, what's wrong?" She knew there was something the moment she looked at my face.

"Oh, Mama Arlene. We're going away. We're leaving Mineral Acres for good!" I rushed into her arms.

I told her everything quickly, including my suggestion I remain behind and live with her and Papa George. We hadn't even moved from the doorway before I had it all said.

"Oh," she said nodding. "So that's why she was asking me about George's condition. Well, come in a moment," she said.

"Where is Papa George?" I asked, not seeing him in his favorite oversized chair watching television and smoking. Before she could reply, I heard his heavy cough from their bedroom.

"He's a bit under the weather tonight," she said. "The doctor wanted him in the hospital, but you know Papa George. He wouldn't go. When did you say you were going?"

"Today! Right now!"

"Right now? But she never said . . . Right now?" The realization shocked her almost as much as it had me. Her small hands fluttered up to her throat like two little song birds. She shook her head in disbelief.

"She wants you to keep our things until we send for them," I explained.

"Of course. I'll take good care of everything. Oh Melody," she said, actual tears flowing from her eyes now. "We'll miss you. You're the grandchild we never had, the child we never had."

"I don't want to go," I wailed.

"You got to go with your mother, honey. She needs you."

"She doesn't need me," I said defiantly. "She has Archie Marlin."

"Archie Marlin? Oh." She took on a look of disapproval and sadness, her eyes darkening.

"What's going on out there?" Papa George called from his bedroom.

"You better go say good-bye to him." The way Mama Arlene said it put an icicle in my chest, chilling my heart. I walked slowly to the bedroom doorway and gazed in.

Papa George looked tiny under his comforter. Only his head, crowned with that stark white hair, showed. He coughed violently for a few moments and spit into a metal tray at the side of the bed. Then, he took a deep breath and turned to me. "What are you women jabbering about?"

"We're going away, Papa George," I said.

"Who's going away?"

"Mommy and me . . . and for good," I said.

He stared, took another breath, coughed a bit and then pushed hard to get himself into a sitting position.

"Where she taking you?"

"We're going to see my daddy's family. They live in Cape Cod."

The old man nodded. "Well, maybe that's best. Leaving on quick notice, though, ain't you?"

"Yes. I haven't said good-bye to any of my friends and I haven't been to the cemetery yet."

He thought a moment and then reached over to his night table drawer. He took something out and beckoned for me to come closer.

"I want you to have this," he said and handed me a gold-plated pocket watch. I had seen it once or twice before and knew that on the inside was the inscription, To George O'Neil, Ten tons of coal! "It still keeps good time," he said. When the watch was opened, it played one of Papa George's favorite tunes: "Beautiful Dreamer."

"I can't take that, Papa George. I know what it means to you."

"It will mean more to me to know Chester Logan's little girl has it now and forever," he said, urging me to take it. I reached out and clutched it in my hand. "This way, you won't be able to forget me."

"Oh Papa George, I can't ever forget you," I moaned and threw my arms around him. He felt so small, all skin and bones, and his hug was barely anything. I was shocked. It was as if he were wilting, disappearing right before my eyes.

He started to cough again and pushed me back so he could lower himself under the blanket. I waited for him to catch his breath.

"Send us postcards," he said.

"I will. I'll write every day."

He laughed. "A postcard now and then is all we need, Melody. And don't forget to play that fiddle. I didn't spend all that time teaching you for nothing."

"I won't."

"Good," he said. He closed his eyes. "Good."

Hot tears streamed down my cheeks. I felt

as if my lungs would burst, the ache was that deep. I turned and saw Mama Arlene standing in the bedroom doorway, her tears falling just as hard and fast. She held out her arms and we hugged. Then she followed me out.

Mommy and Archie had finished loading his Chevy. He slammed the trunk closed and got behind the wheel. Mommy came over to Mama Arlene.

"I didn't know you meant you would be leaving this soon, Haille."

"It's just worked out that way, Arlene. I guess Melody already asked you to look after our remaining things, if you can."

"I'll keep an eye on the place, sure."

"Once we're settled, I'll see about getting what else we want. Where's George?"

"He's lying down," she said.

"Oh."

They exchanged a knowing glance that made me weak in the knees.

"Well, I'll call and I'll drop you a line now and then," Mommy promised.

My mind was racing. There was too much to think about. "Mama Arlene. I'm going to leave my school books on the kitchen table. I'll call my friend Alice and she'll come by to get them and my library books, okay?" I asked.

"Of course, dear."

"Here's the keys to the trailer." Mommy

handed them to Mama Arlene. She took them reluctantly. Her gaze went to me and her lips trembled.

"I better go put the books on the table, Mommy," I said.

"Hurry. We want to be on the road. We've a lot of distance to cover," she said. "Go on. I'll wait here with Arlene."

I ran back to the trailer and entered. For a moment I just stood there gazing around. Yes, it was a tiny place to live and our furniture was very ordinary. Yes, the rugs were worn, the curtains thin, the wallpaper faded. The faucets dripped and the sinks were stained with rust at the drains. The heat never worked right and in summer, the place was an oven. I had wished and wished to have a real house instead, but this had been home to me, and now I felt as if I were deserting a poor old friend.

Daddy and I had eaten thousands of meals at that small dinette. I had curled up in his arms a thousand times on that worn sofa while we watched television. I blew out candles on many birthday cakes here. In that corner we had decorated our small Christmas tree. Although the pile of gifts under it was never impressive, it was always exciting for me.

Good-bye trailer home, I thought. Good-bye to the sound of the rain's drum beat on the roof while I slept or studied or ate my meals. Good-bye to every creak and groan in the wind; to the funny moaning sound in the plumbing that brought laughter to Daddy and me dozens of times.

And how do I say good-bye to my small room, my small private world? Once, this was my special place and now I was looking in at it for the final time.

I bit down on my lower lip and pressed my palm against my heart, holding in the ache, and then I scooped up my school books and the library books and put them on the kitchen table.

Archie Marlin honked the car's horn. I glanced at everything one last time, pressing it forever into my memory. Archie honked again.

"Good-bye," I whispered to the only home I had ever known. I rushed out the front door, afraid that if I paused or looked back, I would never be able to leave.

"What took you so long?" Mommy complained, her head out the window.

I got into the back seat. It was half covered with some of Mommy's clothes. I put my fiddle on the car floor.

"Be careful of my things," she said.

"Here we go." Archie pulled out of our lot. I pressed my face to the window. Mama Arlene stood in her doorway, small and sad, her hand frozen in good-bye. The tears blurred my vision and some of them ran down the glass. I sat back to catch my breath as Archie spun around the entrance to Mineral Acres and shot onto the road.

"We're stopping at the cemetery, aren't we, Mommy?" I asked.

"What? What for?"

"To say good-bye to Daddy," I replied, my voice filled with desperation.

"Oh, Melody. Can't we start this trip on a happy note?"

"I've got to say good-bye to Daddy!" I exclaimed. "I've got to!" My voice was full of desperation.

Archie looked at Mommy and she shook her head.

"It's on the way out," he said.

"Well, I'm not going in with you," Mommy said. "I can't bear it."

Archie stopped at the entrance to the cemetery. Mommy said it would break her heart again to drive in. It reminded her too much of the funeral.

"We're only waiting five minutes, Melody," she told me.

"Are you sure you don't want to come, Mommy?"

She stared at me a moment, her eyes looking genuinely sad. She gently shook her head.

"I said my good-bye some time ago, Melody. I had to or I couldn't go on with my life."

I opened the door and jumped out, running up the pathway past the monuments until I reached Daddy's stone. I walked up to it and threw my arms around it the way I used to throw them around him. I pressed my cheek to the hard granite and closed my eyes.

"Oh Daddy, we're going, but I'll come back as often as I can. Mommy has to get away. She can't live here anymore.

"I know you would forgive her. You forgave her for everything," I said a little bitterly. "And I know you would tell me to be a help to her, but I can't help how I feel."

I fell to my knees in front of the stone and bowed my head to say a little prayer and then I plucked a blade of grass growing on the grave and put it inside Papa George's pocket watch. It would always be with me, I thought. I kept the watch open so some of "Beautiful Dreamer" would play. Daddy loved that song, too.

Mommy and Archie were honking the Chevy's horn again.

I closed the watch, stood up, and gazed at the mountains in the distance, drinking in the trees and the bushes. I wanted to press the memory of this place into my mind as firmly as I had pressed the blade of grass into the pocket watch.

Then I kissed Daddy's gravestone, leaving some of my tears on top of it before I turned to walk away. I got back into the car without a word. Archie and Mommy both glanced at me and then he turned the car around and we started down the road that would lead us north, first to Richmond.

Mommy squealed with delight as we passed through the town and beyond the sign that read, Now Entering Sewell, West Virginia.

"I'm leaving!" she cried. "I'm really getting out of here. My prison sentence is over!"

I gazed at her and squinted. What had she meant by that? I would have asked, but my chest ached so, I knew my voice would crack as soon as I tried to speak.

Archie sped up. They turned on the radio and began to sing along with the music. Mommy swung around to look at me.

"Oh, be happy, Melody. Please. Be happy, if not for yourself, then for me."

"I'll try, Mommy," I said in a voice barely above a whisper.

"Good."

The scenery whipped by. I barely paid attention, but I saw enough familiar territory fall back to fill my heart with sadness. I gazed through the rear window, watching Sewell disappear behind a hill, and with it, the cemetery in which Daddy rested.

Then I turned around and looked ahead. Trembling, I felt no less frightened and confused than a newborn baby pulled kicking and screaming into the future, terrified at the unknown.

4

The Girl out of the Country

I closed my eyes and lay back in the seat.
Before Daddy was killed, he, Mommy, and I
had gone to the beaches in Virginia a few
times, but other than those trips, we hadn't
traveled many places. I had never been
north, and had only read about and seen
pictures of cities like New York, Washington,
D.C., and Boston. Mommy tried to get me
excited about the trip by telling me we would
see Washington and Boston on the way to
the Cape. Someday, she said, we'll go to New
York City. She said she had been there once
herself, but she went with her elderly adoptive parents who weren't much fun. She
could barely remember it.

"But we'll have wonderful times going to
museums and shows and eating in the famous restaurants. Right, Richard?"

"Absolutely," Archie replied. "Your life is
really just beginning, Melody."

"See?" Mommy said.

As we rode on, I listened to their conversation. Archie talked about the cities he had been to, comparing them, complaining about this one or that one, raving about the others. He claimed to know the best restaurants in New York and Chicago. He had been to Las Vegas many times and Los Angeles at least three times. He bragged about the people in the entertainment industry he had met and gotten to know at the various bars and restaurants where he had worked. He said he was sure he could call any of them on the phone and get them to consider Mommy. Mommy squealed and laughed with delight at all his promises. I couldn't believe she was so gullible, but then I remembered Daddy once telling me that if you want something to be true hard enough, you'll ignore all the proof that it's not so. Mostly, you won't ask questions that give you answers you don't want to hear.

Mommy should be asking Archie Marlin if he was so friendly with all these important people, why didn't he have a better job himself? How did he end up in Sewell? I was tempted to lean forward and fire these questions at him myself, but I didn't want to anger Mommy so I tried to sleep instead.

We stopped for gas, got some snacks and drove until we reached Richmond. Archie bragged about knowing a little Italian restaurant, the owners of which he claimed would surely remember him and give us special treatment. He promised Mommy he would take us someplace special every step of the way. However, when we turned down the street where the Italian restaurant was supposed to be, it wasn't there anymore.

"That's the trouble with these little restaurants," he remarked. "They go in and out of business so quickly. Let's just stop at that roadside diner," he decided and pulled into the parking lot.

I wasn't hungry, but Mommy insisted I eat something. While we waited for our food, I took a closer look at Archie Marlin, trying to understand what Mommy liked about him, especially after she had been married to a man as handsome and strong as Daddy.

Besides having patches of freckles on his face, Archie had them on the backs of his hands as well. His pink skin was interrupted here and there by white blotches. It looked as if he had been splattered with permanently staining milk. I thought his wrists were not much wider than mine or Mommy's, and I laughed to myself at the thought of him lifting a pick axe or a shovel. No wonder the heaviest thing he ever hoisted was a glass of beer.

Archie Marlin was full of nervous energy. He lacked Daddy's strong, quiet, calm manner. Archie's gaze was forever wandering. When he answered questions, he rarely looked at you. He looked down or up at the ceiling or fiddled with a spoon while he replied. While we waited for our food he described how he had once been a Blackjack dealer in a Las Vegas casino. He demonstrated how he would flip cards and hide aces in the palm of his hand. He'd been one of the best Blackjack dealers in the whole city, he said.

"So why did you leave that job?" I blurted, finally filled to the brim with his stories.

"I was underage," he said. "And," he added with a wink, "I was throwing my pay back into the casino looking for the big win all the time, just like the rest of the poor fools. But it was fun for a while."

"It must have been exciting," Mommy said. "The lights, the glamour, all those rich people, the entertainers you must have met."

"Yeah, sure," he said, as if he had been doing that all his life. "I've had some pretty good times in Vegas, but I have a pretty good time wherever I am."

"Then why did you end up in Sewell?" I asked as sharply as I had intended. Mommy threw me a reprimanding look, but I kept my eyes fixed on Archie. He hinged his lips at the corners and smiled like a cat.

"It looked like a nice little town at the time," he replied. "I thought I'd settle down, take it easy. I thought I was ready for the simple life, but I was wrong." He laughed, then

90

Mommy laughed too. "Boy, was I wrong about that."

"There's nothing wrong with a simple life," I snapped. They both stopped laughing. "What's wrong with having a decent job and friends you can count on and a nice house?"

Archie shrugged. "Nothing, if you're seventy-five or eighty."

"That's stupid," I said.

Mommy scowled. "Melody. You apologize. Go on."

"It's all right," Archie said. "She's confused. Remember what they say, you can take the girl out of the country, but you can't take the country out of the girl." He winked at me.

"I don't care if the country stays in me," I muttered.

"That's because you really haven't been anywhere yet. Just wait," he promised. "You'll come around to my way of thinking."

Hardly, I thought. I'd rather be buried forever in a coal mine.

Our food came. I ate sullenly while they jabbered on about the things they were going to see and do. Every time Archie mentioned a new place, Mommy squealed. He had been to Niagara Falls, of course, and he had traveled through Yellowstone and he had seen the Grand Canyon, had ridden over the Golden Gate Bridge and had been to the Grand Ole Opry in Nashville. He had even seen the Alamo, and claimed he had gone riverrafting and skiing in Utah.

"You must be a lot older than you look," I remarked in a casual tone.

"What? Why?" He held his forkful of food at his mouth and waited for my reply, his thin lips stretching into another plastic smile.

"Because if we believe all the places you've been to, you're about a hundred."

The smile finally left his face. "Well, I don't lie, missy," he said. "I can't help it if you've been shut up in a small town all your life." He realized how angry he sounded, glanced quickly at Mommy, and replaced his angry expression with a syrupy smile. "But, thankfully, that's all going to change. Right, Haille?"

"Yes." She shot a fiery look at me. "It definitely is."

I shut up after that. They wanted to have coffee and dessert, but I didn't. I asked to be excused and was permitted to wait in the car. Neither seemed unhappy about getting rid of me. Archie gave me the keys and I left the diner and flopped in the rear seat, fuming and frustrated. They took their time. It was nearly a half hour before they came out, arm in arm, giggling like children.

"How's the country princess doing?" Archie asked as he started the engine.

"Wonderful," I said.

"Good, because we don't want any un-happy country princesses in our chariot, do we Queen Haille?"

"No," she said. "It's against the law to be unhappy, isn't it?"

"Exactly. I, King Archie — I mean, King Richard — do hereby declare all tears and sadness prohibited from our lives from this day forward. Anyone who complains about anything gets a demerit. Anyone who has two demerits becomes the gopher."

"Gopher?" Mommy asked.

"Yeah, you know: go for this, go for that."

Mommy got hysterical with laughter and we were off.

"Where were you born?" I asked Archie after a few minutes on the road.

"Me? Detroit."

"Don't you have any family?"

"Not that I care to remember," he said.

"Why not?"

"Melody," Mommy chastised, "I taught you better than that. You know better than to pry into someone else's personal affairs," she said.

"I wasn't prying. I was just making conver-sation, Mommy. You complained about my being too quiet before, didn't you?"

"Yes, but you don't have to cross-examine Richard, do you?"

"I just wondered if it wasn't the other way around," I said with a shrug.

"What do you mean?" Archie asked.

"I just wondered if it wasn't your relatives that would rather not remember you."

"Melody!"

Archie wagged his head. "She's a card. You're going to do just fine, Melody." In the rearview mirror, I saw his smile fade and his eyes suddenly turn glassy cold.

"She's not usually like this," Mommy explained. "It's all the excitement, I'm sure."

Archie said nothing. He turned on the radio. Darkness grew thicker and we drove into a shower that turned into a downpour. The windshield wipers couldn't keep up and they were apparently worn out anyway. The window became lined with streaks.

"Looks like we won't make as much time and distance as I had hoped," Archie remarked. "Best thing would be to find a motel and pull in for the night."

"Whatever you think, Richard," Mommy said. "You're the seasoned traveler. We're in your capable hands." It was enough to make me want to puke. I stared angrily out the front window into the darkness, interrupted now and then by oncoming car headlights. They made the drops of rain look like slivers of ice that sent shivers down my spine.

About ten minutes later, Archie turned the car into the parking lot of a motel. Rain was falling in sheets by now, so hard we could barely see the motel's neon sign. Archie pulled his jacket over his head and ran through the raindrops to the office door.

The moment he left the car, Mommy turned on me. "Melody, I wish you would treat Richard with respect. He is an adult, you know."

"What did I do?"

"You talked to him as if he was one of your schoolfriends, and I don't want you asking lots of personal questions. It's impolite. If he wants to tell us about himself, he will. Okay?"

"I really don't care."

"Well, start caring. We're going to be together for a long time. We have to get along. We should be grateful Richard is doing all the driving." She leaned toward me, her eyes full of pleading.

"Oh, honey, try to be happy. Soon you're going to see wonderful new things. Think of that," she cajoled. "You should be happy that you're getting this opportunity. It's one I never had. I was forced to live with people I didn't like and endure terrible things."

"Like what?" I asked, my interest piqued.

"Someday I'll tell you," she replied, a distant look in her eyes, the look of someone lost in her memories.

"When will you tell me?"

"When you're old enough to understand."

"I'm old enough, Mommy. I'm fifteen. You should take a good look at me once in a while. I'm not a child anymore."

"I look at you plenty. You're still growing and at a sensitive stage. I remember how it was when I was your age. Trust me." She reached over the seat and put her hand on mine. "I want only what's best for you. You believe that, don't you, Melody?"

"Yes, Mommy," I said, wanting so much to believe her.

The door was pulled open and Archie hopped in, slamming it shut behind him. He brushed the rain off his face.

"Man, what a storm! But we're in luck. This place was almost filled. They had one room left."

"Good," Mommy said.

One room? I thought. All of us in one little room? Archie drove ahead and parked in front of Room C.

"Okay, we're going to have to move quickly. I'll get the door open first and then you girls decide what you need for overnight and we'll just bring that in, okay?"

"A-ok," Mommy said.

He jumped into the rain again.

Mommy turned to me. "What do you need, Melody?"

"Mommy, how can we all sleep in the same room?" I asked, mournfully.

"I'm sure there's two beds, silly."

"But . . ."

"Now start acting like the grown-up you

96

want me to think you are. Concentrate. What do you need?"

"The small suitcase," I replied petulantly.

"All right. Why don't you run inside? Richard and I will bring in all the things we need. Go on, honey."

I opened the door. It raged like a hurricane outside. With my hands over my head, I rushed toward Room C. Its door was wide open and I lunged through it.

I looked around the room. It had dull brown walls, stained near the baseboard. There were two double beds with a dark brown night table between them, on which sat an old fashioned telephone. Behind me were a dresser and a standing lamp with a faded yellow shade. The closet, open, some hangers dangling, was next to the bathroom doorway.

I went to the bathroom and tried to close the door, but it was out of alignment. There was no shower curtain around the tub and there was a long rust stain down its middle, from the back to the drain. Water dripped in the sink, above which was a cabinet with a cracked mirror.

Mommy and Archie came charging in from the rain, laughing. Was everything going to be funny, even this horrible room?

"The bathroom door won't close," I declared. They both stopped laughing and looked at me.

Archie raised his right forefinger.

"That's one," he said.

"One what?" I asked.

"Complaint. One more and you're our gopher for the whole trip."

"Very funny," I said with my hands on my hips. "But what about the door?"

His laugh wound down like a dying lawn mower as he approached to inspect it. "When you close it," he said after a moment, "just lift up on the handle."

"Thank you."

I took hold of the door handle and stepped back into the bathroom, closing the door as he had instructed. It still didn't close tightly, but it would have to do. I heard them both giggling again.

When I stepped out, I saw Archie had a bottle of gin and he was pouring some into two glasses. "This oughta take the chill out," he said.

They tapped glasses and swallowed.

"I just noticed there's no television set in the room," Mommy said. "Did you bring something to read, Melody?"

"No. We left home too quickly, remember? I had to leave my books behind anyway because there was no room in the suitcases," I complained. Archie leapt to his feet.

"That's two! Two complaints! You're the gopher."

Mommy laughed. They clinked glasses again.

"We really need something to mix this with, don't you think, Haille?"

"It would help," she said.

Archie dug into his pocket and produced two dollars.

"Why don't you run down to the motel office and get us a can of tonic water or some ginger ale." Archie thrust the money my way. "Stay under the overhang and you won't get wet."

I looked at Mommy. She sat on the bed, a wide grin on her face. "Be a good sport, honey."

I plucked the bills from Archie's hand and grabbed my coat on the way out the door, thinking I needed to get away from them for a while anyway. Their laughter followed as I slammed the door behind me.

Looking around, I saw how dreary the motel was. The parking lot was torn up in many spots, and the neon sign had some letters burnt out. Closing my coat tightly around myself, I hurried under the overhang, noticing as I went that there apparently *were* other empty rooms.

The office was small. Inside was a red imitation leather settee with slits and cracks in it, a worn cushioned chair, a coffee table, and the counter, behind which sat a short, bald man. He had long, bushy eyebrows and thick lips that looked as pale as day-old dead worms.

When he smiled, I saw he was missing a lot of teeth.

"How can I help you?" he asked.

"I need a can of tonic, please."

"The machine's broke, but I got some in the fridge back here," he said, indicating a room behind his office. "Just tonic water?"

"Yes, please."

"One minute."

He brought it out and I paid him a dollar. I noticed the pay phone on the wall behind the settee.

"Can I have change for the phone, please?"

"Sure thing."

He gave it to me and I went to the phone. He sat again and picked up his magazine, but his attention was fixed on me.

I dialed Alice's phone number, put in the required change, and waited for her to answer. She did so on the second ring.

"Alice, it's Melody."

"Where are you? I tried to call you four different times after school."

"Oh, Alice, I don't know where I am. Some place near Richmond, Virginia."

"Richmond, Virginia?"

I gazed at the man behind the counter. He wasn't pretending to be interested in anything but me now.

I turned so that my back was to him and

spoke as softly as I could. "We left, Alice. Mommy had it all planned. When I got home, she was packing. We're with Archie Marlin," I moaned.

"What? Where are you going?"

"Provincetown, on Cape Cod, at least at first. Then I don't know. Mommy wants to find a new place to live."

"You're gone for good?" Alice asked incredulously.

"Yes." My tears blinded me. "Could you say good-bye to everyone for me, and especially Mr. Kile?" He was my favorite teacher.

"But how will I know where you are?"

"I'll write as soon as it's decided. Oh, before I forget, I left my school and library books on the kitchen table in the trailer. Mama Arlene knows. Would you go by and get them and return them for me, please?"

"Sure. I can't believe this."

"Imagine how I feel. You know I hate Archie Marlin," I said. The operator interrupted to say I needed to put in more change, but all I had left was a nickel. "Good-bye, Alice. Thanks for being my best friend."

"Melody!" she called as if I were drifting away like a ghost.

The connection went dead. I stood there holding the mute receiver, afraid to turn and show the motel manager my tears. I took a deep breath, wiped my face with the back of my hand, and cradled the receiver.

"Really raining out there," the manager commented.

"Yes."

"You folks come far?"

"Sewell."

"Not that far."

I started away.

"You forgot your can of tonic," he said nodding toward the can I had left on the shelf by the telephone.

"Oh, thanks." I went back for it and then paused on the way to the door again. "Are you all booked up here tonight?"

"Booked up?" He laughed silently, his shoulders shaking. "Hardly."

"I thought so," I muttered to myself and left.

When I returned to the room, I found Mommy and Archie dancing to music on the radio. Mommy looked embarrassed for a moment, then smiled. "Richard can make even the dreariest situations happy."

"Here's your tonic water." I thrust the can at him.

"Thanks, princess," Archie said. "Any change?"

I handed him the nickel.

"I needed to call Alice to tell her to get my books," I said. "We owe you ninety-five cents."

"Plus interest," he said winking at Mommy. Then he snapped open the can and poured some into his glass and Mommy's.

"There are other empty rooms," I declared.

Archie paused with a surprised look painted on his crimson face. "There are? That's not what baldy in the office told me. Well, how do you like that? He just wanted to get us into a more expensive room, I bet."

"Wouldn't he be better off renting two?" I asked, snorting.

"Naw. This room is more expensive than two," he asserted.

"What difference does it make now?" Mommy said.

"The difference is I'm tired."

"So go to sleep. We'll put down the lights for you," she said and did so. Then she turned the radio low.

Seeing that I had no other choice, I unbuttoned my blouse with my back to them and took it off. Then I kicked off my shoes, slipped out of my skirt and quickly slid under the blanket. It smelled as if it had been stored in a box of mothballs. I kept my back to them, but I knew they continued to dance, drink their gin, and whisper. I prayed to fall asleep quickly, and miraculously, maybe because I was so exhausted, I did.

But later in the night, my eyelids snapped open. I heard a soft moan and a subdued giggle, followed by the sound of bed springs squeaking. They thought I was asleep, so I didn't turn around. I had heard similar sounds before through the thin walls of our trailer. I knew what they meant then and I knew what they meant now.

How could Mommy let another man put his hands on her and be so intimate with her so soon after Daddy's death? I wondered. Didn't she still see Daddy in her mind, hear his voice, remember his lips on hers? Archie Marlin was so different from Daddy, too. He was a weakling. Couldn't Mommy wait until she met someone with whom she was really in love?

She was just confused, frustrated, afraid to be alone, I told myself. Maybe it would all change when we found another place to live and she was happier with herself. Surely she wouldn't want to spend the rest of her life with a man like Archie Marlin.

I squeezed my eyelids tighter and pressed my ear to the pillow. I tried to think of something else, but their heavy breathing grew louder. Mommy moaned and then they grew silent. Moments later, Mommy slipped into bed beside me.

For now, at least, we were all supposed to pretend I heard and knew nothing. In the morning she would be here in bed with me and Archie Marlin would be in his.

It was a sad way to start a new life . . . lying to each other.

We left the motel as soon as we were all

washed and dressed the next morning. In the daylight, the motel looked seedier. Even Mommy commented. Archie laughed it off, saying, "Any port in a storm. I've slept in lots worse."

"I believe that," I muttered. If either of them heard it, they didn't react. We stopped for breakfast off Route 95 north of Richmond and then continued. I saw the Capitol building in the distance from the highway, but we didn't stop in Washington, D.C., to do any of the sightseeing Mommy had promised. Nor did we go to Baltimore or any city along the way. It was apparent that Mommy and Archie Marlin wanted to get us to Provincetown as soon as possible. I began to think about the family I was about to meet.

I knew very little, of course, but I did know that Daddy had a younger brother who lived on the Cape with his family and that Daddy's family had been in the lobster business for a long time. Daddy's father was retired and he and my grandmother lived in a house too big for just the two of them. That was all I knew. When I asked Mommy how many children Daddy's younger brother had, Mommy said she remembered he had twins, a boy and a girl. Another child had been born after she and Daddy left Provincetown. She couldn't remember if the third child was a boy or a girl, but she did say that she thought the twins were about my age, maybe a year older.

"Daddy's brother got married before you and Daddy?" I asked.

"I think so. Maybe. I don't remember. Please, Melody, don't flood me with questions I can't answer. You'll get all your answers when you get to Provincetown."

"But . . . well, how much younger than Daddy is his brother?"

"A year or so," she said. "He's different," she added.

"What do you mean?"

"You'll see," she said and refused to do anything but leave it at that.

With all this family mystery looming ahead of me, I couldn't help being nervous. Mommy had obviously told them about Daddy's death. Was his parents' grudge over? How come, after all these years, we were finally going to see them?

When I pushed Mommy about why we were finally going to see Daddy's family, she sighed deeply and said, "It's what your father would want now, I'm sure."

I told myself that must be true and I must be strong and do what I could to make things right again among all of us.

"You know," Archie Marlin said as we headed into Massachusetts, "I just realized I've never been to the Cape."

"How is that possible?" I asked dryly.

Mommy flashed her eyes at me, but Archie widened his smile. "I'm not one for sailing or fishing," he said.

"But I thought you went riverrafting," I followed quickly.

"That's not sailing or fishing. That's just a thrill," he replied.

"Cape Cod has its charms," Mommy said, "but the people can be hard. The ocean makes them that way."

"It didn't make you hard," Archie said lustily.

I turned my attention back to the scenery flying by. That night we slept in a much nicer motel. We stayed in a suite and I had the sofa bed all to myself. I was able to wash my hair and shower, too. We ate dinner at the motel and I returned to the room while Mommy and Archie remained in the lounge listening to music and drinking. They stumbled in hours later, giggling and whispering. I pretended to be asleep as they clumsily made their way into the bedroom and shut the door.

Even though the conditions were better, I had a harder time falling asleep. Now that we would be in Provincetown the very next day, and meeting Daddy's family, I had a small trembling inside. Where was my new home to be? I felt like a balloon, floating, bouncing, carried this way and that by the winds of Mommy's and Archie Marlin's fancy. Maybe we didn't have all that much back in Sewell, but now I had nothing: not a friend, not a familiar sight, no one in whom to confide. I had never felt so alone. I could squeeze my eyelids shut until they ached, but I couldn't close out the fears that kept me tossing and turning, fretting in and out of nightmares until the first light of morning streaked through the motel room curtains.

Mommy and Archie slept very late. I washed and dressed and sat reading a visitor's guide, wondering if at least we could do some sightseeing. Finally, tired of being shut up in the stuffy room, I went for a walk around the motel. By the time I returned, Mommy and Archie were awake. We went for breakfast. They were both very subdued, they hardly talked and their eyelids drooped.

"Are we going to do some sightseeing before we go on to Provincetown?"

Archie groaned.

"On the way back," Mommy said quickly. "We want to get to the Cape as early as possible today."

"I thought we were exploring new places," I muttered.

"Oh Melody, please. No complaints today. I'm afraid I had a little too much to drink last night," she said.

I said nothing. After breakfast, we moved mutely, repacking the car and getting in for the drive. I saw many good views of the ocean, especially when we crossed the Cape Cod Canal. It was a beautiful warm day. The sailboats and fishing trollers looked painted on the blue water. As I smelled the salty air, I had the funniest feeling, as if I were truly returning home. Perhaps I was experiencing what Daddy would have felt if he were alive and with me on this journey. I would learn more about him by going to this place. I began to overcome my nervousness and fear. In a way, Daddy would be with me.

Mommy fell asleep as we continued our journey up Route 6. The miles slid by like a long ribbon with no end. When the road signs indicated we were getting closer to Provincetown, a tiny charge of excitement passed through my heart. How could Mommy sleep through this? After all, she was going home, too. Finally, Archie, who had been quiet himself, announced we were close to the tip of the Cape, Provincetown. Mommy stirred, opening her eyes and stretching.

I caught sight of the dunes. "It looks like the desert."

Then Pilgrim's Monument came into view and Mommy told me what it was.

"The pilgrims supposedly landed here first," Mommy said. "The blue bloods make a big deal of that."

"Blue bloods?" I asked.

"People who trace their family history back to the Mayflower. Your father's family," she added disdainfully. "They think that makes them better than the rest of us."

"Is that why you and Daddy left?"

"That among other things," Mommy said and sewed her lips shut.

"Where do we go?" Archie asked.

"Turn left," Mommy ordered.

"Are they expecting us today, Mommy?"

"Yes," she said. "Jacob should be home. I see the tide is in."

"How can you tell?" I asked.

"The waves are breaking on the beach up at the beach grass. See?"

I nodded.

"Fishing boats go out and come back at high tide," Mommy explained. "I remember that much, but don't ask me too much more," she said quickly. It was as if it were painful for her to remember.

Archie followed her directions. We moved slowly through the narrow street, on both sides of which were small souvenir shops, boutiques, restaurants advertising fresh lobster dinners, and taverns with names like The Buccaneer and Mast Head. Here and there were signs advertising bed and breakfast accommodations. The buildings, some of which looked very old, were made from gray cedar shingles. All had Vacancy signs dangling in the breeze.

Mommy explained that it wasn't the season yet, so the tourists really weren't here. "These small streets get so crowded in the summer, it's wall-to-wall people."

"Yeah, just like the Vegas strip," Archie commented.

"Turn here," Mommy directed. We went east on an even narrower street that had small Cape Cod houses on both sides, none with much more than a couple of a hundred feet of rough-looking grass in front. But some had flowers. I saw one with a lilac bush towering as high as its roof. As we rolled along, I heard Mommy mumble, "It seems like a hundred years ago, but not much has changed."

Suddenly, there were no more houses, just a stretch of dunes. I thought we would stop, but Mommy told Archie to continue following the road. It turned north, and then, on the right, just a few hundred yards or so farther, a house appeared. I could see the beach and the ocean not too far away. A flock of terns circled over something on the sand.

"There it is," Mommy said, nodding at the house. There was a light brown pickup truck parked in the gravel driveway, and in front of that a dark blue, four-door automobile with its right rear end jacked up. A tall, lean man with hair Daddy's color was bending over a tire. He didn't turn to look at us, even when we stopped near the driveway.

"That is your uncle Jacob," Mommy said softly.

He finally glanced up. I saw the resemblances in his face, especially in his chin and cheekbones, but he was much leaner in build and he looked older than Daddy, not younger. Even from this distance I could see the deep lines at the corners of his eyes. He had a much darker complexion than Daddy's had been. He stared a moment and then went back to his tire as if he had no interest in who we were or why we were here.

"Should I pull in?" Archie asked.

"Yes," Mommy replied with a deep sigh. "Well, Melody, it's time to meet your family."

5

The Only Mother I Had

Archie slowly pulled into the driveway. Uncle Jacob didn't turn around again until we came to a full stop. Then he stood up and gestured emphatically for Archie to back up.

"I need the room to work here," he explained.

"Sorry," Archie said. He backed up a good ten feet and we all got out of the car. Uncle Jacob, his back to us, continued to work on removing the flat tire.

"Hello Jacob," Mommy said. He nodded without turning around.

"I'll be a while with this," he finally replied, still not looking our way. "Go on inside. Sara's been waiting on you all morning. Thought you were supposed to be here last night." He groaned as he turned the nut on the flat tire. The muscles in his long arms tightened and the muscles in his neck bulged with the effort. The nut loosened and he relaxed again.

"It took longer than we expected," Mommy said.

Uncle Jacob grunted.

Mommy looked at me and then at Archie, who had his lips twisted in disgust. She put her hand on my shoulder and guided me toward the front door. The house was a Cape Codder with a widow's walk that faced the ocean. The trim on the railings and shutters was a Wedgwood blue, but like the cedar siding, it was faded by the salt air. There was a short, narrow cobblestone walkway to the front door.

On the windows were dainty eggshell white curtains, and on the sills were flower boxes full of tulips and daffodils. A bird feeder dangled from the roof of the small porch and a tiny sparrow fluttered its wings nearby, cautiously waiting for us to pass.

Mommy tapped gently on the door. Then, after a moment, she tapped again, a bit harder.

"Just go on in," Uncle Jacob called from the driveway. "She won't hear you. She's in the kitchen, I'm sure."

Mommy turned the knob and we entered. A small entryway led us to the living room on our right. A massive brick fire place consumed most of the far wall. There was a bluish-gray throw rug on the tongue-and-groove floor. A deep-cushioned sofa and the overstuffed chair beside it were the only things that matched. The rest of the furnishings were antiques, which included a well worn rocker, two small pine tables at the ends of the sofa, an old sewing table in the corner, and lamps made of cranberry glass and milk glass. On the mantle were framed photos. Mounted on a dark blue board and hanging over the fireplace, was a swordfish that looked at least seven feet long. Its glass eye seemed to turn toward us as we entered.

"Sara?" Mommy called. "We're here."

We heard a pan being dropped into a metal sink and a moment later, my Aunt Sara appeared in the doorway to the kitchen.

A tall woman, maybe an inch or so taller than Mommy, she wore a long, flowing light blue skirt that made her look all legs. Over her skirt she had a plain white apron, on which she wiped her hands. Her blouse had frilled sleeves and pearl buttons closed almost to the top. The collar parted just enough to reveal her very pronounced collarbone and a thin gold chain that held a gold locket. Her chestnut brown hair hung down over her shoulders. Through it were delicate streaks of gray. Aunt Sara wore no makeup to brighten her pale complexion, and she wore no jewelry but the locket.

She might once have been pretty, but the silvery webs at her temples were deep and her eyes looked a dull, dark brown. The darkness spread to the puffiness beneath her eyes, too. She had a small nose and high cheekbones with gracefully full lips, but her face was thin, almost gaunt.

"Hello, Sara," Mommy said.

"Hello, Haille," Aunt Sara replied without changing her expression. The way Mommy and Aunt Sara gazed at each other made my stomach turn. It was as if they were not only looking at each other across this room, but across time and great distance. Neither made an attempt to hug or even shake hands. A deep silence lingered for a confusing moment, making me feel as if I were floundering in the world of adult quicksand.

What sort of welcome was this? I stood there, full of a thousand anxieties, butterflies panicking in my chest.

"This is my friend, Richard," Mommy said feeling she had to explain Archie's presence first, I suppose. "He was kind enough to drive us here from West Virginia."

Aunt Sara nodded but her eyes quickly went to me with greater interest, her face brightening in anticipation.

"And this is Melody," Mommy added, putting her hands on my shoulders. Aunt Sara's gaze was so penetrating I thought she could look right through me. A small smile, almost impossible to notice, formed at the corners of her mouth.

"Yes," she said nodding as if I were exactly the way she imagined I would be. "She's about Laura's size and height, only Laura's hair was darker and she never kept it that long," she said, sadness making her face long and hollow eyed.

"I'm so sorry about all that," Mommy said softly.

"Yes," Aunt Sara said, still staring at me. I looked to Mommy. What was she sorry about? Who was Laura? Apparently, she knew more than she had admitted about Daddy's family.

"I bet you're hungry," Aunt Sara said to me, a smile returning to her lips. I smiled back, but my stomach was tied in so many knots I didn't think I could ever put food in it. "I've got a chicken roasting. Cary will be home from school soon with May. They're both very excited about your coming here." She turned to Mommy and Archie. "In the meantime, I have some clams steamed for you."

"Oh good. In the years since I've been here, I've never had any good as yours, Sara."

"I don't do anything more with clams than anyone else around here does," she said modestly. "You scrub them and drop them into a clam kettle with just enough water to cover them. No mystery about it," Aunt Sara said, her voice suddenly harder, sterner.

"Maybe it's just the clams here," Mommy said. She seemed awkward and uncomfortable under Aunt Sara's icy glare.

"That's it for sure," Archie said. Aunt Sara raised her eyebrows and looked at him as if she had just noticed his presence.

"Well now, come into the dining room and make yourselves to home," she said.

An antique trestle table stretched nearly the whole length of the dining room. It had a captain's chair at each end and four straight chairs in a perfect line on each side. Lying at the head of the table was a leather-bound Bible. There was a small pine table in a corner of the room with a vase of yellow roses on it. On the wall was an oil painting: a seascape with a lone sailboat moving toward the horizon. I looked closer and saw what looked like a ray of bright sunshine pouring through an opening in the overcast sky with a godlike finger in the center of the ray of light. The finger pointed at the lone sailboat.

"Please take a seat," Aunt Sara said. "That's Jacob's chair," she added and nodded toward the captain's chair at the end of the table where the Bible lay. Obviously, no one else was permitted to sit in it. "Everyone like cranberry juice?"

"It makes for a great mix with vodka," Archie quipped.

"Pardon?" Aunt Sara said. Mommy gave him a reprimanding look.

"What?" He recovered quickly. "Oh, sure

we like it. Thank you." Aunt Sara hurried back to the kitchen.

"Who's Laura, Mommy?" I asked. "Why didn't you tell me about her?"

"It's too sad," Mommy whispered and brought her finger to her lips. "Not now, honey."

Aunt Sara reappeared carrying a pitcher filled with cranberry juice on a tray with three tall glasses, each with two ice cubes. She gave us each a glass and started to reach for the pitcher.

"Let me pour that," Archie volunteered. Aunt Sara nodded to him. She gazed at me again, drinking me in for a long moment, her eyes twinkling with pleasure and approval. It made me feel uncomfortable to be scrutinized so closely. I looked away.

"Do you like clams, dear?" she asked.

"I guess so," I said. "I don't remember eating them."

"She loves them," Mommy said quickly.

"Laura loved them so," Aunt Sara said. She sighed. "I'll go get them."

She returned to the kitchen.

"Mommy?" I said, pleading for information.

"Just wait, Melody. Let everyone get to know everyone before you start asking all your questions." She looked at Archie. "She's always full of questions."

"You don't have to tell me." He gulped

119

down some cranberry juice. "Hey, this is good."

"Cranberries are a big thing here," Mommy said. "I'd like a penny for every one I harvested. I'd be rich."

"You're gonna be rich," Archie promised. Mommy's smile warmed and she turned to me. "Isn't this a nice house, honey? There's a beach right behind it and a dock, too." She took a deep breath and closed her eyes. "I forgot how refreshing the ocean air could be," she said, which I thought was funny. She had never enjoyed our trips to the ocean as much as Daddy had.

"Yeah, it sure cleans the coal dust out of your lungs," Archie said.

Aunt Sara brought in pretty blue-and-white china soup bowls and set them in front of us. Then she brought in the kettle of clams and a bowl of melted butter.

"Please help yourselves," she said. Archie dipped his hand into the kettle quickly and brought out a clam. He plucked the meat with his thumb and forefinger and dipped it in the butter and sucked it down quickly.

"Great," he said.

"Use your fork," Mommy instructed as quietly as she could.

"What? Oh. Sure." He took a handful of clams out of the kettle and dropped them into his bowl, this time digging into the clams with his fork.

Aunt Sara smiled quickly and then looked as if she were at a loss as to what to do next.

"Aren't you having any, Sara?" Mommy asked.

"No. I'm fine. Go on. You eat, Haille." She looked at me again, stabbing me with her penetrating gaze. I nervously reached into the kettle and scooped up a few clams. I put them into my bowl and picked out the meat of one with my fork. Aunt Sara watched my every move, approving with a little nod every gesture I made. I felt like a specimen under a microscope. I looked at Mommy.

She didn't seem to notice or care about the way Aunt Sara was looking at me. "These clams are as wonderful as I remember them. It's been a long time."

"Yes," Aunt Sara said. After a deep sigh, she finally sat in her chair. "Was it a hard trip?"

"Naw," Archie said. "Some rain along the way is all."

"We had an unusually cold winter this year," Aunt Sara said. She looked around. "This house never seemed to warm up."

"How do you heat it?" Archie asked.

"Fireplace, and kerosene stoves. It's an old house, but we've been here ever since."

"Ever since what?" Archie asked.

"Ever since Jacob and I got married," she said. She looked at Mommy a moment. "You haven't changed all that much, Haille. You're still so pretty."

"Thank you, Sara."

"Melody has inherited your best features," Aunt Sara added, gazing at me again. I couldn't help blushing.

"Yes," Mommy said. "Everyone says so."

"Cary, he takes after Jacob, but May looks more like my side of the family. Laura . . . Laura was special," Aunt Sara added softly. Her eyes grew glassy and her gaze grew faraway. Then, suddenly, as if realizing we were there, she turned to me again and smiled. "Are you a good student?"

"Yes, ma'am."

"She's a *very* good student," Mommy said. "All A's."

"Just like Laura," Aunt Sara said. She shook her head. "Cary isn't like his twin sister was. He gets by, but he's not much for being shut up in a classroom. He's more like Jacob," she said. "Give him something to do outside and he'll be happy, no matter how cold it is or how much it's raining. When the Logan men get busy, the world could come to an end around them and they wouldn't know it."

"I know," Mommy said.

Aunt Sara sighed again, so deeply I thought she might shatter like thin china right before our eyes. "I'm sorry about Chester. Might as well tell you that before Jacob comes in. He won't want me speaking about him."

I looked at Mommy. Why wouldn't Daddy's brother permit anyone to speak about him even now, after he was dead? Mommy nodded, as if she had no trouble understanding.

"So how old's Cary now?" she asked, deliberately changing the topic.

"He's sixteen. May was ten last month."

"I bet she's a good student," Mommy said, struggling for conversation. Aunt Sara raised her eyebrows.

"Yes, but she goes to the special school, you know. Cary sees she gets there all right and home all right. He's devoted to her. I think more so since Laura . . . since Laura's been gone," she said.

Again, I looked at Mommy. She shifted her eyes away.

"You don't like the clams, dear?" Aunt Sara asked me, poised to be disappointed.

"What? Oh, yes," I said and dug my fork into another.

"How are Samuel and Olivia?" Mommy asked Aunt Sara. I knew those were my grandparents so I stopped eating again to listen.

"They both suffer from arthritis now and then, but otherwise they're well. I told them you were coming," she said, almost as an afterthought.

"Oh?"

Aunt Sara said nothing more about them. The topic disappeared as quickly as a popped soap bubble, but neither Mommy nor Aunt Sara seemed unhappy about that. I wanted to know more. They had never seen me. Were they curious about me as I was about them?

The door opened and closed. Uncle Jacob appeared, a rag in his hands. The shape of his chin and mouth resembled Daddy's, but he had a longer, sharper nose and larger ears. His eyes were more hazel than green.

"Clams are sweeter this year," he said.

"They're great," Archie said. Uncle Jacob finally considered him.

"This is my friend Richard, Jacob. He drove us here."

Uncle Jacob just nodded and then looked at me.

"She's not as tall as I thought she'd be," he said. The way he said it made me feel as if I had failed at growing properly.

"Melody, this is your Uncle Jacob," Mommy said, her eyes on him.

"Hello," I said, my voice cracking.

He didn't smile. He wiped his hands and stared at me. "Plenty of time for us all to meet later," he declared. "I got to do some work on the boat right now. Sara, send Cary down as soon as he's home." He left through the rear of the house.

"It's very important to look after the boat,"

Aunt Sara explained, with another quick smile. "Well," she continued, "I imagine you plan on staying the night, Haille."

"No," Mommy said quickly. "We have a tight schedule."

"Oh."

Why had we come so far if we were going to leave so quickly? I wondered. Mommy had talked about showing me Provincetown. Before I could ask, we heard the front door again.

"That should be Cary and May," Aunt Sara said. A few moments later, my cousins appeared in the dining room doorway.

Cary was tall and did indeed take after his father. He had the same dark complexion as Uncle Jacob only he had a more sensitive face with much softer features. He had green eyes like Daddy, but because his hair was darker, almost coal black, his emerald eyes seemed brighter. He wore his hair rather long, almost to his shoulders. He was dressed in jeans and a dark blue shirt with the sleeves rolled up to his elbows.

Beside him, still clinging to his hand, was my cousin May. She was small, birdlike for ten, diminutive except for her round, very bright hazel eyes. Her hair, the same chestnut shade as Aunt Sara's, was cut short in a pixie style. She wore a light blue dress with an embroidered bodice and saddle shoes. Her feet were so small, they made her look like a doll. She smiled, but Cary kept a very serious expression on his face, his gaze quickly moving from Archie to Mommy to me. When he fixed his eyes on me, I thought his look softened.

"Well, now, say hello to everyone," Aunt Sara said. "This is your aunt Haille, her friend Richard, and your cousin Melody."

Cary immediately turned to May and began to move his hands. She watched him and nodded when he stopped. Then she turned to us and said, "Hello." She stretched the syllables so that it sounded mechanical.

I couldn't help my look of surprise, but I saw it displeased Cary.

"Yes, she's deaf," my cousin said sharply to me.

"Well, ain't that a shame," Archie muttered. Cary threw him an angry look that, were it a knife, would have cut off Archie's head.

"How was school today, May?" Aunt Sara asked her, signing as she spoke.

May proudly held up a paper with a bright gold star at the top.

"She got a hundred on the spelling test," Cary boasted.

"That's nice, dear," Aunt Sara said. She seemed a bit more uncomfortable with the hand movements than her son was. "Your father wants you to go right down to the dock, Cary," she said. He nodded. "You can visit with everyone at dinner."

Cary turned immediately and signed something to May. She nodded and then looked at me. He glanced at me once more before heading out back.

"Go up and change your clothes, dear," Aunt Sara signed to May. The young girl nodded and signed something back before hurrying off. "Cary takes such good care of her," Aunt Sara remarked with a sigh.

"I didn't know she was deaf," Mommy said softly. "I don't think Chester knew either."

"Yes, she was born deaf. Seems like that should have been enough of a burden for us, but then . . . there was Laura."

A heavy pall fell over the table.

Archie couldn't stand it. "Why don't we go into the town and see the sights before dinner, Haille?"

Mommy nodded.

"Can we take May along?" I asked Aunt Sara.

"Oh, I don't think we should," Mommy said quickly. "We're still strangers to her."

"Your mother is right, dear. It's a little soon," Aunt Sara said. She got up and started to clear off the table.

"Let me help you, Aunt Sara," I said. She turned with surprise.

"Why, thank you, dear, but I can manage fine. Why don't you go and get your things and I'll show you your room now."

"My room?"

Aunt Sara smiled and went into the kitchen. I turned to Mommy.

"My room? What's wrong with her, Mommy? Didn't you say we weren't staying overnight?"

"Let's go outside, Melody," Mommy said in a whisper.

I followed her and Archie out. He headed for the trunk of the car.

"Let me talk to her first, Richard," Mommy told him.

He paused and shrugged. Then he dug a cigarette from his pocket and leaned against the car.

"What's going on, Mommy?"

"Nothing terrible," she replied quickly. "Isn't it pretty here? Look at the view of the ocean you get from the house, and it's not too far from the town, is it?"

"Mommy, what is happening?" I demanded.

"Now just listen carefully, Melody, and don't go into a tantrum." She glanced over at Archie. He looked at his watch. "Let's take a little walk by ourselves," Mommy suggested. She started away. I followed, but I was stretched like a tight wire inside, so taut I thought I might snap in two.

"It really wasn't right for the family to be separated for so long," Mommy began. "It wasn't right that you never met your cousins until now, and it certainly wasn't right for you never to have met your grandparents," she recited. It sounded like something she had memorized.

"So? I thought that was why you wanted us to come here first," I said.

"It was. It is. I mean, yes." She took a deep breath and pressed her lips together. Tears came to her eyes.

"What's wrong, Mommy? What is it?"

"Oh Melody, you know that I love you, that I will always love you."

"I know that, Mommy."

"You know that even though I love you, I always thought it was a mistake for me to have had a child so early in my life. I want to warn you about that," she said sternly. "Don't have children until you're at least thirty-five."

"Thirty-five!"

"Yes. If you're smart, you'll remember that. Anyway, you know that I've tried to be a good mother. I know I'm not the best mother."

"I'm not complaining, Mommy," I said. There were burning tears coming to my eyes now, too. "We'll be all right."

"Oh, I know we will, honey, but first I have to do things. I have to try, don't I? You wouldn't want me to feel I never tried when I had the chance. You wouldn't want me frustrated and shut up in another place like

Sewell, would you? Because if I'm not happy, Melody, I can't make you happy, can I? Can I?" she repeated.

"No," I said. I tried to take a deep breath, but my lungs felt as if ice had entered them and shriveled them with constricting pain.

"Good. So you understand why I've got to go places and meet people and do auditions and learn things," she said.

"You already told me all this, Mommy."

"I know, but . . . well, it's not the kind of life I can put you through right now. You're still in school and you need stability. You need friends and boyfriends and to go to parties and —"

"So, why can't I do that wherever we are, Mommy?"

"Because I'm not going to be anyplace for a while, maybe a long while. I'll have to travel around. If I get an opportunity, I have to pick right up and go. You can't turn down good opportunities, not at my age," she emphasized. "And what would life be like for you under such circumstances, huh?"

"But Mommy —"

"Listen, honey. Imagine just having made some new friends or starting out with a new boyfriend, and me coming home and saying, we're leaving tomorrow. You know now how hard that was this time, how terrible you felt? How would it be feeling that all the time? And then having to sleep in cheap motels and eat on the road and . . . everything. After a while you're just going to hate me, and then I would hate myself, and then I wouldn't try to be someone," she explained. "We would both be unhappy."

She smiled. "I don't want you to be unhappy, honey."

"What are we going to do, Mommy?" I asked and held my breath.

"Well, now here's where everything worked out for us. After your daddy died, I called Uncle Jacob and Aunt Sara and told them, of course, and then I explained what I was going to do with my life now. It was Aunt Sara who suggested it."

"Suggested what, Mommy?"

"Suggested you stay here while I'm off making a career change," she said. "She's very happy to have you and this is a wonderful place to live. You'll make so many new and interesting friends, I'm sure."

"You can't leave me here." I shook my head.

"Just for a while, honey. I'll call constantly and I'll come back for you as soon as I'm established some place. But for now I've got to go off with Archie and I know you're not crazy about traveling with us."

"You mean Richard," I said dryly. "And I know he's not happy about having me travel with you."

"It's not because of Richard."

"Are you going to marry him, Mommy?"

"Of course not," she said, but not with a great deal of firmness. "Anyway," she said, gesturing toward the house, "this will be fine for a while. You'll be staying with family."

"I don't want to stay here, Mommy. I don't want to be away from you," I moaned.

"Oh, you won't be, not for long anyway. I promise." She stroked my hair and smiled and then kissed my forehead. "I just need this chance, honey, and I can't go off and get it worrying about you, too. It wouldn't be fair to you. I'd neglect you even worse than I have in the past. And you're so very smart. You understand, don't you? I have no fear that you'll do well here, too. Everyone likes you, Melody."

I lowered my head slowly like a flag of defeat and stared at my feet. A southern breeze blew, caressing my cheek, making strands of my hair dance around my face. I heard the cry of nearby terns and the roar of the ocean.

Daddy was the glue that had held our little family together. Now that he was gone, we were coming apart.

"I'd rather have stayed home with Papa George and Mama Arlene, Mommy."

"I know. I thought of that, but Papa George is a very sick man. Mama Arlene can't be responsible for a young girl, too. It wouldn't be fair to dump you on her, honey."

I looked up sharply.

"So instead you want to dump me here?"

"No, Melody. Living with your own family for a while isn't the same thing as dumping you some place, is it?"

"These people . . . I don't know them, Mommy, and they don't know me."

"An even better reason to stay with them, Melody. You should get to know them, right? Aren't I right about that?" She waited for the answer she wanted.

"I don't know, maybe. But why didn't we ever speak to them before? Why was Daddy so upset with them?"

"Because they didn't want him to marry me, Melody. I told you. They looked down on me because I was an orphan, adopted. I wasn't one of their bluebloods and your grandparents — your father's parents — wanted him to marry someone else, someone they had chosen. He refused. Chester Logan fell in love with *me* and we got married. Then they wouldn't talk to him and he wouldn't talk to them. Now everyone realizes how foolish they were, I'm sure. They want to make it up to your father, but it's too late for that. The only way they could make up for their bitterness and unpleasantness is to care for you. That's why they were so anxious to do it and why I agreed. I only wish you'd see the logic in it and let me leave with a happy heart.

"Because if I feel happy about you, I will be able to concentrate on my new career and I'll be able to do things for us faster, Melody," she added.

"What are you going to do, Mommy? You don't even have a specific plan."

"Sure I do. I'm going to be a model and an actress," she said firmly. Then she laughed and spun on her heels. "Did you ever see anyone who is more qualified, anyone prettier?"

"No, Mommy."

"Won't it be wonderful seeing me in magazines or in the movies? Can you imagine telling your friends that's your mother?" She laughed and twirled her hair. She was beautiful. Maybe she would become a model and be in magazines. If I went into a tantrum and stopped her from going without me, she would blame me for failing, I thought. I didn't want Mommy to hate me.

I looked back at the house. Archie paced behind the car impatiently. At least I wouldn't have to be with him any longer. I was the eternal cockeyed optimist, always looking for a rainbow after any sorrowful storm.

"Well?" Mommy said. "Will you stay with the family a while? Will you, Melody?"

"If that's what you want me to do, Mommy," I said in a tired, defeated voice. She clapped her hands together.

"Oh, thank you, honey. Thank you. Thank you for giving me my chance. I won't let you down. I promise, honey."

I nodded and took a deep breath. When I looked at the house again, I saw May come out and look our way. She had a ball and paddle and began to play with them, her eyes trained on me and Mommy.

"What happened to Laura, Mommy?"

"She went sailing one day with a boy and they got caught in a storm."

"She drowned in the ocean?"

Mommy nodded.

"We didn't find out about it until months afterward. Daddy decided to call your uncle then, but he still wouldn't speak to Chester. This house has seen a lot of sadness, just like ours. But they'll be lucky for a while," Mommy added. I looked up at her.

"Why?"

"They'll have you," she said. She put her arm around me and we started back toward the driveway. Archie looked up expectantly and Mommy nodded. Then he hurried to the trunk to unload my bags.

"What about the rest of my things, Mommy? I don't have much."

"I'll get in touch with Arlene and see about having them shipped up here. Don't worry," she said. May was still watching us with great curiosity.

Mommy noticed the girl. "Hello, honey."

May smiled at her but turned quickly to me. Then she thrust her hand at mine and seized my fingers tightly, tugging me to go someplace with her.

"Go on, honey," Mommy said. "Richard and I will see to your things."

"But . . ." May pulled again. I let her lead me away. She quickened her pace when we reached the sand and soon I was running alongside her.

"Where are we going?" I cried, for a moment forgetting her deafness. We were heading toward the dock and the ocean. First, we had to climb to the top of a dune covered with scrub pine. The sand gave way beneath my feet. It was hard to run on the dunes, and before long, I felt my calf muscles ache. Little May didn't seem to have the least bit of difficulty. She was as light as air, remaining ahead of me all the way to the crest of the small sandy hill.

When we reached it, I paused to look at the vast ocean. In the distance two fishing boats trolled toward shore and farther out, a sailboat gracefully glided over the waves, its white sail fluttering. Off to my right there were shacks along the dunes. Above us, a flock of Canada geese flew north in formation against a deep blue sky dappled with smoke-blue puffs of clouds. The sight was invigorating and the fresh sea air seemed to wash the sadness from my heart. This, I thought, was once my father's playground. And now, for a while at least, it would be mine.

May tugged on my hand and pointed toward the dock.

"Car . . . ry," she said. "Come on."

I laughed and followed her down the dune. We continued to run, my chest heaving. Finally we slowed to a walk as we reached the dock.

My uncle's lobster boat bobbed gently in the water. It was a white and gray boat, and although it looked old, it looked very clean and well kept. The boat was named *Laura* and the name had been recently repainted on its side. At first we saw no one, but then Cary came out of the cabin with a pail and a brush in his hands. He had his shirt off and didn't see us immediately. May called up to him.

"Car-ry."

When he saw us standing on the dock, he immediately put down his pail and brush so he could sign to May. Whatever he was telling her, he was telling her emphatically. He looked angry, too.

"Is anything wrong?" I asked. The falling sun gleamed off his shiny brown skin. He looked muscular and hard and wore a silver necklace I hadn't noticed before.

"She knows she can't come down here by herself," he said.

"She's not by herself. She's with me," I replied.

"You're a landlubber," he snapped. "It's the same as if she were by herself." He signed again and May turned and started back toward the house. I stared up at Cary.

"She only wanted to show me," I said.

"She knows better. Take her home," he ordered and picked up his pail and brush. Turning his back on me, he returned to what he had been doing. I fumed for a moment and then hurried to catch up to May, who was walking much more slowly with her head down. I grabbed her hand when I caught up with her and she smiled.

"It's all right," I said. She tilted her head. She had beautiful hazel eyes, bejeweled with flecks of blue, green, and gold on the soft brown. "Your brother shouldn't have gotten so nasty," I added, but she looked confused and I felt frustrated. I was speaking loud, as if that mattered. It made me feel stupid. I glanced back once and saw Cary looking after us. Behind him, the sky was turning a dusky lavender.

"If it's so dangerous around here," I muttered, "why live here?"

I pounded my feet into the sand and clung to May's hand as we returned to the house. When we arrived, I found Mommy and Archie waiting by the car. May released my hand and ran into the house.

"Where did you go, honey?" Mommy asked.

"Just for a walk to the dock to see the lobster boat, but that was apparently off limits for May," I said. "Cary isn't very nice."

"Oh, I'm sure it's just because you two don't know each other yet," Mommy said.

"Haille," Archie said raising his eyebrows.

"Honey," Mommy said stepping closer so she could take my hand. "Archie and I think we should start out now so we can get back down to Boston. He has someone for me to meet there tonight."

"You're leaving now? But what about dinner?"

"We're just going to grab something on the highway," she said.

"Didn't you want to look at the town and —"

"Oh I know this town," she said laughing. "Don't forget how long I lived here."

"But . . ." I looked at the house and then back toward the ocean. "Don't you want to talk with Uncle Jacob?"

"I think he'll be happy to avoid it right now," she said. "We put your things in your room. It's a very nice room, honey, nicer than what you had in the trailer. The window looks out on the ocean. Aunt Sara is going to see to it you get enrolled in the school and the school will get all your records from West Virginia easily enough. I've already signed the papers I needed to sign

139

to give Aunt Sara the authority," Mommy added.

"When?" I asked, astounded at how much had really been done already.

"Um, just now. Aunt Sara found out what had to be done. She's very excited about having you."

Archie got into the car and started the engine. My heart began to beat wildly like a jungle drum.

"Mommy?"

"Now don't make this any harder than it has to be, honey. I'll be calling you in a few days to tell you where I am and what I've been doing, and before you know it, I'll be coming back for you."

"Time ticks," Archie called.

"Can't you stay a little longer?" I pleaded. My heart was doing flip-flops.

"A little longer isn't going to make any difference to you, but it will make a lot of difference to us because we have to drive so far, honey. Please."

She hugged me, but I kept my arms at my sides. Then she kissed me quickly on the forehead.

"I don't have to tell you to be a good girl. I know you will be. See you soon," she added and turned toward the car.

"Mommy!"

I ran to her and hugged her tightly, clinging to her, clinging to the only life I had known, clinging to the memories of our laughter and tears. Maybe she wasn't the best of all mothers, but she was the only mother I had, and there were nice times, too. There were the picnics and the dinners, the Christmases and birthdays. All I could remember now was being a little girl and clinging to her hand as we walked through the streets of Sewell. Everyone looked at us; Mommy was so beautiful and I was so proud.

"Melody," she whispered. "*Please,* honey."

I let her go and backed away.

She smiled. "I'll call you soon." She walked quickly around the car to get in.

Archie smiled at me. "Don't do anything I wouldn't do, kid," he said and winked.

"There's not much you wouldn't do," I replied. He laughed.

"Going to miss you, princess. I got no one to be my gopher." He laughed and backed the car out of the driveway. I took a step forward.

Mommy turned as they pulled away, waving.

Another picture to press down into my memory. I watched as the car disappeared down the street. I stood there, still in disbelief.

Then I heard the door open behind me and I turned to see Aunt Sara nervously wiping her hands on her apron. "Laura always liked to help set the table. Would you like to help?"

I nodded and she smiled.

"I thought so."

She went back inside. I lowered my head and followed. I felt like someone who'd been cast off a boat. I was searching desperately for a lifesaving raft.

6

Laura's Things

Aunt Sara had the dinner dishes on the kitchen counter and the silverware piled next to them. She folded linen napkins. The kitchen was as long as it was wide, with pots and pans hanging on the wall, two metal sinks side by side, a large cast-iron stove, and a refrigerator. There was a pantry off to the left. The late-afternoon sunlight poured through the large window on the west end, providing the only light.

"I'm putting out my better china tonight," she said smiling as she meticulously folded the napkins. "Your arrival is a special occasion. Set out five places," she told me. "You'll sit directly across from May and next to me. That's where Laura used to sit."

"Where is May?" I asked.

"May went up to her room, probably to start on her homework. She's a diligent student. Laura taught her that."

"She took me to the dock and Cary yelled at her," I said.

Aunt Sara nodded. "He won't permit any-one else to take her near the water. He's afraid." She took a deep breath and held her right palm against her heart. "We're all just a little more afraid," she muttered.

I gathered the dishes and brought them to the dining room. I felt I was sleepwalking. Was this really happening? Had Mommy truly gone and left me here?

When I returned to the kitchen to get the silverware and folded napkins, Aunt Sara was checking the chicken. Something sim-mered on the stove. Potatoes baked while pies cooled on the windowsill. The hustle and bustle in Aunt Sara's kitchen gave me a warm feeling. Everything smelled wonder-ful. I had been too nervous this morning to eat much of a breakfast, and except for the few clams I had nibbled when we first ar-rived, I had eaten very little all day.

"Laura loved to cook with me," Aunt Sara said as she worked. "While other girls her age were off giggling over boys, she was home, helping. She was always like that, even as a little girl. You never saw a more selfless person, worrying about everyone else before she worried about herself.

"You know what Jacob says?" She turned to me. "He says the angels must have been so jealous of her, God granted them their wish and took her to heaven sooner than planned."

She smiled, her face softened, her chin quivering. Tears glittered in her eyes.

"I'm sorry," I said. "I'm sorry I never got to meet her."

"Oh, yes. Wouldn't that have been wonderful?" She thought a moment and then sternly added, "You should have met."

I wanted to ask her why we hadn't, why this family had been so bitter and mean to each other, but I thought it might be the wrong time to bring up such questions.

She took a deep breath. "You better put out the silverware, dear."

After the table was set, Aunt Sara said she'd take me to my room. "Your things are already there. I want to show you where to put them away and all that you can use, too."

"Use?" I wondered what she meant as I followed her up the short stairway leading to the second floor. The steps creaked and the railing shook as we ascended. At the top was a small landing.

"May's room and Cary's room are down that way," she said pointing right. Without windows, the hallway was dark. "Jacob's and my room is the last room on the left and your room, which was Laura's room, is right there." She pointed to the first door on the left. "That's the bathroom, of course," she added, curtly nodding at the doorway across from what was to be my room.

"Here you are." She stood back after opening the door. I gazed in slowly, shocked at what I found. The room was cluttered with things that had once belonged to my dead cousin. It looked as if she had just died yesterday. The walls were covered with her posters of rock and movie stars, the shelves crowded with stuffed animals and ceramic dolls. There was a collection of ceramic and pewter cats on one shelf. Below the shelves was a small table with a miniature tea set and a big doll in a chair.

It was a very pretty, cozy room, with pink wallpaper spotted white. There was a canopy bed, just like the bed Alice Morgan had, only the headboard didn't have a heart design. The bedding, comforter, and pillows all matched the mauve shade of the canopy, and at the center of the two fluffy pillows was a large, stuffed cat that looked almost real and very much like the one I had brought.

There was a vanity table with a large mirror and a matching dresser. In one corner was a desk and chair. An open notebook lay on the desk and beside it was a pile of school textbooks and what looked like library books.

Why weren't they ever returned? I wondered.

The sliding doors on the closet were open, so I could see the garments hanging inside. On a hook next to the closet doorjamb was a pink terrycloth robe. The slippers were at the foot of the bed.

Two open windows, one on each side of the bed, faced the ocean. The breeze made the curtains flutter and wave. The scent of the sea air overpowered the vague, sweet perfume I smelled when first looking into the room.

"Isn't it beautiful?" Aunt Sara said.

"Yes."

"I want you to be comfortable here," she said. "Use anything you want and need. It would be a great joy to me to see you wearing one of those pretty dresses. Try one on," she said anxiously. "They look just your size."

I shook my head gently.

"I don't know if I should, Aunt Sara." Despite its recently lived-in appearance, the room felt more like a shrine to a dead girl.

"Of course you should," she said, her eyes full of panic because I had suggested otherwise. "That's why I wanted you to stay here. There's so much going to waste and now it won't. If Laura were standing right here beside us, she would say, 'Cousin Melody, use anything you want. Go on.' I can almost hear her saying that." She tilted her head as if to catch someone's voice in the breeze. "Can't you?" She wore a strange, soft smile.

I walked into the room and looked more closely at everything. On the desk was a pile of letters wrapped in a rubber band. The brushes and combs on the vanity table still had strands of dark brown hair twirled through them. On the top of the dresser was a framed picture of my cousin Laura standing at the front of the house holding a bouquet of yellow roses.

"That was her sweet sixteen picture," Aunt Sara explained. "Taken almost a year ago now. Laura and Cary's birthday is next month, you know."

Cary would be seventeen. "Is Cary a senior?"

"Yes. Laura would have been the class valedictorian and have made the speech on graduation day. Everyone says so."

I looked more closely at the girl in the photograph. Aunt Sara was right. Laura had been very pretty. She had Cary's eyes and they had similar noses and mouths, with the exact same shade of dark brown hair. Laura's features were smaller, feminine, dainty. She looked about my height and weight, but not as full as I in the bosom. Staring at the photograph, I understood why Uncle Jacob told Aunt Sara the angels were jealous, however. Laura had a glow in her face, a soft, spiritual quality that made her look as if any moment she might sprout angel wings and fly away.

"She was very pretty," I said.

"Yes."

"And who is this?" I picked up a wallet-size

photograph of a brown-haired boy that was wedged in the frame of Laura's sweet sixteen photograph. He was handsome.

"That was Robert Royce," Aunt Sara said. She sighed yet again. "He was taken along with Laura that terrible day."

"Oh. How horrible!"

"How horrible," Aunt Sara parroted. She gazed around the room. "I haven't touched anything in here except to dust and clean. It's just as it was the day she died. Please try to keep everything where it is, Melody dear. Put everything back exactly where you found it. But as I said, use whatever you want.

"I suppose you could use a little rest after traveling so long and so far. Dinner is in an hour. Jacob likes us all to look nice come the evening meal. I left this drawer for you to put your own things in," she said showing me the third drawer in the dresser, "and you can find enough space in the closet for what you have brought, I'm sure."

"Mommy said she was going to have my other things sent," I said.

"Until she does, use these things," Aunt Sara said gesturing at everything. "Tomorrow morning," she continued, "I will take you to the school to get you enrolled. It's not far. You can walk home with Cary and May every day, just as Laura did."

Aunt Sara turned, paused in the doorway,

and then marched back to the closet.

"I might suggest something for you to wear to dinner." She sifted through Laura's garments. "Now this, yes, this would be perfect." She held out a blue dress with a white collar and white cuffs on the three-quarter sleeves.

"It looks as if it might be tight here," I said holding my hands on my ribs.

"Oh no, it won't be. This material gives a bit, but even if it is, I'll let it out for you. I'm a talented seamstress," she added with a laugh. "I used to adjust all of Laura's clothes. I made her this dress." She pulled a pink taffeta off its hanger to show me. "She wore this to a school dance."

"It's nice."

"Perhaps you'll wear it to a school dance, too." She gazed at it a moment before returning it to the closet. She hung it between the exact same two dresses, right where it had hung before she retrieved it to show me.

She lay the blue dress on the bed and stepped back.

"What size is your foot?"

I told her. She looked disappointed.

"Laura had smaller feet. It's a shame for you not to be able to use any of her shoes."

"Maybe May will get to wear them," I suggested.

"Yes," she whispered, looking heartbroken. "Anyway," she said, "I'm sure the dress will fit. Welcome to our home, dear."

Before leaving, she again paused in the doorway.

"It's so wonderful knowing all these things will be used and loved again. It's almost as if . . . as if Laura sent you to us." She smiled at me and left.

A chill passed through my breast. I felt like an intruder in this bedroom. It was still Laura's room. My small suitcases were stacked beside each other against the wall and my fiddle in its case was resting on top of them. There was so little of me here, so much of Laura.

I unpacked, putting my own stuffed cat next to the one already on the bed. They looked as if they'd come from the same litter. I put my teddy bear above them on the pillow, too. Then I hung up what clothes I had brought and used the drawer Aunt Sara had cleared for me.

When I was finished, I went to the window and stared out at the ocean and the beach. Cary and Uncle Jacob walked back from the dock. Cary still had his shirt off and had tossed it over his shoulder. His shoulder gleamed in the sunlight as he plodded along with his head down. Uncle Jacob appeared to be lecturing him about something.

Suddenly, as if he knew my eyes were upon him, Cary gazed up at the window and for a strange moment, it was as if Laura herself were gazing up at me through his emerald eyes.

I jumped when I heard someone behind me. May stood in the doorway.

"Hi," I said and waved. She came into the room with a book. She plopped on the bed and opened the book, pointing to a page. I sat and gazed at her math text. "You want help?" I asked. I pointed to the page and to myself and then to her. She nodded, signing what I assumed meant, "Yes, please help me."

"This is just figuring percentages," I muttered. "It's easy."

She stared at me. I kept forgetting she couldn't hear a single word. What would it be like, I wondered, to live in the world and never hear a bird sing or music, never know the comforting sound of a loved one's voice. It seemed unfair, especially for a little girl as nice as May.

"Okay," I said nodding. I gestured at the desk and she followed. I sat with her standing beside me and began to do the problems, struggling to explain what I was doing. Despite my difficulty to communicate, she appeared to understand my guidance, carefully reading my lips. When she did a problem, she quickly followed my lead. She was clearly a bright girl.

We did another problem and again she picked up my suggestions quickly.

"What's going on?" I heard and turned to see Cary in the doorway.

"I was just helping May with her math homework."

"I help her with her math," he said. "She can't hear you. It makes it too difficult for her," he said.

"She's doing just fine with me."

He signed something to May and she looked upset. He signed again and she shook her head.

"If she doesn't do well, it will be your fault," Cary snapped and walked away.

"He's not very friendly," I muttered.

May didn't see my lips move, but she was apparently not bothered by Cary's attitude. She smiled at me and went to my suitcases, inquisitively tapping on the fiddle case. She looked at me curiously.

"It's a fiddle," I said. I opened the case and took out the bow. Her eyes widened with surprise. How horrible, it occurred to me: she won't be able to hear me play.

But she urged me to do so anyway. I smiled and shook my head, but she seemed to plead with those big eyes.

"But how can you . . . ?" I was confused.

She nodded at my fiddle.

I shrugged, picked up the bow, and played.

May stepped closer. I ran the bow over the strings and played a jaunty mountain ditty. Slowly, she raised her hand and put her fingers on the fiddle. She closed her eyes.

She's feeling the vibrations, I realized, and sure enough, her head moved slightly up and down with the undulations in the rhythms. I laughed happily and continued.

Suddenly, Cary was at my door again, buttoning a clean white shirt. "What are you doing with her now?" he demanded.

I stopped, lowering the fiddle. May opened her eyes with disappointment and then turned to see what I was looking at.

"She wanted to know what this was and then she wanted me to play it for her."

"That's a pretty sick joke," he said.

"She was listening through her fingers," I began to explain, but he shook his head and walked away again.

I fumed.

"Your brother," I told May, "is a . . . a monster." I exaggerated my eyes and twisted my mouth when I pointed to the doorway. She looked at me, shocked for a moment, then when she realized what I meant she laughed.

May's sweet laughter calmed my temper.

"I better get ready for dinner," I told her and pointed to Laura's dress. I pantomimed bringing food to my mouth. She nodded and scooped up her math book and papers to go off and get dressed herself.

I put my fiddle away, thinking about Daddy, recalling him, Papa George, and

Mama Arlene sitting on their patio and listening to me practice. How I missed them all!

Aunt Sara had made it sound as if dressing for dinner was very important in this house. I went to the bathroom and washed up, then returned to my room's vanity mirror to fix my hair. I wanted to clear away all of Laura's things and make room for my own, but I remembered Aunt Sara asking me not to move anything. I found small places for my own stuff and crowded everything in together.

Laura's blue dress was snug, especially around my bosom. I had to leave the top two buttons undone, but it was somehow important to Aunt Sara that I wear it.

Maybe it was because I was wearing this clinging dress, but when I gazed at myself in the mirror, I had a new sense of myself, a feeling that I had reached a level of femininity. Despite the way Mommy always talked about herself, I felt guilty being proud of my looks, my figure. In church the preacher called it a sin of pride.

But as I ran my hands over my bosom and down the sides of my body to my hips, turning and inspecting myself, I thought that I just might look pretty. Perhaps I, too, would turn men's heads the way Mommy did. Was it sinful to think like this?

A loud rapping on the door shattered my

moment of introspection, making me feel as if I had been caught doing something naughty.

"It's time to come down," Cary growled. "My father doesn't like us to be late."

"I'm coming." I fixed a loose strand of hair. I opened the door. Cary and May stood outside in the hallway, waiting.

I saw his look of surprise. The mask of sternness and fury shattered. He looked handsome with his hair brushed back. He wore a tie and a nice pair of slacks.

"That's one of Laura's dresses," he whispered.

Panicky butterflies were on the wing again, battering my brain with doubts, buffeting my heart with indecision. Perhaps I shouldn't have put on her dress. Maybe I was violating another unwritten code in this confusing house.

"Your mother picked it out for me to wear to dinner," I replied.

The answer satisfied him and his face softened. May took my hand. Cary glanced at her and then pivoted and strutted to the stairway, leading us down. May signed to me and I imagined she said, "You look very nice."

Uncle Jacob was seated at the table. His hair was wet and brushed back, parted in the middle. He was cleanly shaven and wearing a white shirt, a tie, and slacks. Cary glanced at me before sitting. May followed. I hesitated.

"I'll see if Aunt Sara needs help," I said. Uncle Jacob nodded and I went into the kitchen. "Can I help you bring the food to the table, Aunt Sara?"

She turned from the stove.

"Of course, dear. That's what Laura always did." She nodded at the bowls of vegetables and the potatoes, the bread and the cranberry sauce.

I started to bring out the food. Uncle Jacob had his Bible open and was silently reading. Cary and May sat ramrod straight, waiting, but Cary's eyes lifted to follow my movements around the table. The last thing I brought in was a pitcher of ice water. I poured some in everyone's glass and then sat as Aunt Sara brought out the roast chicken. She smiled at me and took her seat.

"Let us give thanks," Uncle Jacob said. Everyone lowered his head. "Lord, we thank you for the food we are about to enjoy."

I thought that was it when everyone looked up, but Uncle Jacob handed Cary the Bible.

"It's your turn, son."

Cary shot a look at me and then gazed at the pages Uncle Jacob had opened for him.

"What man of you having a hundred sheep, if he lose one of them, doth not leave the ninety and nine in the wilderness and go after that which is lost, until he find it?"

Cary read in a voice so hard and deep, I had to look twice to be sure he was reading.

He continued. "And when he hath found it, he layeth it on his shoulders, rejoicing.

"And when he cometh home, he calleth together his friends and neighbors, saying unto them, Rejoice with me; for I have found my sheep which was lost."

"Good." Uncle Jacob took the Bible. He nodded to Aunt Sara and she rose to serve the vegetables, beginning with Uncle Jacob.

As he cut the roast chicken, he finally looked at me. "I see that you're settled in," he began. "Your aunt will give you a list of your daily chores. Everyone pulls his weight here. This ain't a Cape Cod rooming house." He paused to see if I was listening closely.

"I did most of the chores in our house in West Virginia," I said firmly.

"You lived in a trailer, I understand," he said, putting the chicken on May's plate.

"There was still lots to do, cleaning, washing, cooking."

"I bet there was." He shook his head. "Haille was never one for doing home chores." He paused and turned to me. "What was that music I heard before?"

"I was playing my fiddle for May."

Uncle Jacob raised his eyebrows as if I had said the most astonishing thing. "Who taught you how to do that? Chester wasn't musical." He paused and then added, "Although Dad says his Pa was."

"Papa George taught me," I replied, quickly explaining who he and Mama Arlene were.

"So he was a coal miner, too?" He shook his head. "I don't know how anyone could shut himself inside a mountain for his daily bread," Uncle Jacob said. "Especially someone who was brought up on the ocean, breathing God's freshest, cleanest air. It's what we were meant to do. We weren't meant to live like moles."

"It wasn't something Daddy wanted to do," I replied.

Uncle Jacob grunted. "You make your bed and then you lie in it."

I was afraid to ask what he meant. We all started eating.

My uncle paused after a few moments and looked at me again. "This year, we're going to have our best cranberry crop. If you're still here in the fall, you can help harvest."

"Cranberry crop?"

"We got a bog just over the hill here." He nodded toward the north end. "Helps supplement what I make lobstering. That ain't what it was when my father had his fleet of boats working."

He nodded at Cary. "Cary can tell you all about the cranberry harvesting. We're not millionaires, but it's easier than clawing black rocks from the earth's gut," he muttered.

My eyes went to Cary. His eyes were on me. He shifted them quickly away and I looked at May. She smiled. The one bright spot at the table, I thought.

Then I looked at Aunt Sara. She hadn't yet eaten a bite of supper. She had been staring at me the whole time, smiling.

I helped Aunt Sara with the dinner dishes and silverware, then decided to take a walk. The entire time I was in the kitchen, Aunt Sara went on and on about Laura, describing how much of a help she had been and how good she was at making cranberry muffins and jams. Aunt Sara wanted me to learn how to do everything Laura had been able to do. I didn't mind, I suppose, but it was strange being constantly compared to my dead cousin. If I voiced any hesitation, however, Aunt Sara would stop whatever she was doing and smile at me.

"But you have to try, dear. Laura would want you to try." She said it with such certainty. It was as if she could still speak to her drowned daughter. It gave me the willies.

Leaving the kitchen, I felt drained, but I had more tension ahead of me. I had to walk through the living room to the front door. Uncle Jacob sat in the rocker reading a newspaper. He looked up sharply when I appeared.

"Dishes done?" he demanded.

"Yes, Uncle Jacob."

"Well, then take a seat there and we'll have our talk now." He folded his paper and nodded at the settee across from him.

"Our talk?" I slowly entered the room and sat. He put his newspaper on the sea chest table, tapped the ashes from his pipe into a seashell ashtray, and sat back in his rocker, gazing more at the ceiling than at me.

"When Sara told me Haille wanted to bring you here to live a while, I was against it," he admitted frankly. "It didn't surprise me none to hear that she was trying to avoid her responsibilities. That was the only Haille I ever knew. But Sara had her heart set on this, and Sara has suffered far more than a decent, hardworking woman like her should. We can't question the burdens God gives us. We've just got to bear them and go on.

"Sara," he continued, fixing his cold, steely gaze at me, "thinks God sent you here to help fill the hole in our hearts we got from Laura's passing. You ain't never going to fill that hole. No one can fill that hole. But Sara's got a right to hope, a right to put her tears to bed. Can you understand that?"

"Yes," I said meekly. I held my breath.

"Good. I want you to promise never to disappoint Sara. You got off to a good start

161

here helping out with dinner like you did without anyone having to tell you to do it. It's the way Laura would have behaved.

"Laura was a good girl. She read her Bible, said her prayers, did well in school, and never gave us none of the grief some of the young people today are giving their folks. I never caught her smoking . . . anything," he added. His eyes burned with warning. "And she never drank beer or whiskey outside of this house. If she went on a date, she was always home the proper time and did nothing about which we would be ashamed to hear."

I let out the breath I was holding. Surely, Laura wasn't a total saint, I thought. I dared not suggest it.

"This is a small town. Everyone knows everyone else's itches and scratches. What you do reflects on us and we'll hear about it, you can be sure of that."

"I didn't get in trouble back in West Virginia, and I won't get in trouble here. I won't be in Cape Cod very long," I promised confidently.

He grunted. "Good. I'll hold you to that. Do your chores, do well in school and mind Sara, then we'll all be fine." He reached for his pipe and stuffed new tobacco into it.

"I didn't even know until today I was going to be staying here," I said.

His eyes widened. "That so?"

"Yes. I thought we were coming here only to visit."

He nodded, thoughtful. "Haille always had a lot of problems with the truth. It was like hot coals in her hands."

"Why don't you like my mother? Is it only because she didn't have ancestors that went back to the Pilgrims?"

"We're all sinners," he said. "Our first parents, Adam and Eve, caused us to be cast from Paradise and wander the earth struggling with pain until we're granted mercy. No one's better than anyone else."

"She said you treated her poorly because she was an orphan," I threw back at him.

"That's a no-account lie," he snapped.

"Then why didn't you and my daddy talk all these years?"

"That was his doing, not mine," Uncle Jacob said. He lit his pipe.

"What did he do?"

"He defied his mother and father," he replied, a hard edge in his voice. "It says in the Bible to honor thy mother and father, not defy them."

"How did he defy them?"

"Your mother never told you?"

"No."

"And my brother, he never said nothing about it either?"

"Nothing about what?" I asked.

He tightened his lips and pulled himself

back in the chair. "This ain't a proper conversation for me to have with a young woman. The sins of the father weigh heavily on the shoulders of his sons and daughters, too. That's all I'll say about it."

"But . . ."

"No buts. I've taken you in and asked you to behave while you stay. Let's leave it at that."

I held back my tears.

He lit his pipe again, took a few puffs, and looked at me. "Sunday you'll meet my parents. We're going to their house for dinner. You be on your best behavior. They ain't happy I took you in."

It was as if an electric shock had passed through me. What sort of grandparents were these? How could they hold a grudge so deeply?

"Maybe I shouldn't go," I said.

He pulled the pipe from his mouth sharply. "Of course you'll go. You'll go anywhere this family goes as long as you're living under this roof, hear?" His eyes seemed to sizzle as they glared at me.

"Yes, sir," I said.

"That's better." He rocked gently but continued staring at me.

I started to rise from the chair.

"It ain't proper to leave without first asking permission."

I sat again.

"May I please go?" I asked in a brittle voice. I felt like bone china myself and feared I would shatter any moment.

"This place you lived in West Virginia —"

"Sewell."

"Yeah, Sewell. It's in the back hills, ain't it?"

"Hills. Yes, I suppose."

"Where those families have those rotgut whiskey stills and feud and marry their cousins."

"What?" I started to smile, but saw he was deadly serious. "No, it was just a coal mining town," I said.

He snorted with skepticism. Then he leaned forward, pointing at me with the stem of his pipe. "There are places in this country, havens for the devil where his own do his work. The fiend's at home there as much as he is in Hell itself," he added. "It don't surprise me Chester went to such a place directly after leaving here with Haille." He sat back again and took a puff on his pipe, rocking and thinking a moment. "Maybe Sara is right. Maybe God did send you here to be saved."

"My daddy was a good man. He worked hard for us," I said. "He was no sinner."

Uncle Jacob continued to rock and stare. Then he stopped. "You might not even know what a sinner is. You've been brought up a Godfearing girl?"

165

"I went to church with Daddy."

"That so? Well, maybe Chester made his peace with the Lord before he was taken. I hope so for his soul's sake."

"My daddy was a good man. Everyone in Sewell liked him. More than his own family," I added, but Uncle Jacob was lost in his own thoughts. He didn't hear me.

He blinked and looked at me again. "Who was this man brought your mother here?" he asked.

"A friend of hers who knows people who can help her," I offered weakly. He heard the doubt in my voice and shook his head.

"She know him before or after your daddy's death?" he asked, his eyes small and suspicious.

"She knew him before, too," I reluctantly admitted.

"Thought so." A wry smile was smeared over his lips.

I looked away so he couldn't see how thick my tears were getting. It stung my eyelids to keep them from flooding my cheeks. "May I please go now? I want to take a walk," I pleaded.

"Don't go far or be out there long. Sara has to take you to school tomorrow and get you started."

I rose. I wanted to turn and shout at him. I wanted to scream back and say "Who do you think you are? I thought you said no one is better than anyone else. What makes you so perfect and how dare you judge my daddy and mommy and say such things?" But my tongue stayed glued to the roof of my mouth. Instead, I fled the room and hurried out the front door. I felt like a coiled fuse attached to a time bomb. Sooner or later I was bound to explode. However, right now I wished I could run into my father's steel arms.

But there was only the strange darkness to greet me. Except for the light from the windows of the house, there was nothing to illuminate the street. Behind the house, the dunes were draped in thick darkness. A sea of clouds had closed away the stars. The wind twirled the sand. Beyond the hill, the ocean roared.

This world was completely different from the world I had lived in all my life. I felt cold and alone, without the trees and songbirds and flowers of my past. Instead, I heard the scream of terns. Something ghostly white flapped its wings against the wall of night. Someone could have easily pluck my nerve endings and hear them twang like my fiddle's strings.

Embracing myself, tears streaking down my cheeks, I walked over the cobblestones to the driveway and then went a little way out toward the dunes and the sea. I stared up at the sky, hoping for sight of a star, just one star of hope and promise. But the ceiling of clouds was too thick. Nothing but darkness greeted me everywhere.

I wondered where Mommy was tonight. Was she thinking about me? Surely her heart was as heavy as mine was at this moment.

Or was she drinking and dancing and laughing with Archie someplace? Was he introducing her to so many exciting people that I never came to mind?

I wanted desperately for her to call me on the telephone.

I started to turn to go back into the house, when Cary appeared out of the darkness like some night creature. I gasped when his silhouette first took shape and then gazed with astonishment when he drew close enough to be caught in the dim light from the house windows.

He looked just as surprised to see me.

"What are you doing out here?" he demanded.

"I'm just taking a walk. Where were you?" I asked.

"I had to check something on the boat and didn't want to have to do it in the morning," he said, walking toward me.

"But it's so dark out there."

"Not for me. I've been back and forth over that piece of beach in storms and in darkness more times than I care to remember," he said. "You get to know it as well as the back of your hand and your eyes get used to the darkness." He stared at me for a moment. "You look cold."

"I am cold," I said. I was shivering more from emotional ice than from the weather.

"So why don't you go inside?"

"I am going."

"Fine," he said curtly before continuing toward the house.

"Why don't you like me?" I asked. He stopped and turned back to me.

"Who said I didn't like you?"

"I did."

"I don't know you enough to not like you," he said. "Wait until I get to know you and then ask me again," he added.

"Very funny." I started back to the house. "How do I learn sign language?"

"You want to learn sign language?" he asked with surprise.

"Of course. How else will I communicate with May?"

He considered a moment.

"There's a book I'll give you," he said.

"Could you give it to me now?" I followed quickly. He glanced at me again.

"Yes," he said and continued toward the house. I was right behind him, but he walked quickly to stay ahead. When we entered, he went to speak to Uncle Jacob and I went up to my room where I found Aunt Sara waiting for me at the closet.

"Oh hi, dear. I thought I would choose a dress for you to wear to school tomorrow. This one is the one Laura wore the last day she attended school," she said holding out a dark blue, ankle-length dress. It had a matching belt. "It should fit you perfectly."

"I brought some of my own things to wear, Aunt Sara, things I wear to school."

"But this is such a nice school dress. Laura often wore it," she insisted.

"All right," I relented. It really was a nice dress.

"That's good, dear. Well, do you feel a little more at home now?"

"It's very different here," I said. "But you've been very kind," I quickly added before she took on a look of disappointment.

She smiled and put her hand on my cheek. "You're a very pretty young lady, a sweet girl. It is like having Laura back." She drew me to her to hug me and kiss my hair. "Have a restful sleep, dear, so you can be fresh and ready in the morning. Good night." She kissed me again.

Aunt Sara was fragile, but she was a nice lady. I wanted to make her happy, but I was frightened by the look in her eyes, too. She expected too much of me. I could never be the daughter she had lost.

How ironic, I thought sadly. My mother gave me away so nonchalantly and Aunt Sara would cut off her right arm to have her daughter back for an hour.

I threw myself down on the bed and buried my face in the comforter. I was lying there, forgetting the door was still open, when I heard a knock and looked up quickly.

"Here," Cary said. He tossed the book onto the bed. "Don't lose it or spill anything on the pages," he instructed. His eyes lingered on me for a moment and then he turned away quickly, as if in pain, and marched down the hallway to his room.

I gazed at the sign language book and then I sat up, took a deep breath to help swallow back the tears, and opened the cover.

May would never hear the sound of my voice, but right now I thought I was as small and as vulnerable as she was. It seemed she would be the only one in this house who would understand how deep my well of tears went.

I sat at the vanity mirror and practiced the hand movements until my eyelids drooped. It had, after all, been one of the longest days of my life, second only to the day Daddy died. After I put on my own nightgown, I realized it was too sheer for me to walk around in, so I put on Laura's terrycloth robe and went to the bathroom.

When I came out, Cary was waiting to go in. He had the strangest expression on his face, a pleasant look of surprise.

"Is May asleep?" I asked.

"I put out her light and say good night first," he replied.

"I learned how to sign good night. Can I try?"

"Don't keep her up," he said, returning to the bathroom.

I went down the hall to May's room and looked in. She was in bed, reading a young adult novel. I had to move up to the bed for her to see me. She lowered the book and smiled. Then I signed good night.

Her face beamed and she signed back. Then she held out her arms. I embraced her and kissed her cheek, signed good night again, and left her room. Cary glanced at me and as we passed in the corridor I said, "Good night."

"Good night," he mumbled, sounding as if I had forced him to say it.

It brought a smile to my face.

I returned to my room, closed the door, and slipped under the comforter. The windows were still open, but I didn't mind the breeze. It was a comfortable bed, the sort I could snuggle in.

I gazed at Papa George's pocket watch, running my fingers over its outside. Then I opened it carefully and touched the blade of grass I had taken from Daddy's grave. The watch tinkled its tune. It gave me comfort.

I didn't want to think of anything sad. I didn't want to remember Mommy driving off.

I didn't want to hear Uncle Jacob's harsh words, yet they rang in my ears. "The sins of the father weigh on the shoulders of his sons and daughters?" What sins?

Outside the window, the sound of the ocean's waves stroking the shore resembled a lullaby. In the darkness of the room, I wondered about Laura falling asleep to the same rhythmic ocean song. I wondered about her hopes and dreams, and her fears, too.

Then suddenly, I couldn't help crying for my mother. I closed Papa George's watch and put it back on the night table.

I took a deep breath and then I signed good night to myself. I closed my eyes and hoped for the magic of sleep.

7

"Grandpa" Cary

Sunlight filtered through the wall of morning fog. First it trickled, then it poured through my bedroom windows: lifting darkness and sleep from my eyes. I blinked and stared at my new surroundings, feeling still embroiled in an elaborate dream. This entire journey, Mommy's leaving me in the home of my estranged relatives, my waking in my dead cousin's room, had to be part of some nightmare I had suffered after Daddy's death. Surely, if I blink again, I thought, I will be back in Sewell. Any moment I might wake up, get dressed, have breakfast, see Mama Arlene and Papa George, and then be on my way to school. I'll just close my eyes, take a deep breath, make a wish, and when I open them again, all will be as it was.

But the door of the room opened before I could make my wish. Aunt Sara stood there, her lips formed in an O, her eyes wide. Her palms rested on her chest. Then she blinked rapidly and smiled down at me.

"Good morning, dear," she said. "I'm sorry if I frightened you, but when I opened the door and looked in and saw you there in Laura's bed . . . just for a moment it was as if Laura hadn't . . . Laura was still here. Did you sleep well? But of course you did," she said, answering her own question. "Laura's bed is so comfortable, isn't it?"

I rose on my elbows and then sat against the headboard and ground the traces of sleep from my eyes.

"What time is it?"

"Oh, it's early. We rise early. Jacob wanted me to wake you with everyone else, but I told him you had such a trying day yesterday you needed a little extra sleep. Cary and your uncle Jacob have been up for more than an hour preparing the boat. I've already made them and Roy breakfast."

"Roy?"

"Jacob's assistant."

"Oh. Then May is up, too?"

"Yes, she's eating breakfast." Aunt Sara spotted something and entered the room. "She and Cary will be off to school soon. But that's all right." Aunt Sara went to the dresser and moved a picture of Laura back to the exact place it had been. She turned to me. "You and I will have a little time together and then we'll walk to school, stopping at Laura's grave in the cemetery. I visit her every morning." She returned to the doorway. "Come down as soon as you're ready." She took a deep breath and closed her eyes. "It's going to be a glorious day. I can feel it."

She left and closed the door. I gazed at the picture on the dresser. I had obviously not put it back exactly where I had found it.

The room was brightening with the strengthening morning light. More than ever I felt that I was invading a shrine. I felt guilty enjoying the things my cousin Laura should be enjoying — her bed, her clothes, her beautiful vanity table.

Nevertheless, after I showered, I put on the dress Aunt Sara had chosen for me to wear on my first day in a new school. I had seen how important it was to her that I do so and I didn't have the heart to refuse. I gazed at myself in the mirror. Were there any resemblances between me and my dead cousin? There were none I could see beyond the general things: both of us being about this height and weight when she was my age. Our hair color wasn't the same, nor our eyes, nor the shapes of our faces.

Cary and May were already gone by the time I went downstairs.

"I knew that dress would fit. I just knew it!" Aunt Sara flitted around the kitchen excitedly. She had prepared something she called flippers, fried dough that accompanied my eggs. It was good. She sat and sipped coffee, watching me eat, describing the town, the school, the places Laura enjoyed, the things Laura liked to do.

"She was always in the school plays. Were you ever in a school play?"

"No, but I was in the school's talent show, playing my fiddle."

"Oh. Laura wasn't musically inclined. She sang in the chorus, but she didn't play an instrument." She thought a moment and then smiled. "I imagine she could have though. Laura could do just about anything she put her mind to.

"I was so different," Aunt Sara continued. "I only went as far as high school. My father didn't believe a young girl needed much formal education. My mother wanted me to go to college, but I didn't know for what. I was never the best student. It was finally decided I would marry Jacob and be a homemaker."

"What do you mean it was decided?" I asked.

"Jacob's father and my father were close. They were matchmaking Jacob and me before we went to high school." She followed that with a light laugh that reminded me of tinkling glasses.

"But weren't you in love with Uncle Jacob?"

"I liked him, and my mother always said love was something you grow into rather than something that explodes in your heart the way romance novels and movies portray it. Real, lasting love, that is." She nodded, her face firm. "It makes sense. That's why there are so many divorces nowadays. People claim to fall in love rather than grow into love. Growing into love takes time, commitment, dedication. It's as Jacob says, marriage and love are just other kinds of investment."

"Investment? Love?" I nearly laughed at the idea.

"Yes, dear. It's not as silly as you think it sounds."

"My father fell in love with my mother," I insisted. "He told me so many times."

"Yes, I know," she muttered sadly and looked away.

"Isn't it true that everyone in the family was upset about it only because my mother was an orphan?"

"Who told you that?" A curious, tight smile appeared on Aunt Sara's face.

"My mommy."

"No one disliked your mother for being an orphan. That's silly. Everyone was always kind to her, especially Samuel and Olivia."

"I don't understand. Why else did this family stop talking to my daddy? Wasn't it just because he married her?" I continued.

Aunt Sara bit down on her lower lip and then rose and began clearing the dishes.

"Uncle Jacob told me my daddy didn't

honor his father and mother. Wasn't that what he meant?" I pursued.

"I don't like to talk about Chester and Haille." Aunt Sara was near tears. "Jacob forbids it." She took a deep breath, as if the subject stole the air from her lungs.

"I'm sorry. I don't mean to upset you," I told her. She took another breath and nodded.

"It's over and done. As Jacob always says, we've got to go with the tide. You can't fight the tide. Now you're here and I would like you to be happy with us." She turned, smiling again. She could flip emotions like someone surfing television channels. "Okay, dear?"

I pouted for a moment. Why was it all such a great secret? What more could there be?

"Let's get ready to go to school, dear."

I nodded, rose from the table, and went upstairs to take one last look at myself. I had my hair brushed down and tied loosely with a light pink ribbon I had found in Laura's vanity drawer. I dabbed some of her cologne behind my ears, but decided not to wear lipstick. I noticed that the tiny freckles that were under my eyes looked more prominent. There was nothing I could do about that. Cake makeup only seemed to emphasize the freckles.

Going to a new school and making new friends was terrifying. I had seen how other girls who had moved to Sewell were sometimes treated the first few days and how nervous and timid most of them were. I always felt sorry for them and tried to help them get oriented quickly, but some of my friends felt threatened by new faces. Boys were always more interested in fresh faces, at least for a while, and every girl who had a steady boyfriend was paranoid.

Aunt Sara was waiting at the foot of the stairs. Just as I started to descend, she stopped me. "You're going to need a pen, a pencil, and a notebook. They're on Laura's desk, honey," she instructed.

I hesitated, then returned to the room. Taking the pen and the pencil was fine, but the notebooks all had Laura Logan written on their front covers in big, black letters. Many of the pages were written on, too. I'll take one for now, I thought, and get a new notebook later.

Aunt Sara was pleased. "Laura usually made her own lunch for school, but since you had so little time this morning, I decided to give you the money to buy your lunch." Aunt Sara put two dollars into my hand.

"Thank you, Aunt Sara."

"I want you to be happy." She kissed me on the cheek. "You look so pretty, so perfect. Like Laura."

We started toward town. The fog had burned away and left a turquoise sky dabbed with puffy clouds moving quickly with the wind. There were many fishing boats and sailboats in the bay, and off in the distance, gliding against the horizon, was a large cargo vessel. To my left, junipers on a hill swayed in a melancholy rhythm. Aunt Sara explained that just beyond the bend in the road was the cemetery.

"We won't be long," Aunt Sara said as we turned in the direction of the cemetery. There were two rectangular granite columns at the entryway. Atop each column was a sculptured bird that looked like a raven. The cemetery road was gravel and forked just after the entrance. We went left and then again left, stopping at the Logans' plots. Laura's headstone was a soft shade of gray. Under her name, Laura Ann Logan, and her dates was inscribed, Let the saints be joyful in glory: let them sing aloud upon their beds.

Aunt Sara knelt at the grave site and placed a deep red wild rose against the monument. She closed her eyes and prayed and then she turned to me and smiled.

"Laura loved the red rose most. As soon as they bloom, I bring them to her."

"I like them, too," I said.

"I knew you would," she replied, her eyes bright.

She stood up and wiped off her skirt. Before we left, I noticed two fresh stones with the names, Samuel Logan and Olivia Logan engraved on them. Beneath the names were the dates of birth but no dates of death.

"Aren't those my grandparents?" I asked, astounded.

"Yes, dear. Samuel put the stones in this year to be sure it would be done the way he wanted it done." She laughed. "The Logans don't trust anyone, even their own. Samuel wanted to be sure he was facing the east so the rising sun would warm his plot every morning."

She took my hand as we left the cemetery. She was quiet for a while, but when the school came in view, she began to talk excitedly again, describing how much Laura had liked school and her teachers and how much they had liked her.

"They almost called school off the day of her and Robert's funerals. So many students wanted to be there, and teachers, too."

We marched up the walkway to the main entrance and entered. A sign directed us to the principal's office. Aunt Sara had made an appointment, so we were expected. The principal's secretary, Mrs. Hemmet, greeted us with a warm smile and gave me papers to fill out while we waited to see the principal, Mr. Webster.

"So this is your niece?" Mrs. Hemmet said to Aunt Sara.

"Yes. Isn't she pretty?"

Mrs. Hemmet nodded. She was a thin, spidery woman with long, skinny arms and salt-and-pepper hair cut into short curls that hung on her scalp like tiny springs. While I filled in information on some forms, Aunt Sara and Mrs. Hemmet discussed the town, the upcoming tourist season, and the fall's cranberry harvest. Aunt Sara gave Mrs. Hemmet the letter Mommy had written authorizing Aunt Sara to act as my guardian.

"All right," Mrs. Hemmet said, perusing my paperwork, "I'll send for your school records right away."

"You'll find she's been an excellent student," Aunt Sara assured her. She had accepted that on faith, but I was confident everyone would be pleased with my grades.

"Unless something has to be changed," Mrs. Hemmet continued, "this will be your schedule."

She handed me a card listing my classes, rooms, and teachers. Then she knocked on the principal's door and announced our arrival.

Mr. Webster was a short, stout man, with light, thinning brown hair, a firm mouth, and thick bulbous nose, red at the bridge where his thick-framed glasses rested. His cheeks had a crimson tint and his dark brown eyes were roofed with bushy eyebrows. He greeted Aunt Sara warmly and scrutinized me for a moment before offering his hand and a smile.

"Please sit," he said gesturing at the chair in front of his desk. Aunt Sara sat in the one beside it. "West Virginia, eh?" he said, gazing at my file. "Coal mining country. Tell me a little about your school there."

I described it simply. He wanted to know more about my extracurricular interests than my schoolwork, it seemed, and when I told him I played the fiddle, he raised those bushy eyebrows, gazed at Aunt Sara, and then nodded at me.

"That will be different," he said. "We have an annual talent show to raise money for scholarships at the end of the school year. I hope you'll participate."

"I'm sure she will," Aunt Sara offered.

"Well then, your being Sara and Jacob Logan's niece, I don't think I have to tell you to behave yourself, Melody, but here's our school code and our rules to follow." He handed me a pamphlet. "Look it over and if you have any questions, don't hesitate to come knocking on my door. Good luck and welcome."

I thanked him. When I came out of the office there was a diminutive girl with a caramel complexion and shoulder-length ebony hair waiting in the outer office. She had eyes as black as her hair. She wore a necklace made of tiny seashells and a light blue blouse, matching skirt, and sandals with no socks. Her toenails were polished in bright pearl.

"This is Theresa Patterson," Mrs. Hemmet said. "Theresa's one of our honor students. She'll show you around today."

"Oh Theresa, how nice that you're going to help Melody," Aunt Sara said. "I remember how Laura used to help you with your work sometimes."

"Hello, Mrs. Logan," Theresa replied. She didn't crack a smile. She was a very serious looking girl, pretty but dour to the point of seeming angry. She turned to me. "You have a schedule card?"

"Yes." I showed her. She gazed at it, then nodded. "All my classes. Let's go. We're missing the American history lecture and Mr. K. doesn't like to repeat himself," she said. She started away. I looked at Aunt Sara.

"Have a nice day, dear."

I nodded and hurried to catch up with my obviously reluctant guide.

"Why did you get here so late?" she asked, her face forward as she marched down the corridor.

"I had to visit with my aunt this morning. She wanted to bring me to school herself and she always stops at the cemetery first to spend a moment at my cousin Laura's grave. She drowned almost a year ago."

Theresa glanced at me, her right eyebrow raised.

"Don't you think I know that?" She paused and turned. "Don't you know who I am? Why they picked me to show you around?"

I shook my head.

"No."

"I'm Theresa Patterson. My father is Roy Patterson. He slave-works for your uncle Jacob, so naturally they just assumed I should slave for you," she added and walked on.

Welcome to your new school, I thought and hurried to catch up with Theresa.

School was not much different here from what it had been in Sewell, I decided. The desks were the same type and we had even been using the same history textbook, so I wasn't behind the other students. In fact, I had read enough ahead to actually raise my hand and answer a question the first day, even though I was full of a thousand anxieties. The teacher, Mr. Kattlin, whom the students called Mr. K., was obviously impressed. Theresa simply offered me a smaller smirk.

"Did you take algebra, too?" she asked as soon as the bell rang to end the period.

"Yes."

"Good. Then I won't have to do much," she commented. "Let's go. Math is all the way at the end of the corridor and we often get surprise quizzes. I like to look over last night's work before class starts," she added.

It turned out I was actually a chapter ahead of the class in algebra, but I didn't volunteer any answers this period. The teacher did spring a quiz on the class, and I surprised him by offering to take it, too. Some of the other girls who had been in my history class looked annoyed with me. I was afraid that if I did better than they did, the teacher would use me to mock and chastise them. I had seen my teachers back in Sewell do that.

After math we had our lunch break and Theresa showed me to the cafeteria.

"I've got my own lunch," she told me and showed me her brown bag. "Buying lunch is too expensive for all of us."

"All? How many brothers and sisters do you have?"

"I have two sisters and a brother, all in elementary school, and my father doesn't make enough money."

"Oh. Your mother doesn't work too?" I asked.

"My mother's dead," she said sharply. "I'm going to get a seat over there," she said nodding toward a table in the rear where other students with dark complexions sat. "But you probably don't want to sit with the bravas."

"Bravas?"

"Half black, half Portuguese," she explained and walked away, leaving me in line.

I looked for Cary and saw him way on the other end sitting with two boys. He was a senior so I knew he wouldn't be in any of my classes, but I was hoping we would at least see each other at lunch. He looked my way, but made no gesture for me to join him. Instead, he continued to talk to his friends.

Alone in a large room full of strangers, most of whom were staring at me, made me feel like the proverbial fish out of water. What better place to feel like that, I thought, than Cape Cod? The idea brought a smile to my face and I turned toward the food counter.

"Hi." A tall, slim, brown-haired girl appeared beside me. She had the brightest blue eyes I had ever seen and a pretty smile. "I'm Lorraine Randolph."

She offered me her hand and we shook.

"Melody Logan," I said.

"I know. This is Janet Parker." Lorraine nodded at a dark brunette who had harder features and dull hazel eyes. She had two prominent pock marks on her forehead, too, and, being large breasted, was quite a contrast to Lorraine Randolph.

"Hi," she said.

"I'm Betty Hargate." The shortest of the three pushed herself between Janet and Lorraine. She had her dark blond hair cut in a page boy and wore a cap to match her designer blouse and skirt. There was a puffiness under her eyes and a twist in her mouth that made her look as if she were smirking. Her small nose looked as if it had been planted at the last minute of birth between her bloated cheeks. She was the only one of the three who wore earrings. She had a gold necklace and a ring on every other finger, too.

"Hi," I said.

"So you're Grandpa's cousin, huh?" Betty asked.

"Grandpa?" I smiled, confused.

"Cary Logan. We call him Grandpa," Lorraine explained.

We moved down the food line.

"Cary? Why?"

"Because he acts like it," Betty explained. "Don't you know your own cousin?"

"We just met, actually," I replied, and chose my lunch. I moved quickly, not comfortable with Betty's tone of voice. They followed and Lorraine asked me to sit at their table. I wanted to walk over to Cary's table even though he hadn't invited me, but I didn't want to turn down any prospective new friends, either.

"How come you just met Cary?" Janet asked before putting half her hot dog into her mouth.

"We lived too far away from each other for

our families to see each other." That seemed to satisfy them.

"So you never knew what he was like then," Betty concluded.

"What do you mean: what he's like?" I asked. "I don't understand."

"All he cares about is working with his father and saying his prayers. He doesn't smoke or drink, never goes to any of our parties. He talks to us as if we're all . . ."

"What?" I asked.

"Jezebels," she said. They all laughed.

"What?"

"Didn't he tell you about Jezebel?" Janet asked.

I shook my head.

Betty leaned toward me. "Jezebel was the wife of Ahab and worshiped pagan gods."

"It means wicked woman," Lorraine explained.

"If you don't know your Bible, you're in for hell and damnation living with Grandpa," Betty said.

"I know my Bible," I said defensively. "I just didn't understand why Cary would call you that."

"You will, once you get to know him better and he starts calling you that," Betty told me.

I gazed at Cary. He was looking at us with some interest. He didn't smile, but when our eyes met, he seemed to soften and nod slightly.

I continued eating my lunch, answering questions about life in Sewell, West Virginia, the music I liked, movies and TV shows I watched. The girls acted as if I had come from a foreign country.

"You can forget about television as long as you're living with the Logans," Janet said.

"Why?"

"They don't have a television set, right?"

I thought about it for a moment and then was amazed that I hadn't noticed myself. "No, they don't. I wonder why."

"Television is full of sinful acts," Betty quipped.

"Grandpa doesn't even know what the Beatles sang. He still thinks we're talking about insects," Lorraine said. Their laughter attracted the attention of everyone around us. I felt guilty sitting here listening to them mock Cary.

"You shouldn't make fun of him," I said. "He and his family have suffered a great loss."

They all stopped smiling and laughing.

"You mean Laura," Betty said.

"Yes. Did you know her well?"

"Of course we knew her," Lorraine said. They exchanged glances as they continued to eat. Silence fell over our table and those who had been looking at us, listening and smiling along with them, turned back to their own conversations.

"My aunt is still very upset," I continued, angry at how cruel and insensitive they seemed to be. "It was a terribly tragic accident, wasn't it?"

The three glanced at each other. Janet wiped her lips with her napkin and gulped down her apple juice. Lorraine's eyes shifted quickly from mine, but Betty sat back, stretching.

"Better ask Grandpa about it," she said. The other two looked shocked that she had said it.

"What do you mean?"

She shrugged.

"Just ask him about Laura and Robert. They were using Grandpa's sailfish when they got caught in the sou'wester," she replied as if that explained it.

"Sailfish?"

"It's a shell with one sail on it," Lorraine said.

"Not the sort of boat to be in when bad weather hits," Betty continued. "Grandpa knew that better than anyone. He was born on a wave and came in with the tide."

They laughed again.

"I don't understand. What are you trying to say?"

"We're not saying anything," Betty replied quickly, her smile evaporating. "And don't tell anyone we did."

The bell rang. I stared at the three of them

for a moment and then stood up.

"Where do we dump our trays?" I asked.

"Just follow Theresa. She knows how to clean off tables," Janet told me.

I rushed from their annoying laughter. It was making my blood boil. I followed the others to an opening in the wall where trays and dishes were placed. Theresa waited for me there.

"Making new friends?" she asked dryly.

"More like new enemies," I responded. Her eyebrows lifted. I thought I even detected a small, tight smile on her lips.

"English is next," she said. "We're reading *Huckleberry Finn.*"

"I read it."

Theresa paused and turned to me. "You did? Good. Then maybe you can help me for a change."

"I'd love to," I shot back, my voice as tight and firm as hers.

She stared a moment and then she smiled warmly for the first time. Her pearl black eyes brightened and she laughed. I laughed, too.

Betty, Janet, and Lorraine stared at us with amazement as they walked past and down the corridor.

"Do the witches from *Macbeth* have English now, too?" I asked Theresa.

"Witches?" She gazed after Lorraine, Janet, and Betty. "Oh. Yes."

"Good," I said firmly.

We walked on, Theresa talking more freely now about our teachers, our classes, and the way things were.

Cary waited outside the school building at the end of the day. He looked up sharply when I appeared.

"My mother wants you to walk home with May and me," he explained. "But you don't have to if you don't want to."

"I do," I said. He started walking quickly.

"Are we walking or running?" I asked, keeping up with him.

He glanced at me.

"I don't like to be late for May," he said.

"She doesn't know how to get home by herself?" I asked innocently. He stopped and spun on me.

"She's deaf. She might not hear a car when she crosses the street."

"I bet she would look carefully first," I said. "She's a bright girl."

"Why take chances?" he said.

"She needs to feel she can be on her own," I told him.

"She's only ten. There's plenty of time for that. Besides, we're wasting time standing here and arguing."

"We're not arguing," I said keeping up with his pace. "We're only having a conversation."

He grunted like Uncle Jacob and kept his

194

face forward as he took long strides.

"I see you made friends with the most popular girls at school already," he commented.

"I'd rather be friends with Theresa Patterson," I replied. He shot a glance at me, a look of surprise on his face.

"She's a brava."

"So?"

"If you hang out with them, the others won't be as friendly. You won't be included in their gossiping and you'll never get invited to their wonderful parties."

"I'll risk it," I said. Although he didn't turn back to me, I saw a smile form.

May was waiting patiently for us at her school. She broke into a wide, happy smile when she saw I had come for her, too, and I signed hello. She ran to us, but Cary began to sign quickly. Whatever he told her calmed her down and she walked along holding tightly to his hand. I was at a great disadvantage not knowing the language of the deaf. I made up my mind to learn as much as I could as quickly as I could.

Aunt Sara stood at the front of the house when we arrived. She rushed to us, her face full of expectation. I could tell that the way she was gazing at us as we all came walking up the street made Cary uncomfortable. I heard him mumble something under his breath, and then he quickened his pace, tugging May along.

"How was your day, children?"

"The same as always," Cary muttered and walked through the gate and past her quickly. May paused to tell Aunt Sara her school news. Her fingers and hands moved so quickly, I wondered how Aunt Sara could keep up. She didn't seem to be paying much attention either, because as she nodded and smiled, her eyes were focused on me.

"It's so good to see three of you come down the street instead of only two. Was school okay? Did you make new friends, dear?"

"It's hard to make friends the first day," I replied, without revealing anything in my tone of voice.

"Of course," she said. "Would you like something cold to drink? Laura and I would enjoy a glass of iced tea about this time of the day."

"That sounds nice. Did my mother call?" I asked hopefully.

Her smile wilted like a flower without sunshine and water. "No, dear, not yet."

I tried not to look disappointed. "I'll just go and change into something else. I'd like to see the cranberry bog."

"Oh, yes. It's right over the hill. Maybe Cary will take you," she suggested. May tried to get Aunt Sara's attention and interest again. Her hands resembled small fluttering birds, but Aunt Sara babbled on about her quiet afternoons with Laura. By the time I got to my room, Cary was emerging, dressed in a worn pair of pants, dirty sneakers, and an old shirt.

"I've got to go help my father with today's catch," he said as he passed. I was standing in the doorway. "I don't have time to take someone sightseeing."

"Can I help?" I called after him, but he was bouncing down the stairs and didn't reply.

Why did he avoid me? Coming home from school, he had looked embarrassed walking with me at his side, and whenever he spoke to me, he always looked at something else. Was I that detestable? I was sure it had something to do with his resenting my being in Laura's room, using Laura's things. I couldn't wait for Mommy to call so I could at least get the shipment of my other things.

I changed into my own jeans and blouse, loosened my hair, and put on my older pair of sneakers. May had already changed out of her school clothes and was waiting for me. She signed something I didn't understand.

"Wait," I told her and scooped up the book on sign language. "You and I will practice, okay?" I said holding up the book.

She nodded and I took her hand. As we descended the stairs, Aunt Sara called from the kitchen.

"Is that you, dear?"

"It's May and me," I replied. She appeared with only one glass of iced tea in her hand. "Come, sit with me a minute on the porch," she said, handing me the glass.

"Thank you, but doesn't May want any?" I held up the glass. May started to nod.

"May has something to do," Aunt Sara said harshly. She gestured at her and May's smile faded. She looked at me a moment and then ran to the rear of the house.

"Where's she going?"

"May helps with the laundry, folding towels and putting away the linens. It's her chore. Everyone has a list of chores," Aunt Sara said.

"Where's mine?"

"Oh, there's time enough for yours, dear. I want you to get settled in first."

"It's not fair," I said looking after poor May. "Maybe I can help May."

"No, dear. She'll be fine. Come." Aunt Sara led me to the porch. "Tell me all about your day at school. Laura used to describe everything so well that I felt I had been right there beside her," she said with a short, thin laugh. She sat in a rocker and I sat on the small bench.

A tiny song sparrow perched itself on the red maple tree and paraded as if to show off its plumage. The afternoon sun had fallen behind a thin layer of clouds, and a cool breeze passed through my clothes, giving me a sudden chill. I looked toward the beach where the sunshine was still strong.

I told her how I felt about my teachers and how I thought I really wasn't behind in my schoolwork, how I was even a little ahead in some classes. She listened attentively, but she looked disappointed, as if I wasn't telling her what she really wanted to hear.

"You didn't make friends with anyone yet?"

"Theresa Patterson's nice," I said and she grimaced.

"You should make friends with the daughters of the better families in town, dear. That way you'll get to meet nice, respectable young men." She smiled. "I'm sure you will. You're too pretty not to succeed. It's what I always told Laura, and sure enough . . . sure enough . . ." She hesitated as if she had forgotten what next to say and then she turned abruptly toward the ocean. "We're going to have a neap tide tonight, Jacob says."

"What's a neap tide?"

"It's when the moon's at its first or third quarter. It's at its third quarter. The breakers could be as high as seven feet. Stay away from the water tonight," she added. She sighed deeply. "Laura went out on the neap tide and never came back. I never laid eyes on her face again." She shook her head slowly. "Only Robert's body was recovered."

"But Laura has a grave," I said.

"Yes. I had to have a monument for her, a place for her spirit." She smiled. "Only a clamshell's toss away as you saw. I can go there whenever I want and talk to her. I told her all about you last night, so I'm sure her spirit's looking over you. That's why I know she'd want me to give you this." She dug in her dress pocket. "Hold out your left hand, dear," she ordered. I did so slowly and she put a gold charm bracelet around my wrist and locked it on before I could resist. "Oh, it looks perfect on you."

"I can't take this," I said. "It isn't right."

"Laura wouldn't want you to have it if it weren't right. It will bring good luck. You know why, don't you?"

I shook my head, afraid to even guess.

"You were born June twelfth, right?"

"Yes," I said, holding my breath.

She widened her smile.

"Don't you know, dear?"

"Know what?"

"Laura was born June twentieth. You're both Gemini. Don't you see?"

I shook my head, still holding my breath.

"Gemini, the twins. That was Laura's sign, that's Cary's sign, and it's your sign," she said. "Isn't that wonderful?"

"I don't know anything about astrology," I said.

"One night when it's clear, I'll show you your constellation. Laura and I loved to see it in the night sky." She gazed up as if it were already night and the sky were blazing with stars. May timidly appeared in the doorway. Aunt Sara asked her if she had completed her chore and she signed back that she had.

"Maybe May can show me the cranberry bog?" I suggested. Aunt Sara nodded, disappointed that I didn't want to sit and talk some more. She reluctantly told May my request. May beamed, took my hand, and urged me to follow her.

"Come right back!" Aunt Sara called from the porch.

"We will," I promised.

"I've got nice flounder for tonight's dinner. It was one of Laura's favorite meals," she cried.

May pulled harder. I laughed as we broke into a run around the rear of the house and over the pinky-mauve and pearly pebbles toward the hill. Toward the ocean I could see Cary on the boat working with his father and Roy Patterson. It looked as if he was gazing our way, but he didn't wave.

May lead me to the top of the hill. We paused and I looked down at the cranberry bog. It was all in blossom. It looked like a second sea of pale pink. May gestured wildly with her hands. I was sure she was explaining the planting, the flooding, the draining, and the harvesting of the berries. It was frustrating not to understand.

I sat her down beside me on the top of the hill and opened the book about sign language. If we worked together, I thought, I would make faster progress. We were still practicing gestures when Cary and Uncle Jacob returned from the dock.

"Hey!" Cary barked. "Get her back to the house." He made some gestures and May stood up.

Using my new skills, I thanked her. She hugged me.

When I looked back, I saw Cary glaring at us. He lowered his head and then plodded after Uncle Jacob. I took May's hand and we followed.

"May showed me the cranberry bog," I told him when we entered the house. He was in the living room with Uncle Jacob. "It's beautiful."

He snorted. "See if you still think it's beautiful when it comes harvest time." He cut past me quickly to go upstairs.

"If I'm still here," I called after him. Couldn't I say anything that would please him?

"Go see if Sara needs any help with dinner," Uncle Jacob commanded. He didn't even say hello and he had no questions for me about my first day at school. He snapped his newspaper and sat back to read.

May looked at me, wondering, I was sure, what all the dark faces meant. I smiled at her reassuringly. Then I heard the phone ringing.

Oh let that be Mommy, I prayed. I had never longed to hear her voice so much. No matter what her faults were, how much she had annoyed or disappointed me before, I would be grateful for the sound of her voice.

Uncle Jacob lifted the receiver reluctantly and said hello. His eyes were on me.

"I said go help Sara," he ordered. I took a step past the doorway, but paused to hear him talk.

"Yeah," he said, "She's here. She's looks a lot like Haille. Guess you'll see for yourself soon enough," he added. "It's bound to bring back memories."

Suddenly, I felt eyes on me and turned to look up the stairs. Cary was standing there glaring.

"Eavesdropping isn't very ladylike." He went back upstairs, leaving me feeling cold.

I choked back my tears and went into the kitchen, where I was sure Aunt Sara waited to tell me how she was preparing Laura's favorite meal.

8

A Stormy Warning

As we had at dinner the night before, we began with a prayer and a Bible reading. Uncle Jacob gazed at Cary, glanced at May, and then turned to me. "You might as well start right off," he said. "It's your turn."

"My turn?" I looked at Aunt Sara.

"He wants you to read an excerpt from the Good Book, dear. Laura always followed Cary."

"I could read again if she doesn't want to," Cary volunteered with a smirk.

"It's all right," I said quickly. "I'd like to read. What do I read?"

Uncle Jacob handed me the Bible with his thumb on the section he wanted read.

I began. "Who can find a virtuous woman? For her price is far above rubies.

"The heart of her husband doth safely trust in her, so that he shall have no need of spoil.

"She will do him good and not evil all the days of her life."

I gazed quickly at Cary because I felt the heat of his eyes on me as I read.

"She seeketh wool, and flax, and worketh willingly with her hands."

"Yes," Uncle Jacob said nodding, obviously pleased with how I read.

Cary glanced down as I continued until the chapter was completed.

"Good," Uncle Jacob said. "Words to remember. Amen." His eyes fixed on me. I knew what he thought of my mother. Did he choose this chapter because he thought I would be just like her? I was afraid to ask.

As soon as we began to eat, Uncle Jacob and Cary got into a conversation about the lobster catch and the construction of more traps. While they talked, I tried to converse with May. I saw Cary watching us out of the corner of his eye, and something I did brought a smile to his face. But Uncle Jacob suddenly looked furious.

"Will you tell your daughter to eat and not talk at dinner," he commanded Aunt Sara. "It's distracting."

"Yes, Jacob." Aunt Sara signed his orders to May, who immediately dropped her gaze to her food and stopped trying to communicate with me.

It occurred to me that I had yet to see Uncle Jacob use sign language with May. Up until now, it had been only Cary, Aunt Sara, and I.

"I'm sorry," I said. "It was my fault. I am trying to learn sign language."

"Well do it after dinner," Uncle Jacob snapped and turned back to Cary to talk about the new traps.

After dinner I helped Aunt Sara clear away the dishes and put away the food. She went on and on about the wonderful things Laura had learned to do with fish.

"Got so her filleted bass was good enough to be in a contest. You should have tasted her fish pie, too. The crust always came out so light. That girl had magic in her fingers."

"I cooked for my daddy often," I said.

"Oh, did you, dear? Yes, I bet you did. I don't remember Haille being much of a cook. She had other things on her mind."

"Like what?" I pursued.

"Not fit to discuss." Aunt Sara sewed her lips shut.

"What's that mean?" I demanded.

She shook her head and then gazed at the doorway before lowering her voice to a whisper. "Truth is, Jacob don't even like me mentioning her and those days."

"Well, I'd like to hear more about her," I said.

"No you wouldn't dear. I must show you some of Laura's needlework," she said to change the subject. "Did I tell you she used to do that? I have it all in my bedroom on the walls, but there is one she never got to finish. It's in my closet. Have you ever done needlework?"

"No," I said, sulking.

"Oh you should try needlework, dear. I bet you would be good at it, too."

"I don't think so," I said. "Is there anything else I can help you with, Aunt Sara?"

"What? Oh. No dear, thank you," she said. "That's right. You have to do homework now, don't you?"

"Yes," I said.

"Then go on, dear. I'll see you before I go to sleep," she said.

I hurried upstairs. When I ascended the stairway, I noticed a ladder had been lowered from the roof above the second floor landing. It led up to a door in the ceiling. I approached slowly and gazed up at the lighted attic. Curious, I started up the rungs and stopped at the top to peer into the room. Two oil lamps illuminated a table and a chair, chests, boxes, all sorts of antiques and old paintings. But the most interesting thing to me were the model boats constructed of balsa wood. One was partially completed on the table. The others were lined up on shelves, all painted, too, and some with tiny sailors manning the sails.

There was a very worn looking couch on the right and a telescope pointing at the sole window.

"What are you doing?" I turned to see Cary

staring up at me from the bottom of the ladder.

"I was just wondering what was up here. Do you do the boats?"

"First, they're not boats, they're ships. And second, the attic is a private place, if you don't mind."

"I'm sorry." I started down the rungs, but slipped on the next to last one and fell into his arms. For a moment our faces were inches apart. The moment he realized he was holding me in his arms, he released me and I landed hard on my feet on the floor.

"That's why I don't like anyone going up there," he said moving past me quickly. "It's dangerous." His cheeks were crimson.

"I'm sorry. Is that your hobby?" I asked before he reached the top.

He dropped a "Yes," back at me before pulling the ladder up after him.

"I don't have the measles or anything you know!" I cried.

He hesitated a moment before closing the door.

"Good riddance!" I marched to my room, and lost myself in my homework. Once in a while, I heard the sounds of Cary moving above me. I gazed up at the ceiling and listened until he grew quiet again.

The telephone rang below in the living room. I waited, holding my breath and then, I heard Aunt Sara call my name.

"Telephone, dear."

"Mommy!" I cried. "Finally!" I hurried down the stairs.

"It's Haille," Aunt Sara said. "Hurry, it's long distance."

I rushed to the living room. Uncle Jacob sat in his chair, smoking his pipe and thumbing through a mail-order catalogue. He glanced at me and then back at his pages, but he didn't get up. Aunt Sara stood in the doorway, watching. I would have no privacy for this phone call. Nevertheless, I seized the receiver. "Mommy?"

"Hi Honey. See, I told you I would call you first chance I got. Aunt Sara says you've already started school there and you said you were right up with the work."

"Yes, Mommy. Where are you?"

"We're on our way to New York City," she said excitedly. Her voice dropped. "The people in Boston weren't available when they told Richard they would be so we never met them, but he has people for me to meet in New York and then in Chicago. After that we'll head for Los Angeles."

"Los Angeles? But Mommy, when will I . . . when will we be together again?" I asked my question as quietly as I could.

"Soon, honey. Real soon, I promise."

"I could still meet you someplace, Mommy. I could take a bus and —"

"Now don't make things harder than they

are for me, honey. I've already suffered a serious disappointment. Please, cooperate."

"But I need my things," I said. "You didn't leave me any money, Mommy. I can't call my friends. I can't call Alice or Mama Arlene. It's long distance."

"I'm calling Mama Arlene as soon as I get to New York," she promised. I heard a horn blaring and someone shouting.

"Coming!" Mommy shouted back. "I've got to go, honey. I've already held us up longer than I should have. I'll call you as soon as I can. Be good, honey. Bye."

"But Mommy —"

The phone went dead. I held it tightly. Silent screams stuck in my throat and tears froze behind my eyes.

"Hang it up properly," Uncle Jacob instructed. "I'm waitin' on an important call."

I cradled the receiver with my back to him and walked out of the living room quickly, not glancing at Aunt Sara either.

"Just a minute, there," Uncle Jacob growled. "Get yourself right back in here, young lady."

I sucked in my breath, turned, and marched back. My heart thudded madly, drumming out a tune of fright in my ribcage.

"Yes sir?"

"It's proper to thank people when you use their things. Sara ain't your secretary."

"I'm sorry. Thank you, Aunt Sara."

"You're welcome, dear. Is everything all right with Haille?"

"Yes," I replied.

"Good."

"Humph," Uncle Jacob grunted.

"I'll bring you a glass of hot milk tonight," she offered.

"You don't have to do that, Aunt Sara."

"I always brought Laura a glass of warm milk. I bring one to May as well." Her huge scared eyes stared woefully at me. I glanced at Uncle Jacob. He looked ready to pounce.

"Oh, then thank you, Aunt Sara."

Her face brightened, the darkness evaporating from her eyes. I forced a smile and hurried up the stairway. When I reached my room, I closed the door behind me and threw myself on the bed, burying my face in the pillow to smother my sobs.

I didn't want to be here! I hated it! No wonder my father stopped speaking to his family. He was nothing like Uncle Jacob. I would be happier if Mommy had dumped me in an orphanage, I thought. My shoulders shook with my muted crying. Suddenly, I felt something touch my shoulder and I turned quickly to see little May staring at me, her face full of fear and sympathy. She had come in so quietly that I had not heard her. Her hands moved rapidly, wondering why I was so unhappy. What made me cry?

"I miss my mother," I said. She tilted her

head. I let out a deep breath and located the book on sign language. I found the gestures and produced them. May nodded and signed how sorry she felt for me. Then she offered me a hug.

How sweet, I thought, and how sad that the only one in this house who made me feel at home was the only one who couldn't hear the sound of my voice.

Nor could she hear the sounds of scuffling and footsteps above, but she saw where my gaze had gone and understood.

"Car . . . ry," she said and demonstrated the construction of a model ship.

"Yes. Do you go up there?" I signed. "Or doesn't he even let you up there?"

She thought a moment and then shook her head.

"No?"

She shook her head and gestured "only . . ." She pointed to Laura's photograph.

"Only Laura?" May nodded. "Only Laura," I thought aloud and gazed at the ceiling. May grunted and then gestured about his great sorrow.

I gazed at the ceiling again. Cary was in pain, I thought, and for a moment at least, I stopped feeling sorry for myself.

May returned to her room to complete her school work. After I finished mine, we practiced sign language until it was time for her to go to bed. I washed and dressed for bed myself and then Aunt Sara brought my glass of warm milk. There was something rolled under her arm. She took it out and showed me Laura's unfinished canvas of needle-work. It was a picture of a woman on a widow's walk gazing at the sea.

"Laura drew the picture herself," Aunt Sara explained. "Isn't it beautiful?"

"Yes," I said.

"Don't you want to finish it for her, dear? I can't get myself to do it," she said with a deep sigh.

"I'd be afraid I would mess it up, Aunt Sara."

"Oh, you won't, I'm sure. I'll just leave it here and bring up the threads tomorrow and show you the stitch."

"I never did something like that before," I said, but she didn't seem to hear or care.

"My goodness," she said, her gaze falling on the two nearly identical stuffed cats. "Where did this one come from?"

"It was mine, a present from my daddy. I brought it with me in my suitcase."

"Isn't that remarkable. Cary won the other one for Laura at a fair one summer. And this Teddy bear you brought along, too?"

"Yes."

"Geminis," she said. "All of you."

She gazed around the room sadly, looked at me, smiled and then left, after wishing me a good night's rest.

I was tired. It had been an exhausting day, my emotions on a rollercoaster. I had gone through the tunnel of fear, been angry, sad, and curious. I enjoyed being with little May and appreciated that she sincerely welcomed me. That was the only ray of sunshine in this gloomy world of sadness.

Impulsively, I picked up my fiddle and played a mournful tune. It was the mood I felt and the music came from deep within me. I closed my eyes and pictured Daddy sitting on the sofa in our trailer living room, a small smile on his face, his eyes full of pride as I played. Afterward, he would pull me to him and give me one of his bear hugs, smothering my cheek and forehead with kisses.

Suddenly, there was a loud rapping on the wall.

"Stop that noise!" Uncle Jacob ordered. "It's time for everyone to sleep!"

My memories of Daddy popped like soap bubbles. I put away the fiddle and crawled under the comforter. Then I turned down the oil lamp, closed my eyes, and listened to the roar of the ocean. The house was very quiet for a few moments, and then I heard what I recognized as the distinct sound of someone sobbing.

"Just go to sleep!" Uncle Jacob commanded gruffly, his voice seemingly coming out of the walls.

The sobbing stopped.

The ocean came roaring through my window again, the same ocean that had taken Laura from this house and the melancholy world in which I now found myself.

Following Aunt Sara's instructions the next morning, I made lunches for both Cary and myself. It was something Laura always had done and I assumed it was to be one of my chores. We were to have a sandwich and an apple, and we were given fifty cents to buy a drink. May's lunch was provided for her at the special school.

When we left the house, May took my hand instead of Cary's. He paused for a moment, visibly annoyed, but said nothing about it.

"Let's go. We don't want to be late," he muttered and plodded along ahead of us, moving so quickly, May practically had to run to keep up. We dropped her off first and then started for our school. I tried to make conversation.

"How long have you been constructing model ships?" I asked. He glanced at me as if I had asked a stupid question.

"A long time and they're not toys," he added.

"I didn't say they were. I know grown-ups can have hobbies, too. Papa George used to carve out flutes from hickory branches. He even made my fiddle."

"Why do you call this person Papa George?" he said disdainfully. "He's not your grandfather. This Sunday you'll meet your grandfather."

"Papa George is the only grandfather I've known. He and Mama Arlene are my real grandparents as far as I'm concerned," I replied firmly.

"Don't they have any children of their own?"

"No."

"So why didn't Haille leave you with them while she went rushing off to become a movie star?" he asked, his eyes sparkling wickedly.

"Papa George is very sick. He suffers from black lung," I replied.

He grunted. "That's a convenient excuse," he said.

Furious, I seized him at the elbow and pulled him to a stop, spinning him around. He was genuinely shocked at my outburst of physical strength. I shocked myself.

"It's not an excuse. He's very sick. I don't know why you don't like me, Cary Logan, and the truth is, I don't care to know. If that's the way it has to be, that's the way it has to be, but don't think I'll let you ridicule me or say bad things about the people I love."

He went from astonishment and shock to what looked like appreciation and pleasure, before returning to his stoic self.

"I can't be late for school," he said. "I already have two demerits."

He walked on and I hurried to catch up.

"*You* have two demerits? What for?"

He was silent.

"What did you do?" I pursued, keeping pace with him. I was curious what possible infraction of the rules Mr. Perfect could have committed.

"Fighting," he finally replied.

"I wonder why that comes as no surprise?" I said. I couldn't resist.

He glared at me and I thought if looks could kill, I'd be long dead and buried. Then he pumped his legs harder, remaining a foot or two ahead of me the rest of the way to school.

Theresa Patterson was friendly and spoke to me between classes, but since she didn't have to be my guide any longer, she stayed with her own friends. She didn't have to say it, but I knew if she brought me along, her friends might resent it. Just as in my school, and probably in most schools, clumps of girls and boys clung to each other in cliques, feeling safer and more comfortable hanging around with those whom they perceived to be their own kind.

At lunch I sat at a table alone until Lorraine, Janet, and Betty brought themselves and two other girls over to join me. I saw by the mischievous twinkle in Betty's eyes that they had been plotting something.

"So after nearly two days here, how do you like our school?" Lorraine asked innocently.

"It's okay. The teachers are nice," I said.

"Are the boys better looking than the boys in West Virginia?" Janet asked.

"I haven't had a chance to look," I said. When they all looked skeptical, I added, "It's hard starting someplace new during the last quarter of the year. I've got to take the same finals you will take."

One of the new girls looked sympathetic, but Betty tucked in the corner of her mouth and said, "You don't look like you're going to have a problem with schoolwork."

"Grandpa might have a problem, though," Janet said. "He's barely passing. He might not graduate, I hear."

"Billy Wilkins told me Grandpa is going to fail English," Lorraine said nodding.

"Maybe you can tutor him," Betty suggested.

"That's right, like show him how to do it," Janet said. They all laughed.

"What's that supposed to mean?" I asked. The girls glanced at each other and ate.

"Do you sleep in the same room?" Betty asked me.

"Same room?"

"With Grandpa? We heard Laura and Cary

slept in the same room ever since they were born."

"Of course not," I said. "And they didn't."

"I wouldn't be so sure about that," Lorraine said.

"Laura had a very nice room. That's the room I use. None of you have ever been in my aunt and uncle's house?"

"No," Betty said.

"Laura was a very strange girl," Janet offered. "That whole family's strange."

"She didn't want to do anything with girls her age," Lorraine said. "She was like an old lady — cooking, cleaning, canning fruit with her mother."

"I hardly saw her at any of our dances," Janet complained.

"Robert Royce was the only boyfriend she ever had," Lorraine said.

"Unfortunate for him," Betty added.

"Whereas, Grandpa has never been with anyone we know," Janet said.

"Now we have someone who will tell us," Lorraine said, eyeing me. "Tell us, Melody."

"Tell you what?"

"Does Grandpa spend a lot of time in the bathroom, maybe sneaking in with girlie magazines?"

More laughter. The blood rushed to my neck and face.

"When he goes to sleep, do you hear the bedsprings squeaking?" Betty continued.

The girls giggled.

"You're all disgusting," I said. Their laughter stopped.

"Oh come on, Melody. I'm sure you're curious about him, too," Janet said.

"He's not bad looking," Lorraine offered gazing across the cafeteria at Cary. He stared back at us. "Maybe you can get him to loosen up, relax. We could help you."

"What do you mean?" I asked.

The girls were quiet a moment, all eyes on the teacher monitor. Betty nodded at Lorraine. She opened her school bag, which she had set between me and her, and took something out quickly. Then she pressed it into my hand. I gazed down at what looked like one of Papa George's self-rolled cigarettes.

"I don't smoke," I said.

"That's not a cigarette, stupid," Betty said. "And keep it below the table so Mr. Rotter doesn't see."

"What is it?"

"It's a joint," Lorraine whispered loudly.

"I don't want it," I said and tried to give it back, but she pushed my hand away.

"Just keep it in case you get a chance to offer it to Grandpa. It'll loosen him up."

"Just tell us what happens, that's all," Betty said.

"Put it away, quick," Lorraine said as Mr. Rotter started down the aisle between the tables.

Little butterflies of panic fluttered in my head. Gazing around, it seemed as if everyone were looking at me, waiting to see what I would do.

"Hello, girls," Mr. Rotter said smiling down at us. "Are you making our new student feel at home?"

"Yes, Mr. Rotter," Lorraine fluttered her eyelids.

"Is that true, Melody?" he asked me.

I was afraid my voice would crack. "Yes sir," I said.

"Good. Good." He continued through the cafeteria. I let out my breath.

"Very nice. You did well," Betty said. The other girls apparently agreed.

"We're having a beach party Saturday night. We'll meet about eight at Janet's house. You want to come? It will be a chance for you to meet some normal boys," Betty said.

"I don't know if I can. I'll ask my aunt."

"Don't tell her where you're going," Janet said, "or she won't let you come. Just say you're coming over to my house to study for a test. That always works."

"I don't like to lie," I said.

She smirked. "You haven't been living with the Logans long. After a while, you'll get to like it."

The bell signalled the end of lunch period.

221

Everyone rose to leave. I was the last to get up, not realizing until that moment, that I still had the joint of marijuana clutched in my hand. I dropped it into my sandwich bag and then dropped the bag in the garbage can on the way out of the cafeteria.

At the doorway, someone bumped into me hard, and I turned to look into the most perfect face I had ever seen. His blue eyes were positively dazzling and his smile was the warmest and sweetest I'd ever seen. Strong, full lips were turned up gently at the corners, revealing teeth as white as piano keys. A wave of dark brown hair floated over his forehead. He was tall and broad in the shoulders with a narrow waist. His face wasn't as tanned as Cary's, but he had a creamy rich complexion and looked like a male model or a movie star.

"Excuse me," he said. "Did I hurt you?"

"No. It's all right."

"I'm afraid I had my mind on my upcoming European history exam. I'm not usually this clumsy."

"It's okay. I'm fine."

"You're the new girl, right?"

"Yes," I said smiling.

"I'm Adam Jackson."

"Melody Logan," I returned.

"Welcome to Provincetown," he said. "I see you've already made friends with some of the girls. Are you going to their beach party

Saturday night?"

"I don't know. I . . . I'll see."

"I hope to see you there," he said. His face glittered with a handsome smile as he moved away to join his friends, who, I saw, included a very pretty brunette. She glared at me as she threaded her arm through his and moved him down the hall and away. I stared after him until Lorraine nudged me. The girls had been standing nearby, watching.

"Be careful," Lorraine said. "That's Adam Jackson."

"I know. He told me."

"Did he tell you he puts a nick in the bow of his sailboat for every girl he takes to bed?"

"What?"

"One more nick and that boat might sink," Betty added. We continued toward class before I could catch my breath.

"But maybe she won't mind becoming one of Adam's nicks," Janet quipped. "Would you, Melody?"

"What?"

Everyone laughed again. I was beginning to feel as light and helpless as a balloon caught in a crosswind, blown one way, then another. And I had been here only a couple of days!

Mr. Malamud, my chemistry teacher, spent some time with me after class to be sure I was up-to-date with the class. It was my last period of the day. Cary wasn't waiting for me when I finally emerged from the building. I gazed around for a few moments and then hurried along. I assumed he had picked up May from her school already, so I just took the shortest route back.

"Oh Melody, dear, I was worried about you," Aunt Sara said when I entered the house. "Cary and May have been home a while."

"I had to stay after school for a few minutes to get some extra help from my science teacher," I explained.

"You should have let Cary know," she told me.

"I don't see or speak to Cary much after we arrive at school, Aunt Sara, and that's not all my fault either," I added. I went upstairs to change into a pair of jeans. I found the needlework picture spread out on the bed with a box of colored thread beside it. Moments later, Aunt Sara was in the doorway.

"I'll show you how to make the stitch," she said.

"I'm really not good at this, Aunt Sara."

"Once you start, you will be, I'm sure," she insisted. I was about to continue my protest when Cary appeared in the hallway behind her.

"If she doesn't want to do it, don't keep forcing it on her, Mother," he snapped. Aunt

Sara's mouth fell open and her hand fluttered up to the base of her throat.

"I didn't mean to . . . I —"

"It's okay, Aunt Sara," I said, shooting my own sparks of anger from my eyes, "I'd be happy to learn."

Cary took on a look of amusement that added fuel to the fire before he hurried down the stairs and out of the house. Aunt Sara smiled and came into the room to demonstrate the needlework. I picked it up quickly and did enjoy it.

"As soon as this is finished, I'll get a frame for it and put it up with the others," Aunt Sara promised. "But you don't have to work on it now. You've been cooped up in school all day. Go get some fresh air. Laura liked to walk on the beach and hunt for seashells."

May was still completing her chores so I went out by myself. The sky still had patches of deep blue, but most of it had become covered with what looked like storm clouds, bruised and sooty puffs that rolled angrily from the horizon. The ocean looked more tempestuous, too. I could see Cary and Roy Patterson on the lobster boat bobbing beside the dock. I walked out a little way. Cary left the boat and started back toward me and the house.

"There's going to be a storm," he said as he approached. "It's a nor'easter," he added, continuing past. I said nothing and contin-

225

ued to walk toward the ocean. "Didn't you hear what I said?" he called.

I turned.

"Look at the sky. Even a landlubber like you should be able to see rain comin'."

"Don't call me a landlubber."

He smiled. "Well what are you?"

"I'm a person, just like you, only I was brought up in a different place. I'm sure you wouldn't know your way around a coal mine, but I wouldn't call you silly names just to pump myself up."

"I'm not doing it to pump myself up."

I turned away. To my surprise, he was at my side in moments. "Keep walking in this direction and you'll get caught in a downpour. Look at the breakers. The ocean is talking to us, telling us what to expect. See how the terns are heading for safer ground, too."

"Where's Uncle Jacob?" I asked, gazing toward the dock.

"He took today's catch into town. It wasn't good. Only four good-size lobsters in the traps."

"How do lobsters get trapped?" I asked.

"We bait them with stinky dead fish and set them on the ocean bottom. The lobster crawls into the living room and gets caught."

"Living room?"

"That's what we call that part of the trap. Later, we pull up the traps and if the lobsters meet the measurement, we prepare them to take to market."

"How do you prepare them?"

"Well, you got to put rubber bands on the claws so they can't pinch. One claw is a cruncher claw, strong, dull; the other is like a scissor, sharp and quick."

"I didn't know they were so dangerous."

"It's not really so dangerous if you're careful. I've been pinched a bit, but only once had blood drawn." He showed me his right hand. I could see a faint scar along his forefinger.

"Did Laura go lobstering with you?" I asked. He blinked rapidly and turned toward the ocean.

"No, not much," he replied.

"She didn't know the ocean as well as you did?"

"We should go back to the house. There goes Roy." Cary nodded at the tall, broad black man who hurried away from the dock.

"Where do the Pattersons live?"

"In the saltbox houses on the other side of town."

"What happened to Theresa's mother?" I asked.

"You're stuffed full of questions, aren't you?"

"Wouldn't you be if the shoe was on the other foot and you just arrived?"

His lips made that tiny turn up again and

he permitted his eyes to stay on me for a few moments longer.

"I guess," he finally admitted. "Theresa's mother died in a car crash coming home from work. She was a chambermaid in a hotel in North Truro. Terrible accident. Man driving a tractor trailer lost control in the rain and crossed the road. Smacked her clear into the other world. Dad says it was meant to be."

"How can something so terrible be meant to be?"

"It's what my father believes," he said.

"Is that why he doesn't seem one bit sad about my father's death, even though my father was his brother? It was meant to be?"

Cary was silent. He kept his head down and kicked some sand. A particularly loud tern cried at the approaching storm.

"And your sister's death," I pursued. "Was that also meant to be?"

He looked at me, his eyes glistening with tears.

"I don't like talking about Laura's . . . Laura's disappearance."

"If you keep sadness and pain bottled up, it swells and swells inside you until you burst," I said. "Mama Arlene told me that."

"Yeah, well I never had the pleasure of meeting Mama Arlene," he replied. "I'm going back to the house. Do what you want."

"Why did your father stop talking to my father?" I demanded, my hands on my hips. He hesitated and then turned. "He told me my daddy defied his parents. What did he mean by that? What did my daddy do to them?"

"I don't know."

"But Aunt Sara and Uncle Jacob must have talked about it often."

"I don't listen in on their private talks," he said. "Besides, it's over and done, why talk about it now?"

"I know. You've got to go with the tide."

He widened his eyes and lifted his eyebrows.

"Well," I continued, "sometimes you have to swim against the tide and just be strong enough to get past it, too. Sometimes, you don't give up and give in."

"Really?" he said, amused by my defiance.

"Yes, really."

"Well, first chance I get, I'm going to take you out in my sailboat and let you buck the tide."

"Good."

He shook his head, his smile widening.

"The girls in school told me Laura and her boyfriend went out in your sailboat. Was that so?"

The smile quickly faded. "I have a different sailboat now. And I told you," he said, turning away, "I don't talk about Laura's disappearance with anyone. Especially strangers."

I watched him walk away, shoulders sagging, his head bent, his hands clenched in fists.

The wind grew stronger and whipped past me, catching my hair. Sand began to fly from the beach into my face. The small patches of blue had disappeared from the sky, now completely overcast with dark, brooding clouds. I could feel the ocean spray even this far from the beach. It all began to terrify me. How could weather change so rapidly?

I started for the house, bucking the wind, every step harder than the one before it. My feet slipped on the sand that gave way beneath them. It was harder than walking on ice. The wind was so strong, my eyes began to tear. I had to keep them closed and pump my legs hard. I tried to run. My blouse flapped over my breasts and ribs.

Just before I reached the house, the first sheet of rain tore down, washing over me. I screamed and ran harder for the front door. When I burst in, Cary stood in the hallway, a look of glee in his eyes, an "I told you so" written on his lips.

"I hate it here!" I screamed at him and charged up the stairway.

The wind howled around the house and whistled through it. I thought it might take the roof off, but at the moment I didn't care. Let the sky fall, let the rain swell the ocean and wash over this place, I thought. I embraced myself at the window, watching the trees bend to the point of breaking. The rain came down like bullets fired by God. The street was being pounded. I shuddered and stripped off my blouse. Then I rushed to the bathroom to get a towel for my hair.

Moments later, when I emerged, Cary was in the hallway. He glanced at me before I realized I was standing there in my bra. I draped the towel around myself.

"I'm sorry," he said. He looked repentant. "I shouldn't have left you out there."

"It was my own fault. I didn't listen," I admitted. "Where's May?"

"She's in her room. Sometimes, it's a blessing to be deaf," he said. "She can't hear how hard it's raining and blowing."

"How do you say it's raining?" I asked.

He demonstrated. "This means it's raining hard," he added and showed me. Then he smiled. "Not the same thing as being out there, huh?"

I relented and smiled. "No."

"Maybe you ain't such a landlubber after all," he allowed. He blushed before going to his room. It was the closest he had come to giving me anything akin to a compliment.

Daddy would say, "Be grateful for the little things."

I went into my room to work on the needlepoint until it was time to help Aunt Sara with dinner. Before it was time to go down, I heard a knock on my door.

"Yes?"

Cary poked his head in.

"I just thought I'd let you know what we do in case it's still raining in the morning."

"What do we do?"

"We walk faster," he said. For the first time since I had come to Provincetown, I heard the sound of my own laughter.

9

Something Special

It rained most of the night. Twice, the loud drumming of the drops on the windowpanes woke me. I heard Aunt Sara come to my door after the second time. She stood there gazing in at me, her face in shadow, her head silhouetted against the dim hallway light. I said nothing and she finally closed the door softly.

The rain stopped just before morning. After I dressed and went downstairs, I was surprised to find most of the windows crusted with salt. It reminded me of ice and I remarked about it at breakfast. Aunt Sara said it wasn't unusual after a storm.

"The salt even peels the paint from our window casings. The weather is hard on us, but we endure it."

"The weather's hard on people everywhere," Uncle Jacob declared. "But it's good to us too, and we should be grateful for our blessings. Mark that," he said sharply, waving his long right forefinger at us like some Biblical prophet.

"I can help you clean the windows after school today," I told Aunt Sara.

"Why thank you, dear. It's kind of you to offer."

"Kind? She should do nothing less," Uncle Jacob fixed his eyes on me. "Most young people today don't know what it is to have regular chores and responsibilities. They think everything is owed to them just because they were born."

I wanted to snap back at him and tell him I hadn't been brought up to be spoiled and selfish. I did plenty of work around our home in Sewell, and I often helped Mama Arlene and Papa George with their housework, too. I never asked them anything for it and I never expected anything. It was enough that they gave me their love.

I glared back at Uncle Jacob, the crests of my cheeks burning. He didn't know me. He had hardly spoken ten minutes to me my whole life. What right did he have sitting there on his high and mighty throne and lumping me in with all the spoiled young people he saw in town?

Cary must have sensed those words were at the tip of my tongue, for he shot me a look of warning before I had a chance to part my lips. I stared at him a moment and saw a gentle, but definite shake of his head. I looked down at my hot cereal and swallowed back my anger, even though it threatened to get stuck in my throat and choke me all day.

"Your father is an ogre," I told Cary as we left for school that morning.

Cary didn't reply for a few moments and then said, "He's just afraid, that's all."

"Afraid?" I nearly laughed. "Your father? Afraid of what?"

"Of losing another one of us." Cary marched on, his lips tight, his eyes so focused on the street ahead he barely glanced at me the remainder of the way to school. Despite what Cary said, I think he was ashamed at how his father sometimes behaved.

Since it was Friday, at the end of the school day, Betty, Lorraine, and Janet reminded me about their beach party Saturday night. I said I would try to go, but I reminded them I couldn't go without permission.

"Then you won't be there," Betty predicted. "You'll miss a great time."

"I can't help it. I have to ask my uncle and aunt first. My mother left them in charge of me."

"Just do what Janet told you to do: tell them you're going over to her house to study," Lorraine instructed. "A little white lie is no big deal. We all do it."

"It sounds like more than a little white lie. If my uncle found out I lied —"

"He won't find out," Betty assured me. "We don't tell on each other."

"Of course, if you tell Grandpa, he'll turn you in," Janet said.

"Stop calling him Grandpa," I snapped. "He's not anything like an old man."

"Oh? Why do you say that? Do you know something we don't?" she asked quickly. The girls all smiled, waiting with expectation for my reply.

"No," I said.

"Did you get him to smoke the joint?"

"No."

"He didn't see it and tell your uncle, did he?" Lorraine asked quickly.

"If my uncle even thought I had something like that —"

"He'd turn you over to the police," she suggested.

"He'd turn his own mother over to the police," Betty added. "Do you still have it or did you smoke it yourself last night?" Betty asked.

"No, I didn't smoke it." I didn't want to tell them I had simply thrown it out.

"You can smoke it at the beach party," Janet said.

"Let's go, girls," Betty said.

"Be at Janet's house at eight. You won't be sorry. Adam Jackson will be at the beach party," Lorraine sang back at me as they all walked off.

I watched them go down the hallway and then I hurried out to meet Cary and walk home. I wanted to tell him about the party and ask his opinion, but I was afraid even to mention it. I knew how much he didn't like these girls, but I wanted to go. I had never been to a beach party and I had to admit, Adam Jackson's eyes had been in my dreams last night.

I decided to wait until after dinner when I was helping Aunt Sara with the dishes. She had done all the windows herself, even the upstairs ones. "I would have helped you," I told her.

"I know, dear, but don't fret about it. Work gets me through the day. Jacob always says idle hands make for mischief."

I shook my head. What sort of mischief could she ever commit? And why did she permit her husband to treat her as if she were another one of his children and not his wife, his equal in this house? She did everything he asked her to do and as far as I could see, she never uttered a single complaint. He should worship the ground she trod upon and he should have been the one to have done the hard manual labor. My daddy would have done it for my mother, I thought. The more I learned about this family, the more it was a mystery to me.

"Aunt Sara, I was invited to a party Saturday night."

"Oh? A party? Already? What sort of party? Birthday? School party?"

"No. Some of the girls in my class are having a hot dog roast on the beach," I said. "It starts about eight o'clock."

"What girls?"

I gave her the names. She thought a moment.

"Those are girls from good families, but you'll have to ask your uncle," she said.

"Why can't you give me permission?"

"You'll have to ask your uncle for something like that," she replied. I could see that the very idea of her solely giving me permission terrified her. She busied herself with the dishware. If I wanted to go to the beach party, I would have to talk to Uncle Jacob about it. There was no avoiding it.

He was in the living room reading his paper after dinner as usual. I approached him with my request. "Excuse me, Uncle Jacob," I said from the doorway.

He slowly lowered the paper, his eyebrows tilting and the skin folding along his forehead. I couldn't recall speaking to Daddy without seeing a smile in his eyes or on his lips.

"Yes?"

"Some of the girls in my class at school are having a party on the beach tomorrow night and they have invited me. Aunt Sara said I should ask your permission. I would like to go. It's the fastest way to get to know people,"

I offered as a practical reason.

He nodded.

"It don't surprise me you'd like to go to a party where they'll be no adults supervising."

"What do you mean?"

He leaned forward with a wry smile. "Don't you think I know what goes on at those beach parties: how they drink and smoke dope and debauch themselves?"

"De . . . what?"

"Perversions," he declared, that irritating forefinger raised like a flag of righteousness again. "Young girls parade around with their revealing clothing and then roll around on blankets with young men to lose their innocence. It's pagan. While you are under my roof, you will *live* decent, *look* decent, and *act* decent, even if it flies in the face of your instincts." He snapped his paper like a whip. "Now, I don't want to hear another word on it."

"What instincts?" I asked. He ignored me. "I am decent. I've never done anything to shame my parents."

He peered over the paper at me.

"It would take something to shame them, I suppose, but I know what's in the blood, what's raging. If you give it free rein, it will take you straight to hell and damnation."

"I don't understand. What's raging in my blood?"

"No more talk!" he screamed. I flinched and stepped back as if slapped. My heart began to pound. A white line had etched itself about his tightened lips as the rest of him flamed with bright red fury. I had never seen rage inflamed by so small a spark. All I had asked was to go to a party.

I turned away and marched up the stairs. The girls were right, I fumed. I should have just lied and said I was going to Janet's to study. Lying to such a man wasn't wrong. He didn't deserve honesty.

Cary was at the foot of the attic stairway, waiting for me to reach the landing.

"What was all the yelling about?"

I told him and he snorted.

"You should have asked me. I would have spared you his reaction to such a request."

"Why is he so mean?"

"I told you. He's not mean, he's just . . . afraid."

"I don't understand. Why should he be so afraid?"

Cary stared at me a moment and then blurted, "Because he believes it was his fault and that he was being punished." He turned away to go up his ladder.

"What was his fault?" I drew closer as he moved up the rungs. "Laura's death? I don't understand. How could that have been his fault? Was it because he gave her permission to go sailing that day?"

240

"No," Cary said, not turning, still climbing.

"Then I don't understand. Explain it!" I demanded. My tone of voice turned him around. He gazed down at me with a mixture of anger and pain in his face.

"My father doesn't believe in accidents. He believes we are punished on earth for the evil we do on earth, and we are rewarded here for the good we do as well. It's what he was brought up to believe and it's what he has taught us."

"Do you believe that, too?"

"Yes," he said, but not convincingly.

"My daddy was a good man, a kind man. Why was he killed in an accident?"

"You don't know what his sins were," he said and turned away to continue up the stairs.

"He had no sins, nothing so great that he should have died for it! Did you hear me, Cary Logan?" I rushed to the ladder and seized it, shaking it. "Cary!"

He paused at the top and gazed down at me before pulling up his ladder.

"None of us knows the darkness that lingers in another's heart." He sounded just like his father.

"That's stupid. That's another stupid, religious idea," I retorted, but he ignored me and continued to lift the ladder. I seized the bottom rung and held it down. He looked

241

down, surprised at my surge of strength.

"Let go."

"I'll let go, but don't think I don't know what you're doing up there every night," I said. His face turned so red I could see the crimson in his cheeks even in the dim hallway light. "You're running away from tragedy, only you can't run away from something that's part of you."

He tugged with all his strength, nearly lifting me from the floor with the ladder. I had to let go and the ladder went up. He slammed the trapdoor shut.

"Good riddance!" I screamed.

May, locked in her world of silence, emerged from her room with a smile on her face. In my mind, she was the luckiest one in this damnable home.

She signed to me, asking if I would let her come into my room. I told her yes. She followed me in and watched me angrily poke the needle and thread into the picture her sister Laura had drawn just before she died. As I worked I glared up at the ceiling and then down at the floor, below which my coldhearted uncle sat reading his paper. After a while the mechanical work was calming and meditating. I began to understand why Laura might have been entranced with doing so much of it. Everyone in this house was searching for a doorway.

May remained with me until her bedtime, practicing communicative skills, asking me questions about myself, my family, and our lives back in West Virginia. She was full of curiosity and sweetness, somehow un-scathed by the turmoil that raged in every family member's heart. Perhaps her world wasn't so silent after all. Perhaps she heard different music, different sounds, all of it from her free and innocent imagination. When her eyelids began drifting downward, I told her she should go to bed. I was tired myself. I felt as if I had been spun around in an emotional washing machine, then left in a dryer until my last tear evaporated.

Cary lingered in his attic hideaway almost all night. I was woken just before morning to the sound of his footsteps on the ladder. He paused at my doorway for a moment before going to his own room.

He was up with the sunlight a little over an hour later and had gone out with Uncle Jacob by the time I went down for breakfast. Aunt Sara said they were going to be out lobstering all day. I walked to town with May and we spent most of the afternoon looking at the quaint shops on Commercial Street, then we watched the fishermen down at the wharf. It wasn't quite tourist season yet, but the warm spring weather still brought a crowd up from Boston and the outlying areas. There was a lot of traffic.

Aunt Sara had given us some spending money so we could buy hamburgers for lunch. She didn't mind my taking May along with me. She saw how much May wanted to be with me, and I was growing more confident with sign language.

Aunt Sara remarked at how quickly and how well I had been learning it. "Laura was the best at it," she told me. "Even better than Cary."

"What about Uncle Jacob?" I asked her. "Doesn't he know it?"

"A little. He's always too busy to practice," she said, but I thought it was a weak excuse. If my daddy had to learn sign language to communicate with me, nothing would be more important, I thought.

About midday, I counted the change I had left and went to a pay phone. It wasn't enough for a call to Sewell, but I took a chance and made it collect to Alice. Luckily, she was home and accepted the charges.

"I'm sorry," I told her. "I don't have enough money."

"That's okay. Where are you?"

"I'm in Provincetown, on Cape Cod, living with my uncle and my aunt."

"Living with them? Why?"

"Mommy's gone to New York to get an opportunity as a model or an actress," I said. "If she doesn't get a job there, she's going on to Chicago or Los Angeles, so I had to stay here and enroll in the school."

"You did? What's it like?"

I told her about the school and about my life at my uncle's house, Laura's disappearance and death, and May's handicap.

"It sounds sad."

"It's hard to live with them, especially with my cousin Cary. He's so bitter about everything, but I keep telling myself I won't be here long."

"What are the girls like at school?"

"They're different," I told her. "They seem to know more about things and do more things."

"Like what?"

I told her how they had given me a joint of marijuana in the school cafeteria.

"What did you do? You haven't smoked it, have you?"

"No. I was scared. Actually, I was terrified when a teacher came to our table. Afterward, when the girls weren't looking, I threw it in the garbage."

"That's what I would have done," Alice said. "Maybe you should stay away from them."

"They invited me to their beach party tonight, but my uncle won't let me go."

"A beach party!" She hesitated and with some envy said, "Sounds like fun. Maybe you're going to like living there after all."

"I don't think so," I said. "I wish I were back home."

"I was passing the cemetery yesterday and I thought about you so I went in and said a little prayer at your father's grave for you."

"Did you? Thank you, Alice. I miss you."

"Maybe, if you're still there, I can come up to visit you this summer."

"That would be great, but I expect to be gone from here by then. Mommy's coming to get me as soon as she gets settled. Which reminds me, have you seen Mama Arlene? Mommy was supposed to contact her to send me my things."

"I saw her, but George is real sickly."

"I know."

"I think he may be in the hospital."

"Oh no! Would you please tell Mama Arlene I called?"

"I'll go right over to see her," Alice promised.

I gave her my uncle's name and telephone number and she promised to call me the next weekend.

"I really have no friends since you left," she admitted at our conversation's end. It brought tears to my eyes. After I hung up, May wanted to know why I was crying. I tried to explain, but I really didn't know enough sign language to reveal all the pain in my heart. It was easier just to go home.

When we arrived, Aunt Sara explained

that dinner was going to be different this night. Uncle Jacob had invited another lobster man and his wife, the Dimarcos. May, Cary, and I were to eat first and be gone by the time the adults sat at the table. I thought that was a blessing and was grateful for a meal without Uncle Jacob glaring at me as if I were one of the Jezebels he saw on every corner.

However, late in the afternoon, Cary and Uncle Jacob returned home in a very happy mood. Apparently, they had one of their best days at sea, a catch of fifteen lobsters as well a dozen good-size striped bass.

To celebrate, Cary declared that he, May, and I were going to enjoy a real New England feast: clam chowder, steamed muscles, grilled striped bass, potatoes, and vegetables. Cary said he would prepare the fish himself outside on the barbecue grill. "Mother's busy with her own dinner. We can have our own picnic," he said.

"Fine," I told him.

"It won't be as exciting as the beach party, I'm afraid."

"I said, fine."

He nodded and told May, who was very pleased with the idea.

"You two can set the picnic table, if you like."

I nodded without smiling, even though I was happy with the idea.

Cary went about preparing the meal meticulously. He was much better at it than I had expected. None of the boys I had known in West Virginia knew the first thing about preparing fish and vegetables. He thanked me when May and I finished setting the table. I decided to make civil conversation.

"I still don't understand how you fish for lobster," I said standing nearby and watching him grill the fish. "You don't need a pole?"

He laughed.

"We don't fish for them exactly. We set traps at the bottom of the ocean floor and attach buoys that float above."

"How do the other fishermen know which trap is theirs and which is yours?"

"Each lobster fisherman has his own colors on his buoys. We're using the same colors my great grandfather used. They sort of belong to our family, like a coat of arms or something. Understand?"

I nodded.

"After we bring up a trap, if there is a lobster in it, we measure it with a gauge from its eye socket to the end of its back. An average lobster runs anywhere from two to five pounds. My father once brought up a trap with a lobster in it that weighed over thirty."

"Thirty!"

"Yeah, but someone else trapped one

closer to forty last year. Lobsters with eggs on their tails have to be thrown back in immediately. We have to do all we can to keep up the supply. It takes about seven and a half years for a lobster to grow to decent size."

"Seven and a half years?"

"Uh huh," he said smiling. "Now you know why we grow and harvest cranberries, too."

"Is this what you want to do for the rest of your life?" I asked him.

He nodded.

"You don't want to go to college?"

"My college is out there," he said pointing toward the ocean with the fork.

"There's more to life than just fishing and sailing, and there are wonderful places to visit on land, wonderful things to see."

"I see enough here."

"I never saw someone so young act so —"

"What?" he asked quickly. I swallowed back the words and chose less painful ones. "Grown up."

He nodded.

"Go on," he said. "If you want to call me Grandpa, too, you can. I don't care."

"You're nothing like a grandpa."

He looked at me curiously for a moment. I felt, since he was being honest, I should be. "But you're too fixed in your thinking for someone your age. You should have a more open mind about things."

"Sure," he said. "And be willing to smoke dope and drink and waste my time just like those other jerks in school."

"They're not all jerks, are they?"

"Most are."

"You can be pretty infuriating," I told him.

He shrugged and began serving the fish. "I don't bother anyone and just ask they don't bother me," he said. "Let's eat."

He made sure May had her meal first. The way he took care of her, saw to her needs and happiness, softened my frustration and anger toward him.

"How hard was it for May when Laura died?" I asked him as we sat at the picnic table and began our meal.

"Real hard," he said.

"Poor thing. To have such a tragedy on top of her handicap."

"She does fine," he said angrily.

"No one is saying she doesn't, Cary. You don't have to jump down my throat. There is such a thing as being too protective, you know."

"You can never be too protective," he replied. "Once you go out there, you'll understand." He nodded toward the ocean.

"When am I going out there?" He was silent. "I've never been on a sailboat. Daddy used to take us to the beach, but Mommy hated boats so we just went swimming and got suntans."

"What a bunch of tourists," he quipped.

"You shouldn't make fun of the tourists. They buy your lobsters, don't they?"

"And ruin everything, litter the beach, poison the water, make fun of us."

"I think you'd be happy just being a hermit," I concluded. It didn't faze him. He shrugged.

"This is good," I told him after I ate some of the fish, but it sounded like a complaint.

"Thanks," he said without any feeling.

"You're welcome," I growled.

We ate silently, shooting darts at each other with our eyes, but when we turned to May we saw her staring at us and smiling a wide smile of amusement. Cary's eyes shifted to mine. We gazed at each other a moment and then we had to laugh.

It was as if a sheet of ice had cracked and let in some warm air. Our conversation lightened up and I talked about the scenery. I was taken with the apricot glow of the sunset as we looked out over the ocean. I hadn't realized how beautiful the ocean could be. That pleased him and he revealed that when he was a little boy he and Laura would lie on their backs in their father's rowboat at dusk and watch the sky change colors.

"It seemed magical," he said.

"It is."

There was real warmth in his eyes and I

thought the girls were right: he was good looking when he wanted to be. Suddenly, though, he became self-conscious and quickly reverted to his serious, hard look. However, after dinner when I helped him clean up, he surprised me by suggesting we walk into town with May for some frozen custard.

"And see what damage the outsiders are doing," he added.

"And what money they're leaving with the local merchants," I added. He hid his smile, but I caught it.

For the first time, when we walked with May, he allowed her to hold both our hands. Cary led us a different way that took us past high grass, bushes, and scrub oak trees. I heard the peepers in the marsh.

"Theresa and her brother and sisters and her father live down there," he pointed when we turned a corner.

I gazed at a street that wound east. The houses were small and the grass in their yards was spotty and rough. Closer to the town, the houses were nicer, with real lawns and flowers, like yellow tea roses in a bed of Queen Anne's lace, dark purple iris, and hydrangeas.

The Cape was truly amazing. Toward the ocean, there were rolls and rolls of sand that looked as dry and sparse as any desert, but a short distance away were oak trees, blueberry bushes, red maple trees, and houses with lawns full of crocus clusters, emperor tulips, and sprawling lilac bushes. It seemed like two different worlds. Cary said there was often two kinds of weather. It could be stormy on the east with the sun shining brightly on the west.

Perhaps the differences in the land explained the differences in the people, I thought, some hard, frugal, with religious ideas carved in stone; others carefree, impulsive, jolly, and hungry for fun and excitement. Some lived to work and some worked just enough to live.

At night the little town was exciting, especially with all the people, the music from the bars and restaurants, the carloads of tourists yelling to each other, the crowds down at the dock. My eyes went everywhere. He bought May her frozen custard and asked me if I wanted one, too. I did. He got himself one as well.

May wanted to go to the dock and watch the deep-sea fishermen try to entice the tourists to hire them. I had never been in a real tourist town at night before, and was taken with all the lights, and the way store owners and desert tour operators barked at the people, tempting, cajoling, practically begging for their business.

"I hate those desert tours," Cary remarked when a jeep load rolled by. "Once, a couple of jeeps pulled up behind our house and the guide pointed to my mother and Laura, describing them as native fishermen's women."

"So, that's what your mother is, right?"

"She's not a freak for tourists to gape at, no," he said, "and Laura certainly was not. How would they like a sightseeing bus coming around to their backyards and having people gape at them while they did their housework?"

I nodded, understanding some of his anger.

"You're right. That isn't nice." He looked appreciative, but quickly checked his smile and gazed at May.

"Better get back," he said. "May's sleepy."

When we returned to the house, Uncle Jacob was entertaining his fisherman friend in the living room while their wives chatted in the kitchen. We went directly upstairs. May went to sleep quickly.

"Thanks for the custard and the walk," I told Cary in the hallway.

He stared at me a moment.

"Are you very tired?"

"No, not very," I said.

"Want to see something special?"

"Sure."

"Come on," he said, leading the way down the stairs. We stepped quietly through the house, but Uncle Jacob heard us and came to the living room doorway.

"Where you going now, son?" he asked.

"Just going to check the bog," Cary replied.

Uncle Jacob looked at me, his eyes growing smaller before he nodded softly and returned to his company.

Cary said nothing. He hurried out of the house and led me over the grounds to the hill. When we reached the top, he paused and we gazed at the bog. The moonlight played tricks with the blossoms. They dazzled like jewels in the night.

"What do you think?" he asked.

"It's beautiful."

"I thought you might like it."

To our right the ocean roared in the darkness. I embraced myself.

"Cold?"

"A little," I admitted.

"I bet you really wanted to go to that beach party," he said.

"I've never been to one."

"All they do is smoke dope or drink around the fire. Some of them go off into the darkness, of course."

"Don't you want a girlfriend some day?" I asked him.

"When I find someone sensible, I'll speak to her," he replied.

"No one's sensible?"

"And pretty, too," he admitted. He stood there with his hands in his pockets, kicking the sand and occasionally glancing at me and then at the ocean. "What about you?"

"What?"

"Did you have a boyfriend back in West Virginia?"

"For a while I was going steady, but after Daddy died . . . I stopped going to school dances and things."

"Yeah, I didn't want to do anything after Laura died. I didn't want to work or ever go back to school."

"That was the only good thing about us leaving Sewell," I told him. "Not having to go to the places Daddy and I used to go to anymore, not having to look at the coal miners and wait for him to come home."

He thought a moment. "I couldn't leave here ever."

"Most of the young people I knew were always talking about getting away from home someday."

"Not me. This is where I belong, where I was meant to be. I got saltwater in my blood."

I laughed.

"I probably won't graduate anyway," he added.

"Why not?"

"Doing pretty bad in English."

"Badly."

"What?"

"You're doing badly, not bad."

"See what I mean?"

"Maybe I can help you. I'm a very good English student."

"It's probably too late. If I don't pass the final —"

"Then you'll pass it," I told him. "I'll help you every night. Okay?"

"I don't know. I don't know if I even care."

"You've got to care! Besides, I'm sure you'll do well if you try."

He smiled.

"I understand Laura was a very good student. Did she help you?"

He looked away instead of answering and then he turned back and started down the hill. "Let's go back to the house."

I followed him. When we entered the house again, Uncle Jacob asked Cary in to talk about the lobster business with them. I told them good night and went to my room to read. A little while later I heard Cary go up to his attic hideaway. I listened to him scuffle about and then all grew quiet, but for the muffled voices of Uncle Jacob, Aunt Sara, and their friends below.

My eyelids felt heavy. I dozed off, woke up, went to the bathroom, returned, and dressed for bed. After I put the lights out, I gazed out the window and saw the moon walk on the ocean. How beautiful. Had Laura looked out this window and been thrilled by it? What was she really like? I had

Aunt Sara's constant descriptions, comparisons, and remarks, but somehow I thought there was more to her daughter than she knew.

Cary knew, I thought. She had been his twin, but he was afraid or unwilling to talk about her. It would take time, but more importantly, it would take trust. I wondered if I could ever get him to trust me with the secrets of his heart. I knew he had secrets buried deeply.

I closed my eyes and lay back on my pillow and thought about Mommy. Where was she tonight? I swallowed back my tears and pressed for sleep to keep myself from thinking sad thoughts.

Was that what Cary did every night?

10

A Cocoon of Lies

The next morning, Sunday, we went to church then came home and prepared for our visit to my grandparents as if we were going to visit royalty. Aunt Sara explained that everyone had to wear his and her best clothes and be prim and proper.

She paraded through the room explaining what I was to wear and how I was to wear my hair and carry myself. "Olivia doesn't like women to have their hair loose and down. She says it makes them look like witches. Use the bobby pins and combs to wrap your hair neatly. And no makeup, not even lipstick. You can wear the charm bracelet, of course, but rings and necklaces, and especially earrings don't belong on young ladies, she says."

"Is that what you think, too, Aunt Sara?"

"What I think doesn't matter when we go to Samuel and Olivia's home," she replied. "Jacob's pleased when they're pleased."

"And you? When are you pleased?"

Aunt Sara paused and gazed at me as if I had asked the most ridiculous question. "I'm pleased when Jacob's pleased, as any wife would be."

"I hope that my husband will want me to be happy, too, and care about my feelings as much or more than he cares about his own. My daddy was like that."

"Oh dear, don't say things like that in front of Jacob. Especially not today," she warned.

"Maybe I shouldn't go along," I said. Alarm sprang to her eyes.

"You have to go! It's Sunday. We always go to Samuel and Olivia's for Sunday brunch," she said. "Why, Laura used to look forward to going. Olivia always has wonderful things to eat. Laura loved the tiny cakes with frosting and jelly in the center, and Samuel always gave her a crisp five-dollar bill when we left. She was the apple of his eye. She was . . ." She paused to take a deep breath.

For a moment she seemed locked in a daze. Then her eyes snapped closed and open and she spun around. "Try to keep your shoulders back and your head up when you walk. Olivia hates the way young people slouch today. She's always saying posture shows character and embellishes good health."

"No one's ever said I slouch."

"No, you don't, but just be more attentive to it. Well, I must see about May."

I took a deep breath and rose, feeling even more nervous this morning than the day I had first arrived. When I finally thought myself dressed well enough and looking somewhat the way Aunt Sara wanted me to, I descended the stairs to find the family waiting in the living room. Everyone was still dressed in their church clothes.

Uncle Jacob wore a dark blue suit and tie and Cary wore a light blue sports jacket, tie, and slacks. His shoes were spit shined. May looked sweet in her pink cotton dress with her hair tied in a pink ribbon. She wore black patent leather mary janes. Aunt Sara had on a dark blue, high-necked dress with a belt at the waist. As usual she wore no makeup and only the locket for jewelry. Her hair was pulled back in a severe bun and held there with a bone-white comb.

They all stared at me when I entered. I was being inspected. I waited for approval. Cary's eyes widened and then went darker before he looked away. I was sure it was because I was wearing another one of Laura's dresses — this time a pretty cream-colored one. I couldn't wait for my own things to arrive.

"Well, she looks very nice, doesn't she, Jacob?" Aunt Sara asked meekly.

"Aye," he said reluctantly. "Did you talk to her about her behavior?"

"Not yet," she said.

"What have I done now?" I asked.

"It's not what you've done. It's what you might do," Uncle Jacob remarked. Then he turned to Sara. "Well, do it and then come out," he said rising. He nodded at Cary, who got up quickly, took May's hand, and left.

"Just sit a moment, dear," Aunt Sara said. "There are a few other things you must remember."

"What other things?" I sat on the settee.

"Olivia, your grandmother, is very particular about how children behave in her home."

"I'm not a child," I said. "I'm nearly sixteen."

"Oh, I know, but until you're married yourself, she thinks of you as a child." Aunt Sara obviously spoke from her own experience.

She stood before me like a teacher in school. "Most important, speak only when you are spoken to. Olivia thinks it's rude for a young person to demand answers from adults or give an opinion without being asked to do so. And especially, never, never interrupt when someone else is speaking."

"I don't," I said.

"Good. Remember to say please and thank you and never sit with your legs apart. Put your hands in your lap. At the table be sure to bring the spoon and the fork to your mouth and not vice versa, and remember to keep only one elbow at a time on the table. Always dab your lips with your napkin after you put something in your mouth. Sit with your back straight and don't stare at people," she recited as if she had memorized some etiquette book. "Do you understand everything?"

I nodded.

"It doesn't sound as if I'm going to enjoy myself very much," I muttered. She went white.

"Oh dear, never say such a thing. Please! Keep such thoughts under lock and key."

"Don't worry, Aunt Sara, I've never embarrassed my parents. I won't embarrass you." I rose, my legs very reluctant, and left the house. Cary and May waited in the rear of the car. I got in beside May.

"How far away is it?" I asked Cary softly.

"About twenty minutes."

My teeth were actually chattering in anticipation of Grandma Olivia's disapproval and rejection. But why? I was finally going to meet my father's parents, my real grandparents. I should have been excited. All the grandparents I ever heard of loved their grandchildren dearly.

But, I reminded myself, our family is different.

From the outside, my grandparents' house did not look cold and impersonal. It was a large, wooden clapboard house.

Aunt Sara said that the house was very old

and prestigious, the original portion having been built around 1780. Cary shook his head and raised his eyes toward the car ceiling when Aunt Sara went into her lecture about the house, a lecture I guessed Grandma Olivia had given her so many times it was stored forever in her memory.

The grounds were certainly the prettiest I had seen on the Cape. The beautifully cared for green lawn was uncommon, and the flower garden was the most elaborate with its baskets of gold, purple pansies, roses, and geraniums. There was a small duck pond to the right with about a dozen or so ducks in it. Most impressive were the large, blooming red maple trees. Between two on the far right was a bench swing with a canopy over it.

We stopped in the driveway and got out. Aunt Sara immediately brushed a loose strand of my hair back and straightened the shoulders of my dress.

"Leave her be," Cary muttered.

She stood next to Uncle Jacob as he rang the bell, the three of us standing behind them. A moment later the door opened.

I set eyes on my grandfather for the first time in real life. Up until now, all I had seen was that old photograph of my daddy.

Grandpa Samuel was still a tall, straight-standing man with a proud, strong demeanor. I saw my daddy's resemblance in his face immediately. Daddy, as did Cary, shared his green eyes. Grandpa Samuel's hair was mostly gray, but he still had a full head of it. It was trimmed neatly at the ears and sides, with the top brushed back. There was a trace of a wave running through it.

Daddy had had the same straight, firm nose, but Grandpa Samuel's lips were thinner and his chin more carved. He had Daddy's large hands and long arms, and for a man his age, I thought he had very firm, full shoulders.

"Hello, Jacob, Sara," he said. He gazed past them quickly to focus on me. I thought I saw a small smile at the corners of his mouth, the same light and gentle twist that Daddy often had. He looked quickly at Cary and May. "Children."

"Hello, Papa," Cary said.

"Hello . . . Pa pa," May said.

"This is Melody," Aunt Sara said stepping to the side to bring me forward.

"Pretty girl. Lot of Haille in her, eh Jacob?"

"Aye," Uncle Jacob replied glancing at me.

"Hello, Melody," my grandfather said.

I didn't know whether I was to shake his hand or curtsey or just nod.

"Hello," I replied. "I'm pleased to meet you." I almost added, "finally." He nodded, holding that small smile on his lips.

"Well, come on in," he told us and stepped

back. "Olivia's seeing to the brunch, of course."

We entered a short, marble-floored entry-way with paintings on both sides: pictures of the Cape and boats, pictures of sailors. The house was full of the perfume of flowers.

Grandpa Samuel showed us to the room on the right, the sitting room. It looked like a showcase in a furniture store window. The oak floor was so polished I was sure I would be able to see my face in it if I looked down. On every table, on every shelf, there were expensive-looking glass pieces, vases, and occasionally, photos in silver and gold frames. I just glanced at them, but they looked like pictures of my grandfather and grandmother when they were younger, and some pictures of Uncle Jacob, Aunt Sara, Laura, Cary, and May. There were no pictures of Daddy.

"Sit with Cary and May over there," Aunt Sara instructed. We took the settee on the right. Grandpa Samuel sat in the chair and Aunt Sara and Uncle Jacob sat on the settee across from us. Although he kept his eyes on me, Grandpa Samuel spoke to Uncle Jacob.

"So how was your week, Jacob?"

"Fair to middling," he replied. "We had a good day yesterday, eh Cary?"

"Yes sir," Cary said. He shot a glance at me.

Grandpa Samuel nodded. Then he turned toward me. "So you're Melody. How old are you?"

"Fifteen, almost sixteen."

"Aye, that would be right." He thought a moment and then smiled. "I hear you can play the fiddle. My grandfather played the accordion. I ever tell you that, Sara?"

"No," she said, her eyes wide.

"I've told you the same before," Uncle Jacob snapped at her.

"Did you? I don't remember your speaking about your grandfather playing the accordion, Jacob."

"Aye, he was good at it," Grandpa Samuel said, directing himself to me. "I can still remember hearing his jolly tunes."

"There are better things to remember than a lazy fisherman," I heard a sharp, small voice say. We turned to the doorway to see Grandma Olivia. She stood a little over five feet tall, and wore a pale yellow dress. Her snow-white hair was pulled back in a bun as severely as Aunt Sara's, which only made her eyes look bigger and her forehead look wider. There were tiny age spots clustered at the foot of her hairline and on her cheeks. Without lipstick, her lips were a dull pink. Below her jaw, her skin hung loosely like a hen's.

There was no bend in her back, and because she had such a regal posture, she looked taller, sturdier than I was sure she was.

"You're early," she accused, gazing at us, her eyes fixing tightly on me.

"We were ready, so we came," Uncle Jacob remarked.

"Early's better than late," Grandpa Samuel said. She shot a look at him and his smile faded quickly.

"Well, then," she said, nodding at Sara, "make the proper introductions."

"Yes, Olivia." Aunt Sara turned to me. "This is Melody, Haille's Melody."

Haille's, I thought. Why not Haille and Chester's? Was even my father's name forbidden in this house?

Aunt Sara nodded at me to tell me to stand. I rose and Grandma Olivia came closer. She drank me in, gazing at me from head to foot quickly, and nodded to herself to confirm some previous notion.

"Looks healthy. Tall, too, with good posture."

Tall? I wasn't so tall, I thought, but then I realized almost anyone would be tall to her.

"Well then, what do you say?" she asked.

I glanced at Aunt Sara who nodded and smiled.

"Hello, Grandma Olivia," I replied. The words appeared to sting her. She tightened her body and lifted her shoulders.

"We'll eat even though we're a bit early,"

she said, "and you'll tell me all about yourself. Samuel," she ordered and he rose. Cary and May stood and Aunt Sara got up quickly with Uncle Jacob.

For a moment I felt as if we were all in some army and Grandma Olivia was the general. She started out and we followed. We crossed the hallway to the dining room.

It was a beautiful room, with dark, oak-paneled walls and a glossy, long cherrywood table. All the chairs were upholstered with high backs. The china looked very expensive and the candle holders looked as if they were made of real gold. The silverware was heavy. Everyone had a linen placemat and linen napkins.

Cary, May, and I were put on one side, Aunt Sara and Uncle Jacob on the other. Grandma Olivia sat at the far end of the table and Grandpa Samuel on the other end. A maid brought out the brunch.

It began with a tossed salad, glittering with plum tomatoes and the greenest peppers and lettuce I had ever seen. Long loaves of bread were sliced and placed on silver serving plates. Everyone was given tall glasses of ice water. Following that, a large dish of perfectly arranged jumbo shrimp on a bed of lettuce was presented. There were small, cold potatoes, asparagus spears, and then two beautifully roasted ducks, all sliced.

Grandma Olivia took tiny portions of

everything, but Grandpa Samuel ate as much as Uncle Jacob and Cary. I felt Grandma Olivia's eyes on my every move and recited Aunt Sara's instructions for etiquette at the dinner table to myself as I chewed, sipped, and reached for things.

"So then," Grandma Olivia said suddenly, as if we were all still in the midst of a conversation that had previously begun. "Haille called?"

"Yes," Aunt Sara said. "The other night she spoke with Melody."

Grandma Olivia turned her cold, steely eyes on me. "Where is your mother?"

"She called from someplace between Boston and New York," I replied.

"And how long does she intend to carry on like this?" she asked.

I shook my head. "Carry on?"

"Pretending she's doing something with her wretched life," she explained.

I felt the heat rise into my neck and face. "She has auditions, meetings, appointments," I said. "She's trying to become —"

"A what? A model, an actress?" she interrupted with a small, thin laugh. Then she looked at Grandpa Samuel. "An actress she's always been," she said. He looked away and she turned back to me.

"Your father left you and your mother no money after all these years of so-called honest labor?"

"We had something, but expenses were high for us and Mommy needed things and —"

"Wasteful. Never changed a bit," she muttered. "What did she look like?" she asked Aunt Sara.

"Oh, she's still very pretty, Olivia. Maybe she can be a model."

"Ridiculous. With her posture? Cary," she snapped, deciding to move on to someone else at the table, "how is your schoolwork now?"

"Not much better than it was, Grandma, I'm afraid," he said.

"Well, what do you plan on doing about it, Cary? You don't have all that much more time left, do you?" she asked.

"I'm thinking of being tutored," he said, shifting his gaze to me. I saw the small smile on his lips and smiled, too. Grandma Olivia caught the look between us and turned to me again.

"You are a good student, I understand?"

"Yes, Grandma. I've always been on the honor roll."

"Hmph," she said and shook her head. "Your mother didn't even graduate from high school, you know."

I looked up quickly.

"Yes, she did," I said.

Aunt Sara made a tiny gasp and brought her napkin to her lips. She shook her head slightly at me. Was I supposed to just sit by and let Grandma Olivia say untruths?

"She told you that, did she?"

"Yes," I said.

She smiled that cold smile again, twisting her thin lips until they looked as if they would snap. "That girl never could distinguish between reality and illusion. No wonder she's gallivanting around the country trying to be an actress or a model," Grandma Olivia continued.

How do you know so much about my mother? I wanted to ask. You who disowned my father after he married her. But I lowered my eyes and nibbled on my food instead. Then I gazed at May, who sat eating and staring ahead with a soft smile on her face. I wondered if either Grandma Olivia or Grandpa Samuel knew how to communicate with her. All I had seen so far were smiles and nods from Grandpa Samuel. Grandma Olivia barely acknowledged her, from what I had seen.

We ate in silence, with everyone but Grandma Olivia keeping his eyes on the food before him. Finally, Grandpa Samuel looked up.

"The word I been getting," Grandpa Samuel said to Uncle Jacob, "is there'll be a good tourist season this year with the price of travel overseas going up and all."

Uncle Jacob nodded. "Aye. I heard that the hotels were looking good. There'll be lots of garbage to clean off the beach come this fall," he added. I knew where Cary got his attitude about the outsiders.

"How are the cranberries coming along?" Grandpa Samuel asked.

"They look good. We're anticipating a decent crop."

"Does she expect to leave you here over the summer?" Grandma Olivia suddenly asked me.

"I don't know," I said. "I hope not."

She raised her eyebrows.

"And why is that? Aren't you being treated well at my son's home? They gave you Laura's room, I understand, and you're even wearing her things, aren't you?"

"Yes, I'm being treated well," I said quickly. "I just meant I would like to be with my mother. I miss her."

She smirked. "A girl your age should have a home and not be living out of a car running on someone's pipe dreams," she muttered.

"We had a home and we'll have another one," I said, my voice full of defiance.

"What kind of home did you have in West Virginia?" she asked, not intimidated by my tone of voice.

"We lived in the trailer park. Daddy worked very hard in the coal mine. I never went hungry."

"And your mother, what did she do?"

"She worked in a beauty parlor."

"That figures," Grandma Olivia said. "That woman could wear out a mirror."

Before I could respond, Grandma turned quickly to call the maid. "The adults will have coffee in the sitting room, Loretta."

"Yes, ma'am."

"Bring out some ice cream and some of the petit fours for the children," she ordered.

Children? I looked at Cary to see how he liked being referred to that way. He tucked the corner of his mouth in and gazed at the wall.

"Lucky for you that your Aunt Sara saved all of Laura's clothing," Grandma Olivia told me. "She always had such nice things."

"Mommy's sent for my things," I replied. I glanced at Aunt Sara and saw the hurt look on her face. "Although I am grateful for what Aunt Sara has given me to use. I'm just sorry about the circumstances."

Grandpa Samuel nodded, his look softening.

Grandma Olivia raised her eyebrows. "And what do you know about the circumstances?" she demanded.

"What? Well, I was told —"

"Olivia, must we go through this again?" Grandpa Samuel asked softly.

Grandma Olivia snorted. "Jacob says you can play the fiddle well," she said. I was shocked. Uncle Jacob had said something nice about me? "Maybe one day you'll come over and give us a concert," she added. My jaw nearly dropped. Was she serious?

She stood up. "Let's go into the sitting room for coffee, Samuel," she commanded.

"Right, dear," he said rising.

The maid brought out three dishes of ice cream for Cary, May, and me and served them with a plate of small cakes, the ones Aunt Sara told me Laura had loved.

"Sorry, we only have vanilla ice cream," Grandma Olivia remarked. "Cary, you can show Melody the grounds when you're finished, and entertain yourselves outside. But don't track in any dirt. Make sure May understands," she concluded.

"Okay, Grandma," he said and signed instructions to May.

"How is she?" Grandma asked, remaining at the table and looking at her with pity.

"She's doing very well, Grandma," Cary said, before his parents could reply. Grandma Olivia nodded, shook her head as if to drive the thoughts away, and led the adults out of the dining room.

I felt a ceiling of oppressive gray clouds and heavy air, too thick to breathe, go out with her.

"You should call this place the Ice House," I remarked.

Cary smiled. "She's not as tough as she makes out."

We ate the dessert and, I had to admit, I

did like the small cakes. "This house itself is very nice, nicer even than Alice Morgan's."

"Who's she?"

"My best friend back in Sewell." I gazed at the pretty things, the antique hutch filled with expensive crystal, the beautiful chandelier above us, and the rich, large paintings on the walls.

"How did Grandpa make so much money?" I asked Cary.

"A great deal was left to Grandma Olivia when her parents passed away. Grandpa had a fleet of fishing vessels, including five lobster boats. But, he lost most of them during bad times. Luckily, my father had his own by then. Come on. I'll show you around."

He signed to May and she gulped down one more spoonful of ice cream. I took her hand when she came around the table. Cary led us through the house, down the corridor, past the door to the kitchen, past a den-office on the right, finally to a rear door. It opened on a small porch.

Behind the house was a large gazebo, some benches and a rock garden with a small fountain. The rear of the property was on the beach and there was a dock with a large sailboat and a small motorboat tied to it.

"This is a beautiful place," I declared.

"Aye. They actually have a small cove here

so it's not as rough as it is up and down the beach."

We walked down to the dock and looked at the ocean. The waves were gentle. Milk-white streaks of clouds lay against the blue sky. To the right against the shoreline were large rocks.

"See the mussels clinging to those rocks," Cary said pointing. They were dark purple against the stone. On the sand, seagulls strutted about searching for clams. I saw one circle the rocks and then drop some-thing from its beak. The moment what it had dropped hit the rock, it swooped to retrieve it.

"What is that bird doing?"

"Seagulls drop the clams on the rocks to break the shells and then drop to eat them as soon as they hit the stone. Smart, eh?"

I shook my head in amazement, not only at what I saw, but at how much Cary knew about nature.

I looked down the beach to our left. A large sailboat bounced over the waves, its sail flapping in the breeze. "I can understand why my daddy wanted to go to the seashore so much. He missed this."

Cary nodded, glanced at me, and then checked the knot on the rope that held the motorboat to the dock. May signed to us she was going to look for seashells.

"Not too far," Cary signed. She nodded and

directed her attention to the beach.

"Our grandmother sure hates my mother, doesn't she?" I said.

Cary kept his watchful eyes on May. "Looks that way," he admitted.

"Do they often talk about her and my daddy?"

"Hardly ever," he said. He started for the beach and I followed.

"I can't understand what my daddy could possibly have done to make them so angry. Why shouldn't a man have a right to choose the woman he loves to marry? Why did they have to disown him? She's very cruel, or are you going to tell me it's simply because she's afraid, too?"

He spun around, his eyes filled more with pain than anger. "Grandma's bark has always been worse than her bite," he said. "After you're here a while, you'll see that, too. It takes her a little time to warm up to strangers."

"I'm not a stranger. I'm her granddaughter, whether she likes it or not."

He looked away. May was close enough to the water for the tide to just touch her feet. "Damn!" He rushed to her and pulled her farther back. I thought he was unnecessarily rough with her and said so. Then I took her hand and we walked away. I told her I would help her find seashells. Cary followed.

"She can't swim, you know," he said in his defense.

"She can't swim?"

"No. Even if she could, the undertow can sometimes pull the strongest swimmer out to drown."

I kept us a good distance from the water.

"I understand why you are so protective of her, Cary, and it's a good thing, a loving thing, but you've got to let her breathe."

He stared at me. The wind made the strands of his hair dance around his face. I felt the sea spray on my own. Above us, the terns circled and cried.

"I know why the family had nothing to do with your father and why he and your mother ran off," he confessed.

"You do?"

"Yes." He knelt down and plucked a shell out of the sand and handed it to May. "It wasn't something anyone told me," he continued. "I learned about it all in bits and pieces over the years just being nearby when they would discuss it.

"When my father realized what I had learned and knew, he pulled me aside one day and forbade me to ever mention anything, especially in my grandparents' presence."

"Tell me." I asked softly.

"Your mother should have been the one to tell you, or your father, but I'm sure they were too ashamed and afraid," he added.

My heart seemed to stop and then start, and accompanying that came a thumping that made my blood rush to my head.

"Ashamed of what? What had they done?"

"Married," he said.

"So? Are your parents and our grandparents so conceited, so arrogant, that they can look down on someone who wasn't from what they call the best families? Someone who was an orphan? Just who do they think they —"

"Your mother was an orphan, yes. But she never told you the truth about who her adopted parents were."

I held my breath.

"What do you mean? Who were they?"

"Grandma and Grandpa," he said. "Your mother and your father grew up like brother and sister, and when they found out she had become pregnant with you, it was even more of a disgrace."

I shook my head and nearly laughed aloud.

"That's stupid. That's some ridiculous lie your father told you to cover up for the disgraceful and disgusting way they treated my daddy."

"It's the truth," he insisted.

"No!" I put my hands over my ears. "I won't listen to another horrible word."

May stared at me, her face in a grimace.

She started to sign quickly, asking what was wrong. I shook my head at her.

"I thought you should know so you would understand why everyone has these feelings about your mother and father. Maybe you won't blame Grandma and Grandpa and my father and mother so much."

"I blame them more!" I screamed at him. "More for lying."

"They're not lying," he said softly. "I'm surprised those gossipmongers in school haven't said anything to you. It's an old story, so maybe they don't know, or maybe they just don't realize who you are."

I shook my head and backed away from him. "You're just getting back at me for what I said about May. You're cruel. I hate you," I said. "I hate you!"

I ran down the beach, tears streaming down my cheeks. I ran as hard and as fast as I could, my feet slipping and sliding in the sand. I even splashed through some water without caring, and then I fell forward on the sand, exhausted, my chest feeling as if it would explode. I took deep, hard breaths.

He had to be lying, or passing on their lies. Why wouldn't Mommy or Daddy ever have told me?

Moments later, Cary stood at my side. "I knew I shouldn't have said anything."

"You shouldn't have said anything so stupid," I retorted, looking up at him. He stood holding May's hand. She looked frightened, as if she might start to cry herself. I got to my feet and brushed off my clothing.

"When we get back to the house, I'll show you something," he said. He turned and started away. I took May's hand and we followed.

At the rear door, Cary paused. "This way." He took us around to the north side of the house where there was a metal cellar door. He reached down and pulled it open. There was a short, cement stairway that led to another door. "It's the basement."

I hesitated. He went down the stairs and opened the next door, stepping in to pull a cord that turned on a swinging, naked bulb. When I walked down the stairs, I saw the basement had just the ground for a floor, but there were metal shelves against the old fieldstone foundation. I passed through cobwebs. There was a dank and musty odor.

"This is under the oldest section of the house," Cary explained. "I think it was once the fruit and vegetable cellar. Something like that. Laura and I used to think of this as our clubhouse. We didn't mind the dampness or the spiderwebs and mice."

"Mice?"

"They've scurried into their hiding places by now." He smiled, then stepped across the small room to one of the metal shelves and pulled a carton off the second shelf, lowering it to the basement's dirt floor. The cardboard, left in this clamminess, was soft and nearly ripped under his touch as he opened the box slowly.

"Here," he said, waiting for me to approach. I took slow steps, my chest feeling as if I had swallowed lumps of coal that now lay stuck against my heart. May remained at my side, clinging to my hand. I gazed into the box. It was filled with photo albums. He took out the first one and opened it.

"Your parents were gone by the time Laura and I had discovered all this, of course. When we asked Grandma Olivia about these pictures, she forbade us ever to come in here again. We didn't for a long time," he said.

I looked at the pictures. They were old photos taken of children, two boys and a girl.

"This is your father and your mother and this is my father," Cary pointed out. He turned the pages, which contained pictures of Daddy, Mommy, and Uncle Jacob as they grew older. The resemblances became sharper and clearer with every turn of the page. "Your father was always a big guy, huh? And your mother, she was pretty from the start," he said.

Tears streamed down my cheeks as he slowly turned the pages, revealing pictures taken at lawn parties, on the swing bench, near the flower gardens, pictures on sailboats and fishing boats. There were school pictures, as well as group family pictures.

I shook my head in disbelief.

"I'm sorry," he said. "I'm sorry you never knew the whole truth."

I bit down on my lower lip and sucked in air through my nose, ignoring my hot tears. He put the albums back in the carton, neatly closed it, and placed it back on the shelf.

"There's a lot more here, but maybe some other time," he said.

I turned away, releasing May's hand. It felt as if I had let go of a lifeline and I was now drifting in space. Dazed, I went back to the cement steps and up into the daylight, vaguely hearing Cary put out the light and close the basement door behind us. I stared out at the glittering sea, the ocean looking like a floating mirror, mesmerizing.

A cocoon of lies had been spun around me. Cary had sliced it open and I was looking out at the world with different eyes.

But more was yet to come. I sensed it, and that ominous dread put thunder in my heart. I would know it all, I vowed, no matter how damning the truth might be.

11

He Says I'm Pretty

Cary stepped up beside me and stood there for a few moments without speaking. Two terns flew by. Their cries sounded like screams to me. Maybe that was because I felt I was screaming inside myself. In moments my world had gone topsy-turvy. The blue sky now looked gray. The soft blue water had turned to ice.

"I'm sure my parents were unaware that you didn't know about Haille, Melody. At least, I never heard my father say anything. I'd appreciate it if you didn't let them know I was the one who told you," Cary said.

I spun on him so sharply, he winced as if he expected to be slapped. "I guess I could lie and tell them Mommy had told me all this. Or I could pretend someone at school told me. Maybe I just figured it all out myself, right? I mean, everyone here grows lies as abundantly as the cranberries. I have lots to choose from, don't I?"

He nodded. "I understand how you feel."

"Do you?" I snapped, the skin on my face feeling hot and sunburnt.

"Yes," he replied firmly. His green eyes grew dark, but held me with their sincerity. "I do, Melody. When I first realized you didn't know the whole truth about your parents, I was shocked. Even before today, I thought about telling you because I was tired of hearing you complain about how my father treated your mother and your father, but —"

"But what, Cary Logan?"

He looked away, swallowed, and then turned back.

"I didn't want to happen just what is happening now," he blurted.

"And what's that?" I demanded, hands on my hips. Out of the corner of my eye, I saw May watching us, confusion on her face. "Well?" I demanded.

"I didn't want you hating me," he confessed.

My heart continued to thump, but the steel in my shoulders and back softened. I relaxed and looked back at the ocean.

"I don't know what you mean," I muttered.

"I don't remember the story, but I remember the lesson the teacher taught," he continued. "It was something about how we always hate the messenger who brings us bad news. That's why we hate to deliver it."

"I don't hate you for telling me the truth," I said. "But I *am* angry, mostly at my mother.

286

She should have told me everything before she brought me here and dumped me on the family that hates the sight of me."

"No one hates the sight of you. How could anyone blame you? But you're right: your parents should have told you," he said, nodding. "They should have trusted you with the truth about their past and all that had happened. I guess my father hit the nail on the head: they were ashamed of themselves. That's why they ran from here to live in West Virginia after they had gotten secretly married."

"But . . . I just don't understand it all." I shook my head. "Why did Grandpa Samuel and Grandma Olivia take my mother into their home and adopt her if they considered her inferior? And even though my parents lived like brother and sister, they weren't brother and sister. Why was it so terrible, terrible enough to disown my father, to hate him so much that none of you even mourns his death?"

"Look, I don't know details. As I said, no one likes to talk about it. Maybe now your mother will tell you everything," he concluded. "You can ask her."

"Yes, I will ask her," I moaned, "if she ever calls me or comes for me."

"I'm sorry, Melody," he said. "It all stinks like a rotten fish."

I gazed into his now softened emerald eyes

and saw how deeply he felt my pain.

"Thank you for caring," I said. His eyes brightened and a small smile formed on his lips.

May stared up at me, waiting for an explanation. My outbursts and anger had frightened her. Why should someone so innocent and sweet be hurt by my miserable mood? I thought.

"Everything's all right," I signed and reached for her hand. She grinned from ear to ear.

"We better go back inside now," Cary said. "They'll be looking for us." He told May to be sure her shoes were clean before we all re-entered the house.

"There are the children," Aunt Sara said as we appeared in the living room doorway. "I was just going to call you. Where did you go, Cary?"

"We took a walk on the beach."

"Find any interesting seashells?" she asked me. "Laura always found the most unusual ones, didn't she, Jacob?"

He grunted.

It was so hard looking at them all, now that I knew more of the truth. Grandma Olivia sat in the oversized high-back chair, her arms on the arms of the chair, her back straight. She looked furious when she gazed at me. I felt her eyes burning through me. I don't care what Cary says, I thought. She hates me. She hates the sight of me because she can't look at me without seeing my mother. I couldn't wait to leave.

On the other hand, Grandpa Samuel's face was softer, a small smile on his lips. "You take your cousin sailing yet, Cary?" he asked.

"No sir."

"There's no hurry," Aunt Sara said, her voice fluttering with fear.

"I can't think of anyone I would trust more in a sailboat than Cary," Grandpa Samuel said, his eyes still fixed on me. Cary blushed. "He's the best sailor the family's ever had, eh Jacob?"

"Aye," Uncle Jacob said. "That he is." He slapped his hands on his knees and stood. "Well, I guess we had better be moving on." He glanced at Aunt Sara and she rose quickly. Then he looked at Cary.

"Thank you for the brunch, Grandma," Cary said quickly, prodded by his father's look of expectation. Uncle Jacob's gaze moved to me.

"Thank you," I said, my lungs so hot I didn't think I could make sounds. I wanted to add sarcastically, "Thank you for keeping my mother and father's pictures buried in a carton in the basement. Thank you for hating your own son so much that you won't even mention his name, much less mourn his death. Thank you for blaming me for anything and everything they did." But I swallowed back the thoughts and turned to watch May signing her thank you. They barely acknowledged her. Maybe that was their way of pretending she didn't have a handicap, I thought. Another lie was being added to the piles buried in the Logans's sea chests and dark closets.

"I'll call you during the week, Sara," Grandma Olivia said, barely turning her head, "and tell you when the dinner will be."

"Fine, Olivia. Thank you," Aunt Sara said. She looked at Uncle Jacob for direction. When he started out, she followed. I noticed no one kissed anyone good-bye, just as no one had kissed anyone hello. Only Grandpa Samuel followed us to the door.

"Have a good week, Jacob," he said.

"Thanks, Dad," Uncle Jacob replied. He shook his father's hand and started for the car, all of us following.

"I'm looking forward to hearing you play your fiddle," Grandpa Samuel called to me. "Bring it with you when you come to dinner."

I gazed back at him. He was smiling warmly, his eyes twinkling. We had barely exchanged any words or spent any time in each other's presence, but I thought he seemed too nice to have disowned my father, too nice to carry anger in his heart so long and so firmly.

"Did you have a good time, Melody?" Aunt

Sara asked me after we had all gotten into the car. Cary glanced at me nervously.

"Yes, Aunt Sara. The food was wonderful and this is a beautiful place," I recited dryly.

"Isn't it though? I love coming here. Laura used to visit Grandpa and Grandma Logan often. In time you will, too, I'm sure."

"I'm not so sure," I muttered under my breath. Cary was the only one who heard me, but he didn't say anything.

"We've all been invited to dinner this week. Isn't that nice?" Aunt Sara said. No one, not even Uncle Jacob, replied. We drove home in silence, with May the only one comfortable in such a muted world, I thought.

It was a relief to change out of formal clothes and put on dungarees, sneakers, and a sloppy blouse. I had felt so constrained in Laura's clothes. Aunt Sara treated them like holy garments. I buttoned my own blouse halfway down and tied the front ends in a knot at my waist, just the way Mommy often tied her own. My mind still reeled from the discoveries and revelations about my parents.

When did they first realize they were in love with each other? Was it really like falling in love with your brother or your sister, even though they weren't blood relatives? How did they tell Grandpa and Grandma Logan? There was so much I didn't know about my family. I felt like someone who had been living with strangers.

Everyone else was still changing when I stepped out of my room. I knew May was looking forward to spending time with me, but I craved solitude. I hurried down the stairs and out of the house. Confused, angry, and frightened, I dug my feet into the sand and furiously marched toward the ocean. The breeze whipped through my hair. Large, puffy clouds blocked the sun. I felt a bit chilled and realized I should have worn more than a cotton blouse. But I didn't want to turn back.

On the hard-packed sand of the beach, the tide rushed up so fast I had to leap out of the way to dry ground. It was as if the ocean itself were snapping at me. I took off my sneakers and socks and waded through the water, oblivious to the cold. If I came down with pneumonia, it would be Mommy's fault. No one would care anyway. I fumed so hard I imagined smoke pouring out of my ears.

How could Mommy not tell the truth? Didn't she think the day would come when she would have to admit to all the lies?

Surely Daddy would have eventually told me everything. He was just waiting for me to be old enough. Daddy wouldn't have wanted to see me hurt this way. But Mommy must have realized I would hear the whole story while I was here. All she worried about was getting away and doing her thing, becoming famous.

"It's not fair!" I shouted at the ocean. My words were drowned by the roar of the waves.

I didn't realize how far I had walked until I turned to look back at the house. I folded my arms across my breasts and sat on a dry mound of sand, staring across the ocean waves. There was a constant breeze, but the sky wasn't as cloudy as it had first seemed. The weather here changed so quickly it was as if a Cape Cod magician controlled it. I sensed the sun was stronger down by the water, reflecting off the sand. Like a Ping-Pong ball, I was bouncing from warm moments to cool ones. The breeze brushed the tears from my cheeks. I sighed so deeply I thought I might snap like a brittle piece of china. I even envisioned my face shattered in pieces like some alabaster puzzle. All the king's horses and all the king's men . . . couldn't put poor Melody together again.

Suddenly, I saw and heard a motorboat skipping over the waves, the spray flying up around it. Whoever was driving it turned it sharply toward the shore and sped up, heading directly toward me. I watched with curiosity as it drew closer until it was near enough for me to realize who was driving. Adam Jackson waved. He shut off the motor and the boat drifted in with the tide.

"Hey!" he called, his hands cupping his mouth. "What are you doing out here all by yourself?"

The boat lifted and fell until he was nearly to shore.

"Just taking a walk," I shouted back.

"I thought it was you. I have great eyesight, huh?" He laughed and then held up a pair of binoculars. "Come on. I'll take you for a spin."

I shook my head. "No, thank you."

"Come on," he urged. "You'll have fun."

"How will I get to the boat? I'll get soaked to the bone and shrink to death."

He laughed and hopped out. He was wearing a tight black bathing suit and a light blue polo shirt, which was getting wet, but he didn't mind. He pulled the boat closer until the bow hit the sand. Then he took off his shirt and threw it into the boat before he beckoned.

"Come on. I'll make sure you don't get too wet."

"I don't think so."

"You don't look too happy," he said. "A ride in this thing will drive your gloom away. You have the Adam Jackson one hundred percent guarantee."

I looked toward the house. Aunt Sara and Uncle Jacob would have a fit if they saw me get into the boat, but Adam's shoulders gleamed invitingly in the afternoon sunlight.

I stood up, my heart thumping.

Why not? I thought. I'm not a prisoner here. "Okay," I said impulsively.

"Good," he cried. "Hurry up. The Atlantic Ocean isn't exactly a bathtub yet," he said laughing and pretending to be shivering in the water.

I rolled up my dungarees as high as I could, cradled my sneakers and socks in my arms, and then stepped into the water. The tide kept rising, however, and I screamed and retreated. He laughed and rushed forward, scooping me into his arms before I could protest. Then he carried me to the boat as if I weighed nothing and gently lifted me over the edge. Once I was in, he pushed the boat out, pulled himself up and swung over.

"See. Barely a drop on you."

"I can't believe I'm doing this."

"What's the big deal?" he said shrugging. "Boats, water, fishing . . . they're as common as breathing to us Cape Codders, and now that you're becoming one, too, you have to get used to it all or risk forever being known as an outsider. And you know how we treat outsiders," he said. He widened his eyes as though that would be a fate worse than death. He laughed and started the motor.

The boat lifted and fell with the waves so sharply, I had trouble standing.

"Isn't it too rough today? I feel as if I'm in an egg beater."

"Call this rough? Hardly." He started the engine. Then he patted the seat beside him. "Sit up here so you get a good view. I'll even let you steer if you want."

"Really?"

"Sure. Come on, sit," he urged and I did so. "I haven't been out much myself this year," he said. "I'm glad I had the desire to do so today." He turned to me with a twinkle in his soft blue eyes. "It wasn't just an accident finding you on the beach, you know."

"Oh?"

"It's fate, what's meant to be," he said with a wink. And then he gunned the engine so fast and hard, the front of the boat lifted and we hit the water with a hard bounce.

I screamed. I had to cling to him, but he didn't seem to mind.

"Do you have to go so fast?" I cried. The spray was hitting us and the wind made my blouse flap so much, I thought it would tear off. My eyes were tearing, too.

"Of course," he said. "You want to get a thrill, don't you? Going slow is not for people like us."

People like us? I thought. Who did he think I was?

The boat bounced so hard each time it hit the water, I was afraid it might fall apart. My heart was pounding. Finally, he slowed down and told me to try steering myself. He slid over and I took the wheel. Then he

296

pulled himself around, straddling me, and reached over my shoulders with both his arms to put his hands over mine.

"I'll show you how to do it first," he said, his cheek against my cheek. He was wearing some wonderful-smelling aftershave lotion. The water, the breeze, the scent of the ocean and his lotion made me dizzy. I felt myself spinning, but it was wonderful and exciting. For a while anyway, I could forget the secrets and the lies.

He accelerated slowly and I turned the wheel, impressed and fascinated with my power to direct the boat. I was so entranced with it that I didn't pay much attention to his lips moving over my ears and down my cheek.

"You're delicious," he suddenly said.

"What?" I pulled to the side to look at him. He was staring at me, those remarkable eyes drinking me in, then swallowing me down. I quickly fastened one of the buttons of my blouse that had opened, but my garments felt flimsy and transparent under his piercing gaze. It took my breath away. Without warning, the boat bounced sharply, tossing him into my lap. We both screamed and he recovered quickly enough to drop the speed and straighten the bow. We caught our breaths and the boat bobbed gently. This far away from shore, the water was calmer and more inviting.

"You have to keep your eyes on what you're doing," he said.

"And you have to keep yours in your head. I have pupil prints in places I'd rather keep unblemished."

He laughed and leaned back. "You sure talk funny sometimes, but it's refreshing. All the girls here sound the same. Everything's groovy, know what I mean?"

I nodded.

"Why didn't you come to the party last night?" he asked. "I kept looking for you."

"I couldn't," I said. "I wanted to, but —"

"Your uncle and aunt wouldn't let you?"

"Something like that."

"I figured." He shook his head. "Must be hard for you. I bet you feel as if you're in some kind of a prison or a nunnery, huh?"

I didn't say anything.

"All the girls are jealous of you, you know."

"What? Why?"

"I heard them talking about you last night, saying how pretty you are."

"They did not."

"Swear," he said raising his hand. "It's true. You're about the prettiest girl I've seen and I've seen quite a few." He leaned toward me. "I've even gone out with college girls, but you've got that one-in-a-million look about you, the magic that makes for movie stars and models. I heard from the grapevine that your mother is a model. Now I understand."

I sat there with my mouth gaping open. I had never heard a boy in our school talk like this and certainly never about me.

"Wait a minute," he said before I could respond. He got up and went to a cabinet to take out a camera. "I'd like to get a few shots of you just the way you are, natural, the wind in your hair."

"What do you want me to do?"

"Just sit there. Steer the boat and be yourself." He aimed his camera and snapped pictures. "These will be worth something someday after you're famous."

I laughed and shook my head. "I am not so pretty. I have freckles and my ears are too big. I'll never become famous."

"Adam Jackson knows pretty women and I'm telling you, Melody, you're one of 'em. Don't argue with an expert." He kept on looking at me with that gleeful smile in his eyes. He was making me very nervous.

"Can I make it go faster again?" I asked.

"I knew you would want to. Just move the lever ahead slowly."

I did so, getting better at controlling the boat. He even gave me a compliment about it.

"You've got your sea legs," he said and ran his palm down the side of my right leg. "And they're really nice." He laughed at the look on my face. "You better get used to compliments, Melody. They're going to rain down on you like a hurricane as you get older and prettier."

The blood rushed to my face. Was he just saying these things or did he really mean them? He put his arm around my shoulder and helped steer with his other hand. He held me tighter, drawing me against him until I felt his breath on my cheek again and then the soft touch of his lips.

"I think you better take me back," I told him, my voice close to cracking. "My aunt will be turning over rocks looking for me." He laughed.

"Okay, but only if you promise to meet me tomorrow night about eight o'clock."

"Meet you? Where?"

He thought a moment.

"Meet me right there where I found you sitting, or are you afraid to walk the beach at night?"

"I'm not afraid," I said quickly. "It's just that —"

"You might not be able to get out? Don't let them treat you like a child," he said, his eyes narrowed.

"I don't," I protested, but in my heart, I knew he was right.

"Then it's settled. I'll bring a radio and a blanket and something to drink."

"Something to drink?"

"Something to keep us warm. You've done that before, haven't you?" he asked.

"Sure," I said, not even positive what he meant. Was he going to bring a thermos of hot chocolate, coffee, tea, or did he mean whiskey?

"I thought so. You have a more sophisticated look about you. I'd like to hear what it was like growing up in West Virginia. My college friends tell me that girls from the coal mining towns know the score. The girls here like to think they're so sophisticated. They talk a good game, but when it comes right down to playing it, they're not home. You know what I mean?"

"No," I said.

"Sure you do."

"I'd better get back."

"Aye, aye, Captain," he replied sitting up quickly and saluting. I laughed as he hurriedly took the controls and turned the boat around. "You want me to put you back where you were or closer to the house?"

"Better put me back where I was," I said. "My aunt would turn inside out if she saw me riding in a motorboat, and my uncle would put a ball and chain on my ankle."

"The Logans are strange, and not because of what happened to Laura. They were strange long before that."

I wanted to see just how much he knew and how much the people here gossiped. "You mean about my mother and father?" I asked.

"No." He shook his head. "I don't know much about them, except what I was told in school. I'm sorry about your father. That must have been a terrible accident, too."

"It was."

"You've got a lot of good reason to be sad, Melody, but you're too beautiful to remain melancholy long." He brought the boat as close to the shore as he had brought it before. My heart skipped beats when he smiled at me again. Then he hopped out. "Sit on the side," he ordered. "Don't worry. I won't drop you."

I clutched my sneakers and socks and did as he said. He scooped under my legs again, this time holding me tighter around the waist. Our faces were inches apart. I thought I would drown in his eyes. He leaned in and kissed me softly on the lips.

"No fair," I said. "I'm trapped like a cat up a tree."

He laughed. "That's right. And if you don't kiss me back, I'll drop you in the ocean." He pretended to let go and I screamed. "Well?"

"All right, but just once," I said. This time, our kiss was long and his tongue moved between my lips, grazing mine. It sent a chill down my spine, but it wasn't unpleasant.

"I've got to get back," I said, practically whispering. My heart pounded so hard, I thought I wouldn't be able to get out the words.

"No problem," He gracefully moved through the water and set me down on dry land. "Until tomorrow night." His face turned serious. "I'll see you in school tomorrow, but I'd rather we kept this our little secret. If we don't we'll have company. I know these kids here. They can be pains in the rear end. Besides, I like secrets, don't you?"

"No," I said quickly and so firmly, he raised his eyebrows.

"Not even secrets of the heart?"

I didn't want to tell him that I had never really had any, so I just shrugged. He laughed. "Bet you just got a sea chest full of love secrets," he teased.

"You'd lose." I started backing away. "I have to go. Thanks for the ride."

He stood there, watching me walk quickly over the sand. Then he turned and waded through the water to his boat. I stopped to watch him accelerate and spin through the waves. I felt as if I had stepped in and out of a movie. He had been right about the boat ride. The dreariness that had washed over me had dried up with my tears. I had a new bounce in my step as I hurried over the beach toward my uncle and aunt's house, wondering if I would have the nerve to meet Adam Jackson tomorrow night.

"Where were you, honey?" Aunt Sara

303

asked as soon as I entered the house. She was in the doorway of the living room. She looked at my sneakers and socks in my hand. I had simply forgotten to put them on or roll down my dungarees.

"I just took a walk on the beach," I said quickly.

"You shouldn't go anywhere without telling your aunt or me," I heard my uncle Jacob cry from behind her in the living room. "Your aunt shouldn't have to go looking for you, hear?"

"Yes," I said. "Sorry," I told Aunt Sara and ran up the stairs before she could ask or say anything else. Cary heard me pound the steps and came out of his room.

"You all right?" he asked as I turned down the hallway.

"Yes."

His eyes grew smaller with interest and he stepped closer, a textbook in his hand.

"I heard you run out, but by the time I put on my sneakers, you were over the hill. I figured you wanted to be alone, maybe to sort things out," he said.

"Sort things out?" I started to laugh. "It would be easier to unravel a bee hive."

He nodded and then his eyes widened with interest. "You look like you got some sun."

I couldn't keep my eyes from shifting guiltily away. Did he notice the flush on my face, the excitement in my eyes? Daddy used to say they were like little windowpanes, with my thoughts as clear as newsprint.

"You were walking in the water?" Cary continued nodding at my sneakers in my hand and my rolled up dungarees. Tiny grains of sand were in between my toes.

"I'm tired," I said moving to my room. "I'm going to rest before dinner."

"Melody?"

I turned.

He held up the book.

"I was wondering if after dinner you might —"

"That's your English textbook?"

"Yes. We have a test tomorrow on clauses. The only clause I know is Santa Claus," he said glumly.

"It's not really hard. I'll show you some tricks my teacher in West Virginia showed me."

"Thanks."

"Where's May?"

"She's doing her homework, too," he said. I nodded and went into my room, softly closing the door behind me. For a few moments I stood there, reining in my emotions. I had gone from anger and sadness to excitement and thrills. I couldn't be more confused about this place, I thought. My family was hard and unpleasant, but May was sweet and hungry for love, and Cary

. . . Cary was more sensitive and caring than he let on. The ocean could be cold and gray, and no thunderstorm in West Virginia was as frightening as the storm we had had the other night — the nor'easter Cary called it. Yet today, the ocean was delightful, exciting and the beach was warm and inviting.

Didn't I hate it here? Didn't I want to just run away?

And yet, Adam Jackson's handsome face lingered before my eyes and his compliments echoed in my ears. Was I really as pretty as he said I was? I gazed at myself in the mirror. Was there as much potential beauty as he claimed he saw? Was he making up what he had told me the other girls thought of me? I didn't want to become conceited, and yet, I didn't want to underestimate myself and become some mousy creature with no self-confidence, terrified of life like . . . like Aunt Sara hovering in Uncle Jacob's dark shadow.

I sat at the vanity table and thought and then I gazed down at the pile of letters bound with a rubber band. They were Laura's letters from her boyfriend. I had no right to look at them, and yet, I couldn't help wondering what sort of a relationship they had had before their tragic end.

I took off the rubber band and opened the first envelope. The handwriting was pretty, an almost artistic script. The letter had been written on blue stationery.

Dearest Laura,

I had a wonderful time yesterday. I don't know how many times I've walked on that beach, but yesterday, with you, it suddenly seemed more beautiful than ever. I didn't mean to take you away from your work. I know Cary was upset with me for just appearing unexpectedly. When I get a chance, I'll apologize to him for stealing you away and leaving him with all the lobsters and fish.

But I'll never apologize for taking you anywhere. I'm glad you feel the same way about me that I feel about you. I've felt this for a long time, but I didn't have the courage to tell you. Don't ask me why I have it now. I think it's because of the way you smiled at me in the cafeteria that day. It gave me all the nerve I needed.

I'm not used to writing letters to girls or anyone. Actually, you're the first girl I've ever written a letter to, not counting my cousin Susie. I know it's hard for you to talk long on the telephone. Besides, it's kind of exciting receiving letters from you, too. I'm just nervous about mailing the letters and maybe having someone else read them. You know who. He never seems to be happy to see me around,

*even when I'm not taking you away from
helping your father.*

*Maybe, when he feels about a girl the
way I feel about you, he'll be more understanding. I know what you meant
when you said you were afraid of how
you felt about me sometimes. It's a bit
overwhelming, but I'm not ashamed of it
and never will be. I hope you feel that,
too. I promise, I'll try to control myself
more, but you know what they say about
promises lovers make. Just kidding,
only, please don't hate me for loving you
more than I should.*

*I like writing to you, Laura. I see your
face in front of me as I think of the words.
It makes me want to write to you all
night. Until I see you, hold me in your
heart.*

*Love,
Robert*

Tears filled my eyes. Would I ever have
anyone love me as much as Robert Royce
loved Laura? If they had something so beautiful, why did they have to die so tragically
and so young? I sighed and thought about
reading another letter, but there was a
sharp knock on my door. I guiltily stuffed
the letter back into the envelope.

"Yes?"

Cary entered. His gaze moved from me to

the pile of letters and then back to me.

"My mother says you have a phone call. A girl friend from Sewell."

"Alice!" I jumped up. "Thanks."

I went downstairs quickly, forgetting that I still hadn't put on my sneakers and socks. This time, Uncle Jacob wasn't sitting near the phone, ready to listen. Aunt Sara held the receiver away from her as if it were a forbidden object that might contaminate her.

"Jacob doesn't approve of young people gossiping on the telephone," she whispered. "Don't be long."

"Thank you," I said and took the receiver. "Alice?"

"Hi. Was it all right for me to call now? Your aunt sounded upset."

"It's all right. I'm happy to hear from you so soon."

Aunt Sara gave me a look of warning and stepped gingerly out of the room.

"I miss you and I miss Sewell," I added as soon as she was gone. "More than I ever expected."

"Oh? Well, I don't have good news. Papa George is in the hospital and when I asked Mama Arlene about your mother and your things, she told me she hasn't heard a word from your mother since you all left."

"Mommy never called her?"

"Not yet. I thought I had better tell you."

"How is Papa George doing?"

"He's in intensive care. He's very sick, Melody. I'm sorry."

"I should be there," I moaned. "I don't know what to do."

"What can you do?" Alice asked in her habitual blunt manner.

"Nothing until Mommy calls me."

"You really hate it there?"

"There's a lot happening, Alice."

"Tell me," she pleaded.

"I can't. Not on the phone. I'll write you a letter."

"Don't wait. Write it tonight."

"Melody, dear, not too long," I heard Aunt Sara say through the wall. She was probably just on the other side of the door all the while, I thought.

"I've got to hang up, Alice. Thanks for calling."

"Write me and I'll call you the moment I hear that your mother called Mama Arlene," she said quickly.

"Thanks. Bye."

I cradled the receiver just as Uncle Jacob came through the front door. He saw Aunt Sara standing in the hallway and me by the phone.

"Was that your mother?" he asked me.

"No. A friend from Sewell."

He glared at Aunt Sara.

"She wasn't on the phone long, Jacob."

He grunted. Then he noticed my bare feet.

"We don't walk through the house half dressed here," he said. For a moment I didn't understand. "Your feet," he said nodding at them.

"Oh. I just came down quickly. It was a long-distance phone call and —"

"A decent girl always thinks about those things first," he chastised.

"I am a decent girl," I fired back.

"We'll see," he said, undaunted, and started up the stairs. "Getting dressed for dinner," he muttered toward Aunt Sara.

"Okay, Jacob. We'll have a good Sunday dinner," she promised. "Don't worry," she whispered to me. "He'll soon see that you're as sweet as Laura was, and then everything . . . everything will be wonderful again," she added. Her eyes glittered with hope. "Hurry and get cleaned up and dressed so you can set the table, dear."

I watched her walk away with that fragile smile on her face. Aunt Sara had wrapped herself snugly in her illusions, but illusions, I thought, were just dressed up lies. Someday the weight of the truth would come down on her glass house and shatter her dreams even more.

I didn't want to be here when all that happened. I wanted to be far away. I wanted to be in a place where people didn't have to lie to each other to live with each other.

Was there such a place? And even if there were such a place, could I, a daughter born in a world of deceit, ever hope to find it?

With Daddy dead and gone and Mommy off searching for her own private dreams, I felt like an orphan, a hobo begging for a handout of love. No wonder my eyes saw Adam Jackson's eyes and my ears were so receptive to his words.

I'll meet him tomorrow night, I thought defiantly. Not even one of Cape Cod's treacherous nor'easters could keep me away.

12

An English Lesson

At dinner everyone appeared to be in a subdued mood, even May. After Uncle Jacob read his selection from the Bible, we ate in near silence. I thought the heavy atmosphere in the house might be a result of the weather. Although it wasn't raining, a thick fog had rolled in on great billowing waves. It shrouded the landscape, turning everything cold and dreary. Once again, the weather on the Cape surprised me with its fickleness and its ability to change so abruptly. I wondered if there was any way to tell right now what it would be like tomorrow night. Would it rain and thus put off my rendezvous with Adam Jackson?

"Does it often get foggy like this at night?" I asked as innocently as I could. Uncle Jacob raised his eyebrows. Aunt Sara smiled as if I had asked the silliest little question, and Cary looked amused. "This time of year it often does."

"Weathermen might as well toss the dice,

313

as good as they predict these days," Uncle Jacob muttered. "Better off just listening to the creak in your bones."

"Aye," Aunt Sara said. "More potatoes, dear?"

"No thank you, Aunt Sara," I answered.

"I won't be having coffee tonight," Uncle Jacob announced as if the whole country were awaiting his decision. "Got a big day tomorrow. Getting up early to bring the boat to Stormfield's in North Truro for an engine tuneup."

"I could skip school tomorrow," Cary offered immediately. He glanced quickly at me because he knew I understood why he would like to cut classes. He hoped I wouldn't say anything. There was no reason to worry. It was none of my business and I certainly wouldn't want to be responsible for getting him in trouble with Uncle Jacob. I wouldn't do that to my worst enemy.

"No need," Uncle Jacob said, rising. Cary's face folded in disappointment. "Roy and I can handle it. Well," he said stretching, "I'll just have a pipeful in the den and go up to bed. I'd like a peaceful night," he added glaring at me as if I were a noisy teenager who played rock music late into the evening.

I rose to help Aunt Sara with the dishes. May wanted me to go to her room and help with her homework, but I explained I was helping Cary study for a test tomorrow. She looked disappointed, so Aunt Sara offered to help her. She still looked disappointed, but I could see she was too considerate to hurt her mother's feelings.

After we had put away the dishes, I went up to my room and waited for Cary. I had just a little of my own schoolwork left and finished it quickly.

He knocked on my door and peeked in timidly. "Got time now?" he asked.

"Yes." I pulled a chair up alongside my own at the desk. "Sit here."

"I hate this stuff," he complained as he entered. He tried to narrow his vision just to me and the desk, but his eyes flitted from one side of the room to the other, the look on his face sad and as painful as a raw wound that refused to heal. He caught me scrutinizing him. "I don't come in here often," he confessed. "Anymore."

"I understand," I said.

Skepticism clouded his face and gave birth to a small frown. Did he think that because I had no brother or sister, I couldn't appreciate what it was like to lose someone I loved?

"It was really hard for me to look at things in our trailer that reminded me of my father after his terrible accident," I explained. Cary's skepticism faded as I went on. "I was closer to him than I am to my mother. And when he died, I thought the world had come

315

to an end. It still doesn't seem the same. Nothing does."

He nodded, his eyes softening. "I wish I could have gotten to know him."

"I wish you had too. I wish this family wasn't so vindictive."

He tilted his head.

"Vin-what?"

"Cruel," I continued. "When you love someone, you don't hate them to death for mistakes they make. You try to understand them, help them, and if that doesn't work, you feel sorry for them. But you don't disown them forever and pretend they never lived."

He stared at me a moment and then he smiled and shook his head gently. "That's something Laura would say. She always looked for the good in everyone. The girls at school mocked her, ostracized her, were jealous of her, but she was always nice to them. We had lots of arguments about it," he said. "It was practically the only thing we argued about. We agreed about most everything else."

"Even Robert Royce?" I asked quickly. When he looked at me this time, there were shadows in the emerald depths of his eyes.

"That was something entirely different. She was blinded by —"

"By what?" I asked, intrigued.

"Blinded by his lies, his phony charm, his handsome face," he replied bitterly.

"How did you know he was a phony?" I asked. His letter to Laura seemed sincere.

"I just knew," he insisted. "She always listened to me. We were close and not just because we were twins. We really did like the same things and feel the same things. We didn't have to speak to each other lots of times either. We just looked at each other and understood. She would smile at me or I would smile at her and that was enough.

"But after Robert . . ." His gaze drifted, his eyes growing smaller — darker — when he looked at Laura's picture on the dresser.

"What happened after Robert came into her life?"

He turned to me, his watery eyes hard. "She changed. I tried to help her see, but she wouldn't listen."

"Maybe what she saw she liked," I offered softly.

He grimaced. "Why is it that girls who are normally smarter than boys are so dumb when it comes to boys?" he asked me.

I stared at him. He blinked his eyelids rapidly. He had long, perfect eyelashes, which most girls I knew would die to have.

"That's a matter of —"

"What?" he interrupted.

"I was going to say opinion, but it's really more a matter of the heart."

He blew air through the side of his mouth. "Matters of the heart," he said disdainfully.

"An excuse for stupidity."

"Cary Logan, are you going to sit there and tell me you don't believe in love? You don't believe two people can fall in love?"

"I didn't say that exactly," he retreated. "But it's silly to think you can fall in and out of love the way you . . . you catch a cold."

"From what I understand, that doesn't sound like a good description of Laura. She didn't have lots of boyfriends, did she?"

"That's not the point. She thought she was in love and that he loved her, but . . . Let's just say I know it was a mistake, okay, and leave it at that." He glared down at his textbook. "I hate this stuff. What does it have to do with what's important?"

"It's important to understand our language so we can express ourselves," I said, my voice hard and firm. Like a splinter, Cary had a way of getting under my skin.

He grimaced again and raised his eyebrows.

I wasn't intimidated by him.

"You're not just going to spend all your life talking to lobsters, Cary Logan. You're going to have to talk to your customers, too, and if you sound as if you don't know what you're doing, they won't believe in you, no matter how good a fisherman you are."

He broke into a smile. "Don't get so mad."

"I'm not mad. I'm —"

"What?" he teased.

"Mad," I said. "Why should you have to be talked into educating yourself? We don't live in the Dark Ages. Even up here in Cape Cod heaven where everyone is supposedly so perfect, people still need to be educated," I snapped.

He laughed. "Okay, help me talk to my customers."

I gazed at the page.

"Clauses are easy to recognize. Just test them. If they don't have a subject and a verb, throw them back in like a lobster that's too small."

His smile widened. "I like that. That, I can understand."

I went over what a subject does in the clause and then what the verb does.

He listened, tried some examples, and then widened his eyes. "I understand what you're saying. I just don't understand how you know whether it's an adverb or an adjective."

"Test it again," I told him. "Here's one way: if you can move it around in the sentence, it's an adverb. Look at this one: Because I got sick, I had to go home. I had to go home because I got sick. See?"

His eyes lit up.

"Yeah."

"Your teacher never showed you that?" I asked.

"I don't remember. I guess I wasn't paying

as much attention to her as I paid to you. Maybe you should be a teacher."

"Maybe I will. Do those exercises at the end of the chapter. I'll correct them when you're finished."

"Yes ma'am."

I went to the closet to sift through the clothing. Tomorrow, I would wear one of my own things, I thought, not that I had much from which to choose. How could Mommy not have called Mama Arlene yet? She knew I needed my clothes.

"Laura always looked really good in that," Cary said. I hadn't known he was watching me. I held a light yellow cotton dress in my hands. "You thinking of wearing that to school?"

"I might just wear a pair of jeans and a blouse I brought with me," I said.

"Laura never wore jeans to school. My father didn't think it was proper."

"Well he's not my father," I replied. "And I'm not Laura."

He shrugged. "I'm just telling you."

"Are you finished with the exercises?"

"No, I —"

"Then finish," I commanded.

"Right," he said turning back.

I smiled to myself and considered the yellow dress again. It had a square collar with frilled sleeves and a gently billowing skirt. I imagined it might look nice on me. I *did* want to look nice for Adam, I thought.

"Finished," Cary declared.

I put the dress back and went to the desk. He had one mistake, but even I might have made it, I thought. "Not too bad," I said.

"I hope I can do it tomorrow."

"You will. Just remember the tricks," I told him.

"Thanks," he said standing. "I owe you one." He thought a moment. "Maybe I'll do what Grandpa suggested this weekend."

"What's that?"

"Take you sailing. Would you like that?"

I thought about Adam. What if he invited me to go motorboating again?

"I . . ."

My hesitation jarred him. "Don't if you have better things to do." He turned for the door.

"No, it's just that I've never really gone sailing."

He looked back at me. "Whatever. If you want to, we'll do it."

"We'll go over the material again on the way to school," I told him.

He rolled his eyes. "Can't wait," he said and left.

A little while later I heard him go up to his attic hideaway. I didn't know for certain, of course, but I was willing to bet that he spent more time up there alone since Laura's death than he had when she was alive.

We all retreat to different attics when we're unhappy, I thought. I was still looking for mine.

Uncle Jacob had eaten his breakfast and left by the time May, Cary, and I went downstairs the next morning. I decided to wear Laura's yellow dress, and when Cary saw me in the hallway, he said I looked very nice.

"It's not going to rain, is it?" I asked him.

"No. It's going to be a nice day and a pretty nice night," he told me. I breathed relief and felt a tingle of the excitement of anticipation.

Downstairs, Aunt Sara was frenzied. Grandma Olivia had called last night and told her the dinner would be tomorrow night. Apparently, from the way she spoke, I understood that dinner at my grandparents' house wasn't merely dinner, it was an elaborate affair. There would be someone else there, some highly respected member of the community. We would all have to be on our very best behavior, be well dressed, and be more polite than the Queen of England.

"Don't forget Grandpa wants to hear Melody play her fiddle," Cary teased. Aunt Sara gasped and gazed at me with abject terror in her eyes.

"Oh, I don't think he meant this particular dinner," she said in a voice just above a whisper.

"Sure he did," Cary continued, deliberately

raising his own voice. "We all heard him, Ma."

Aunt Sara shook her head. "But Olivia didn't . . ."

"It's all right. I don't want to bring my fiddle anyway," I said.

"Grandpa's going to be disappointed," Cary warned. "He might just send you back for it. Why don't you bring it along and leave it in the car, just in case," he pursued.

Aunt Sara shook her head again, this time more emphatically. "Jacob might be upset. I don't know if —"

"I'm not bringing it along, Aunt Sara. Stop worrying," I declared firmly. I gazed at Cary, whose green eyes sparkled with mischief.

May wanted to know what we were all talking about so intensely. Cary signed and explained, mimicking my playing the fiddle. Her eyes lit up with encouragement.

"See, Ma, even May wants her to bring it along, and she can't even hear."

"Oh dear," Aunt Sara said, wringing her hands.

"Stop it," I told him sharply. "You're going to get me into trouble."

With a tiny smile on his face, he finished eating his breakfast quietly. On the way to school, I chastised him. "You shouldn't tease your mother that way, Cary Logan."

"I wasn't teasing. I'd like you to play your fiddle, too. It will spice up the dinner party.

I've been to enough of them at Grandma's to know what to expect. They could use some excitement."

"Well under the circumstances, I'm not feeling much like fiddling. It only reminds me of my daddy and Grandma Olivia's house is no place to be thinking about him," I said bitterly.

Cary's impish grin faded. "Maybe if they heard you play and learned more about your father after he and Haille left here, they'd be more inclined to feel sorry about things, too," he offered.

"They should feel sorry! My daddy's gone and the damage that was done is done forever and ever."

Cary was silent. The subject sank deeply in the pool of our thoughts. We dropped May at her school and continued to our own, reviewing the material Cary would have on his English test. As soon as Cary and I arrived at school, we split up. Fortunately, he didn't hear the girls heckle me when I went to my locker. I'm sure he would have become very angry.

"We missed you Saturday night," Janet said. "Too busy darning socks or something?"

"Or did you have to make cranberry muffins?" Lorraine asked.

"I tried to come," I told her. Betty closed in beside her and Janet to listen to my explanation. "But my uncle wouldn't let me go."

"We told you he wouldn't. We told you to lie," Betty said. "But you're just like Laura, aren't you? You're too goody-goody to have any real fun. It must run in the family or something — Grandpa, Laura and now you. I bet the mute is the same."

"She's not a mute," I snapped, my face filling with blood so fast I thought I would blow the top of my head off. "She's deaf, but she can talk."

"I've heard her talk. Who could understand that?" Betty said. The others agreed.

"If you take the time, you can understand her. She's a bright, sweet little girl."

"Right. Anyway, we all had a good time. A certain boy was heartbroken that you weren't there," Lorraine said, a twisted smile on her lips.

As if on cue, Adam sauntered down the corridor and paused when he reached us. All three of the witches from *Macbeth* fluttered their eyelashes and beamed their most seductive smiles, but his eyes were on me.

"Good morning, girls. Exchanging feminine secrets or can I listen in?" he asked with that beguiling smile. Even early in the morning, he looked perfect enough to have just walked out of an aftershave advertisement in a men's magazine.

"We were just telling Melody about what a great beach party she missed," Janet said.

"That's right. It was a great party," he agreed, his eyes still fixed on me.

"Debbie McKay certainly had a good time," Betty said. "Didn't she, Adam?"

"You'll have to ask her," he replied with a nonchalance that made the three giggle.

"I'm sure we'll find out," Lorraine said. "Debbie's the kind who kisses and tells. See you later, Melody," she sang.

"Yeah, see you later," Betty echoed. The three walked off, leaving me with Adam.

"Now you know why I want you to keep the things between us secret," he said looking after them. "The gossipmongers around here work overtime. I'll walk you to homeroom," he offered when I closed my locker. "Everything else all right? You didn't get into trouble after our ride yesterday, did you?"

"No," I said.

"Good."

I noticed everyone's interest as we continued down the corridor. Even Mrs. Cranshaw, the librarian, peered at us over her thick lenses.

"I really had a good time with you," Adam said softly. "Did you like it, too?"

"Yes, I did."

"Good. Until eight o'clock," he whispered at the homeroom door. "Don't disappoint me." He squeezed my hand and walked away.

My heart pounded. Was I really going to

meet him? Did I have the courage? His lips had the lure of forbidden fruit, but oh, how luscious, ripe, and delicious was the promise they had left on my own when he held me in his arms and kissed me! I sighed.

When I turned to go into the classroom, I saw each and every girl was looking my way. All looked curious, many looked envious.

"That didn't take long," Theresa Patterson said coming up behind me as I walked to my desk.

"Pardon?"

"For Adam Jackson to find a new fish," she muttered, walking by.

The girls in this school, I thought, gave the word catty a new meaning. Adam wasn't wrong about that. Cary had told me much the same thing.

I didn't see my cousin until lunch time in the cafeteria. When I did, he looked very excited and happy. He had taken his English test and for the first time, he felt confident of the results afterward.

"Every time I considered an answer, I could hear your voice, your advice. It didn't seem as hard as I thought it would be."

"Good," I said. I looked past him toward the cafeteria's entrance, hoping to spot Adam. I expected he would want to sit with me, but when he came in, he was with some boys and they all went to a table on the right. He gazed my way and smiled. He looked as if he were holding court. Cary saw the direction of my interest and my expression of disappointment.

"Thanks for your help," he said dryly and started away.

"Cary," I called. He turned. "Mind if I sit with you? I'd rather skip my new girl friends for the moment."

I could see they had a place open for me at their table, but it would have been like delivering myself to the Spanish Inquisition, torture chamber and all.

Cary shrugged and looked in Adam's direction. "Suit yourself," he said. "It won't be the most exciting table, though." I followed anyway and he introduced me to two of his friends, Billy Beedsly and John Taylor. Their families were also in the lobster and fish business. They asked me a lot of questions about coal mines, but they were frustrated by my limited knowledge of the industry.

"My father was stuck down in the shafts, locked away from sunlight and air, and I hated thinking about it. He didn't like talking about it much either."

"Why did he do it then?" Billy asked. Cary and I exchanged knowing looks.

"It was the best work for the money at the time," I offered and then Cary managed to change the subject.

At the end of the day, Cary eagerly waited for me, a wide, satisfied grin on his face.

"I wasn't sure you were going straight home," he said, obviously pleased that I was alone.

"I am. You look as if you have a secret."

"Oh, I do," he said starting away quickly. I had to walk fast to catch up.

"Well, what is it?"

"Nothing much."

"Cary Logan." I seized him by the elbow and spun him around. "Tell me this moment."

"Mr. Madeo stopped me in the hall as I was on my way out of the building to tell me he corrected the English tests already. I got a ninety-eight! He wanted to congratulate me and ask me how I had done it. I told him I had a great tutor and he said, 'Don't stop working with her.' "

"Oh Cary. Ninety-eight!"

"It's the best test grade I ever got!" he exclaimed.

"See. You can do it if you want to."

He shrugged. "Thanks to you. Anyway, I decided you were right. I have to learn how to talk properly and be educated if I'm going to be a businessman." He was grinning from ear to ear.

"Congratulations. I'm so happy for you."

"Let's celebrate," he said. "Let's do something special tonight after dinner. I'll take you to town for custard."

My heart sank into my stomach. He saw

the expression plain as day on my face.

"What?" he asked.

"I already made a promise to someone," I said.

He nodded. "Okay," he said and walked ahead.

"Maybe tomorrow night," I offered, running to catch up.

"Sure," he said. "But let's wait and see. You might have made another promise by then." He shut up like a turtle, his shoulders rising, his neck sinking. It made me feel sick inside. I realized how much it must have taken for him to reveal his feelings to me. Since Laura's death, he was all clammed up.

I felt pinched by contradictory emotions. They were like scissors cutting me in half. One part of me was full of excitement — counting the minutes to my rendezvous with Adam — while another part of me longed to share Cary's elation and be part of his return to trust, to hope, to a world where there were sunshine and stars and not the gloom of his tragic memories. Just for tonight, I thought, I wished I could duplicate myself and be in two places at once.

But I couldn't, and there just wasn't anything to do about it but feel sorry.

Cary walked ahead of me all the way to May's school. When he saw her run to me, he just kept walking. "See that she gets home all right," he called behind himself.

"We're coming. Wait up!" I cried.

But he didn't slow down and May was full of questions and stories. I had to watch him round the bend and disappear, his shoulders still scrunched up, making him look like an old man. It brought tears to my eyes, but I held them back and put on my best smile for May, who chatted away with her hands all the way home.

Cary remained down at the dock with Uncle Jacob until just before dinner. As usual, I helped Aunt Sara prepare the meal, but right before Uncle Jacob and Cary returned, the phone rang. Aunt Sara answered it and called out to me excitedly.

"It's your mother, dear!"

My heart stopped and then started again, pitter-pattering so quickly, I thought I wouldn't have the voice with which to speak. I walked slowly into the living room and took the receiver from Aunt Sara, wondering if the wires could hold the heat of the words I wanted to scream over them.

"Hello," I began.

"Hi, honey. I just have a couple of minutes, but —"

"Don't you dare rush off again, Mommy. Don't you dare."

"Oh Melody, we're in Los Angeles and I'm —"

"How could you lie to me so much?" My throat started to tighten almost immediately. I thought I would choke before I got out my words. "How could you have kept your real adoptive parents a secret? Why didn't you ever tell me you and Daddy grew up together?"

After a short pause, she replied, "Your father didn't want to tell you all that, Melody. He wanted to protect you from all that was unpleasant."

"Don't put it all on him, Mommy. He's dead. He can't answer."

"Well, it wasn't just me! He wanted it that way, too," she proclaimed.

"Why?" I cried. "Why not tell me the truth about how you really met and fell in love? Why not tell me why the family was angry?" I demanded. The tears were burning under my lids.

"Chester thought you were too young to understand."

"But I'm not too young now! Why did you leave me here without telling me the truth, the whole truth about you and Daddy? How could you do that?"

She was quiet a moment and then she admitted, "I didn't think you would stay if I told you all that, Melody, and I didn't have much choice at the time. If you are as old as you claim you are, you'll understand."

"Mommy, these people hate you and they hate Daddy for what you two did. How can I stay here?"

"Uncle Jacob will never throw you out, Melody," she said. "And he has no right to be so high and mighty, believe me. Don't let him talk down to you. Don't be a trouble-maker, but don't take his . . . garbage."

"I can't stay here, Mommy, and I want to know more. I want to know everything."

"You will. I promise. You're obviously old enough now to know our side of the story. Who told you anyway, Jacob, Sara, or Olivia?"

"I saw your pictures. Grandma Olivia put all the pictures of you and Daddy in car-tons," I told her. "They don't mention Daddy's name, they don't talk about his accident. It's horrible."

"Olivia's doing, I'm sure. The whole time I lived there, I could never call her anything but Olivia, you know. I could never call her mother," she said with bitterness.

"But why did they take you into their home? Why did they adopt you?"

"It's a very involved story, honey. That's another reason why I couldn't get into it before I left Provincetown. Just hold out a little longer. Put up with their snobbery a little longer," she pleaded.

"Mommy, you never called Mama Arlene to get my things sent up here."

"I'll do it right after I hang up," she prom-ised.

"And Alice called and told me Papa George

was in the hospital, very sick."

"It was expected, honey."

"Mommy, I can't stay here. Please come back for me or send for me. I'll meet you anywhere and put up with anything, travel, running about from city to city. I'll never complain about anything. I promise. I swear."

"Melody, I'm in Los Angeles! I'm in Holly-wood! I have appointments, auditions. Can you imagine? Something wonderful is going to happen and soon, just as I told you. Give me a little longer. Finish school there, at least. Then, during the summer months —"

"Mommy." Tears streamed down my face. "Why did they hate you for marrying Daddy? Why didn't they accept it? You weren't blood relatives."

"We disobeyed Queen Olivia," she quipped. "Just stay out of her way. She'll die soon and put everyone out of their misery. *Ooo*," she said, "I just hate talking about them. They made us suffer. Get everything you can out of them. They owe you. That family owes us more than it can ever repay. Do your own thing and ignore them. Uncle Jacob won't throw you out."

"Mommy —"

"I have to go, honey. I have an appoint-ment. I'll call Arlene. I promise."

"But where are you? How can I reach you?"

"We haven't settled into one place yet. I'll

let you know," she said. "When we're to-gether again, we'll have a long talk, a grown-up talk, and I'll tell you everything, every last crummy detail. Be good, honey."

"Mommy!"

The click sounded like thunder.

I shouted louder. *"Mommy!"* I squeezed the neck of the receiver with all my might and screamed into it again.

Aunt Sara came running.

The front door opened and Uncle Jacob stopped in the corridor with Cary right be-hind him.

I was crying hysterically now, bawling without control.

"What's going on here? What's the mean-ing of this outburst?" Uncle Jacob de-manded.

"She was talking to Haille," Aunt Sara explained.

"Well I won't have this sort of emotional display. Stop it!" he commanded.

I cradled the receiver slowly and then wiped my cheeks with the back of my hand, glaring at him. The fury in my eyes took him aback and he blinked.

"Go clean yourself up," he ordered, "or you won't have any dinner."

"I don't want any dinner. I don't want anything from you," I said through clenched teeth.

Uncle Jacob reddened. Cary's mouth fell

open and Aunt Sara gasped.

"I don't want anything from this . . . this horrible family." I ran from the living room.

"See!" Uncle Jacob cried after me as I started up the stairs. "And you thought she was like Laura. That's Haille's daughter."

I stopped abruptly and turned, glaring down at him.

"What's wrong with being Haille's daughter? Why do you always say that? What did she ever do to you?" I demanded.

He looked at Aunt Sara and then at me. "She didn't do anything to me. What she did, she did to herself and to Chester."

"What? *What?*" I screamed.

"Go up to your room until you calm down," he said, visibly shaken. I didn't move. What was it Mommy kept saying: he would never throw me out? How did she know? What made her so sure? Every time I uncovered one secret, there were ten more bundled beneath it, I thought. "Go on," he ordered.

"I'll go where I like when I like," I said defiantly. My boldness surprised us both and left him stuttering for the right words. I trembled, but tried to look calm so I could continue to face him.

"Ah, suit yourself," he finally said. "I'll have none of it. You wanted her here, you put up with her," he told Aunt Sara. Then he waved his hand as if chasing flies and marched through the house. Cary stared up at me, a stunned look on his face.

"Oh dear. Oh dear, dear," Aunt Sara mumbled.

"I'm sorry, Aunt Sara," I said. I took a deep breath. "I have to rest for a little while."

She looked up at me sadly and shook her head. "It was all going so well, wasn't it, Cary?"

"Let her be," he said and followed after Uncle Jacob.

I turned and continued up the stairs to my room. Behind the closed door, I let my tears of sorrow, tears of fear, and tears of loneliness flow freely.

I was on my stomach on the bed so I didn't hear May knock and then come in to see me. I felt her little hand on my shoulder and turned sharply. She looked as if she was about to cry because I was crying.

"What's wrong?" she signed.

I smiled through my tears. "I'm all right," I told her. "I'll be all right."

Then I sat up and hugged her, clung to her as tightly as I would cling to a life raft in a sea storming with turmoil.

13

Angry at Them All

Mainly because I didn't want May to be upset any more than she was, I went down to dinner. I had no appetite. The heavy atmosphere of the night before was nothing compared to the cemetery stillness that pervaded the dining room tonight. It was so quiet I could hear Uncle Jacob crunching his food between his back teeth, and Aunt Sara's little whimpers between her bites and swallows. The tapping of silverware, clanking of dishes, and pouring of water created the most noise. Everyone spoke in monosyllables or short sentences whenever he or she spoke.

"Bread, Jacob?"

He grunted yes.

"Would you like more chicken, Cary?"

"No, Ma."

Cary watched my every move. I ate like a bird, pecking at my food, keeping my eyes down. I didn't know whom I was more angry at: Mommy, Uncle Jacob, my grandparents.

Maybe I was equally angry at all of them. I was even angry at myself for agreeing to remain here. How could I have believed Mommy's promises? One lie spun another when it came to the Logans, and Mommy had caught their lying disease.

Aunt Sara tried to cheer me up by talking about the Blessing of the Fleet, a June festival that took place yearly in nearby Provincetown. She said there would be lots of boats, people in costumes, great food and games. Whenever she asked Uncle Jacob about something, he would simply grunt a yes or a no, his eyes mostly on me. I sensed that I had scratched a scab on his memory when I had screamed my questions at him in the hallway. He didn't look irritated as much as stunned.

Aunt Sara made a final attempt to inject some joviality into our dinner by mentioning Cary's English test result. Uncle Jacob expressed surprise and approval, but when Cary explained that it was all because of my tutoring, Uncle Jacob grew dark again.

"Laura used to help Cary like that, too. Remember, Jacob?" Aunt Sara said smiling.

"I remember," he said. "I have something to do at the dock." He pushed himself away from the table and stood. "Don't make me any coffee."

"I'll have some hot water steaming for tea for you when you return, Jacob," Aunt Sara promised. He glanced at me once more, then left the room.

"If you have homework, you don't have to help me with the dishes tonight, Melody," Aunt Sara said. She was trying her best to make things right again. I felt sorry for her, but even sorrier for myself.

Cary's eyes were fixed on me. They were strangely haunted. Was he still angry at me or did he feel sorry for me? From the day I arrived, I had felt Cary carried deep secrets in his heart, secrets that resembled chunks of lead weighing him down, making him grow older faster. It was why he seemed so bitter all the time and why the girls at school saw him as Grandpa.

"I do have something to do tonight, Aunt Sara," I said. "I'm going to study for a test with a friend."

Cary looked down, his head lowering as if in prayer.

"Oh? Well . . . yes, Laura did that once in a while. Who was it she studied with, Cary? Sandra Turnick?"

"Yeah," he said quickly, but he didn't look up.

"She has a sister in your class, doesn't she, Melody? Is that who you're studying with tonight?"

"No," I said. Cary lifted his eyes and gazed at me. "It's someone else. Janet Parker," I said. Cary looked disappointed and once again dropped his gaze to his plate. "But first, I promised May I would do some homework with her," I added.

Aunt Sara smiled. "That's nice of you, dear. I'm sure May appreciates it."

She signed to her and May signed back, expressing her enthusiasm. I went upstairs with her and worked with her on her reading and speaking exercises. At a quarter to eight, though, I had to leave. I explained that she would probably be asleep when I returned, so I kissed her goodnight.

Cary had gone up to the attic. I heard him moving about while I worked with May, but now he was quiet, still. I found a blue cardigan sweater to wear over Laura's yellow dress. It was a little over sixty degrees outside, but the sky was clear with a three-quarter moon that put a bone-white glow over the sand.

"Don't be too late, dear," Aunt Sara called from the living room when I headed for the front door.

"I won't," I promised. My heart was pounding, both from the excitement and from guilt. I hated lying to her, but there was no doubt in my mind what her and Uncle Jacob's reactions would have been if they had known I was planning to meet a boy on the beach.

They have no right to restrict me, I told myself. This family, especially, has no right

341

to tell me what I should and shouldn't do. Never before did I feel as much on my own, as much in control of my own destiny. Mommy had deserted me, lied to me, ignored my feelings and my needs. She knowingly left me with people who looked down on us. She had left me to fend for myself. And that's just what I would do, I told myself.

All my life I had believed in being honest. I believed in the ultimate goodness of people, only to find out that my own parents had deceived me. Who did I have but myself? I thought. Driven by my rage as much as I was drawn by Adam Jackson's magical eyes, I bounced quickly down the steps and walked away from the house. I looked back once. I thought a curtain in an upstairs window moved, but other than that, there was no sign of anyone watching, so I veered left onto the beach and plodded through the sand. I quickly discovered it was easier to walk with my shoes off. The sand, still holding on to the day's sunlight, felt warmer than the air.

As I drew closer to the ocean, I saw the moon walk on the water and heard the roar of the surf. The water looked inky, mysterious and the stars on the horizon blazed with a brightness that filled my heart with even more excitement. In moments I was far enough out on the beach to sense the solitude. The Logans' house was lit up, but looked toy-like and distant after another few minutes of my walking away from it.

I went up and down the hilly terrain. At the top of the dune, I gazed toward the place on the beach I had been when Adam had first found me. I saw the glittering flames of a small bonfire and my heart thumped. Would he be surprised to see that I'd actually come, I wondered. I was surprised, myself.

When I drew closer, I saw his motorboat anchored on the beach and heard music from his radio. He was sprawled on the blanket, his hands behind his head, and he was gazing up at the sky. He wore a white polo shirt and a pair of white shorts. He was barefoot. If he heard me approach, he didn't show it. I stood beside him for a moment before he slowly turned, his face glimmering in the moonlight with that polished smile. He sat up.

"I'm glad you came," he said. "It's a great night. It would have been a shame for you to miss it." He patted the space beside him on the blanket. "Did you have any trouble getting out?"

"No," I said. "I dug a tunnel."

He laughed. "Great. So?" he said after a moment, "Are you just going to stand there? You didn't come all this way to watch me lie on a beach blanket, did you?" he asked.

"Maybe. Don't forget my uncle and aunt don't allow television in their house."

He threw back his head and roared with laughter. Then he grew serious and gestured for me to come to him. "It's very cozy on this blanket."

I lowered myself to my knees and put my shoes down before sitting on the blanket, close to the edge.

He stared with a quizzical look on his face and then he shook his head, still smiling. "Aren't you the tease?" he said. "All right, I'll play hard to get, too." He lay back on his hands to look up at the sky.

"I'm not a tease."

"Of course you are. All girls are."

"Well, it's not true about me."

He turned over and braced his chin on his hand to gaze at me. "Really? Well, why do you work so hard at being beautiful if not to have boys look at you longingly?"

"I don't work so hard at being beautiful."

"I imagine you don't," he said nodding. "You are what I would call a natural beauty. That's why all the cats in school are clawing at you. So," he said, sitting up again, "tell me about your life in coal-mineville. Leave a boyfriend crying in his beer when you came to the Cape?"

"No."

"I'll bet. Well, his loss is my gain." He snickered. "Come a little closer. I won't bite," he said. "You want me to beg? Is that it?" he asked when I didn't move.

"I don't want you to beg, no."

"So?"

I shifted on the blanket until I was beside him.

"Now that's better. At least I can smell your hair." He put his nose to my head and then kissed my forehead. "And I can look into those terrific eyes. You know you turn me into jelly, don't you?"

This time, I had to laugh. "Don't you mean cranberry sauce?" I asked.

That brought a wide smile to his face. His blue eyes seemed to sizzle as they blazed down at me. "You're smart as well as beautiful. A rare jewel." He kissed me on the lips, but I was so tense I thought he would hear my nerves twang.

He gazed at me with a curious smile, then he leaned over to his right where he had a cloth bag. He produced a bottle of vodka and two glasses. Then he dipped his hand into the bag and came up with a jar of cranberry juice. "How'd you know I had cranberry juice? Some little bird at school whisper in your ear?"

"I didn't know."

"It's a great drink with vodka. My father's favorite. Let me fix us a couple."

"I don't like drinking whiskey," I said quickly.

"This isn't whiskey. It's vodka. Doesn't stink on your breath as much, and when you cut it with the cranberry juice, you hardly notice it. But it sure makes you feel good. I'm sure you've had it, right?"

"Of course," I said, even though I never had. All I had ever tasted was Mommy's gin and I never could understand how or why she liked it so much.

After he made the drinks and handed me my glass, he tuned the radio to a station that played softer music.

"Let's make a toast," he said tapping his glass against mine. "To us. To good times and good weather forever."

I took a sip. He was right. It didn't taste as bad as Mommy's gin.

"So where did you used to go at night with your boyfriends in West Virginia: old coal mines?"

"Sometimes," I said, even though the very thought of going into a coal mine at night was terrifying. I didn't want him to think I wasn't as experienced or as sophisticated as the girls here.

He brought his glass to his lips and urged me to bring mine to my lips. "Keeps you warm inside," he promised. I drank some more. "Was the sky as beautiful at night in West Virginia?"

"Yes."

"But you didn't have the ocean. The ocean

346

makes the sky look better, doesn't it?" He moved closer, putting his arm around my waist. I looked at the sky where it merged with the horizon. The water was glimmering and the stars did seem brighter than ever, some actually twinkling on the water. He nudged my cheek with his nose and kissed me softly on the neck.

A flow of warmth rushed down over my shoulders to my breasts. Nervous, I drank some more. Then I pulled a little away from him.

"I like this song," I said. "Don't you?"

"What? Oh, yeah." He reached for the bottle of vodka and refilled my glass. "Feels good, right?"

"Yes."

"Let's see, this time we'll toast to . . . the end of school. May it come quickly and put me out of pain." He clinked my glass again. "Quick, drink or we won't get our wish," he urged. I took a long sip and thought this time the vodka was a lot stronger.

"I thought you were a good studious — I mean student," I said.

He laughed. "I do all right. Adam Jackson does just enough to make his father happy with his grades," he bragged.

"Isn't your father a lawyer?" I asked him.

"Yeah, but don't worry. I won't sue you if we don't have a good time tonight."

"Do you want to be a lawyer?" I asked

quickly as he leaned over to kiss me.

"Maybe. I don't know. My father wants me to be." He brushed his lips against mine and then turned abruptly and lowered his head to my lap so he could look up at me. "You look great from down here," he said. He reached up and fingered the buttons on my cardigan sweater. I put my hand over his. "You're not cold, are you?"

"A little," I said.

"Take another drink. Go on," he urged. "You won't be cold long."

I did and he smiled. His finger undid one button and then another.

"You looked great in this dress today," he said. "Like a fresh flower. I was jealous at the way some of my friends were looking at you."

His finger traced the valley between my breasts. Then he lifted himself slowly, reached behind my neck, and gently brought me down to meet his lips. It was like a kiss in the movies, his lips pressing against mine, his tongue moving between my lips, the music around us, the stars above us. I felt warm all over. My mind reeled. He took my glass of vodka and cranberry juice from me, urged me down to the blanket, and then turned so he was lying face down over me.

"I just knew you and I would click," he said.

"How did you know?"

"Adam Jackson knows women."

"You talk about yourself as if you were someone else." I giggled. "I never heard anyone do that."

"Simple explanation," he said, shrugging, "I'm bigger than one person."

He lowered his lips to mine and kissed me long and hard, his right hand moving over my ribs to my breasts.

"You are delicious," he said. My pulse was racing. I looked past him at the stars and they seemed to blur and merge. He kissed my neck, then lowered himself so he could move his tongue under my collar, toward my breasts. I felt him lift me gently and find the zipper behind my dress. I started to resist, but the zipper flew down and he quickly nudged my dress over my shoulders, driving his mouth to my breasts.

It was as if I were on a magic carpet and not just a beach blanket. It seemed to lift both of us off the sand and begin to turn in a counter-clockwise circle. He had the straps of my bra down and was manipulating the hook with surgical expertise. It popped and his hand moved up under the garment instantly, lifting it away. Before the air could touch my naked bosom, his lips were there, nudging, strumming my nipples.

I felt a weakness in my legs as his legs

moved in between and forced mine to separate. It was happening so fast — the blinking, out-of-focus stars were falling like a downpour of diamonds around us, the blanket was spinning, his hand was under the skirt of my dress and his fingers were toying with my panties. The roar of the ocean covered my small protests and he was saying, "You're perfect. I knew we would be great together."

But this wasn't romantic and lovely. This frenzy of passion frightened me more than it excited me. Too fast, I thought. It's happening too fast.

I pushed at his chest and shook my head, but he smothered my exclamation with his lips, jabbing his tongue harder into my mouth. I nearly gagged, and when he pulled back I screamed. "Stop it!"

"What?" he cried. "You wanted this, didn't you? Otherwise, why would you come here? Just relax. Lie back and enjoy Adam Jackson."

My arms were too small and weak to hold back the weight of his upper body. I started to cry as he lifted me easily and began to slip my panties down my thighs. I was shaking my head and pleading. I could hear his heavy, hard breathing and I tried to turn my mouth from his, but he seemed to have grown in size. I saw him in the same distorted way I saw the stars. He resembled a great jellyfish spreading over me, encompassing me.

"Please . . . stop!" I pleaded.

He pulled his head up to look down at me disdainfully.

"You are a tease," he said, "and Adam Jackson is not to be teased."

I thought I would pass out beneath him. My eyes rolled, my mind went dark for a moment, and then, suddenly I felt him rise off me, his head going back first and then his lower body lifting. I opened my eyes to see Cary pulling him away, clutching his hair, and grasping his right arm. He jerked him so hard he fell back on the sand.

"Get off her!" he cried.

Adam turned over on the beach quickly and got to his feet. I sat up, my stomach gurgling. The two boys faced each other. Cary's hands were clenched into small mallets. With his shoulders hoisted like a hawk, he stepped toward Adam.

"Come on," he said. "Let's see how you protect that precious handsome face of yours."

"Get out of here!" Adam whined. "She wanted it," he said pointing at me. "She came here, didn't she?"

Cary gazed at the bottle of vodka on the blanket.

"You got her drunk, you bastard. You took advantage of her."

Cary lunged at him and Adam jumped back.

"You're crazy!" he cried. "Your whole family's crazy, including her!" He backed away. "I'm not going to fight over her." He continued to back toward his boat. Cary stood glaring at him. Then he turned, reached down for the bottle of vodka, and heaved it in Adam's direction. The bottle smashed against the side of the boat and splattered.

"You're out of your mind! You'll be sorry," Adam threatened, but he pushed his boat away from the shore and quickly jumped into it when Cary threatened to come after him. "This isn't the end of this. You'll hear from me!" he screamed.

"Sue me!" Cary retorted, his hands on his hips.

Adam started his engine and turned the boat away. A moment later he was bouncing over the water, fleeing.

I turned over on my left side and buried my face in the blanket. I felt Cary kneel down and touch my shoulder.

"You all right, Melody?" he asked softly.

"No," I said. I felt sick and embarrassed and suddenly very, very tired.

"Come on. I'll help you home," he said.

"I don't want to go home. That's not my home!" I cried. "I don't have a home!"

"Sure you do. You're with us until your mother comes back."

"I don't care if she ever comes back."

"Sure you do."

"Stop saying sure I do. You don't know what I want. None of you know or care."

"I care," he insisted. "Come on," he urged. He started to zip up the back of my dress. "You'll feel better after you walk a while."

"I'll never feel better. I don't want to feel better. Just leave me here on the beach and let the water come in and pull me out to sea. I'd rather drown."

He laughed. "Come on. You're just a little drunk."

"I am not drunk," I said and spun around, only when I did, the whole world spun with me and kept spinning. I moaned and fell into his arms. The gurgling in my stomach turned into a volcano and it began to erupt. He held me as I heaved. All the vodka I had drunk on top of a relatively empty stomach came up like molten lava. It burned its way up my throat and poured out of my mouth. The pain of heaving doubled me over. If it had not been for Cary holding me, I was sure I would have fallen face forward into the sand.

Finally, it stopped. I took deep breaths, gasping for clean air.

"You all right now?"

I was feeling better after getting rid of the vodka. I nodded and he lowered me to the blanket.

"Just rest a moment," he said.

I took shorter breaths, the heaviness in my chest lessening, but there was an ache in my eyes and my stomach felt as if I had been punched a dozen times. The good thing was that the spinning had stopped.

"How did you find us?" I asked, starting to realize all that had happened.

"I followed you. I had a suspicion you were going to meet that creep," he said. "He has trouble keeping his bragging tied at the dock. He was telling some of his friends that he was going to have a good time tonight on the beach and he would have a big story for them tomorrow. He didn't mention your name, but I was afraid it was you, and then, when you told me you couldn't go to town with me because you had made other promises, I was even more suspicious. That lie you told at dinner clinched it. I knew you wouldn't go to Janet Parker's house to study."

"I'm sorry," I said. "I'm sorry I made trouble for you."

"No trouble for me," he said with a laugh. "Trouble for Mr. Perfect."

"He threatened you."

"He'll be too embarrassed to tell anyone what really happened. Don't worry."

I tried to sit up.

"Think you can walk?" Cary asked.

"Yes," I said. He had pulled the zipper of

my dress up, but my bra was still undone. For the moment it didn't matter. I started to stand. He came around behind me and lifted me at the elbows until I was on my feet, but I wobbled and fell against him.

"Whoa," he said. "Steady as she goes. Seas are a bit rough tonight."

"Maybe I should be wearing a life jacket," I said and he laughed. We started away. "What about the blanket and the radio and all?"

"Leave them to the ocean. She has a way of cleaning up the messes left on her beaches," he said. He held my right arm as we continued walking.

"I must look like a mess," I said. "My stomach feels as if I swallowed a beehive."

"We'll get you home and to bed, but you'll probably feel crummy in the morning."

"Your mother will be very upset with me, and if your father sees me —"

"He won't," Cary promised.

"It's too soon. Your mother will wonder why I'm back from studying already."

"We'll smuggle you in," he promised.

I walked with my eyes shut, my head against his shoulder, feeling heavy with the burden of shame I carried. He held me as if I were made of spun glass and any second I'd break. When I stumbled, he held me even tighter and more firmly. It seemed to take forever to go back over the hill, and then when we started to descend the second one, he abruptly stopped. "Wait."

I opened my eyes.

"What?"

He squinted at the darkness.

"My father," he whispered. "He's coming back from the dock."

"Great. Now all I'll hear is how this proves I'm my mother's daughter. He'll have me reading the Bible all night."

"Shh! Just don't move for a moment." Cary was quiet a long moment. "All right, he's just about to the house. Let's go to the boat for a little while," he said. "You'll clean up and straighten up and then we'll go in. Come on. You'll be all right," he promised. His words spread a magic shawl of comfort about my shoulders. I relaxed and followed his direction.

He turned me right and we moved down the hill toward the ocean again. Moments later, we were at the dock. He helped me onto the lobster boat. It bobbed gently in the water, but I was still too unsure of myself to walk without Cary's support.

"Easy." He guided me into the cabin, leading me to a cushioned bench. He turned on a small oil lamp. "How are you doing?"

"I feel as if I'm stuck on a runaway roller coaster. My ribs ache, my head feels like a hunk of coal, my stomach wants to resign from my body . . . I've never been drunk before. Lucky you were there for me," I said. "Thanks."

He stared at me. "I hate guys like Adam Jackson. They think everything's coming to them because they were born with silver spoons in their mouths. They all oughta be harpooned, or taken out to sea and left there floating on their egos."

I laughed, but it hurt and I moaned.

Instinctively, he reached for my hand. "You want a drink of water?"

"Yes, please," I said and he rose to get it. That was when I looked down and saw the mess I had made on the front of my dress. "Oh, Cary, look. Aunt Sara will be devastated. One of Laura's dresses. It will be stained."

He turned and gazed at me. He thought a moment. "I got a tub on deck, and some soap. We'll scrub it clean and then I'll put it on the kerosene heater for a half hour and that'll dry it enough." He poured me a glass of water and handed it to me. "In the meantime," he took a rubber raincoat off a hook, "you can wear this."

I drank the water.

"I'll go fill the tub and get a brush."

"I'll wash it," I said. "You don't have to do that."

"It's all right. If I can wash smelly fish guts off the deck, I can wash off some used vodka."

"Ugh," I said, laughing.

He left, and I took off the dress, fastened my bra and put on the raincoat.

"All set," he called out.

"I'll do it," I insisted.

"You sure?"

"Yes."

He took me to the tub and I scrubbed the dress clean while he lit the kerosene heater in the cabin. When I thought the dress was clean enough, I brought it in and he draped it carefully over the heater.

"Shouldn't take too long," he said. I sat on the bench. He went to a closet and took out a pillow. "Here," he said placing it on the corner of the bench. "Lie back, close your eyes, and rest."

"Thank you. You're a regular rescue service," I told him.

He sat at the base of the bench, his back against it, his arms around his legs. The small flame in the oil lamp flickered, making the shadows dance on the walls of the cabin. I could hear the water licking at the sides of the boat. The pungent odor of seaweed and salt water was as refreshing as mint at the moment. I took a deep breath and sighed.

"I'm a mess," I said.

"You're not. You're bright and pretty. Everything is going to be all right." He said it with such assurance, I wondered if everyone else could see my future clearer than I could. "Don't feel bad about what happened. Guys like that fool girls every day," he added bitterly.

I thought about Laura and Robert Royce and imagined that was what Cary meant.

"I read a letter Robert Royce wrote to Laura," I confessed.

"That garbage?" Even in the dim light, I could see his frown.

"It didn't seem like garbage, Cary. I read only one, but I thought he was sincere."

"He knew how to use sincerity to get what he wanted," Cary said sharply. "He was a conniving, sneaky —"

"How can you be so sure?"

"I can," he said firmly.

"I'm not even confident about people I've known all my life, people I've seen on a daily basis. You can't possibly know what things Laura and Robert said to each other, what they told and promised each other, and from what I've learned about her, she must have been a very bright person, Cary. Maybe you were just —"

"Just what?"

"Overly worried. It's only natural, I suppose. Tell me about the accident."

"There's nothing to tell. They went sailing, a storm came, and they got caught in it."

"They had no warning?"

"They were out there too long. He was probably . . ."

"Probably what?" He didn't answer. "Cary?"

"Probably trying to do to her what Adam Jackson tried to do to you tonight. She resisted and he kept her out there and they got caught in the storm. He's responsible for what happened. He's lucky he died too, otherwise, I would have killed him with my bare hands. In fact I wish he hadn't died. I wish I could have been the one to kill him."

I was quiet for a moment. His shoulders, hunched up with rage, relaxed a bit.

"Don't you think that if Robert Royce were that sort of a boy, Laura wouldn't have continued seeing him, Cary?" I asked softly. "I certainly don't want to be alone with Adam Jackson again."

He didn't reply for a while. Then he sighed, lowered his head and shook it. "She was confused, is all. She was in a rush to have a boyfriend."

"Why?"

"Because of those . . . busybodies in school always teasing her about not having one, saying nasty things to her about . . ."

"About what?" I held my breath.

"About us. They spread dirty stories about us and she thought it was because she didn't have a boyfriend. So you see, she didn't really like Robert that much. She was just trying to please everyone and get them to stop. She thought it was bothering me and she blamed herself."

"That's terrible," I said. He nodded. "Why did they make up those stories about you two?"

"Why? Because they're dirty, mean, selfish. They couldn't understand why Laura and I were so close, why we did so much together and for each other. They were jealous so they made up stories. They're as responsible for her death as Robert was," he concluded.

"I'm sorry, Cary." I touched his shoulder.

He nodded. "Don't bother reading any more of those phony letters. They're full of lies. He wrote and said whatever he thought would get him what he wanted," Cary assured me.

"Why doesn't your mother throw them out, then?"

"She wouldn't touch anything in that room. For a long time afterward, she refused to believe Laura wasn't coming back. They've never found her body, so she refused to accept her death. And then, my father had the gravestone put in and forced her to go there with him. Finally, she accepted that much, but she still clings to the room, to her things, her clothes. I was surprised she wanted to take you in and let you stay in Laura's room, but it's almost as if she thinks . . ."

"What?"

"Laura's come back through you. That's another reason why my father hasn't been the most hospitable person. It's not that he dislikes you for any reason."

"There's a reason," I said prophetically. "Something happened that has made him so bitter about my mother, and I want to know what it was. Do you know anything else?" I asked.

"No," he said quickly. Too quickly, I thought.

"Then, I'll just have to ask our grandparents to tell me everything."

He turned, a look of disbelief on his face.

"You wouldn't just come out and ask them?"

"Why not?"

"Grandma Olivia can be . . . tough."

"So can I," I said firmly. "When I have to be."

He laughed.

"Maybe you shouldn't, Melody," he said after a moment, his smile gone. "Maybe some things are better left below deck."

"Secrets fester like infections. After a while they make you deathly sick, Cary. That's the way I feel. It's the way you felt when people were making up stories about you and Laura," I said searching for a way to make him understand how important it was to me.

"I tell you what," he said, reaching for my

hand. "I'll make you a promise. I promise to try to find out as much as I can about your parents, too."

"Will you? Oh thank you, Cary."

He held on to my hand. "It's okay," he said. "You're probably right. You probably should know everything there is to know about the Logan family."

I smiled at him. "When I first came here, I thought you hated me."

"I did," he confessed. "I knew why my mother wanted you here and I felt bad about it, but . . ."

"But?"

"You're very nice," he said. "And the only cousin I have, so I have to put up with you."

"Thanks a lot."

"Let's check the dress," he said and got up. "It's not completely dry, but it's dry enough. You'll get by with it."

"Thanks," I said rising. He handed me the dress and I started to take off the raincoat.

"I'll wait outside," he said.

I changed, hung up the raincoat, and joined him on the deck.

"How do you feel?" he asked.

"Tired and wobbly, but a hundred percent better than I did, thanks to you."

"Let's go home," he said taking my hand. He didn't let go until we were at the house.

"How do I look?" I asked him, brushing back my hair.

"Fine," he said gazing at me in the glow of the porch light.

Uncle Jacob was in the hallway when we entered. He was heading for the living room with a mug of tea in his hand. He paused and looked at us, his eyes growing small and dark.

"Where were you two?" he asked.

"I met Melody coming back from studying with her friend," Cary said quickly.

Uncle Jacob's gaze shifted from Cary to me and then back to Cary before he continued toward the living room.

"Get home as soon as you can tomorrow," he said. "Lots to do."

"Okay," Cary said.

Aunt Sara appeared in the kitchen doorway.

"Oh, hi. Is everything all right?"

"Yes, Aunt Sara," I said. "I'm tired and going to sleep."

"Good night, dear," she said.

Cary followed me up the stairs.

"I'm sorry you had to tell your father a lie, Cary," I told him at my door.

"It was only half a lie," he said. "You were on the way home." He smiled.

"Good night and thanks again," I said. I leaned over and kissed him on the cheek. He blushed. I flashed the best smile I could and retreated to my room. He was still standing in the hallway when I closed the door. I heard him pull down his attic steps and go upstairs.

I changed and dressed for bed. I hated the sight of myself in the mirror and wondered if those shadows under my eyes would be gone by morning. Nothing felt as good as the mattress and covers. My eyelids were like two steel doors slamming shut. The last thing I remembered was wishing Cary hadn't lied for me. It all starts with little half lies and then it grows until, until . . . you become like Mommy and lose track of the difference.

It won't happen to me, I vowed.

It won't.

The chant worked like a lullaby. The next thing I knew, I was fluttering my eyelids at the flood of sunlight penetrating the window curtains and nudging me to start another day.

14

A Helpless Creature

Unfortunately, Cary wasn't right about Adam Jackson. It was true that his ego had been bruised, but his embarrassment over my rejecting him turned into something uglier. By the time Cary and I had arrived at school, Adam's lies had spread like a brush fire in a drought. The moment I saw the expressions on the faces of girls like Lorraine, Janet, and Betty, I knew something mean and vicious had been poured into their ears and would soon be poured into mine.

As soon as we entered the building, Cary sensed the negative electricity in the air. He hovered about me like a nervous grizzly bear. Usually, when we arrived at school, he would scamper away to join his few friends, but today Cary lingered at my side while I organized my things at my locker. Nearby, the girls watched us, giggling. Other boys walking by held smirks on their faces and twisted their lips as they whispered. I marveled at how completely Cary could ignore everyone when he wanted to. For him, they didn't exist at the moment. He heard no evil and saw no evil. If he looked in their direction, he gazed right through them.

"Good morning, Cary," Betty said as she passed us with Lorraine and Janet.

"Good morning, Cary," Lorraine echoed.

"Good morning, Cary," Janet mimicked.

Something slippery and ugly obviously was hidden beneath their wide smiles. Cary didn't respond. He escorted me to my homeroom and was there at the sound of the bell to walk with me to my next class.

"You don't have to be worried about me," I told Cary after I found him waiting in the hallway outside my first period classroom.

"Oh, I'm . . . not," he fumbled. "I was just nearby and thought I might as well walk along with you as with anyone."

"Thanks a lot," I said, smiling at his clumsy effort to explain his presence.

"I mean, I like walking with you, it's just that —"

"You're usually too busy?"

"Yes," he said, grateful for my suggestion.

Although he wasn't there after my next period ended, he wasn't far behind in the corridor. It was nice having him look after me. For the moment at least, I felt as if I had a brother.

In my classes and in the hallway when I

passed from room to room, I noticed how the girls kept their distance, and in class, I saw them looking at me and passing notes. But no one said anything. When I entered the cafeteria at lunch time, however, I found Janet, Lorraine, and Betty waiting anxiously, their eyes sparkling with glee.

"You're kind of cozy with Grandpa today," Betty teased immediately. "Any special reason?" She swung her eyes toward her friends.

"Cozy? I don't know what you mean," I replied. I stepped toward the counter to get a container of milk, but I caught the way they traded smiles and glances as they moved behind me in the lunch line.

"We heard you've taken Laura's place in more ways than one," Janet whispered in my ear. It made the hairs on my neck stick up.

"What?" I turned to confront them.

"You're still carrying her notebook," Lorraine pointed out, "and you wear her clothes."

"You sleep in her room, use her things," Betty recited.

"And whatever she did with Cary, you're doing," Janet concluded.

I felt the blood rush so quickly to my face, my cheeks burned.

"Whatever she did with Cary? What's that supposed to mean?" I demanded.

"You know." Betty rolled her eyes.

"I don't know because my mind isn't in the gutter. What are you saying? Who told you these things?"

"Who else, but the eyewitness?" Betty said with the firmness of a prosecutor. She nodded toward Adam Jackson who had come in with his crowd of buddies. He strutted across the cafeteria, his shoulders back, his face full of himself when he glanced my way. I saw a wicked, twisted smile take shape on those perfect lips.

"Eyewitness?"

"No sense pretending with us anymore," Lorraine said stepping closer to me. "Adam told us what he found you two doing on the beach last night."

"He did what?"

"He said he was riding in his motorboat, saw the bonfire and pulled up before you two had a chance to make it look innocent," Betty detailed.

"He told you that?"

"Surprised he told?" Janet asked.

"He described how you begged him not to, and promised him something good if he didn't," Betty added.

"Is that what you did back in coal country, bribed boys with your body?" Lorraine asked.

I tried to speak, but the words choked in my throat. I shook my head instead. Out of the corner of my eye, I saw Cary watching with concern. He looked as if he was about to get up. Panic nailed my feet to the floor, but I knew I had to do something and fast, otherwise there would be a terrible scene in front of the whole student body.

"Those are lies," I finally said. "The real truth is he's just angry at me for not doing what he wanted me to do on the beach last night. Really!"

"Really?" Betty quipped. "Is that why you and Grandpa are like two peas in a pod today? Practically holding hands? If he were any closer to you, he'd be under your dress."

"It's disgusting," Janet followed. "You're first cousins, aren't you?"

"The Logans give the Cape a bad name," Lorraine declared. The other two nodded.

"What are you waiting for?" Betty said, shifting her eyes toward Cary. "He's waiting for you. The two of you can hold hands under the table. Or do whatever else you do."

The three laughed and moved ahead to get their food. The moment they did, other girls gathered around them to feed on the gossip like chickens in a pen.

I felt my heart pounding. Everyone was looking at me, waiting to see what I was going to do. Cary was still watching from the table where he sat with his two friends, an expression of deep concern on his face. I hesitated. If I went to him, all these tongues would surely cluck, but sitting with the girls today was like putting myself in a Roman Coliseum. They would eat me alive.

"Aren't you going to sit with him?" Janet asked nodding in Cary's direction as she carried her tray past me.

Theresa was walking by with her friends.

"I promised Theresa I would sit with her today," I said loud enough for her to hear. She turned with a look of surprise, but lost it quickly when she saw the expression on my face and the three witches from *Macbeth* closing in. She waited for me to join her.

"Thanks," I whispered. "I especially don't want to sit with them today. All they want to do is make fun of Cary and me," I explained.

"Oh." She wore a knowing look.

When we were at the table and had taken our sandwiches from our bags, I leaned closer to her. "Why did you say 'oh,' like that?" I asked. "Did you hear dirty gossip, too?"

"There's never a bad day's catch when it comes to dirty gossip around here," she said, "especially when it's about Cary Logan. He and Laura were often the hot topic around here."

"Why?"

"There are other brothers and sisters here, dozens," she continued gesturing at the students in the cafeteria, "but none of them

371

behaved as if they had invisible handcuffs tying them together. Anyone will tell you, so it's not like I'm letting a two-pound lobster out of the trap. If Cary could have followed her into the girls' room, I think he would have."

"Wasn't that all just an exaggeration?"

"No. They came to school together, they sat next to each other in every class, they sat with each other at lunch time, they sat with each other in the library, they left school together. The first time I saw Laura at a school party, she came with Cary," Theresa added, "and even danced with him. She danced with a couple of other boys, but she danced with her brother first."

"Maybe he thought she was too shy and just wanted to make her comfortable, or maybe he was too shy," I said. There had to be a hundred other reasons besides the one she was suggesting.

Theresa snorted.

"Well, she did have a boyfriend, didn't she?" I pointed out.

She bit into her sandwich and then shook her head.

"You really are like a stranger to your own family, aren't you?"

"Yes," I admitted.

"When Laura started to see Robert Royce, it was a comedy show for these gossips. Cary would sit by himself or with those nerdy friends across the cafeteria and glare at Laura and Robert. He plodded through the hallways with a chin down to his ankles. The other boys started teasing him and he got into a few fights."

I looked across the cafeteria at him and saw he was still staring at me with deep concern. My heart beat in triple time. Had he heard the stories about us?

"So now that Laura's gone, they just picked up on you," Theresa said.

"With someone else's help," I added glaring across the cafeteria at Adam. He was obviously elaborating on his lies, gesturing emphatically and nodding in Cary's direction.

"They don't ever stop. They'd eat each other to the bone if they could. But Cary and Laura," Theresa said, "they gave them something to chew on." She shook her head again. "It was as if they didn't care, as if they thought no one could touch them with nasty words and looks. I couldn't understand it."

"Your father works with my uncle and with Cary, what does he think?"

She pulled back a moment and gazed at me indignantly. Then she calmed and sat forward again. "He doesn't talk about the Logans except to say they are hardworking people," she remarked with an and-that's-that tone.

"I don't know which one of them first suggested it," I said, nodding at Janet, Lorraine, and Betty, "but they implied that Cary had something to do with Laura and Robert's accident. They made it sound as if he deliberately put them in harm's way."

"Some people think that," Theresa said.

"Do you?"

She ate for a while and then she sighed. "Look, I didn't exactly hang out with Laura Logan or Robert Royce. Laura was always polite and nice to me and I liked her, but she sat on one side of the world and I sat on another one. Cary . . . he sat somewhere in outer space. I'm not swearing for anyone, but I'm not spreading any gossip, so stop asking all these questions."

She paused and turned completely to me so her back was to her friends. Then, in a low voice, she added, "Just like the rest of the bravas here, I mind my own business. What happens in the homes of the rich and famous isn't my concern. My daddy taught me that was the best way to stay out of trouble. Now don't you go telling anyone I said anything else, either," she warned with cold ebony eyes.

"I wouldn't do that."

"Good." Theresa turned back to her food.

I had barely touched mine. Was no one on our side? I gazed at Cary again. He looked so lost and lonely. In my put-away heart, I thought it wasn't fair. It wasn't fair what they were saying about him and me and what had happened to him.

I nibbled my sandwich, my stomach feeling like a tight drum. Theresa talked to her friends for a while and then gazed at me. The hard shell she had formed over herself cracked a bit.

"Look, it doesn't make sense that Cary would do something that would hurt Laura just to get at Robert Royce, does it?" she asked me.

"No."

"So? Don't let them drive you nuts about it. The trouble with them," she said, nodding at Janet, Lorraine, and Betty and their friends, "is they have nothing real in their lives so they make up soap operas. Maybe I'm not as rich as they are and I don't live in as nice a house, but I'm not anxious to trade places."

I smiled. "I don't blame you," I said.

Her smile widened. "Just ignore them and maybe they'll get bored or start on someone else," she suggested.

But it wasn't going to be that way for a while, and they were just getting started building their fire of pain. While Theresa and I spoke, neither of us had noticed that notes were being passed from table to table in the cafeteria. At each table they reached, everyone quickly stopped talking and leaned in to read the slander. Soon, the girls at Theresa's table grew curious and one of them got hold of one of the notes. She read it and passed it down to Theresa.

Printed on the slip of paper was: Incest is best. Just ask Cary and Melody.

I felt as if my lower body had evaporated. I had no legs. I would never be able to get up from the table. The cafeteria was buzzing with loud chatter and laughter. My heart was pounding so hard, I thought I could hear it drumming over the noise.

"Bitches," Theresa muttered. Her friends nodded. Again, everyone's eyes were on me. I shifted my gaze slowly toward Cary. Someone had tossed one of the notes over to his table. After he read it, he crumbled it in his fist and turned to me. I shook my head to say, "Don't pay it any mind. Ignore it," but I could see he was fuming.

"Cary!" I called when he stood up. His gaze was fixed on Adam Jackson across the cafeteria. "Oh no," I muttered.

"Don't get in his way," Theresa warned me. "I've seen him pull up a net full of ten-pounders as if it were a net full of nothing more than balloons."

"This is just what they want," I wailed. Cary's determined strut across the room silenced the cafeteria. The lines in his face were taut and his shoulders were raised. One of the teacher monitors, Mr. Pepper, looked up from his newspaper curiously as Cary marched past him.

I got up as Cary rounded the table beside Adam Jackson's. Adam sat there, smirking, his arms folded over his chest.

"Careful," Theresa said touching my arm as I started after him.

"You spread a bunch of filthy lies about us today, didn't you?" Cary accused, loud enough for everyone to hear.

"Hey, if you're embarrassed by the truth, don't blame me," Adam said.

"What's going on there?" Mr. Pepper called. If he moved any slower, I thought, he'd make a turtle look like a cheetah.

Cary didn't waste words. His whole body had turned into a fist — it was that tight. He reached across the table and grabbed Adam at his collar and literally lifted him from his seat and pulled him over the table, knocking trays of food everywhere.

Adam struggled to break free of Cary's grip, but it was as firm and rigid as lockjaw. Adam looked like a fish out of water, twisting and turning, flailing about, kicking up his feet and swinging his arms wildly.

Cary turned him over and pinned his arms to the table. Everyone drew back. Mr. Pepper finally put on some steam and reached the table, shouting. "Stop that this instant! Cary Logan . . . Stop!"

Cary ignored him. He gazed down into Adam's terrified face.

"Tell them the truth! Tell them!" he

screamed. "Was there anything between me and Melody? Was there?"

"Cary Logan, let him go," Mr. Pepper cried, but he didn't touch Cary. It was as if Cary were on fire and Mr. Pepper knew he would burn his hands. "Go get the principal," he shouted at one of the nearby students, who reluctantly turned, disappointed he would miss the action.

"The truth!" Cary screamed down at Adam and raised his fist over his face. To Adam, it must have looked as if a sledgehammer were about to fall on his precious handsome visage.

"All right. Nothing happened. Nothing happened! I made it all up. Satisfied?"

Cary relaxed and Adam sat up quickly, now indignant and embarrassed. He started to say something, but when Cary turned back to him, he shrank quickly.

"Mr. Logan, you march yourself right down to the principal's office this instant, you hear?" Mr. Pepper said.

Cary didn't acknowledge him. He looked at me. "You all right?" he asked.

I wasn't sure I had any breath in my lungs. I nodded, reserving my words.

"If anyone else bothers you, tell me later," he said loudly. Then, moving like a prisoner condemned to the gallows, he marched ahead of Mr. Pepper toward the door.

The moment he left, the cafeteria burst

into a storm of chatter.

"Satisfied with yourselves now?" I asked Janet, Lorraine, and Betty as I reached their table on the way back to Theresa's. They were too frightened to reply. "Adam Jackson invited me to meet him on the beach last night. I made the mistake of doing so and he tried to rape me," I told them. Their eyes bulged. "He talked me into drinking vodka and cranberry juice and got me drunk."

I saw from Janet's expression that she believed me. Maybe she had had a similar experience.

"Cary arrived just in time and drove Adam away. He literally tore him off me," I told them. "This is his revenge and you and your mean gossip helped him. Now Cary's in bad trouble. Thanks a lot." I turned on my heel and went back to Theresa.

"That Adam Jackson better watch his step or Cary's going to make him fish bait," she said.

"He'll only get himself into more trouble and it's all my fault," I wailed. I plopped into my seat just as the bell rang. The sea of chatter flowed out of the cafeteria with the students. The teachers in the afternoon classes would have a hard time keeping their attention today, I thought. I waited until most everyone was out before getting up to follow. Theresa lingered behind with me.

"What will they do to him?"

"Probably suspend him again," she said.

I felt just dreadful. I sat half dead in my seat in all my classes, barely listening, never answering a question. I couldn't wait for the day to end, and when it did, I found Cary waiting for me outside, his hands in his pockets, his head down, pacing back and forth like a caged animal. The moment he saw me, he perked up.

"You all right?" he asked quickly.

"Yes, but what happened?"

"I got two days vacation," he said.

"Oh Cary, near the end of the year when you need the review for your tests? This is horrible."

"It doesn't matter," he said.

"Yes it does. I'm not going to let the principal do this to you. It's not fair. He should see the nasty notes that were passed around."

"He saw them. It didn't make any difference. He told me I didn't have a right to lose my temper and take things into my own hands."

"He's right," I said.

"I told him it hadn't happened to his family so he could say that."

"What did he say?" I asked, shocked at his courage.

"He stuttered a bit and then said that wasn't the point. But don't worry. I'll walk you to school anyway and be here for you afterward and if Adam Jackson or anyone bothers you —"

"I won't tell you," I said. "You'd . . . you'd turn them into fish bait," I declared, using Theresa's language. He nodded, pleased with the description.

"Exactly, and they know it."

We started away.

"I appreciate your protecting me, Cary, but I hate to see you get into trouble."

I saw a smile take form on his lips.

"How can you be happy?" I asked him.

"This is the way it used to be between me and Laura," he said softly. Then he lost his smile. "Until Robert stepped into her life."

I said nothing. We walked on, each chased by troubled thoughts.

Cary didn't have to tell Aunt Sara and Uncle Jacob what had happened at school. The principal had called and told Aunt Sara before we returned home. Uncle Jacob was still down at the dock and didn't know yet, however, and Aunt Sara was visibly shaken just with the thought of what would happen once he found out. She wrung her hands and shook her head in despair.

"Don't worry, Ma. I'll tell him myself. I'll go down to the dock now," Cary said.

"How did this happen, Cary? You haven't been in any trouble for a long time, and it's so close to graduation."

I was about to take the blame, but Cary spoke first. "This boy was saying ugly, disgusting things about us and our family around the school, Ma. I did what I had to do."

"Why was he doing that?"

"Because he's a shark who needs to be harpooned, and that's all there is to say." Cary glared at me with eyes of warning.

"Oh Melody, was it dreadful for you, too?"

"Yes, Aunt Sara. I'm sorry Cary's in trouble, but the other boy was at fault."

She sighed.

"What are we going to do? All this happens on the day we're going to your grandparents for dinner. Don't mention anything about this to them," she told us fearfully.

"I won't if you won't," Cary promised. He winked at me and went up to change his clothes.

May, who had learned only bits and pieces about everything, was desperate to know what had caused all the commotion. Neither Cary nor I had told her much on the way home since neither of us was in the mood to talk. I explained it to her as best I could, leaving out the nasty details of the rumors.

She signed back that she was sorry Cary was in trouble again. It had always made Laura sad and it made her sadder still, she said. In her large, shadowed brown eyes lingered more dark secrets and sufferings than a child her age should know, I thought. And with her handicap, most of them remained trapped in her heart.

"Go up and try on your dress for tonight," Aunt Sara told me in a tired, defeated voice. "We have to do our best under the circumstances."

"Yes, Aunt Sara."

She followed me upstairs. The dress hung with a slip on the closet door. On the floor beneath them was a brand new pair of shoes she had bought to match the dress, since Laura's shoes wouldn't fit me.

"Aunt Sara, you shouldn't have done that. I could have worn something that would match my own shoes."

"No, this was the last dress I made for Laura," she explained. "She never got a chance to wear it."

"Oh."

I looked at the dress with different eyes. It took on a strangely spiritual feel, like the dress of a ghost. It was an ankle-length, straight beige silk dress with a Victorian collar that had a lace neck.

"Besides," Aunt Sara said, "we're all going to dress with extra care tonight. Olivia and Samuel are having Judge Childs as their guest. She called especially to tell me so we would all look our best. He was a state supreme court judge, you know. He's retired now, but maybe you've heard of his son, the artist Kenneth Childs."

"No." I shook my head and stared at the dress. I could almost see Laura in it.

"I just thought you might have, because you've been here a while and he's one of our most prominent sculptors. His work is in the Provincetown Artists museum and it's in all the good galleries."

I shook my head.

"The Childs have always been good friends with Olivia and Samuel. Kenneth practically grew up with Chester and Jacob, he was at their house so much. Judge Childs's wife died two years ago. His other sons and daughter all live in Boston. Kenneth's brothers and sister don't have much to do with him, but Kenneth was the judge's favorite even though he didn't do anything with his law degree. The judge and his wife gave him enough money to do his art. They supported him for a quite a while and there are some hard feelings in the family because of it. Jealousy, I imagine."

She sighed deeply.

"Every family has its hardships. I wanted you to know a little about it so you don't say anything out of place, if the judge asks you a question."

"Why are we always on pins and needles when we go to my grandparents', Aunt Sara?" I asked. It seemed to me that time spent with family should be the most relaxing time of all.

"Oh, we're not on pins and needles. We're just trying to do the right thing, say the right thing, look the right way. It's what —"

"What Grandma Olivia wants," I provided. "I'm surprised she has any friends at all."

"But she does! She has many friends and they all come from the best society."

"That doesn't always mean they're the best friends to have, Aunt Sara."

She smiled as if I had said something only the most inexperienced young person might utter.

"Go on, dear, try on your dress. I want to be sure it fits and there's no need for alterations," she urged.

Betty, Lorraine, and Janet's words haunted me as I took the dress down and began to take off my clothes. "We heard you're taking Laura's place in more ways than one." But what else could I do? I had nothing nicer than this to wear. Of course, none of my other things had arrived.

The dress fit a little snugly in the bosom, but other than that, it was perfect.

"I think we can get by with it as it is," Aunt Sara said, scrutinizing me. "How does it feel?"

"It's fine, Aunt Sara."

"Good, and the shoes?"

"They're fine," I said.

"Then you're all set. I'll see to May. We'll

be going about five," she told me.

After she left, I stood there gazing at myself in the mirror. It was a nice dress — beautiful in fact — and at any other time, under any other circumstances, I would be happy to wear it, but right now it seemed as if I were wearing a shroud. I couldn't shake an eerie feeling.

The more I learned about Laura, the more I touched her things, read her letters, wore her clothes, the more I felt I was disturbing her peace and stirring up things better left uncovered, buried at the bottom of the sea along with her and her lover.

I was dressed, my hair brushed, and ready. Cary and Uncle Jacob had yet to return from the dock. May looked very pretty in her pink taffeta dress with matching shoes. She and I sat in the living room waiting while Aunt Sara paced nervously in the hallway. "Where are they? They have to get ready and we're going to be late."

I couldn't help wondering if something terrible had happened after Cary told his father about his being suspended. Finally, the door opened and the two entered. Cary gazed into the living room and then ran up the stairs without a word.

Uncle Jacob paused and peered in at us. He fixed his eyes on me and nodded. "I knew it wouldn't take you long to get him in trouble," he said.

"It wasn't her fault, Jacob," Aunt Sara responded. "It was that nasty Adam Jackson's fault."

"I warned you," he told her. "I warned you what it would be like having Haille's daughter."

I shot up as if I were sitting on an ant hill.

"Why do you keep saying that? What's that supposed to mean?" I demanded.

"Ask your mother next time she calls," he said. He looked at Aunt Sara. "I got to clean up and get dressed. No time for this nonsense now." He started up the stairs.

"Why does he keep saying that, Aunt Sara? I have to know what he means."

She shook her head, pressing her lips together as if she were afraid the words would escape.

"I'm not going anywhere until I get some answers," I insisted.

"Oh dear, oh dear. Why does all this have to happen before we go to Olivia and Samuel's?" She sat on the sofa and started to cry. May ran to her to hug her. I felt just terrible as she sobbed and May stroked her hair lovingly, concerned. "You look so beautiful in that dress, too," she wailed. "What have we done to deserve this? What have we done?"

May looked up, confused, hurt, tears building in her soft eyes. All I seemed capable of doing was hurting everyone.

"All right, Aunt Sara. I'm sorry. I'll go."

She sucked back her tears and dabbed her cheeks with her handkerchief. Then she smiled.

"It's going to be all right," she said. "Once everyone gets to know you better, it will be fine. Look how nice Laura's dress looks on you. That's no coincidence. It's an omen, a good omen. Jacob will realize it, too. Fishermen are very aware of good and bad omens. You'll see."

I just stared. She sighed and patted May's hair.

"My pretty little seashell," she said, kissing her daughter. She held her to herself and rocked for a moment. "We all deserve some happiness now, dear. Don't we?"

"Yes, Aunt Sara," I answered.

"Then it's settled. We'll all be happy," she said. It was as if she believed words themselves could change the world around us.

She left to wash her face and straighten her hair. May sat beside me and we looked at one of her books together. Cary came down the stairs and stood in the doorway. He was dressed in a blue suit and tie and looked very handsome.

"You look nice," I said.

"I feel as if I'm in a strait jacket." He tugged on his shirt collar. "I hate wearing a tie. I feel like . . ."

"A fish out of water," I suggested.

"Aye. I'm going outside to wait," he said. "It's my favorite time of day."

"Okay, we'll come along." I signed to May and she closed her book and followed, taking my hand. We strolled in front of the house.

Just over the western horizon, the sun was a rich saffron color, almost orange. The wispy clouds resembled veils of light cotton being pulled across the azure sky. Terns called over the ocean. The breeze was constant, but warmer than usual.

I had to admit Cape Cod was a beautiful place. How it must have broken my father's heart to leave.

Cary glanced at me, and his glimmering eyes met mine.

"Your father's right, you know," I said. "It was my fault."

"Don't start that again," he warned.

"After school ends, I'm not staying here," I told him. "No matter what, I'm leaving. If my mother doesn't want me, I'll go live with Mama Arlene back in Sewell. I'll get a part-time job and help out, but I can't stay where I'm not wanted, where I can only make trouble for people I like," I said.

A tiny smile took form on his lips. "Summer's the best time of the year up here. You can't leave. Besides, I'm depending on your help come cranberry season."

I shook my head.

Everyone refused to face reality here, I thought.

May suddenly began to tug my hand hard and gesture toward the beach.

"What is it, May?" I put my hand over my eyes and gazed. "Cary? Why are those people gathering down there?"

"Where?" He looked. "Oh no, not again," he said, and started over the sand.

"What is it?" We hurried to keep up with him. A thousand yards or so away, a number of people circled something big and dark on the beach. "Cary?"

"It's a beached sperm whale," he called back. He broke into a trot. May and I tried to keep up.

Nearly two dozen people had already reached the pathetic creature. It was at least fifty feet long. It lay on its side, its one visible eye open, bulging. It was gigantic and powerful looking, but right now it was helpless, dying. Most of the people, tourists, who had come to see it were timid and remained a dozen feet or so away, but some young teenagers demonstrated their bravado by rushing to it and slapping their hands on its body. Cary drew closer, keeping far enough back to prevent his shiny good shoes from getting wet. I drew closer with May.

"What happened?"

"It beached itself," he said.

"Why?"

"Lots of theories about that. Some think they become ill and seem to know that coming to shore or beaching will help them die."

"Does it look sick?"

"I don't know."

"What other reason might the whale have for doing this?" I asked.

"Whales have a built-in sonar system with which they navigate deep water. Sometimes, when they're in water only one hundred or two hundred feet deep, it disturbs the sonar and the whales get echoes and become confused, so they end up beached."

"What's going to happen? Can't it swim away with the tide?" I asked.

"The problem is when they reach land like this, the weight of their bodies is so great it crushes their lungs or hampers their breathing so much they become overheated and die. It looks as if that's what's happened here."

"Oh Cary, isn't there anything we can do?"

"You think you can push that back out to sea?" he said. "And even if you get him back into the water, he'd probably wash up again down shore. Anybody send for the Coast Guard?" he asked the crowd.

"Somebody said something about that," a tall man replied.

"If they come, they might try to do something. If they don't show up soon . . ."

"What?"

He gazed around. The kids were still tormenting the whale, slapping it, going up and gazing into its eye, one threatening to poke the eye out with a stick he had found on the sand.

"Stop it!" I screamed.

They paused for a moment, saw it was only me, and continued their pranks.

"That's not so bad," Cary said. "People sometimes come down at night and start to cut off pieces while the whales are still alive," he explained angrily.

"Oh no, Cary."

We heard a car horn and looked back. Uncle Jacob and Aunt Sara had pulled down the road and were gesturing.

"We've got to go," he said.

"This is horrible, Cary."

He sighed. "I know," he said, turning away.

"Cary?"

"We'll come back later, after we return from Grandma's," he promised. He stared at the whale for a moment more and shook his head. "Not that we can do anything. Come on," he urged.

I followed, but after a few steps, I looked back at the helpless giant creature that had somehow found itself trapped on this beach. It was probably too confused and stunned to realize what had happened and what was soon to come.

Just like me, I thought walking slowly behind Cary and gazing back every few moments: beached.

15

Cary's Attic Room

Perhaps it was because of the family secrets that had begun to unravel around my heart: something frail within me cracked and ached as we turned up the driveway to my grandparents' house. I was on the verge of hysterical crying. Tears blinded my eyes. I turned away and stared out the car window so May wouldn't see how close I was to sobbing.

From what I now knew, I envisioned my parents, not much older than Cary and I, secretly holding hands and secretly pledging their love for each other in the shadowy corners of Grandma Olivia's house. Had Uncle Jacob always known? Was that one of the reasons he was so angry at my father?

Uncle Jacob shut off the engine.

"Now remember, best behavior," Aunt Sara instructed, signing the same to May.

"If we behaved any better, Ma, we'd be in heaven," Cary quipped.

Uncle Jacob glared at him and Cary quickly looked away.

The car beside Uncle Jacob's in the driveway was much older, but so clean and shiny, it looked newer.

"The judge is already here," Uncle Jacob muttered. "He keeps this car better than most people keep themselves. There's a man knows the value of quality craftsmanship." He looked at Cary to drive home his lesson.

Grandma Olivia hired special servants for her formal dinners. A butler came to the door. He was a tall, slim man with a narrow, pointed nose and round, dark brown eyes. His hair was curly but so thin, I could see his scalp and the brown spots beneath the piano-wire strands when he bowed.

"Good evening, sir. Madam," he said with a smile that looked smeared across his face with a butter knife. He held the door open, gazing at all of us to see if any of us had a coat or a hat for him to take. We didn't. "Everyone is in the sitting room, sir," he said. He led us to it as if Uncle Jacob didn't know where it was. Aunt Sara thanked him and smiled back, but Uncle Jacob acted as if the servant weren't even there.

Grandma Olivia was in her high-back chair looking like a queen granting an audience. She wore an elegant black velvet dress and a rope of pearls with pearl earrings. Her hair was held back in a severe bun by a pearl comb decorated with small diamonds. Grandpa Samuel was more casual. He sat with his legs crossed, a tall glass of whiskey and soda in his hand. He wore a diamond pinky ring in a gold setting that glittered in the early twilight that poured through the open curtains on the window. His dark suit looked rather dapper, I thought. As before, he had a wide, warm smile when he looked at me.

On Grandma Olivia's right side sat a distinguished looking elderly man. His gray hair still showed traces of light brown. It was neatly trimmed and parted on the right. He wore a tuxedo and a bow tie. When Judge Childs turned to us, I saw he was still a handsome man. His face was full and his complexion robust with wrinkles only in his forehead. He had light brown eyes that dazzled with a glow more like those of a man half his age.

"You're late," Grandma said before anyone else could utter a word.

"We had a problem with the boat that kept us busy," Uncle Jacob said.

Grandma Olivia didn't consider that a valid excuse. "Boats can wait, people can't," she replied.

"Now, now, Olivia, don't be too harsh on those who still do an honest day's labor these days," the judge chided. "How are you, Jacob?"

"Fair to middling, I suppose," Uncle Jacob said. He nodded at his father, who still had his pleasant smile. "And you, Judge?"

"At my age, you don't dare complain," Judge Childs replied.

"Oh, come now, Nelson," Grandpa Samuel said, "you're only a year and a half older than I am."

"And you're no spring chicken, Samuel," the judge retorted. They both laughed. Then the judge turned with interest toward me. "Well now, Sara, you've got another chick under your wing, I see. And a pretty one at that."

"Yes, Judge." Aunt Sara put her hands on my shoulders and pulled me forward. "This is Melody. Haille's Melody."

"Looks just like her," the judge said, nodding. "Just as I remember her at that age. Hello, Melody," he said.

"Hello."

"How old are you now?" he asked.

"I'll be sixteen in a few weeks."

"Oh, that's nice. Another June birthday celebration."

"Kenneth's a Gemini, too, isn't he?" Aunt Sara asked the judge.

"Oh Sara, not that astrology again," Grandma Olivia warned. Aunt Sara shrank back.

"Well, he was born June eighteenth. Does that mean anything?" the judge asked.

"Geminis are May twenty-first to June twentieth," Aunt Sara said in a small voice, her eyes full of fear as she glanced quickly at Grandma Olivia.

"I see," Judge Childs said. "I'm afraid I don't keep up with that star business." He shook his head at Grandpa Samuel and Grandma Olivia. "My maid Toby won't start her day without first checking those predictions in the newspaper."

"Nonsense and stupidity, ramblings of the idiotic," Grandma Olivia said.

"I don't know," Judge Childs said shrugging. "Sometimes, I wonder what's better. Most of the fishermen I know are quite superstitious. Speaking of that, how's the lobstering been so far this year, Jacob?"

"Erratic," Uncle Jacob said. "With all the pollution, the oil spills, I doubt if my grandchildren will be doing much lobstering."

The judge nodded sadly. Aunt Sara directed Cary, May, and me toward the settee as the butler approached to see what sort of cocktail Uncle Jacob wanted.

"I don't drink," he said sharply.

"You oughta ease up on that, Jacob," Judge Childs said. "Doctors are now saying a drink a day is good for the heart. I know I followed that prescription even before it was the fad."

"My son's afraid to cloud his judgment," Grandpa Samuel said.

"And he's always had good judgment," said Grandma Olivia. "Especially moral judgment," she added, sending sharp arrows his way with her eyes.

Grandpa nodded. "That he has, that he has."

I noticed that throughout most of the conversation Judge Childs kept his attention fixed on me and held that soft, small smile on his lips. Finally, as though no one else were in the room talking about anything else, he asked me how my mother was doing.

"How would she know?" Grandma Olivia snapped. "Haille's off to be a movie star."

"Is that right?" the judge asked, still directing himself to me.

"Many people have told my mother that she was pretty enough to be a model or a movie star," I said. "She has auditions and meetings in Hollywood."

"Is that so?"

"Likely story." Grandma Olivia looked at Uncle Jacob, who nodded and sneered with a face that was nearly a replica of his mother's. My daddy had taken after his father much more than his mother, whereas it was the exact opposite for Uncle Jacob.

"She was one of the prettiest girls in Provincetown," the judge said. "Don't forget that beauty contest. I was one of the judges."

"What beauty contest?" I blurted out. Aunt Sara brought her hand to her mouth to cover a gasp. I was breaking a rule: I was speaking before being spoken to.

"Your mother never told you?" Judge Childs asked.

"Apparently, her mother told her very little," Grandma Olivia said with a twist in her thin lips.

"Oh, some company or another — I forget which one now — sponsored a Miss Teenage Cape Cod contest and it ended up here, with your mother one of the five finalists. They paraded around in their bathing suits and pretty dresses and answered questions with their eyelids batting." He laughed. "None of the other four had a chance, did they, Samuel?"

"Not a chance," he said nodding.

"Hardly an accomplishment to talk about now," Grandma Olivia said.

"Oh, we all thought it was a lot of fun back then, Olivia. You had a celebration here, didn't you?" he reminded her. She glanced quickly at Grandpa Samuel.

"That wasn't my idea. I went along with it, but I never thought it was anything to brag about."

"Why, as I recall, Provincetown folks were proud that one of their own took the prize. You know how people get competitive, especially with those Plymouth Rock folk," Judge Childs added winking at me. "Didn't she get a trophy or something? You never saw it,

Melody?" the judge asked me.

"No, sir."

"Maybe she pawned it," Grandma Olivia mumbled just loud enough for us all to hear.

"There wasn't a boy in town who wasn't in love with Haille in those days," the judge continued. Grandma squirmed in her chair. "That's when Kenneth started camping out on your front lawn." He laughed.

"How's he doing these days?" Grandpa Samuel asked. "I can't recall the last time I saw him."

"Same as always," the judge said shaking his head. "If I didn't go to his studio, I wouldn't see him either. He's married to his work, worse than a monk. I hear that those small clay sculptures of the terns are going for ten thousand dollars. Imagine that, Jacob?"

"I can't," Uncle Jacob said. "Just a lot of foolish rich folk, I guess."

"Kenneth's not complaining." The judge gazed long and hard at me again. "What are your interests, Melody?"

"I'm not sure yet," I said. "Maybe teaching," I added, glancing at Cary. He blushed.

"Good idea," the judge said nodding.

"She plays the fiddle," Grandpa Samuel said. "You bring it tonight?"

I looked at Aunt Sara quickly and then back at him.

"No, Grandpa," I said.

"Oh, that's a shame. I was looking forward to a concert."

"I can go back and fetch it for her," Cary volunteered, that impish smile on his face again.

"There's no time for that," Grandma said, rising quickly. "It's time for dinner. Jerome," she called and the butler popped into the doorway as if he had been dangling just above it.

"Madam?"

"Tell the kitchen we are ready to sit at the table," she commanded.

He nodded. "Very well, madam."

The judge rose and held out his arm.

"Olivia, allow me to escort you," he offered, while throwing me a coy smile.

Holding her head high and her shoulders back, Grandma took his arm. Grandpa Samuel followed behind them and we walked behind him into the dining room.

The table was as elegant and as rich a table as I had ever seen, even in movies. The dishes were on silver platters and there were crystal goblets for the wine. There were three tall candles in each of two silver candelabra as well. Between candelabra was a spray of white roses. For this dinner the judge sat at Grandma's right side and Uncle Jacob sat on her left. Grandpa sat where he had sat before, as did Aunt Sara, May, Cary, and I.

Uncle Jacob said grace, which seemed to

go on twice as long as usual, and the meal finally began. It was orchestrated like a theatrical performance with as many people serving the meal as were eating it, each person seemingly assigned the serving of one course. We began with a caviar appetizer. I was ashamed to say I didn't know what it was, but the judge's eyes twinkled with laughter when Uncle Jacob said, "I always feel guilty eating fish eggs."

"I swear, Olivia," the judge said, "you've raised a saint here."

"Jacob is a good man," she bragged. "We've been blessed."

Uncle Jacob didn't blush at the compliment. He merely looked satisfied. But the judge threw me a smile and a wink. He was the main reason I was feeling relaxed at all.

Jerome poured wine for the adults and the judge offered a toast to everyone's good health and continued happiness. I was impressed with the way he could imbue his voice with senatorial power. There was an immediate sense of authority and strength. He could bring seriousness to a gathering in seconds, I thought.

The appetizer was followed with delicious cream of asparagus soup. While we ate, the judge discussed the local political scene and the fall elections. The adults listened attentively, as if they were party to classified information.

After the soup came a mixed salad of baby field greens and walnuts sprinkled with feta cheese in a raspberry vinaigrette dressing. That started everyone talking about the price of fresh produce, but to me it seemed that money problems were the smallest of worries for this family.

I was surprised when we were served a small ball of orange sorbet. Was the meal over and was this dessert? I wondered. The judge saw the confusion in my face and laughed.

"I don't think your granddaughter is familiar with this culinary custom, Olivia," he said.

"How could she be, growing up in the back hills of West Virginia. The sorbet's meant to cleanse your palette. You know what your palette is?"

"Yes," I said sharply. I glanced at Cary who was scowling at Grandma Olivia. She caught the look on his face and turned back to the judge to talk about the race for governor.

All the kitchen staff and the butler served the entrée, which consisted of roasted quails with wild rice and baby vegetables. There were servants all around us, replacing silverware, fixing napkins, pouring wine and water. One of the servants appeared to be assigned to Grandma Olivia only. The moment she started to reach for something, the maid was there to get it for her. It was truly an overwhelming feast, capped with a dessert that brought an exclamation of delight from the judge.

"Your favorite," Grandma Olivia announced.

It was crème brûlée — something I had never seen nor tasted before. The moment I did, I knew why the judge loved it so.

"Good, isn't it?" he asked me.

"Yes, sir," I said.

"Nothing wrong with enjoying rich things occasionally," he said. "Is there, Jacob?" he asked, enjoying teasing my uncle. I had to admit, I enjoyed seeing him do it.

"As long as you know whom to thank for them," Uncle Jacob said.

"Oh, I do. Thank you, Olivia, Samuel," he said and laughed. My grandpa joined him, but Grandma Olivia shook her head as if he were behaving like a naughty little boy.

"Really, Nelson," she said chidingly.

"I'm just kidding, of course. No one is more thankful than I for my good fortune. I only regret Louise couldn't be with me longer," he added, losing his smile for a moment.

"We all miss her," Grandma Olivia said.

"Thank you, Olivia."

Coffee was served. Cary and I were permitted some. I had never tasted French vanilla coffee, either, but I didn't want to appear as unsophisticated as Grandma Olivia was making me out to be, so I sipped it as if I drank it every day.

When the meal ended, Grandpa suggested brandy and cigars in the parlor.

"This is when we could have heard that fiddle concert," the judge remarked, his eyes glittering at me.

"I could still go fetch it," Cary offered.

"By the time you returned, it would be too late," Grandma said. "Another time."

Cary looked disappointed, but I was relieved. I would have hated to perform before such a critical audience.

"You children amuse yourselves, but do not go out and then track in mud, Cary," she warned.

As the judge passed me, he leaned over to say, "I'll hear that fiddle yet." He winked and followed my grandparents and Uncle Jacob and Aunt Sara out of the dining room. The staff began to clear the table.

"You want to walk on the beach or just sit on the porch in the back?" Cary asked me.

I thought a moment.

"I'd like you to take me downstairs again and show me more of the pictures," I said. He smiled.

"I had a feeling you were going to ask me to do that." He signed to May, who looked excited about the idea. Cary fetched Grandpa Samuel's flashlight. We went out the rear of the house.

We didn't need the flashlight to walk around the outside of the house. The moon was fuller and brighter than ever, turning the ocean into silvery glass and making the sand glimmer like tiny pearls. I could see the horizon clearly delineated against the inky night sky in the distance.

"No wonder ancient people thought they would fall off the earth if they sailed out too far," I said. "It looks so flat." Cary nodded. I took May's hand as he led us around the corner of the house to the basement door.

"Don't let her get her dress dirty," he warned, "or there'll be hell to pay."

I signed the same to May as Cary opened the basement door. He turned on the flashlight, found the light switch for the single dangling bulb, and then beckoned us to follow. Because the shadows were so deep, we still needed the flashlight to find the cartons and sift through them.

"Easy," Cary said when he brought one off the shelf. "The dust is thick. You'll get it all over yourself."

I didn't care about that when I started to dig into the pile of pictures.

"You really do look a lot like your mother did when she was your age, Melody," Cary said. "And you're just as pretty."

I glanced at him and saw how intently he stared at me. May stood by my side as I squatted beside him. We were inches apart and the glow of the flashlight made his eyes glimmer.

"No I'm not," I said. "I could never win a beauty contest."

He laughed. "Sure you could, and I'm sure you will."

"You're beginning to sound like Adam Jackson," I said.

His warm smile evaporated. "I didn't mean to," he snapped.

"I just meant that was the kind of thing he was telling me."

Cary nodded and gazed down at the pictures. "Well," he said softly, "the difference is he didn't mean it. I do."

I kept a smile to myself as I sifted through the photographs. Under the ones I had seen before, were earlier pictures of Mommy and Daddy in boats, on the beach, on swings behind the house. Uncle Jacob was in most of the pictures, too, but he always seemed to be off to the side or even a little behind Daddy and Mommy. I found their high-school graduation pictures and could see how Mommy had developed into the beautiful woman she now was.

She was photogenic: the pictures all caught her in funny, happy poses. I imagined it was Daddy who had taken the pictures, but when I turned one of them over, a picture of Mommy in a bikini posing on the beach, I saw the initials K.C. and the date.

"What does this mean?" I asked Cary. He gazed at it a moment and then smiled.

"Oh, I bet that's Kenneth Childs. Here." He pulled another album from the stack and searched through its pages. He pointed to a picture of a good-looking young man, his arms folded across his chest, leaning against an apple tree. His light brown hair fell loosely over his forehead and lay in long strands down the sides and back of his head. He wasn't smiling. He looked serious, almost angry. "That's him. He doesn't look all that different now. He still has long hair, only he keeps it in a ponytail."

"He does?"

"Uh-huh. Sometimes he wears an earring."

"I don't believe it," I said. "Judge Childs's son?"

"Kenneth is an artist," Cary said. "He can do whatever he wants and get away with it."

I nodded, wide eyed. Cary flipped the pages until he found another picture of Kenneth Childs. In this one, he was at least sixteen or seventeen. He was taller, but his face hadn't changed all that much. He still had long hair and I thought I saw an earring in his left earlobe. He was dressed in a pair of jeans and just a vest with no shirt underneath it.

"Any more pictures of him?"

Cary shook his head.

"He was the one who used to take the

pictures. My father told Laura and me that once."

I stared at Kenneth's photo a moment longer. Then I gazed at the other pictures in the album. There was a really nice one of my daddy and mommy when they were in high school. They sat on a bench in a gazebo, Daddy's arm around her. She had her knees pulled up, her arms around them, and her head was back against his. There was a rose in her hair. Her face was radiant. Daddy looked as happy as I had ever seen him.

"I like this one," I said.

"Do you?" He gazed at the photograph. "They were good looking. Why don't you just take the picture?" Cary suggested.

"Really?"

"Who's going to know?" He shrugged. I looked at May and then ripped the picture from the page.

We looked for a while longer. There were pictures of relatives I had never heard of. Finally, we came to a set of pictures of a mousy-looking woman who continually looked as if she were going to burst into tears.

"And who's this?" I asked.

"That's Grandma Olivia's younger sister," Cary said.

"Really? I didn't see any pictures of her in the house. Does Grandma Olivia have any brothers?"

"No."

"Where does her sister live?" I asked.

He paused as if to decide whether or not to tell me. "She's in some sort of hospital."

"Hospital?"

"She's not —" He pointed to his temple and shook his head.

"She's in a mental hospital?"

"Yeah, I guess. She had a drinking problem and other problems. We don't talk about her much. Grandma Olivia doesn't even like anyone asking about her."

"How terrible."

"I guess so," Cary said. "She was brought here for a little while years and years ago, but she couldn't handle life on the outside. I really don't know much about her," he added.

"What's her name?" I stared at the small-featured woman holding herself as if she thought she might fall apart.

"Belinda," Cary said.

"What a nice name. What's wrong with her?" I looked closer at the photographs. In one she looked more comfortable, even pretty. "I mean, why did she have a drinking problem and other problems? Did anyone ever mention that?" I asked.

"No, not really. I once heard my father say she laughed after everything she said and looked at every man as if he were her long-awaited prince, no matter how old or what he looked like."

"How sad," I said. I studied her face a moment longer and then turned the pages. I hated having to admit it, even to myself, but Grandma Olivia had been pretty when she was younger. Grandpa Samuel was always a good-looking man. As I perused these family pictures that captured moments like birthdays, parties, afternoon outings on boats and on the beach, I wondered about Mommy's childhood. There must have been happy times living in these rich, comfortable surroundings. How I wished she had told me more about them. How I wished there had been an earlier end to the lies.

May was getting fidgety and Cary was afraid she would get dirty moving around the basement so much, so we put the pictures back. I held onto the photo of Mommy and Daddy and we left the basement. We were surprised to find the butler on the back porch, searching for us.

"Oh, there you are. Good," he cried when he saw us coming. "I was sent to fetch you. It appears Mrs. Logan is somewhat under the weather and your father wants to take you all home."

"Ma's sick?" Cary said. He hurried on ahead of May and me.

Aunt Sara had apparently been struck with an upset stomach, and while we were down in the basement, she had spent most of the time in the bathroom throwing up her rich, delicious supper. Uncle Jacob looked distraught and angry.

"Where have you been?" he snapped. "We're going home. Your mother's got the heaves."

"What happened?"

"I don't know."

A maid helped Aunt Sara from the bathroom.

"I'm sorry," Aunt Sara wailed. "I've ruined everyone's good time. I'm sorry, Olivia," she said from the doorway. Grandma Olivia was sitting on the settee, alone in the sitting room. The judge and Grandpa Samuel had been banished outside to smoke their cigars. Grandma Olivia had accused them and their smoke of turning Aunt Sara's stomach.

"Men and their filthy habits," she remarked. "Get her some fresh air, Jacob."

"Right, Ma. Say good night and thank you," he muttered at us. Cary paused in the doorway first and did so. Then May followed, signed, and smiled. Grandma Olivia closed and opened her eyes as a response. They followed Uncle Jacob and I paused.

"What's that in your hand?" she demanded before I could utter a word. Apparently, she had eyes like an eagle.

"An old picture of my mother and father," I replied.

"So Cary's taken you into the basement,"

she said nodding. I thought she was going to become furious. That, on top of everything else, would turn Uncle Jacob into a volcano. However, Grandma Olivia just sighed deeply and shook her head. "I don't know why, but he and Laura used to love spending the most beautiful afternoons in that hole under the house." She caught herself and grew stiff again. "You better hurry along. Sara needs to go to bed."

"Yes, Grandma." My heart was pounding. Cary, May, and Uncle Jacob were at the door following the maid and Aunt Sara out of the house. "I was wondering," I said quickly, so I could hold on to my courage, "if I could come by to see you by myself."

"See me?" She pulled her head back. "When?"

"As soon as possible. Tomorrow after school?"

She looked amused by the idea and then stiffened her lips. I was sure she was going to brush me off, but she turned toward the wall and said, "I'll be in my garden tomorrow afternoon."

"Thank you, Grandma Olivia," I said. "I'm sorry about Aunt Sara." She turned back to me and I forced a smile and hurried after everyone.

Grandpa Samuel and the judge were standing off to the side watching the maid escort Aunt Sara to the car. The smoke from their cigars spiraled into the night.

"Just give her some bicarbonate, Jacob," Grandpa Samuel said.

"That's what comes of a steady diet of plain and simple food, Jacob. Take your wife out for a restaurant meal once in a while," the judge suggested with a grin.

"Feed her poison so she gets used to it? No thank you," Uncle Jacob said.

The judge roared. He looked at me. "Good night, Little Haille," he said. "Don't forget to practice that fiddle."

We got into the car. Aunt Sara had her head back. The maid had given her a wet cloth to put over her forehead.

"I'm sorry, Jacob," she said. "It just all started bubbling in my stomach."

"Let's not talk about it, Sara. It will only make it worse." He drove home as quickly as he could.

For the whole ride back, May sat forward holding Aunt Sara's hand and looking concerned. Cary tried signing that she would be all right, but May remained near tears until we got Aunt Sara into the house and into bed.

Finally, my aunt's color returned and she told us she was more comfortable. She kept apologizing to Uncle Jacob, who finally said it was all right. He thought the food was too rich and admitted he had a hard time holding it down himself.

"Get some sleep now," he declared. May kissed her mother good night and we left the bedroom.

"I'm just going to listen to some news on the radio," Uncle Jacob told Cary. "See that your sister gets to bed."

"Aye," Cary said. He turned to me and I helped him get May into her room and calmed enough to go to sleep. Afterward, we paused awkwardly in the hall.

"I wonder what happened to the whale on the beach," I said.

"Let's change and go see," he suggested.

About ten minutes later, both of us were in jeans and sneakers.

"Where are you going?" Uncle Jacob called from the living room.

"To see about that beached whale," Cary said. "Be right back."

"Make sure you are," Uncle Jacob warned.

We hurried out of the house and over the beach. The absence of a crowd of people indicated something had occurred. When we drew nearer, we saw the whale was gone.

"Coast guard must have come and dragged her out to sea," Cary said.

"Think it's all right?" I gazed over the dark water.

"Either she swam off or sank where they unhitched her," he commented with characteristic Cape Cod bluntness.

"At least she won't be victimized by cruel people."

"Yeah," he said. Even in the darkness, I could feel his eyes on me. "You sure look a lot like your mother in those pictures."

"Thank you," I muttered, looking down at the sand. Then I took a deep breath of the fresh salt air. "I guess I'll catch up on my reading for social studies," I said.

"Catch up? I bet you mean go ahead."

"Something like that," I confessed, and he laughed. "I'll try to see all your teachers and get them to give me your work so you don't fall behind."

"Whatever," he said.

We started back to the house. I walked with my arms folded over my breasts, my head down. Above us, the night sky burst with stars, but I felt afraid to look up, afraid I would be hypnotized and spend all night standing on the beach.

"Say," Cary said, "would you . . . would you like to see my model ships?"

"Up in the attic?"

He nodded.

"Sure."

When we entered the house, we heard a voice on the radio droning about sin and damnation. Both of us peeked into the living room and saw Uncle Jacob slouched down in his chair, asleep, and snoring almost as loudly as the radio. Cary put his finger on

417

his lips and smiled. We walked up the stairway quietly and he pulled down the ladder
to the attic.

"Careful," he said as I started up after him.
He reached down to help me make the last
few steps.

It was smaller than I had thought. On my
earlier quick look, I hadn't seen how the roof
slanted on both sides of the room. He had a
table on which he worked on his model
ships. The completed ships were lined up on
a half dozen shelves. It looked as if he had
done a hundred or so different models. To
the right was a cot and on the left were boxes
and sea chests.

"Careful," he said when I stood up, "Watch
your head." The roof slanted sharply, so I
had to move forward to stand up straight.
"This," he said, going to the shelves, "is my
historical section. They go left to right
chronologically. This is an Egyptian ship."
He lifted it gingerly and held it in front of me.
"About three thousand B.C. It has a double
mast, joined at the top, from which the sails
are hung."

He put it back and lifted another.

"This is Phoenician. They were better ship-
builders. It's called the round boat, one of
the first to depend mostly on sails rather
than oars, and as you can see, it has a larger
cargo space."

I saw how serious he was when he talked

about his ships. His face filled with enthusiasm and brightened. His voice was full of energy and he talked so fast and so much, I was overwhelmed, but I tried to keep up.

He went through the Greek and Roman models, showed me a Norse vessel that he said was used to invade England. He had even constructed a Chinese junk. He said that although it was still used, it lacked three components regarded as fundamental to ships: a keel and stem and stern posts. He lectured and illustrated everything on his models, but I saw that he was most proud of his sailing ships.

"This," he said in a low, breathy voice, "is a replica of the *H.M.S. Victory*, the flagship of the British admiral Horatio Nelson."

"It's beautiful, Cary."

"Isn't it?" He beamed. He put it back carefully and lifted another. "This was Laura's favorite," he said, "the American clipper. This is a replica of the *Great Republic*, built in 1853. These ships set records for transatlantic crossings."

"The parts are so tiny. How do you do it?"

"With great patience," he said laughing. "I renamed this *Laura*," he said and showed me where he had carefully engraved her name on the side. He held it a moment longer and then put it back lovingly on the shelf.

"I've got a lot more here: steamships, container ships, tankers, and of course, luxury liners. Know what this one is?" he asked, holding it up.

"I'm not sure," I said.

"It's the *Titanic*."

I shook my head in amazement.

"You know so much about ships, Cary. You should do better in history."

He grimaced. "One thing has nothing to do with another."

"Did you ever make a report on ships?"

"Yes," he said. "I got an A but I had so many spelling and writing errors, the teacher reduced it to a C."

He put the model back and went to the small window where he had a pair of binoculars.

"Laura and I used to spend a lot of time right here gazing out at the ocean," he said. He handed the binoculars to me when I stepped up behind him and I looked out at the ocean. Way in the distance, I saw a small light.

"What is that?"

"A tanker, maybe heading for England or Ireland. We used to love to imagine where they were going or imagine ourselves on them." He smiled to himself. Then he sat on the cot. "Laura and I spent a lot of time up here. She would lie on this cot and read or study while I worked on my models." He grimaced. "Then she stopped spending time up here after she started going with Robert Royce." His face grew angry.

"She just got interested in boys, Cary. It wasn't weird for that to happen," I said softly.

"Yeah, well, he wasn't the right one."

"How can you be certain?"

"I just am," he said. He had his eyes squinted shut as if trying to drive out some scene scorched on his brain.

I turned to look out the window again. "Then why did you let them use your boat?" I asked with my back to him.

"Laura was a good sailor, almost as good as I am," he said. "She wanted it."

I turned around and looked at him.

"I never said no to Laura," Cary said sadly. "If only I had . . . just that once." He looked at the floor so I wouldn't see the tear escape from his eye.

"I'm sorry." I was close to tears myself. I gazed at the ocean again. It could be beautiful and so deadly. "To lose her like that. It's as if she just disappeared."

"No," he said, so softly at first I thought I imagined it. But when I turned back, he repeated it. "No. It wasn't really that way."

"What do you mean, Cary?"

He stared at me a moment. "I've shared this with no one, not even my parents."

I held my breath.

"After Laura and Robert failed to return, I

borrowed a friend's boat and went looking for them. I looked every day for nearly a week, combing the beach, getting so close to the rocks at times, I nearly crashed into them myself. Then one day something caught my eye."

"What?" I asked, my heart pounding.

He rose and went to one of the chests. He opened it, dipped his hand into it, and came up with a pink silk scarf. "She liked wearing this around her neck when she sailed. I found it floating in the water."

"Why didn't you show your mother?"

"I wanted to keep the hope alive, and then I felt so guilty about not showing it, I never told. It doesn't matter any more. She's accepted the grave. Laura's gone."

I felt the hot tears streaming down my cheeks.

"You're the first person who I thought would understand," he said. He gazed at the scarf and then brought it to me. "I want you to have this."

"Oh no, I couldn't."

"Please, take it and wear it," he said. He pushed it into my hands.

"Thank you," I said softly. "I'll take good care of it."

"I know." He raised his head and our eyes locked. The depths of his pain made me forget my own.

We heard Uncle Jacob coming up the

stairs below. He paused at the attic stairway and then he plodded on to his bedroom and closed the door.

"I'd better go down," I said.

He nodded.

"I'm going to see Grandma tomorrow," I told him. If he could trust me with his deepest secrets, I could trust him, I thought.

"Why?"

"To get her to tell me everything. I'm going after school."

"Do you want me to be there too?"

"No. I've got to speak to her myself. But thanks."

"Remember, her bark's worse than her bite."

"Good night, Cary. Thanks for showing me your models."

He smiled and then abruptly, awkwardly, he planted a kiss on my cheek.

"Careful going down," he said as I lowered myself on the ladder. After I reached the bottom, I looked up at him.

"Good night," I said.

"Good night."

He lifted the ladder as if he wanted to lose all contact with the world below and then he closed his attic door and shut himself up with his memories and his own voices.

Clutching Laura's silk scarf in my hand, I went into her room and prepared for my own dreams, filled with my own memories and voices.

We were alike, Cary and I, haunted by lies and sadness, two sailboats drifting, looking for a friendly wind.

16

Daddy Who?

Although Cary had been suspended from school, he was up and ready to escort May and me the next morning. He carried my books since he didn't have to carry any of his own. It was gray and overcast when we started out. The mist was so thick, we couldn't see very far ahead of us. It was like walking through clouds.

"It will burn off by early afternoon," Cary promised. Despite his being punished for attacking Adam Jackson in the cafeteria and Uncle Jacob and Aunt Sara's disappointment with him, Cary was uncharacteristically animated. He talked continuously, permitting only a few seconds of silence to linger between us. It was as if he thought that silence would make us think and thought would make us sad.

He was especially excited about his plans to build his own sailboat this summer. For now he had to use his father's.

"I've had enough practice building the

models, eh?" he said. He was thinking he might even get into the leisure boat-building business someday.

"I can't depend on the lobster and fishing industry," he explained. "Someday I'm going to be responsible for more than just myself," he added.

I held May's hand and listened, a small smile on my face, as I looked down and walked. Cary continued to voice his plans. He wanted a home just outside the village and he wanted a garden and, of course, his own dock. He would raise a family with at least four or five children and he would take trips to Boston and maybe even New York.

"Provincetown is a good place to raise a family," he assured me. "It really is. I mean, it takes a lot longer for the bad stuff to get up here, and when it does, it can't hide as well as it can other places. Know what I mean?"

I nodded, but before I could speak, he added, "I knew you would. You're so much smarter than the girls around here, and I don't mean just book smart. You have common sense."

"Thank you," I said.

He smiled, sucked in his breath, and looked at the fog.

"It will clear but rain's coming later tonight. I can smell it."

After we brought May to her school, he

insisted on continuing on with me.

"Just to be sure you're okay," he explained.

When we arrived at school, he glared back furiously at any of the students who gazed at us with gleeful smiles on their faces. They turned away immediately and hurried into the building as if to escape freezing cold temperatures.

"You just tell me if anyone bothers you, Melody. Don't let them torment you in any way, hear?"

"I won't."

"I'll be here after school to check on you."

"But I told you I was going to see Grandma Olivia," I reminded him. His eyes grew small with worry and disappointment.

"I know, but I'll just check anyway before you go," he insisted. He gave me my books.

"What are you going to do?"

"I'll work on the plans for my boat," he said. "My father won't let me help him with any-thing when I'm in trouble, as if I might contaminate him." He sounded critical of his father for the first time. "People who've done wrong bring bad luck. Well . . ." He hesitated, looking at the front entrance to the school.

"I'll be fine, Cary. Stop your worrying." I squeezed his hand and rushed into the building. When I turned at the door, he was still standing there, looking after me.

Most of the students kept their distance in the hallway, all gazing at me with some interest. Theresa met me at my locker.

"How did it go for Cary at home?" she asked.

"Not well. My uncle Jacob was very angry. Actually, he's just as angry at me."

"It wasn't his fault or yours. You tell them that?"

"Yes."

"I like Cary," she said. "At least he doesn't put on a phony face," she added, loud enough for some of the girls to hear. Janet, Lorraine, and Betty walked by quickly, just giving me a passing glance.

This day I concentrated only on schoolwork, even though I sensed there was a good deal of whispering and note passing going on behind me. There was just one critical moment in the cafeteria after I entered. The jabber lowered and all eyes were on me for a few seconds. Theresa came up and began talking to me. Then the din in the cafeteria rose again and everyone appeared to go back to his or her business. It left me feeling I had swallowed a spoonful of nails.

Theresa told me that Adam Jackson had tried to recoup his reputation by telling everyone Cary's actions just proved him right. But he stayed away from me, not even glancing in my direction. Toward the end of the school day, I had the distinct sense that everyone had grown tired and bored with this scandal. Some of the students in my classes who had often talked to me about the work did so again. I felt more relaxed and at ease moving through the corridors.

All of Cary's teachers were glad to give me assignments for him, and every one of them said he or she felt Cary could do better if he only tried or cared. Mr. Madeo winked at me and said he was sure Cary would pass his English final if his tutor would stand by him.

"I'll see to it she does," I told him.

True to his word, Cary was waiting after school, his hands in his pockets, his hair over his forehead, his face drawn in a scowl, right at the entrance to the school when the bell rang ending the day.

"Everything's fine," I told him immediately. "It's over, forgotten."

"Sure."

"It is. Here." I thrust the pages of assignments in his hands. "This is your schoolwork, Cary Logan, and I expect you will do it even though you're not attending classes."

He gazed at the papers and then looked up at me and smiled. "You'll make me an A student yet, eh?"

"You'll do it yourself."

We started away and at the end of the street, we paused because I was going to walk to Grandma Olivia's.

"It's not a short walk," he warned. "If I hadn't gotten suspended, my father would

429

have let me use the pickup and I could have taken you, but —"

"I know how far it is. I'll be all right. I want to do it. I have to do it," I said. He nodded and kicked a stone across the macadam.

"You sure you don't want me along?"

"Cary, you have to see to May," I told him.

"She can make her way home alone if she must."

"I once said that and you nearly bit my head off."

He smiled. "I did. I remember. All right, go on, but don't get upset and —"

"Mr. Worry Wart, stop it!" I ordered.

"All right."

I started away.

"Her bark's worse than her bite!" he shouted after me.

"So's mine," I shouted back. He watched me walk off for a while and then he went to fetch May.

It was a long walk, and when I broke out to the main highway, it was harder, because the cars were whizzing by, some so close I felt the breeze in their wake lift my hair. Suddenly, an elderly man driving a rather beaten up light orange pickup truck stopped.

"You shouldn't be walking on this highway," he chastised.

"I have no other way to go," I said.

"Well, get in and I'll drop you off. Come on. My wife would give me hell if she heard I let a young girl walk along here."

I smiled and got into the truck. The seat was torn and there was a basket of what looked like seashells on the floor of the cab, along with all sorts of tools.

"Don't worry about any of that stuff. My granddaughter likes to make things with seashells," he explained.

He had gray stubble over his chin and the sides of his jaw, and his thin gray hair ran untrimmed down the sides of his temples and the back of his head, but he had kind blue eyes and a gentle smile. He reminded me of Papa George. Papa George, I thought, how I missed him.

"So where are you heading with your sails up like that?" he asked.

"My grandparents' house, the Logans," I told him, and his eyes widened.

"Olivia and Samuel Logan?"

"Yes," I said.

"I heard their granddaughter was deaf."

"I'm a different granddaughter."

"Oh. Didn't know. Course, I don't keep company with your folks. I worked for your grandfather once a long time ago. Built a tool shed for him. Paid me on time, too," he added. His truck rumbled along about half the speed of the cars that flew by us, but he didn't care. "Everyone's in a mad rush," he muttered. "Chasing the almighty dollar, but they miss the good stuff along the way."

He smiled at me and then he grew serious as though the thought just crossed his mind.

"You're Chester's little girl?"

"Yes, sir."

"What ever happened to him? No one seemed to know much about him after he left here with your mother."

"He was killed in a coal mine accident," I said, my throat choking up immediately.

"Coal mine? Is that what he left here to do? I never could understand . . ." He gazed at me a moment and saw the sad look on my face. "Sorry to bring it up. Didn't know," he muttered awkwardly. Then he turned into a concerned grandparent again. "I'm surprised to see Samuel Logan lets his granddaughter walk along this crazy highway."

"I just decided to do it on my own," I said quickly.

He nodded, but his eyes remained suspicious. "That's it ahead," he said.

"I know. Thank you."

He stopped and I got out and thanked him again.

"Now you don't walk that highway no more, hear?"

"Yes sir," I said.

"I'm sorry about your father. I just knew him when he was younger, but he seemed

432

to be a fine young man."

"Thank you."

"Bye," he said, and drove off.

I sucked in my breath, straightened my shoulders, reaffirmed my determination, and walked up the driveway to my grandmother's home. Before I reached the front door, a dark-skinned man of about fifty or so came around the corner of the house, pushing a wheelbarrow.

"You looking for Mrs. Logan?" he asked.

"Yes."

"She's around back in the vegetable garden," he said.

I thanked him and went to the rear of the house, where Grandma Olivia was on her knees in her fenced-in garden. She was dressed in a pair of old jeans and she wore a flannel shirt and work gloves. She had a wide-brimmed hat with a few fake carnations sticking up in the rear of it. I was so shocked to see her looking so casual, I paused to watch her dig out weeds. The contrast between the woman who reigned like a queen in the elegant house and this woman with her hands in dirt, wearing old and tattered clothing, was so great, I thought I was looking at a stranger.

She sensed me behind her and turned. "Hand me that iron claw there," she ordered, pointing to a pile of tools nearby. I hurried to do so. "Careful where you step," she said.

"I don't want to lose any of those carrots." She took the tool from me and scratched the earth around a tomato plant. "You walk all the way?" she asked as she worked.

"No, Grandma. Some kind old man in a pickup truck stopped to give me a lift."

"You were hitchhiking?"

"Not exactly."

"You always get into trucks with strangers?"

"No."

She paused and wiped her forehead.

"It's going to rain tonight," she said with the same tone of voice Cary had used when he made his weather prediction. "We need it. I had a better garden last year."

"It looks nice."

She shook her head and stood up. Then she pointed to a small table. There were a mauve ceramic pitcher and some glasses on it.

"You want some lemonade?" she asked.

"Yes, thank you."

She poured me a glass and a glass for herself. Then she sat and looked up at me as I drank.

"All right, you've come to see me. Why?" she demanded.

My lemonade caught in my throat for a moment. I took a deep breath and sat across from her.

"I want to know the truth about my parents," I said. "I'm tired of not knowing the truth and knowing only lies."

"That's good. I can't countenance a liar, and goodness knows, this family's had more than its share of them. All right," she said sitting back. "What is it you want to know?"

"Why do you hate my father so? He was your son."

"He was my son until she stole him from me," Grandma Olivia said.

"But I don't understand that. You adopted my mother, right? You wanted her in your home."

She looked away for a moment.

"That was something I couldn't help. I never wanted her in my home, but I had to have her."

"Why?" I pursued.

She turned back to me.

"Haille was my sister's illegitimate daughter," she said. "My sister was a spoiled, silly girl from the start. My father spoiled her and she grew up thinking anything she wanted, she could have. She couldn't tolerate waiting or disappointment. Her solution was to turn to alcohol and drugs. I always did my best to protect and shelter her from herself, and maybe I'm to blame as much as my father, but I made him a foolish promise on his deathbed: I promised to look after Belinda and see to her happiness."

Her sister was my grandmother? My mind

spun. I tried not to look overwhelmed for fear she would stop talking.

"What happened to your mother?" I asked.

"My mother was a weak woman herself. She couldn't face unpleasantness and always pretended it wasn't there. The truth was my father had three daughters, not two. My mother died of breast cancer. She ignored the diagnosis, just as she had ignored all bad news.

"Anyway, my sister became pregnant with your mother and I made the stupid mistake of having her here during the birth. I made the second mistake of not giving the baby away. My husband," she said bitterly, "thought that would be a horrible thing to do, and he reminded me of my oath to my father on his deathbed. So," she said with a deep sigh, "I took Haille into my home and raised her with my sons, something I'll regret until my dying day."

"Then Belinda is my grandmother?"

"Yes," she said with a nod and a twisted smile. "That wretch living in a home is your grandmother. Go claim her," she said. She looked as if she were going to end our conversation, so I repeated my original question.

"But why do you hate your own son, my father? Because he married his cousin and had me?" I ventured.

She regarded me with a cold, hard stare.

"You think you're old enough for the truth?" she challenged.

"Yes," I said, my heart pounding, my breath so thin I could barely utter the word.

"Your mother grew up here, had the best of everything. My husband spoiled her just the way my father had spoiled my sister. All Haille had to do was bat her eyelashes at Samuel and he'd do her bidding: buy her the dress and jewelry, permit her to go out when I had already said no and on and on. I warned him about her, but he wouldn't listen. She was the little girl I had never given him. Just like all men, he thought he was supposed to spoil his little girl. They confuse flooding them with gifts and their kisses of thanks and hugs as love.

"She had boyfriends. Dozens of boys marched through this house, followed her everywhere, came at her beck and call, groveled for her kisses. Every time I forbade something or punished her for something, Samuel overruled me, and what was the final result? The hand that fed her was bitten."

She paused. The telling of the story was exhausting her emotionally and physically. She sipped some lemonade and shook her head.

"What do you mean, the hand that fed her was bitten?" I asked after she had rested.

"Just like her mother before her, she slept around, and what do you think? She got pregnant, too. With you! Then she did the unforgivable thing." Grandma paused as if to get up enough breath and strength. "She blamed Samuel. She stood before me in this very house and claimed my husband, her stepfather, had slept with her and made her pregnant. Samuel was devastated, but I told him he deserved it for what he had done all those years."

I shook my head.

"I don't understand," I said, the tears filling my eyelids.

She laughed a wicked, short laugh.

"What's there to understand? She thought if she blamed Samuel, she could escape blame herself."

"But my daddy —"

"Your father, my son, turned on his own father. Chester turned on me," she said. "He took her side, believed her, actually believed his own father could have done such a thing. Can you imagine the heartbreak I endured, sitting there in that house and hearing my son tell me he believed that — that whore and not his own father? Can you? I told them both to get out, and as long as he took her side, to stay away. I told him I would have nothing more to do with a son who turned on his own parents that way. He knew Haille's background, but he . . . She beguiled

438

him, too, just as she beguiles everyone she touches.

"Jacob was heartbroken as well. He couldn't believe his brother would do such a thing. They had a terrible fistfight on the beach behind this house and never spoke again."

I shook my head.

"None of this can be true. Why did my mother bring me back here?" I cried through my tears. Grandma smiled and nodded.

"Why? She wanted to get rid of you, dear, and she knew about Sara's loss. Sara's always been a kind person. She was willing to take you in, and Jacob, God bless him for his kindness, too, wants to do nothing but what will make Sara happy again. Haille took advantage of someone in this family once more. It's that simple.

"I kept quiet about it," she continued. "After all, you are my sister's granddaughter, and, remembering the promise I made to my father on his deathbed, I didn't oppose it as long as I didn't have to set eyes on your mother."

I sat there, shaking my head. It had to be more lies, lies built on lies.

"My daddy never treated me as anything but his own daughter," I said. "He loved me."

"I'm sure he did. If he only had remembered his love for his mother and father as well," she said.

I stared at her, trying to make sense of it, slowly realizing what it meant if what she was saying was true.

"If my daddy thought that Grandpa Samuel was my father then . . . he knew he wasn't my daddy," I concluded.

"Precisely," Grandma Olivia said with some renewed energy. "And yet he still ran off with her, he still took her side and turned his back on his own mother and father."

"But . . . who is my father?"

"Take your pick. It could be anyone," she said dryly. "Maybe someday your mother will tell you, only the truth leaves a bitter taste in her mouth. She can't stomach it."

I continued to shake my head.

"I don't believe my daddy wasn't my daddy," I insisted.

"Suit yourself." Grandma Olivia sipped the rest of the lemonade in her glass. "You demanded I tell you the truth and I have. You said you were old enough and I believed you. If you want to continue living in a world of illusions and lies along with your mother, be my guest, only don't come around here accusing anyone of anything.

"What you should do," she said, standing, "is get your mother to come back for you and bear up to her own responsibilities. But I wouldn't get my hopes up." She gazed down at me. "As long as you behave, do as your told, pull your share, Jacob won't throw you out of his house. They tell me you really are a good student, so if you deserve it, I'll see that you get an education. I'll do it for my father, because of the promises I made."

"I don't want anything from you," I said bitterly.

She laughed a laugh that reminded me of glass shattering.

"In time, I'm sure you'll change your mind about that. Just make sure you don't do anything to change my mind about being generous," she warned, pointing her small, crooked little forefinger at me. "That includes making my son and his family unhappy. I'm going in now to wash up. If you want, I'll have Ralph, my handyman, take you home."

I sat there, my shoulders shaking, the sobs rattling my rib cage and throwing a terrific chill over me. I embraced myself.

"I don't have the time to stand here and watch you become hysterical," she said. "When you're finished, come into the house and I'll see to it you're taken home."

She started away. I looked out at the ocean. The heavier cloud cover was making its way toward shore and the wind had grown in intensity, lifting the whitecaps. For a few moments the monotonous way in which the ocean waves slapped the rocks hypnotized me. Terns screamed. I tried to shrink into that small hiding place in my brain where I could feel safe and unafraid, but that place felt like a cage.

I hate Cape Cod, I thought. I hate being here another moment. I rose quickly, but I walked slowly, pensively toward the front of the house. When I looked back, I thought I saw a curtain part and Grandma Olivia gaze out, but the sun dipped behind one of those heavy oncoming clouds, and the shadows that fell over the house darkened the window and, like black magic, changed it into a mirror.

When I reached the highway, I didn't turn toward town. For a long time, I just walked, feeling mesmerized. Cars and trucks whizzed by, but this time their closeness, the breeze in their wake, the loud horns that blared — none of them bothered me.

My daddy wasn't really my daddy. He could be anyone. Is that what Grandma Olivia had said, with spite? How could Mommy have left me drifting in such a hellish place? She really was selfish. I didn't want to believe the terrible things Grandma Olivia had said about her, but in my deepest soul I knew it all made sense. If I honestly faced up to what and who Mommy was now, I would have no trouble believing who and what she was back then. But to make such a disgusting claim, to blame my grandfather for my existence . . . I almost sided with Grandma Olivia and Uncle Jacob.

I don't know how long I walked or how far I actually had gone before I heard a continuous horn blaring and turned to see Cary in his father's pickup. He pulled to the side of the road behind me and hopped out.

"Where are you going? I've been crazy with worry. Everyone has, even Grandma Olivia."

"She told me the truth, Cary," I said.

The sky had become almost completely overcast. The wind was even stronger and the temperature felt as if it had dropped a dozen degrees. I had been shivering without even realizing it. Cary quickly peeled off his jacket and put it around my shoulders.

"Come home," he said.

I shook my head and backed away from him.

"That's not my home, Cary. Your father is not my uncle and your mother is not my aunt."

"What are you saying?" he asked, a confused, half-silly grin on his face.

"Just that. My daddy was . . . my daddy —"

"What?"

"He wasn't my daddy. Mommy was pregnant with me by someone else and she accused —" I had to swallow first before I could continue. "She accused Grandpa Samuel. Daddy believed her and that's why they stopped talking to him. Your father and — my —" It suddenly occurred to me who he was. "My stepfather had a fistfight on the beach and never spoke to each other again. You didn't know that?"

I saw from the expression on his face that he knew something.

"I knew that they'd had a fight, but I never knew why," he admitted.

"Why didn't you tell me that?"

"I didn't want you to hate us and leave," he confessed.

"Well, that's what I'm doing. I'm leaving this place." I turned and started away. He caught up and took me by the elbow.

"Stop. You can't just walk down this highway."

"And why not? I've got to go home," I said. "I've got to see Mama Arlene and Papa George."

"You're going to walk back to West Virginia?"

"I'll hitchhike," I said. "I'll beg rides. I'll do chores to get people to give me lifts or money for bus tickets. But I'll get home. Somehow, I'll get there," I said, my eyes seeing him, but looking beyond and seeing the old trailer house, Mama Arlene waving goodbye, Papa George smiling at me from his bed, and Daddy's grave, the tombstone I had hugged with all my heart before I was forced to leave. "Somehow," I muttered.

"Won't you come home and get your things first? Have a good meal?"

"I don't want to eat and I don't care about those things," I said. "Tell Aunt Sara I'll send this dress back first chance I get," I added and started walking again.

"Wait a minute, Melody. You can't do this."

I kept walking.

"Melody!"

"I'm going, Cary. Not you, not anyone can stop me," I said, full of defiance and anger. I walked and he was silent for a few moments. Then he caught up and walked alongside me. "Why are you doing this, Cary? You can't stop me."

"I know. I'm just thinking about it."

I stopped and turned to him.

"What do you mean?"

He thought and then nodded his head. "All right." He dug into his pocket and came up with a money clip stuffed with bills. "I'll drive you to Boston and give you the money you need for your bus ticket."

"You will?"

"Of course, I will. I'm not going to let you walk down Route Six and hitchhike, and I can see you are determined. Wait here. I'll go back and get the truck."

"But your father will be furious, Cary."

"It won't be the first time or the last, I imagine. He's already going to be mad about my taking the truck," he added and shrugged. "Don't worry about me."

He ran back to the truck and drove up to

me. I got in and we started down the highway.

"It's a long trip back to Sewell, West Virginia, Melody."

"I know, but it's the only real home I've ever known where there are people who love me."

"There are people who love you here," he said. He turned and smiled. "May and me for starters."

"I know. I'm sorry about May. You'll explain it to her. Please."

"Sure. But who will explain it to me?"

"Cary, it was horrible, sitting there and hearing the story and seeing Grandma Olivia's anger. I never felt more like an unwanted orphan," I explained.

He accelerated.

"She shouldn't have done that. She should have made something up, something more sensible, something that wouldn't have upset you this way."

"More lies? No thank you. I've been brought up with lies. I've eaten them for breakfast, lunch, and dinner. It's time for the truth. It's time to get back with people who don't know what lying is."

"Everyone lies, Melody, to someone else or to himself," Cary said.

Raindrops splattered on the windshield. I thought about him having to drive back alone.

"I feel terrible about you doing this, Cary."

"Don't. I would feel terrible not doing it," he said. "Tell me more about what Grandma Olivia said."

I recounted our conversation and he listened attentively, his green eyes growing darker and smaller.

"It makes some sense now, the whispers, the words I picked up here and there."

"It's terrible. I feel as if my insides will be tied into knots forever. I feel betrayed, fooled, Cary. The man who loved me and called me his princess wasn't really my daddy."

"Well, being a father doesn't have to be dependent on blood, does it? He was good to you, wasn't he? You never doubted he loved you. You told me."

I nodded, swallowing back my tears. "Still," I said softly, "it leaves me feeling . . . incomplete. You've got your family name, your heritage. It's so important to you and your family. I see that, even more than I saw it in West Virginia. I'm nobody. I'm Melody Nobody," I said laughing. He looked at me. I laughed harder. "Meet Melody Nobody." My laughter started to hurt and soon turned into tears, sobs that shook my shoulders so hard I thought I would come apart.

He pulled the truck to the side and stopped. Then he slid over and embraced me, kissing the tears off my cheeks and holding me tightly.

"Don't do this to yourself," he said.

I caught my breath and sucked in some air with deep gasps. Then I nodded.

"I'm all right. It's okay. I won't do that again. I promise."

"It's okay to do it as long as I can be next to you," he said, "but I hate to think of you alone out there, crying your eyes out with no one to comfort you, Melody."

"There'll be Mama Arlene," I said.

He stared at me a moment and then slid behind the wheel again. We drove on. Car headlights blinded us in the rain, but he drove relentlessly, firmly.

Cary talked me into stopping for something to eat. I did it for his sake more than my own, although the hot coffee helped and something warm in my stomach gave me needed energy. I lost track of time afterward and fell asleep with my head on his shoulder. When I opened my eyes again, he told me we were pulling into Boston and heading for the bus depot. I sat up and scrubbed the sleep from my cheeks with my dry palms.

Cary went into the bus station with me. We spoke with the ticket seller who, after we explained where I wanted to go, said the best ticket was one to Richmond. There was a shuttle service to Sewell, but he couldn't guarantee the schedule after I had arrived in Richmond.

"Once I get to Richmond, I'll be fine," I said.

Cary paid for the ticket and then insisted I take another fifty dollars.

"Somehow, I'll pay you back," I promised.

"You don't have to as long as you promise to call me from Sewell and then write letters."

"I'll promise you that if you promise me you'll pass all your tests and graduate."

"Big promise, but okay," he said. "You've convinced me to work harder." He smiled.

"That's the bus to Richmond now," the ticket seller announced.

Cary gazed into my eyes, his eyes full of sadness and fear for me.

"I'll be all right once I get home," I said. "Don't worry." He nodded.

"I wish that somehow you had come to think of Provincetown as your home."

"When you have no real family, home has to be where you find love," I said.

"You found it in Provincetown," he said indicating himself.

"I know," I whispered. I leaned toward him and kissed him softly on the cheek. "Oh," I said. "Your jacket." I started to take it off.

"No, please keep it."

"Thanks," I said.

He followed me out to the bus and watched me get on. After I sat at the window, he held up his hand.

"Good-bye," I mouthed through the glass. The bus driver started the engine. Cary's face seemed to crumple, his lips trembling. There were tears on his cheeks, and his tears put tears in my heart. I put my hand against the glass as if I could stop his crying by doing so. He raised his hand. The bus started away. He walked alongside it for a few feet and then the bus turned. He was gone.

I knew where he would go when he got home. He would go to his attic and he would curl up on his cot and he would think of Laura and me and wonder why all that was good and soft in his world seemed to slip through his fingers.

I closed my eyes and thought about Mama Arlene's smile and Papa George and Alice and the warm living room in my old trailer home.

Like a beacon in a storm, the light from those memories held out a tiny spark of hope.

17

There's No Place Like Home

I rode the bus all night. People got on and off at various stops, but I didn't take notice. I was vaguely aware that someone sat down next to me after one stop, but I curled up and fell back asleep. When I opened my eyes again, whoever it had been was gone. It wasn't until an hour or so later, when I was fully awake and moving around in my seat that I realized so was my purse. The shock of it put electric sparks in the air. I screamed so loud, the bus driver hit the brakes and pulled off for a moment.

"What is it? What's wrong back there?" he called. Everyone on the bus was looking my way.

"I can't find my purse with all my money in it," I wailed. It had been right at my feet and I had Cary's fifty dollars in it, the money that was supposed to get me home.

Someone laughed. Most people shook their heads. The bus driver snorted as if to say, "Is that all?" and started away. A small black woman with kind eyes sitting two rows down smiled at me. "You ain't much of a traveler, are you, honey?"

"No ma'am."

"You can't take your eyes off valuable things when you travel, honey. I wear my purse under my dress," she said. She shook her head in pity and turned away.

I sat there stunned and angry. How could someone be so cruel? Another voice inside me asked, "How could you be so stupid?" By now I should have known to trust no one, to depend on no one, to believe in no one. "Expect nothing and you'll never be disappointed," the little voice continued.

It was morning when we reached Richmond. I stepped off the bus, still dazed from the trip and from being robbed. I found my way through the depot and could only look longingly back at the ticket counter where I might have been able to purchase a ticket to Sewell. Now, I had to find my way to the right highway and hitchhike.

I was hungry, and even more so when I passed counters where people sat enjoying their breakfast. My stomach churned as the aromas of fresh rolls, bacon and eggs, coffee, and Danish pastries visited my nostrils. I was tempted to finish a chunk of discarded white bread I spotted on a bus depot bench, but the birds got there before me.

I hurried on, getting directions from a

gentleman in a gray suit who looked as if he were on the way to work. He was in such a rush he continued to walk as he shouted back the route I should take. I followed him like a fish on a hook. I listened to his directions and then shouted my thanks.

I walked along the street, my head down, my limbs still aching from the cramped position I had been in most of the night. At least it wasn't raining. In fact it looked as if it was going to be a nice day. Some time later I reached a turn in the road and a sign indicating the direction to Sewell. Cars flew by with the drivers glancing at me and my stuck-out thumb, but none so much as slowed down. Discouraged, I walked rather than just stand there and wait for another vehicle. Standing and waiting only reminded me how hungry and tired I was. Every time I heard a car, I spun around and jerked my thumb in the air, again with no success. One woman driving by glared at me with such disapproval I thought she might stop her car and get out and lecture me.

There was a lull, then another stream of vehicles. This time a light brown van with dents all over it slowed and pulled up just a few feet ahead of me. I hurried to catch up. When I looked into the van, I saw a man with a rainbow-colored headband. He had a straggly brown beard and wore dark sunglasses. An earring dangled from his right ear and he had a necklace made of what looked like bullet shells. His hair was dirty brown and long, but it looked as if he had either chopped it away from his ears himself or had an amateur do it. He wore a faded gray sweat suit.

"Where you headed?" he asked.

"Sewell."

"I'm not going there, but I'm going nearby," he said.

I thought for a second. The closer I got, the better it would be, I concluded.

"Thank you," I said and opened the door, but to my chagrin, there was no passenger seat.

"You'll have to crawl in back. Someone stole the seat last night," he explained.

"Stole your seat?"

"These seats are in demand and they're expensive. They sell them to chop shops," he said. "If you're coming along, get in. I got to make Jacksonville before nightfall."

I hesitated. No one else had stopped for me and I was tired. I decided to go so I stepped into the van and then crouched to go into the rear. There was a mattress with a ragged sheet placed sloppily over it, a pillow with no pillow case, and a thin, tattered wool blanket. Beside that was a small Sterno stove, some cans of food, packages of bread, cookies, jars of peanut butter, jelly, and jam. There was a pile of clothes to the right and two cartons filled with magazines.

He leaned over to close the door of the van.

"Just find a spot," he said. "You can sit on the bed."

He pulled away quickly and I nearly fell. I lowered myself gently to the mattress. There was the odor of stale food and general mustiness that came from someone living and sleeping in here for some time.

"What's your name?" he called back.

"Melody."

"Great name. You sing?"

"No."

"How come you're hitchhiking?"

"I had my purse stolen while I was on a bus."

"Boy, if I have heard that story once, I've heard it five hundred times. If you're hungry, nibble on anything you want," he said.

I gazed at the food, trying to decide what, if anything, looked clean enough to eat. I thought maybe a piece of bread and a little peanut butter might be all right.

"Thank you."

I dug deep into the package and came up with a slice of bread. It felt a few days old, but wasn't moldy. I wiped off a butter knife and dug out some peanut butter.

"How far you come?" he asked.

"I rode the bus from Boston, but I started out on Cape Cod."

"No kidding." He turned to look at me. "How old are you?"

"Almost seventeen," I said.

"What are you, a runaway?"

"No." I chewed and swallowed. "In fact, I'm going home," I said. He nodded with a skeptical smile.

"Ain't we all," he muttered, and put on some music. I saw him reach over and take something from the glove compartment. When he lit it, I recognized the sweet aroma. "Want a joint?"

"No thank you."

"Gotta stay cool in this world," he said. "Don't let the stress get to you. That's the secret." Then he began to sing it to the tune of "London Bridge is Falling Down": "That's the secret of my life, of my life, of my life, that's the secret of my life, my fair lady." He laughed.

I stopped eating and looked more closely at one of the cartons of magazines. The flap of one was open just enough for me to see what was on the magazine cover. It looked like a picture of a naked little boy.

"Are you in the magazine business?" I asked, realizing he had never told me his name.

"You might say I'm a distributor." He laughed. "But if you're only seventeen, you can't look at those." He turned and smiled. "Now you really want to look at them, right?

That's the way to get someone to buy into your concept — forbid them to do it. Stupid politicians," he mumbled.

His dark eyes were slick as oil, scary. My heart stopped and then started to thump. A clump of ice formed at the base of my stomach and telegraphed chills up and down my bones, making my hands and feet feel numb. I felt as if I couldn't move and the terror that had begun to take form, like some ugly beast in my brain, grew bigger and bigger with every passing second he stared back at me.

"I've been riding for hours myself," he said. "And I forgot to eat. I'll just pull over here and get something."

He slowed the van and turned off the road onto what felt like a gravel drive. I couldn't see the ground because I was so low down, but I did see some trees.

"Here we are, a safe spot," he said. He shut off the engine.

I couldn't swallow. I couldn't breathe. He got up slowly and turned into the rear of the van.

"How's the bread?" he asked sliding beside me.

"Fine," I managed. "If we're stopping, I'll just go out and get some air," I said.

He laughed.

"What's the matter, my house smells?"

I didn't reply.

"You look older than seventeen. I bet you can pass for nineteen, huh? I bet you've done that, gotten into places where you could drink, see X-rated movies."

I shook my head.

"Hey, I've been there," he said jabbing his thumb into his chest. "I understand. Don't worry." He puffed on his joint and then again offered it.

I shook my head. "No thank you."

"It's good stuff."

"No, thanks," I said. He shrugged.

"More for me." He puffed again.

"Can I get out?" I asked.

"Sure." He leaned back so I could get by him, but as I started past him, he flipped his joint into the front of the van and seized me at the waist.

I started to scream as he turned me around hard and slapped me back on the mattress.

"Come on," he said. "Stay inside. It'll be nicer." He laughed thinly.

"Let me go!" I tried to sit up, but he kept his weight on my shoulders and looked me over. The stink of his marijuana, mingled with the sour smell of his body and clothes, reeked down at me, churning my stomach.

"I can get you into a magazine," he said. "I know lots of photographers real well. You can make serious money."

"No thank you. Now let me up."

"Sure, only first you got to pay the fare."

"What fare?"

"I forgot to tell you. This is like a bus. You get on, you pay the fare."

"I have no money. I told you I was robbed."

"There's other ways to pay." He smiled, revealing uneven teeth streaked with green and brown stains.

He slid his hands over my breasts and then moved down to straddle my legs. Desperate and terrified, I found the glass peanut-butter jar and clutched it like a rock. While he explored under my skirt, I swung the jar with all my strength and struck him on the side of the head. The jar shattered, but it stunned him enough to drive him off me and I jumped up. He howled as I dove for the door. My hand found the handle just as his found the hem of my skirt. He tugged, but I flew forward and he lost his grip.

I stumbled from the van, quickly realizing we were a dozen or so yards from the road. When he appeared in the doorway, a streak of blood ran down the side of his face. I got to my feet and ran for the road, screaming for help.

He didn't follow. At the highway, I practically ran in front of an oncoming tractor trailer. The driver hit his horn as hard as he hit his brakes. I got across the road just in time, but his truck came to a stop.

The van backed out of the driveway and

spun around, kicking up gravel. It headed in the direction from which we had come.

The truck driver got out of his cab and strutted angrily toward me. He was a tall, stout man about fifty. "What do you think you're doing? Do you know you could have caused an accident and been killed? Who —"

"That man tried to rape me!" I cried, pointing to the disappearing van.

He stopped and looked after it.

"I got out and ran just as you were coming. I'm sorry." I gasped, trying to regain my breath.

"Who was he?" he asked.

"I don't know. I was hitchhiking."

"Hitchhiking?" He shook his head. "Where are all the parents in this country?"

I started to cry, the realization of what I had just escaped finally hitting me.

"All right, take it easy. Where are you going?" he asked.

"Sewell," I moaned through my tears.

"Is that where your parents live?"

"Yes," I lied.

"All right. Get in my truck. I'm going through Sewell. I'll drop you off. Even though I'm not supposed to take riders," he emphasized. My hesitation infuriated him. "Get moving if you want to get home," he ordered. I walked back with him and got in the truck. He checked the road, shifted, and started away, glancing at me with disapproval. "Don't you kids know how dangerous it is hitchhiking? Especially for a girl!"

"No, sir. I don't do it much, so I didn't know."

"Well, in a way I'm glad you got a good lesson," he said. After a few minutes, his anger subsided. "I've got a ten-year-old girl of my own and it's a battle today raising kids."

"Yes," I said. He glanced at me.

"How come you're so far from home all by yourself?"

"I —"

"You should be in school, right? You ran away, didn't you? And then you realized how good you had it back home and couldn't wait to get back, right?" he said with confidence.

I smiled to myself.

"Yes."

"Thought so. Well, at least you're okay now."

"Thank you," I said. I told him how I had been robbed on the bus and he felt sorry for me.

"There's some cold orange juice in that jug there if you'd like to pour yourself a cup."

"Thank you."

I did. As we bounced over the highway, I lay back. My heart began to beat normally and my body suddenly felt as if I had sunk into a warm bath. I closed my eyes. I heard him talking about his family, his daughter, his younger son, the crazy people on the highways. I must have fallen asleep out of emotional exhaustion, for the next thing I knew, he was poking me gently on the shoulder.

"We're coming into Sewell," he said, and I sat up. I never thought the sight of those hills and trees would be as wonderful as it was at that moment.

We passed the cemetery and rolled into the center of town. All the familiar stores, Francine's beauty parlor where Mommy had worked, the garage, the restaurants, filled my heart with warm joy. The truck driver noticed my happiness.

"You've been away a while, huh?"

"Yes, sir, I have. But I'm back."

"Well," he said, bringing the truck to a stop at a corner, "I got to continue, so I'll let you out. You think twice before you leave home again, young lady. No matter how bad things might seem to be, they're often worse someplace else, especially when you're alone."

"Yes, sir. Thank you," I got out of the truck. He nodded and I watched him drive away. Then I turned and looked at the village as if I couldn't drink it in enough. Some familiar faces turned my way and I waved, even to people who had never said hello to me before. Some waved back, some shook their heads in disapproval. I realized why. It was the middle of the day: I should be in school.

462

I started for the trailer home development, my heart pounding in anticipation. I couldn't wait to set eyes on Mama Arlene and have her set eyes on me. As I walked past the street that led to Daddy's mine, I felt a wave of sadness wash over my renewed jubilation. Going away and coming back didn't change the tragic facts. I climbed the hill that he took every day after work and I thought about how I would wait for him, anticipating, waving, calling him. I almost saw myself ahead, a little girl, excited because her daddy was returning home to sweep her up in his arms and flood her face with his kisses. How she longed for his laughter.

The entranceway to Mineral Acres looked no different, but when I turned up the street to Mama Arlene's, I paused. Her and Papa George's trailer was dark. Its small front patio was covered with fallen twigs, grass, and gravel, something Mama Arlene would never tolerate. I broke into a run and reached the trailer door quickly. It was silent inside. I rapped hard and called, "Mama Arlene! Mama Arlene, it's me, Melody!"

Silence greeted me. I pounded harder.

"Hey," I heard someone say. I turned and saw Mrs. Edwards, one of Mama Arlene's gin rummy partners. She was a woman of the same age. "What are you doing over there?" She came walking from her home. "Oh, Melody. I didn't know it was you."

"Hello, Mrs. Edwards. I was looking for Mama Arlene."

"You've been away," she said as if just remembering. "That's right. Well, dear, Arlene isn't here. She's gone, honey."

"Gone?"

"Gone to live with her sister in Raleigh. She left soon after George passed away."

"Papa George . . . died?"

"Didn't you know? Yes, I'm afraid so. He suffered so. It was for the best," she said, nodding. "Where's your mother, honey? She back, too?" she asked gazing past me.

"What?" I shook my head. I couldn't talk. Dead? Mama Arlene gone?

"Here comes that service man to fix my washing machine," she said, as a truck pulled into the development. "Only two hours late. I got to go see to him. Nice to see you back, honey. Say hello to your mother. Hey there! I'm here!" she called to the driver, who poked his head out of the truck window. She marched away and I turned back to the door of Mama Arlene and Papa George's trailer.

It can't be, I thought. They can't be gone. I peered through a front window and saw the furniture covered and the trailer dark. Disappointment weighed me down. My legs felt as if they were lead. I gazed at my old trailer house. It looked just as deserted.

Where would I go now? Who would I go to? I wondered, but I was too tired and to overwhelmed to care. I went to our old home and tried the front door. There was a For Rent sign on it. Of course it was locked, but all that had happened to me on the trip and the shock of this news put me into a frenzy. I searched the yard until I found a short metal rod, which I brought back to the door. I jabbed it into the small space between the door and the trailer and I pulled and tugged, shaking it and putting all my weight behind it until the door snapped open and I went flying back on the patio. I got up, threw the rod away, and went inside. One way or another I was home again, I thought.

Everything had been turned off in the trailer home: electric and gas, and even water. The cupboards were empty, the refrigerator door left open with nothing on its shelves. Someone, probably the bank, had come into the trailer and removed everything else.

After I had wandered through the trailer, I curled up on the ragged living room rug just about where the sofa had been. I didn't know the time. There were shadows in the corners and whispers in the walls. Time was as irrelevant as honesty, I thought. I lay there sobbing until I fell asleep again. The sound of someone calling my name woke me. I sat up, grinding the sleep from my eyes. The late-afternoon sun was blocked by some high clouds, so the trailer was dark and I could see only a shadowy silhouette in the doorway.

"Melody?"

"Alice!" I cried, so happy finally to hear a friendly, familiar voice. "How did you know I was here?"

"Your cousin Cary called me very late last night. He found my phone number in your notebook and remembered you had mentioned me as your best friend in Sewell."

"Cary?"

"Yes. He told me he put you on a bus and he was very worried that you would arrive safely," she said.

"I almost didn't," I replied and described my nearly disastrous adventure.

"Wow!" she said when I had finished. "You're lucky you got here, but . . ." She gazed around. "Is your mother supposed to meet you here?"

"No. I don't know where Mommy is, Alice," I wailed. I sat on the floor again and she sat beside me just the way we used to sit together on the floor of her warm room in her beautiful house.

"What do you mean, you don't know where she is? Didn't she call you? Didn't she tell you to meet her here? I don't understand," she said.

Finally, I told her my story.

With her eyes widening as I spoke, she absorbed it and then dropped her jaw in amazement and shock. "Chester Logan was not your father? And you don't even know who your real father is?" I shook my head. "What are you going to do?"

"I don't know. I ran away because I was hoping to live with Mama Arlene," I said. "I never heard about Papa George."

"I went to the funeral," she said. "Papa George is buried close to your . . ."

"I know. I don't know what to call him either." I sighed deeply. "I'll just keep calling him Daddy until I find out the truth about my real father."

"You must be starving. Come home with me and get something to eat," Alice urged.

"I am starving, but I know what your parents will say. No thanks, Alice."

"You can't stay here. This place doesn't belong to you anymore. It belongs to the bank."

"I'll stay until they throw me out, I guess. In the meantime, can you loan me some money? I'll buy some food."

She thought. "I know what I'll do. I'll go home and get some food for both of us. I'll tell my parents I'm studying chemistry with Beverly Murden and I'll come back here. I'll bring us some candles, too. It'll be like a picnic. Like the old days, okay?" she said with enthusiasm.

I laughed. How ironic. My predicament provided Alice with the most excitement she'd had in months.

"Okay," I said.

"Your cousin left me a telephone number so I could call to tell him whether you arrived safely. You want me to tell him anything else?"

"Just say thanks, but don't tell him about the other things. I don't want him to know how terrible my trip was, okay?"

She nodded.

"It will take me a little while to get everything together and get back."

"That's all right. I want to go to the cemetery to pay my respects to Papa George and visit my daddy's grave."

"You mean the man you thought was your daddy," she corrected.

"Yes."

"Okay. I'll meet you back here. I'll bring a radio that works on batteries so we can have music. I've got a lot to tell you about the kids at school. Bobby Lockwood's going with Mary Hartman."

"Okay," I said, trying to sound interested, even though it sounded very insignificant to me at the moment.

"I'm glad you're back, even if it's not for long," Alice said, squeezing my hand. "See you in about an hour."

She hurried from the trailer. I followed

soon afterward. The sky became more and more overcast, making everything gray and dreary by the time I arrived at the cemetery. It didn't take me long to find Papa George's fresh grave. Under his name were the dates of his birth and death.

"I'm sorry I wasn't here to see you one more time, Papa George. You were my real grandfather and will always be in my heart."

I kissed the top of his tombstone and then walked down the path to Daddy's. For a long moment I stood there, just looking at the familiar carving. Then I shook my head, the tears running down my cheeks.

"Why, Daddy? Why didn't you tell me the truth?" I glared at the grave. I wanted to be angry, to hate him, but all I could see was his smiling face, his warm eyes, his happiness at the sight of me.

"I'm all alone now, Daddy. I'm really all alone."

I knelt at his grave and said a prayer. I asked that he and Mommy be forgiven for anything terrible they might have done and I asked for mercy. Then I stood up and stared at the tombstone for a long moment until a funny thought came to mind.

"If Papa George is with you, he's bawling you out for sure, Daddy. I can almost hear him."

I sighed deeply and then walked back to Mineral Acres. Soon afterward, Alice arrived bearing bags of food and news.

"Your cousin answered the phone. He said he was waiting for my call all day. He sounds nice, Melody."

"He is. You didn't tell him any of the bad things, did you, Alice?"

"No," she said, but the way she lowered her eyes quickly told me otherwise. "He said he hopes you'll come back."

"You told him about Mama Arlene and Papa George then?"

"He asked me. You didn't tell me not to tell him that," she protested.

"It doesn't matter, I suppose."

She smiled and began to unpack. She had brought two candles and candle holders and we had to light them right away because the twilight — blocked by the heavy clouds — made it very dark in the dingy trailer.

"I didn't know what to bring," she said, "so I brought whatever I could."

Her leftovers included chicken, some cold pasta, fruit, cookies, bread, a jar of honey, tuna fish, and two bars of chocolate. The sight of food reminded me how very hungry I was. Alice, still quite overweight, didn't need any reminders or excuses. Whatever I ate, she ate. As we gobbled away, she related all the stories about the kids at school. She described Bobby Lockwood's new love affair as if it were the hottest relationship in America. Finally exhausted, she begged me to tell her about the students in Provincetown. I was reluctant to stir up the raw memories, but she pleaded and pleaded, telling me how unfair it was for me to have listened to her and not tell her anything. Finally, I gave in and described the last few weeks. She was glued to my every word.

The candles burned down. Darkness closed in around us and with it, the cool air.

"You should at least come to my house to sleep," she said. "You can come back here in the morning if you want. What are you going to do?" She fired her questions at me before I could think of a single idea.

Finally, something occurred to me. "How much money can you lend me, Alice?"

"I could manage to scrape up about a hundred and fifty dollars, maybe a little bit more. I know where my brother keeps some money in a drawer. He won't miss it."

"Good."

"What are you going to do?"

"I'm going to go to Los Angeles and find Mommy," I said.

"Wow." She thought a moment. "A hundred and fifty dollars won't be enough to get across the country, Melody."

"I'll get there. I got here, didn't I?"

She nodded.

"Okay. I'll give you the money."

"Thank you, Alice. You are my one true friend."

"Are you coming to my house to sleep?"

I gazed around the trailer. Even without furniture, it seemed like home again. I could easily imagine where everything had been and I could remember conversations and moments at practically every spot.

"No, I'll just curl up here. You'll get into trouble if your parents find me. I've made enough trouble for enough people."

"But," she gazed around, "can you sleep here?"

"Yes," I said. "I can. Cary's coat is pretty warm."

"All right," she said. "I'll get up a little earlier in the morning and come here with the money before school. I'll leave the radio with you for company."

"Thanks, Alice."

"I'm going to miss you all over again," she said.

"As soon as I get to Los Angeles and find Mommy, I'll write. Maybe you can come visit."

"Yes, maybe," she said, excited with the idea. "Okay. Good night, Melody."

"Good night."

She left, and the candles burned out, leaving me in the darkness, surrounded by memories of Daddy's voice and laughter, Mommy's voice and laughter. I softly wept for a while and then curled up and fell asleep.

I woke in the middle of the night when I thought I heard footsteps. My heart pounded as I gazed into the pitch blackness of Mineral Acres, half expecting to see Mommy emerge from the dark. Something scurried over the floor and I realized it was either a squirrel or a rat trying to work up enough nerve to get to the remnants of our picnic.

That thought made me uneasy and for the remainder of the night I woke up continually, listening and then falling asleep, only to wake up again. By the time the first light of morning came through the dirty, smudged windows, I was almost as tired as I had been when I first tried to sleep. Nevertheless, I rose and used the bathroom, even though the toilet didn't work. I had no choice.

I heard voices around the trailer, other people going to work or to town, so I remained hidden inside, quiet, waiting for Alice. She was true to her word and arrived before going to school.

"You don't look as if you slept too well, Melody," she said when she set eyes on me.

"I didn't."

"You should have come home with me. I worried about you all night. Anyway, here's the money," she said, handing me an envelope packed with bills.

"Thank you, Alice."

"Don't get robbed this time."

"I've learned my lesson, don't worry."

"Well, I better get to school."

"Don't tell anyone about me until I'm long gone," I asked.

"Okay."

We hugged.

"Don't forget to write as soon as you can," she reminded.

"I won't," I promised.

I watched her walk away and then I sat on the floor with my back against the wall, trying to get up the strength and the energy to begin this long and dangerous journey to California. I had no idea about the route or the cheapest, safest means of travel, or even how to go about finding Mommy once I got there.

Finally, I rose and left the trailer, pausing to take one last look at it as I left Mineral Acres and headed to town. On the way I paused at a stream and dipped my hands into the cold water, washing the sleep from my face. I was sure I looked a mess.

The bus depot was in the Mother Jones luncheonette. I ordered a cup of coffee and a buttered roll at the counter. The waitress asked me why I wasn't in school and I told her I wasn't living here anymore, just visiting. Still, I drew a lot of attention. I was afraid to go up to the information desk and ask about routes to California. In the end I decided to take the bus back to Richmond, thinking it would be much easier to plan a cross-country trip from a big city like that. I didn't wait long for the bus.

This time, when I got on, I sat up front near the driver. There weren't many passengers and the driver was talkative. I told him I was going to Richmond to stay with my grand-parents for a few days. Lies, I found, were coming to me easier, now that I was on the run. I didn't like doing it, but I could see how much easier it was than telling people the truth.

At the depot in Richmond, the ticket seller gave me a map that outlined a few different routes. I sat on a bench, trying to figure which route would be the cheapest and fastest. I was concentrating so intently on the bus map, I didn't see or sense that someone was standing right beside me. When my gaze moved off the page and I looked at the feet, I recognized the shoes.

"Cary!" I screamed.

"Talk about luck," he said smiling. I was shocked, but very happy to see his face. "I got off the bus and was just on my way to buy my ticket to Sewell when I saw you sitting here."

"What are you doing here? How —"

"Grandma Olivia was furious when she found out what I did and you did. She gave me the money to buy my bus ticket here and our bus tickets back," he said.

"I'm not going back, Cary," I said. "I'm going to Los Angeles to find my mother and get her to tell me the truth."

"You don't have to go to Los Angeles, Melody. I think I know the truth," Cary said. "Grandma Olivia and I had some down-to-earth talk, and I got her to tell me all she knows.

"I think I know who your father is," he said.

18

Not Alone

"I told you her bark was worse than her bite," Cary said, escorting me to the first bus back to Boston. "The moment she found out what you had done, she summoned me. Boy, did she ever bawl me out! How could I be so stupid as to give you the money to travel alone? Why didn't I bring you right back to her instead of driving you to Boston? How could I let you go back to West Virginia? She made it sound as if I had sent you to work in the coal mines. I thought she would take me out to sea and make me walk the plank."

"What did you do?" I asked him.

"I let her chop up the water until she was exhausted and red in the face and then I calmly stood up and said, " 'Grandma, it was all your fault.' "

"You did?"

We boarded the bus and took our seats.

"Aye, I did."

"What did she do?"

"She flopped back in her seat, so shocked

by my accusation and courage, she could only move her mouth. Nothing came out. Then it was my turn.

" 'How dare you just lay all that misery on Melody like that,' " I told her. " 'What did you expect would happen if you made someone feel less than nothing, if you took away years and years of belief, of the only life she's ever known? She loved Uncle Chester like a father,' I said.

" 'Well . . . well,' she stuttered, 'the girl wanted to hear the truth and so I gave it to her.'

" 'How would you like someone to give it to you right between the eyes like that, Grandma?' I demanded. Then she just stared at me for a moment."

"What did she say?" I asked.

"She said that was exactly what had happened to her. First, with her sister and then, nineteen years later, with your mother, Haille. I told her she should have known better, then. She should have known how it would feel. Then I sat across from her and watched her. She stared at the floor for the longest time without speaking. Finally, she said, 'You're right, Cary. You're a lot older and wiser than I thought. In some ways you're the smartest of all of us.' She straightened up in her chair the way she does, you know, and in that regal voice of hers demanded I go find you and bring you back.

She told me she would give me the money and she wanted me on the road immediately. She said she would take care of my father, not to worry.

"So," he said smiling, "here I am."

The bus started away.

"But I thought you told me you knew who my father was. I thought you said she told you more."

"I was getting to that. I didn't just jump up to do her bidding, you know," he said proudly. It amused me to see how proud he was that he had stood up to his grandmother. "I just sat there and stared at her until she said, 'Are you going after her or not?'

"I thought a moment and said, 'I can't bring her back unless you tell me the truth, Grandma. Otherwise, why would she want to come back?' Well, Grandma Olivia deflated like a punctured blowfish and nodded.

" 'It was your father,' she began, 'who came to me one day after Haille and Chester had left. Even though he had had this terrible fight with Chester — and gotten the worst of it, I might add — he felt very low, very bad that he had lost his brother. The three of them had been inseparable. But not always, Jacob hinted, indicating he knew something more. I pursued this, and he told me that many of the nights Haille was supposed to be spending with a girlfriend, she had been spending at the Childs'.' "

"The Childs'? You mean she was with the judge's family?" I asked.

"Yes, specifically Kenneth. During that last year, Kenneth was in Provincetown a lot," Cary said. "He was going to Boston University undergraduate school. He was supposed to go on to become a lawyer, but he was also heavily into his sculpture and the judge had a studio built for him at their home. Your mother was there almost every weekend Kenneth was there."

"Kenneth Childs is my real father?" I asked.

"It's very likely, from what Grandma said. I didn't get the opportunity to talk about it with my father. I took the money and went off to fetch you, leaving Grandma Olivia to explain it to him."

"But why didn't my mother just tell the truth? Why would she blame Grandpa Samuel?"

"That's something you're going to have to ask her, Melody. She was either protecting Kenneth or herself or —"

"Or what?"

He shrugged.

I sat back, digesting the story. If what he told me was true, then my real father was back in Provincetown and I was going to the right place.

"Have you ever spoken to Kenneth Childs?" I asked.

"I've said hello when I've seen him, but it's not easy to see him. He lives like a hermit on the Point. It's like the judge said the other night: all he does is work."

"He doesn't have a wife or other children?"

"No. Everyone thinks he's strange, but as I told you, they accept it because he's an artist."

"Some artistic hermit living in a beach house away from people — that's my father?" I muttered, stunned with each and every revelation Cary uttered.

"Anyway, at least you'll get a chance to find out the truth now," he said.

I shook my head. Maybe I shouldn't, I thought. Maybe I should live with the lies.

"What am I going to do?" I asked, the reality dropping all around me and over me. "Walk up to him and ask, 'Are you my real father?'"

"I'm not sure. We'll have to talk to my father about it, perhaps," he said.

"Your father?" I started to laugh. "You think he would talk to me about this?"

"Yes," Cary said, his eyes small. "He will or I'll tell my grandmother and she'll wring his neck."

I laughed, just thinking about Grandma Olivia chewing into Uncle Jacob.

Cary smiled. "I'm glad I found you so quickly, Melody."

I nodded and then sighed deeply, the sadness in my heart sprouting its dark flowers again.

"Papa George died," I told him. "There was no one there when I arrived yesterday. Mama Arlene had already moved away to live with her sister. The trailer home was closed, and my old home had nothing in it."

"I know. Alice told me. I'm sorry."

"Alice helped me a lot, but I spent last night in the trailer, sleeping on the floor. I have no idea where my things are. I didn't even think about them. I went to the cemetery, too. It felt so strange. I was angry and sad and . . . confused. Mommy didn't call while I was away, did she?"

"Not when I was home," he said. "How did you ever hope to find her just by going to Los Angeles? It's huge. I hear that even people who live there get lost."

"I didn't know what else to do. I was alone," I said mournfully.

"You're not alone. You'll never be alone. Remember that," he declared, his eyes firm and determined and full of sincerity.

"Thank you, Cary."

He smiled warmly, his eyes soft, loving. Then, he changed expression and took a breath. "Now I'll tell you the truth," he said. "I was shaking in my boots when I snapped at Grandma. I was afraid she would throw me out and call my father and that would be that."

"I thought you said her bark was worse than her bite."

"I did, but that doesn't mean her bite doesn't hurt, too."

The bus rolled on to Boston. I was like a ball in a pinball machine, rolling back and forth, but it wasn't for nothing, I thought. After all, I was unraveling those lies that had been spun so tightly around me, and soon, soon, I would reach the truth. It should have made me happy to realize that, but all it did was make my heart thump and make me tremble inside.

Since I hadn't slept much in the trailer, I dozed for most of the trip, my head on Cary's shoulder. When we arrived in Boston, we had something to eat and then we got into his truck and started for Provincetown. It was nearly morning by the time we saw the town with Pilgrim's Monument ahead of us. The rim of the sun was just peeking over the eastern horizon, turning the sky violet and orange, its bright gold edged with all those heavenly colors. The darkness retreated from the ocean, rising away like a blanket being peeled from a silver sheet. A tanker was silhouetted against the orange sky. It was breathtaking.

The beauty of the Cape, the promise of

revelation and truth, the return after my desperate flight — it all made me dizzy with emotion. I was nervous, afraid, elated, and excited, happy and sad. I didn't know whether to cry or sigh with pleasure, to feel relief or more tension.

"Lucky I was suspended, huh?" Cary said, smiling, as we entered the city limits.

"Lucky?"

"Sure. I wouldn't have been free to go find you. Actually, I would have left anyway and then I might have been suspended because of that."

"Let this be the end of all that, Cary. You've got to graduate."

"Aye, aye, Captain," he said, saluting. We cruised through town and made the turn toward his house. How would we be greeted? Would anyone be awake?

"Maybe I should just sleep on the beach," I said.

He looked at me with a wry smile. "It's time you got a good rest," he said. "You've got a lot to do during the next few weeks. For one thing, you've got to get me through my finals and take finals of your own."

How right he was, I thought. Maybe he was the smartest and wisest of all of us after all.

It was deadly quiet when we entered the house. A small hall light had been left on. We looked at each other and then, as silently as we could, started up the stairs, but the steps creaked like tattletales. By the time we reached the landing, Uncle Jacob, standing in his long nightshirt, was at his bedroom door. We paused. He stared at us a moment and then nodded.

"Get some sleep. We'll talk tomorrow." He retreated to his bedroom, softly closing the door.

"That's his way of saying he's glad we're back safely," Cary explained.

"Well, why can't he just say so? Doesn't he ever show any emotion beside anger? I've never seen him laugh or cry."

"The only time I ever saw my father cry was when he heard Laura was missing. He went off toward the cranberry bog and stood on the hill, sobbing. Then, and at the memorial service. He's not a man to show emotion."

"Except his anger," I reminded him.

"That's just —"

"I know," I said smiling, "his bark not his bite."

Cary smiled.

I had to admit the sight of the soft mattress and comforter was a wonderful sight. I didn't even bother to get undressed. I just plopped onto the bed, hugged the fluffy pillow, embraced my stuffed cat, and fell asleep. I didn't waken until late in the afternoon. Vaguely, I recalled, as if it were a dream, Aunt Sara coming into the room and standing by the bed, gazing down at me, even stroking my hair. I may have groaned and turned over, but I didn't speak, and after a moment, she left.

My bones creaked when I sat up. I felt so scuzzy it was as if I had cobwebs under my arms. A hot shower had never been so marvelous. I washed my hair and brushed my teeth and then got dressed in a pair of jeans and a clean blouse. I smelled the aroma of something delicious even before I came down the stairs.

"You're up! How are you feeling, dear?" Aunt Sara asked.

"I'm fine, Aunt Sara. I'm so sorry," I said quickly.

"Nothing to be sorry about my dear, now that you're home safe again. I have a fish stew cooking and ready for you. I bet you're hungry."

"Starving," I admitted. My stomach churned in anticipation of the good food, the Portuguese bread.

"Just sit at the table and I'll bring it. It's not supper time, but you've got to get something warm in your stomach."

"Where's Cary?" I asked. "Is he still asleep?"

"Cary? Oh no. He was up to take May to school and then return to school himself."

"He must be exhausted," I said.

"It isn't the first time he was up most of the

night and I'm sure it won't be the last. That's a fisherman's life, dear. Cary's used to it."

"Do you know why I left like that, Aunt Sara?"

"No dear." She quickly walked away to demonstrate that she didn't care to know, either. Aunt Sara was definitely the clam in the family, ready to slam shut her shell and ignore anything unpleasant. It seemed almost cruel to make her listen or see what she didn't want to see.

I said nothing. I ate and waited for Cary, May, and Uncle Jacob to return. But before they did, Aunt Sara and I had a surprise visitor. My aunt came running into the dining room as I was finishing my stew.

"She's here!" she cried. "Oh dear, dear, the house is a mess, too," she said, wringing her hands with an invisible dish towel of worry.

"Who's here, Aunt Sara?"

"Olivia," she announced. "She hasn't been here since — since . . . I can't remember." She went rushing about, picking up anything and everything that looked out of place.

Moments later Grandma Olivia came to the front door. Aunt Sara shouted for me to let Grandma Olivia in and I rose, trembling a bit myself. When I opened the door, she stormed past me and walked into the living room.

"Hello Olivia," Aunt Sara said. "It's so nice to see you."

"I want to talk with Melody alone," she snapped.

"Oh, of course." Aunt Sara smiled at me and retreated. Grandma Olivia peeled off her black velvet gloves and sat in Uncle Jacob's chair. She gazed at me with her eyes dark and small. "Sit," she ordered, and I went to the settee. "What did you think you would accomplish with this dramatic gesture — running off like that?"

"It wasn't a dramatic gesture. I wanted to go home."

"Home." She spit the word out as if it filled her mouth with an ugly, bitter taste. She looked away. "Home is here," she said, pointing to her temple, "and here," she added, pointing to her heart.

"I was going to go live with people who don't lie," I said.

"Everyone lies. It's a matter of survival," she declared.

"Then why hate my mother for lying?" I retorted. She widened her eyes.

"I'm not here to talk about your mother. I'm here to talk about you," she said. "As I told you, you are my sister's granddaughter and I made promises to my father."

"I know," I said. "Thank you for being so honest." I wanted to add: and for using the truth like darts.

"I didn't tell you everything," she confessed.

I sat back as she paused.

"My father left both my sister and me a considerable fortune. Most of what you see, what we have, does not come from my husband's brilliant business acumen. Samuel was never a good businessman. To this day I don't think he understands what a profit-and-loss statement is," she said disdainfully. "But that's a different matter. As I told you, Belinda is under a doctor's care. That is eating away at her inheritance, but even if she lives to be a hundred, it won't eat but a small portion of it. The money was well invested and earns good interest. To come directly to the point, your mother would have inherited what was left of Belinda's fortune if I hadn't helped Belinda to see more clearly. Instead, a trust has been formed and you are the heir."

"I?"

"That's correct. It's specifically set up to provide you with your educational needs, your basic needs, until you are twenty-one. After that, you can waste it as you see fit. I'm the administrator of the trust."

"Why didn't you tell me before?" I asked.

"Why? I didn't feel you needed to know all this until you were sufficiently retrained."

"Retrained?"

"Until you had lived with a family in a

moral setting and lost whatever bad habits Haille might have instilled in you."

"She didn't instill any bad habits in me," I replied firmly.

"I wish that were true, but frankly, I don't see how it's possible for you to have grown up as her daughter and not be somehow affected. Anyway, I'm glad Cary got you to come to your senses and return."

"Why?" I challenged. "You obviously hate my mother and hate the sight of me."

"I don't hate the sight of you. I told you why I have the feelings I have toward your mother, but I'm . . . sufficiently impressed with you to believe you have the capability to overcome your unfortunate upbringing. If you will behave and listen to wiser minds, you have a lot to gain, as you now know. It will be a considerable fortune, more than most people make in two lifetimes of hard work. There, now I've given you your incentive and I've welcomed you back," she said, as if that were the prescription to treat her bout of conscience.

"Welcomed me back?" I shook my head and snorted.

"I came here, didn't I?" she protested.

I stared at her a moment. This was the closest she would come to an apology, I thought. Whether it was because of the promise she had made to her father or came from genuine and sincere remorse for telling me things bluntly and causing me to run off, I didn't know.

"I would just ask you for one thing," she continued.

"What's that?" I asked.

"Let the past be the past. Concern yourself with your future. Nothing can be gained by digging up the ugly days and ugly memories," she said.

"I don't know if I can do that," I said. "There are still things I need to know."

Her eyes grew small again and her face firm. She leaned toward me. "I would not like to hear that you were going around Provincetown asking questions and stirring up gossip about the Logan family."

"I wouldn't do that."

"Make sure," she warned. Then she rose. "Stop by the house from time to time to tell me how you are getting along," she said. "Have Cary bring you," she added before leaving the room.

Aunt Sara was in the hallway. "Would you like to stay for dinner, Olivia?"

"Certainly not," Grandma said. She looked at me for a moment and then turned and walked out of the house. It was as if a wind had blown through and shut the door.

"Wasn't that nice?" Aunt Sara said, as if some member of royalty had lowered herself to visit. "Dear, come help me set the table."

I stood there for a moment in a daze. I was

to inherit a fortune? Had Mommy or Daddy ever known? If they had, they couldn't tell me about it without telling me everything else. The more I learned, the more I was amazed by what they had sacrificed to run off together the way they had.

May and Cary arrived only minutes before Uncle Jacob. Cary looked tired but did his best to hide it. May was very excited to see me and was filled with so many things to tell me, her hands never stopped moving. Aunt Sara went on and on about Grandma Olivia. Cary looked at me with surprise and expectation and I whispered that I would tell him everything later. In the meantime, I helped serve dinner. Since I had just eaten, I ate only dessert: a piece of Aunt Sara's blueberry pie.

After I helped clean up, I went upstairs and joined Cary in his attic room. I told him everything Grandma Olivia had told me. He had not known about any fortune.

"I'm not even sure my father knows about that," he said. "That's wonderful, Melody."

"Money isn't very important to me right now, Cary. The truth is, I think Grandma Olivia was hoping I would willingly forget all the lies just so I could get my inheritance. It was as if she were trying to buy me off with the promise of it."

He nodded, thinking.

"Can we talk to your father now? Would he

talk to us?" I asked. I was afraid to approach him myself.

"Let's try," Cary said.

We descended the stairs together and found Uncle Jacob reading his paper and listening to the news on the radio. He looked up, surprised.

"What is it?" he asked.

"Melody has some questions to ask you, Dad," he said. "Because of the things Grandma told her and me about her mother."

"You know how I feel about talking about that." He started to raise his paper.

"Grandma feels we're old enough to know things, why can't you?" Cary challenged. I think he was braver with me standing beside him, only now I felt responsible for any bad feeling between him and his father.

Uncle Jacob thought a moment and then lowered the paper to his lap. He turned off the radio. "You want to hear about your mother? You want to hear the ugly truth?" he said with a note of threat.

"I want to know the truth," I replied un- daunted, "ugly or otherwise."

"All right. Sit," he said, nodding at the settee. We both went to it. Uncle Jacob lit his pipe and puffed for a few moments.

"Haille was always getting in trouble with boys. Either Chester or I had to come to her aid all the time, trying to save her from herself. On more than one occasion, I found her down on the beach with someone doing things I'd rather not describe. I got into fights and so did Chester. We were teased a lot. The family was disgraced a lot, but nothing seemed to change her. She was fascinated with herself.

"Your mother was always a source of misery for my parents," he said, pointing with his pipe. "She was caught smoking, drinking, and doing all sorts of immoral stuff in school dozens of times. If my mother hadn't had influence in this town, they would have thrown Haille out of the public school. She was actually arrested twice for lewd behavior on the beach when she was in high school." He paused. "You still want to hear this?"

I swallowed back a throat lump and nodded.

"About when she was fifteen, sixteen, she got caught with a truck driver out on the dunes. They were going to throw the book at the guy. He was about twenty-eight or so and she was obviously under age. Only, my mother was worried about the scandal, so it was kept quiet and the truck driver was let go. Mother tried to get a doctor to help Haille, the same doctor who was treating Belinda at the time, I recall, but nothing seemed to help. She was a wild creature. She'd do whatever she wanted, whatever she fancied.

Chester and I did our best to cover up for her, to protect her."

He paused and sat back, thinking. The lines in his face grew deeper, his eyes colder. Then he took a breath and continued. "The year she was supposed to graduate from high school, Kenneth Childs began coming up and spending time with us more and more. We liked Kenneth and our families were close. In those days Chester and I thought of him as another brother. Kenneth was going to college in Boston. He would come up weekends. Sometimes Chester and I didn't know he was in town, but Haille always did. She was over at the Childs' lots of times, and sometimes, there was no one else there but Kenneth.

"That was the year she got pregnant. She made up that story about my father. Chester always favored her more than I did, over-looked her sins. He made excuses for her all the time. He refused to believe Kenneth would make her pregnant and not own up to it. Haille filled him with lies about Dad and he swallowed them, because he was so hypnotized with her himself.

"I told him she was a liar and a whore. I told him she once tried to seduce me, and he got into a fight with me. He took her side and they ran off together. That's the story," he concluded, like a slap of thunder at the end of a rain storm.

There was a heavy silence in the room. Cary looked at me.

"Have you ever spoken with Kenneth Childs since?" I asked.

"We've had some words, mainly because of the judge. I went to his mother's funeral, of course, but it's hard for me to look him in the face and not think about what happened."

"Did you ever ask him outright about it?"

"No," he said, "and I don't intend ever to talk about it. You're my mother's sister's grandchild. Your Aunt Sara is fond of you, and from what I hear, you're doing well in school. You're welcome to stay here as long as you need to or until your mother decides to be a mother instead of a tramp. That might never happen, of course, and soon you'll be on your own anyway. But I won't have any more talk about those days in my house," he said firmly. "And I don't want any scandals." He looked at Cary. "Satisfied?"

Cary turned to me. "You want to ask him anything else, Melody."

"No," I said. I was crying inside, the tears falling behind my eyes and over my heart.

Uncle Jacob went back to his paper and put the radio on again. I left the room, pounding up the stairs. I threw myself on the bed and lay there embracing my stuffed cat.

There was a soft knock on my door.

"Yes?"

Cary poked his head in.

"Are you okay?"

"No, but it's all right," I said. "I guess in my heart I knew everything your father said. It's just hard hearing it like that."

Cary nodded. "It'll be all right. Things will be just fine," he promised.

I smiled at him. "Sure."

"I'd better go up and start studying," he said. "I gotta pass those finals."

"Yes, you better. Cary," I said, as he started to close the door. He raised his eyebrows. "One day this week, will you take me to see Kenneth Childs?"

"Sure," he said. "I don't know what he'll do. He doesn't like people coming around much, I know. I hear that when he works, he won't even come to the door."

"Still, I'd like to try to meet him," I said.

"Okay. Nose to the grindstone," he said and left.

I lay there for a long time, just thinking, remembering silly things Mommy had done, recalling her whining and crying and Daddy's soothing her all the time. Then I thought about her with Archie Marlin.

Children inherit so much from their parents, I thought. Would I become like her one day? It frightened and intrigued me. I had to know who my real father was. Then I could

497

learn what part of him I had inherited and whether that part was strong enough to overcome the bad I had inherited from Mommy. To be without a past is almost like being without a future, I thought.

I would know my past. No temptation of a fortune, no threat, nothing would keep me from pursuing the truth.

No one at school knew anything about my trip back to West Virginia. They didn't question why I had been absent. Some of the girls thought it was in sympathy with Cary and his unfair suspension. I didn't say it was, but I didn't deny it. There was a lot of excitement because of the school year's approaching end.

The week before finals was a week mainly for review. At the end of the week of finals, the school would have its variety show, the proceeds of which went toward college scholarships. The principal, Mr. Webster, hadn't forgotten that I played the fiddle. He had Mrs. Topper, the school music teacher who was in charge of the show, ask me to perform.

I tried to get out of it, claiming the truth: I hadn't been playing much these past months.

But Mrs. Topper was desperate. "I barely have enough performers to fill a half hour, much less an hour. I need you. You have to do two numbers," she pleaded. "It's all in good fun and for a good cause. Won't you help us?"

How could I refuse? But this, along with my anticipated visit with Kenneth Childs and my final exams made me more nervous than a flock of hens with a fox at the gate. I couldn't eat. I couldn't sleep. Cary was more excited about my performing than I was. He insisted on watching and listening to me practice. Aunt Sara thought it was wonderful, too, and even Uncle Jacob looked and listened with interest.

I decided I would play one of Papa George's favorites, "Katy Cline," and a traditional Woody Guthrie folk favorite, "This Land is Your Land." I sang when I played, of course. Uncle Jacob looked amazed and Aunt Sara had the widest, happiest smile yet on her face. Cary beamed. I felt sorry for May, but she seemed content just feeling the vibrations when I let her or just watching my face and actions. I didn't think I was good enough to actually perform, but even Uncle Jacob said I was. He hinted that he would attend the show, which Cary said would be a first.

"The only community event I've ever seen him attend is the Blessing of the Fleet."

Cary suggested that on Thursday, after we had brought May home from school, he and I would go to the Point to see if I could speak to Kenneth Childs.

"What are you going to say?" he asked.

I thought a moment. "I'll introduce myself first and then see what he says."

"What if he says nothing? What if he just nods and walks away?"

"I'll find a way to get him to talk to me," I said. Actually, I was excited with the idea of just seeing him, seeing if there was anything about him that reminded me of myself. I couldn't really tell much from the few photos I'd seen.

"The last time I saw him, he had a beard," Cary said. "Laura and I used to go to the beach up there, but I've never been in his house or studio. What excuse are we going to use for driving over to see him?" he asked.

"We'll tell him my mother asked me to stop by to say hello," I replied. Cary nodded and smiled.

"You've been scheming, haven't you?"

"That's all I've been doing lately," I admitted.

"Okay, Thursday," he promised.

My heart was pounding in anticipation.

The night before, I sat at the desk and, after stuffing the envelope with the money Alice had given me, wrapping it carefully so no one would know what it was, I wrote her a letter.

Dear Alice,
You'll be surprised to learn that I didn't

go to Los Angeles after all. My cousin Cary was sent by Grandma Olivia to bring me back to Provincetown and he found me at the bus station in Richmond. I agreed to return when he told me he thought he knew who my real father is. He's an artist who lives in Provincetown. Tomorrow, Cary is taking me to his house and studio and for the first time in my life, I will set eyes on the man who could be my father. I have seen pictures of him when he was younger, but seeing pictures is one thing. Standing before him in the flesh will be another.

I am rehearsing what I will say and how I will say it. You'd laugh if you saw how I pose before the mirror in my room and pretend I'm seeing him. Everything I can think to say sounds silly. I'm afraid he will just look at me and shake his head and maybe shut the door in my face. I don't know how I would feel if that happened.

Apparently, he is a man who keeps to himself, so that just might happen. I'll write to tell you all about it afterward.

Speaking of rehearsals, you won't believe this, but I've been talked into performing at the school's annual scholarship variety show. I'll be playing my fiddle — two tunes. I practice and have played for the family. They all seemed impressed, but I'm terrified.

I'm returning all the money you lent me. It was nice of you to do it and I know now that you are my one true friend. I hope we will always remain friends, no matter how many miles apart we might be.

I still haven't heard from Mommy. When I asked her why she lied to me the last time she called, she sounded frantic and very distant and I have this fear she won't call again. There is a lot she and I have to discuss now, now that I'm old enough to understand. I have heard unpleasant things about her when she was younger — my age and a little older. It saddens and sickens me, but I try not to think about it.

My grandmother has told me that I'm an heiress and that someday I'll have a lot of money. How's that for a surprise? Me, someday rich? Right now, I don't even think about it. It really doesn't seem important.

What's important is that I might be on the verge of learning the whole truth about myself and my family. It frightens me and yet, I know how much I want to know everything.

As I write this letter, I am looking at the watch Papa George gave me. Inside, I placed a blade of grass from Daddy's *grave. Even though I was just there, I feel so far away, not only in miles but in time. It makes me feel that I'm about to become someone else, as if I lived a different life, a life that will soon end. After all, this and a few of the things I was able to bring with me are all that I have from my former life. Of course, I have memories, but they're burning down like candles. I'm afraid of being left in the dark.*

As soon as I finish this letter, I'm going to practice my fiddle and then I'm going to go to sleep and dream of a new tomorrow, where lies crumble like fallen autumn leaves beneath my feet and where promises of happiness and hope sprout rich and green like our mountains and hills in spring.

Say a prayer for me. And thanks for being my truest friend in all the world.

Love,
Melody

I put the letter in the envelope. I played my fiddle and then I crawled into bed and had the dream I told Alice I would have.

Tomorrow would be a new day.

19

Lost and Found

The way to Race Point was along a road so narrow and hidden between two hills of sand, it could easily be overlooked. Cary explained that at Kenneth Childs's request, no sign was posted to designate the road. He was the only one who lived on it and it had become known as Childs Road. After its entrance, protected by the two hills, the road was covered with sand that was six to eight inches deep in spots.

"The best way to navigate this is to let air out of my tires," Cary explained and stopped the truck to do just that.

It was late afternoon and the powder blue sky was streaked with flat, soft clouds that looked like vanilla icing smeared across it in odd shapes. Cary said it meant it was very windy in the upper atmosphere. We went in about three quarters of a mile before we reached the peak of the incline and were able to see the ocean. It looked a darker metallic blue, making its whitecaps whiter.

The beach here was cluttered with twisted seaweed that lay in clumps combed by the fingers of the waves. Terns walked gingerly around and through the seaweed as if they were part of some bird ballet entitled Searching for Food.

"This is one of the best places to find driftwood," Cary said. "Laura and I spent hours gathering strangely shaped pieces. Local artists will buy them from you. Seashells too," he added.

"Where's Kenneth's home?"

"Just to the right here," he explained and we made a turn. Ahead was a smoke-gray cedar saltbox house. The sea air, sun, and rain had faded its black shutters to a light charcoal. Behind the house was another small structure that looked like a barn.

"That's his studio," Cary explained.

I saw no one. The front of the house was spotted with pink wild beach grass, no flowers, no trees. On the side of the house facing us was an upside-down row boat, its hull sun-bleached. There was a dark blue jeep in what served as a driveway. An inky black Labrador was lying on the rear seat and lifted his head with curiosity as we approached.

"That's his dog, Ulysses. He's fifteen years old, half blind and deaf," Cary said. "At least that's what the judge says. His jeep's here, so Kenneth must be home," Cary muttered with some anxiety.

From the moment we had left the house, a small, but persistent trembling vibrated through every bone and muscle in my body. My heart was in a continual drum beat. Cary tried to keep up some conversation, but I could only smile or nod.

"You sure you want to do this?" he asked one final time before turning into the driveway. I nodded and took a deep breath.

Ulysses rose on his legs as if he had to lift three times his weight, but once he was on his feet, he hopped out of the jeep and began barking. It was a friendly bark, not a growl.

"Whenever Laura and I stopped by here, we had the feeling we were being watched, but Kenneth didn't come out but one or two times and then it was just a quick hello and some comment about the weather."

"I'm going to do this," I said firmly. I opened the truck door and stepped out. Ulysses came to me first, his tail wagging. "Hello," I said and patted him. The sight of company excited him and he was licking my hand and rushing back and forth between Cary and me for our strokes and words.

"Some watchdog, huh?" Cary said with a laugh.

I looked at the front door. It was gray and weather-beaten, with no knocker, no buzzer, no indication the inhabitant of this house wanted anyone coming to it.

"You wouldn't think he had any money the way he lives," Cary muttered. "That jeep's about ten, twelve years old, and the furniture in the house looks as if he got it all at a thrift shop. We were never inside," he quickly added, "but Laura and I once peeked through the window. There aren't even any pictures on the walls. All his art is in his studio, I guess. We never got close enough to look in there.

"Kenneth has eyes that can scare you."

"What do you mean?"

"You'll see," he said. "I think. He might not answer the door."

We stared at it. I could see Cary wasn't going to be the one to knock, so I stepped forward slowly over the walkway, which consisted of small rocks. Ulysses stayed at my side, Cary remained a foot or so behind. I knocked and waited.

The roar of the ocean, the waves breaking on the beach, the cry of the terns, and the whistle the sea breeze made was all we heard. I knocked again, louder.

"What'dya want?" Both of us nearly jumped out of our sneakers. We turned to see Kenneth Childs standing at the corner of the house. He wore a pair of jeans, no shoes or socks, and a faded brown T-shirt. He was long-legged and slim. His hair, a little darker than mine, was, as Cary had described, tied in a pony tail, the end of

507

which reached the base of his neck. His full-face beard was even a little darker. He had a wide forehead with deep-set dark eyes and a long, straight nose, under which his strong, firm lips stretched to dip at the corners. I couldn't help staring at his face, looking for more evidence of my own, but it was hard because of that thick beard. To me it was like a mask.

"She wanted to come see you," Cary said quickly, embarrassed and made more nervous by the long silence.

"What for?" Kenneth asked, his eyes on me.

"My mother told me to say hello," I said.

"Who's your mother?" he asked, without softening his face. He was miles from smiling.

"Haille," I said. "Haille Logan."

He stared for a moment longer and then he drew closer. Ulysses went to his side immediately.

"You're Haille's daughter?"

"Yes."

"Haille sent you?" he asked with skepticism. I nodded, positive he could see through my fabrication. "Why didn't she come herself?" he asked me.

"She's not here. I'm here, living with my uncle and aunt," I explained and tried to swallow so my words wouldn't sound so tiny. I couldn't take my eyes off him. His eyes were so hard, as if made of stone. This was what Cary meant, I thought.

"What's your name?" he asked.

"Melody."

His lips softened just a bit. He looked at Cary and then he looked at me.

"I'm going to school here now," I said, too nervous to permit any long silences. "For a while."

"Where's your mother then?"

"She's in California," I said. "She's auditioning to be an actress or a model."

His face finally relaxed.

"That figures," he said. He looked as if he was going to turn and walk away.

"I met your father at my grandmother and grandfather's house," I said quickly. He raised his eyebrows.

"And what did he say when he found out who you were?" he asked.

"He was . . . nice," I replied, not sure what he meant.

"Dad's the most charming man on the Cape," Kenneth said as if it were a basic fact everyone knew. He looked at Cary. "You're Jacob's boy?"

"Yes sir."

"Sorry about your sister. I don't get to hear much news out here, but I heard about that."

Cary nodded, biting down on his lower lip, his eyes glassy.

Kenneth turned back to me. "Are you a good student?"

"Yes, sir."

"Your father here too?" he asked, his face firm again.

"No sir. My father died in a coal mining accident a few months ago."

"Really?" He looked at Cary and then at me. "Coal mine? Where were you living?"

"West Virginia, a town called Sewell."

He nodded.

"Yeah, I knew they had gone south." His eyes were full of thoughts for a moment and then he blinked and looked at me more sharply. "You look a lot like her," he said. "I guess she's still as pretty as she was if she's looking to become a model or an actress."

"She is," I said.

"Well," he said, starting to turn. "Thanks for stopping by."

"Can I see some of your work?" I blurted. Cary's eyes widened. He looked at me and then at Kenneth, who stopped turning and considered.

"Why?" he asked, his eyes small, suspicious.

"I've heard a lot about it," I said.

"You know anything about art?"

"A little, what I learned in school."

"An artist's work is very personal until the day he puts it up for sale in some gallery," he said.

"I know."

"You know?" He widened his smile. "Are you an artist?"

"I play the fiddle and sing," I said. "I don't like doing it in front of people until I'm sure I'm ready. I guess an artist doesn't like showing his work until he is confident it's ready."

His eyebrows lifted again. "That's right." He thought a moment. "Okay, I'll show you something I've nearly completed," he said. "Maybe I need a completely fresh pair of eyes looking at it. I'll let you look at it if you promise to be honest about what you think."

"I don't like to lie about my feelings," I said, my eyes now as firm and as hard as his.

"I bet you don't. Follow me." He started around the house. Cary looked as if he had seen a ghost — shocked, surprised, still afraid. "You can bring him along," Kenneth added without turning back to us.

Between the house and the studio was a patch of beach grass, a bench, and a small, man-made pond in which minnows burst into frenzied swimming when our shadows touched the water. Kenneth opened his studio door and paused.

"Don't touch any of my tools," he warned. I nodded and so did Cary.

The studio was just a large room. On one side were tables and a kiln, and on the tables were his tools and materials. There was a beaten-up tweed settee to our immediate left with a driftwood table in front of it, on which were a large coffee mug and a plate, with a half-eaten muffin on it.

Kenneth's work in progress was to our right. It was a figure about five feet high of a woman whose arms were changing into wings just above the elbow. The face was interesting, her eyes turned upward and her mouth was open as if to express a great sigh. She was naked and it looked as if feathers were growing along her back, sides, and stomach.

"Well?" Kenneth said. "What do you think I'm trying to show?"

"Someone turning into an angel," I said.

He smiled warmly. "Exactly. I'm calling it *Angel in Progress.* I have a lot of detail work left to do yet."

"It's very exciting, especially the look in her face," I said. "It's as if she's . . ."

"What?" He drew closer to me.

"Seeing heaven for the first time."

"Yes," he said, gazing at her. "She is."

"Do you always work in clay?" I asked.

"No. I've done stone, metal, and wood, but here I'm trying to capture and record a fleeting impression, much the way a painter does in a quick sketch. After I'm finished, I'll cast this in bronze."

"How do you do that?" I asked. He checked my expression to see if I really wanted to know. Satisfied, he gestured toward his tools and his kiln.

"In two stages. First, a negative mold is formed, and then a positive cast is made from the negative impression. Plaster is used for the negative mold and bronze for the positive. I call that the slave work, since all the artistic work is completed."

"You do all that by yourself?"

"Yes," he said with a short laugh. "So," he said, his eyes small again, "what do you know about sculpture?"

"Just what I learned in history about the Greeks. Gods and athletes were their favorite subjects," I recited. "I remember our teacher passed around a picture of the *Three Goddesses.*"

He raised his eyebrows. "That's right."

"My best friend's parents have a small replica of Michelangelo's *David* in their house," I said. "But I've never been to a museum and the only galleries I've ever seen are the ones on the street here."

"Take her to Gordon's on Commercial," Kenneth told Cary. "You know where it is?" Cary nodded quickly. "I have some pieces there."

"I'd like to see them."

He nodded. "Well, you've restored my faith in the educational system. Have you ever tried to do anything with art — draw, paint?"

"No."

"Maybe you should," he said. Was he telling me I had inherited some of his talent? I glanced at Cary, who still looked timid and nervous. His eyes shifted from side to side, as if looking for escape routes.

"School's almost over for you, isn't it?" Kenneth asked.

"Yes, just a little more review, finals, and that's it for this year. I graduate next year. Cary graduates this year."

Kenneth looked at him. "What are you going to do with yourself?" he asked him.

"What I do now, fishing, cranberry harvest."

Kenneth nodded. "And you, what do you want to become?" he asked me.

"I think a teacher," I said.

"Not an actress or a model like your mother?"

"I don't think so," I said. He looked pleased. "You were very friendly with my mother once, weren't you?"

"Yes," he said. He gazed at his work in progress. "And with your father and with Cary's father. We all grew up together."

Cary and I looked at each other. In his eyes I could see the tension. Was I just going to come out and ask him if he could be my father?

"Well, I got to get back to work," he said. He walked toward the door to indicate he wanted us to leave. I gazed again at Cary and then I followed Kenneth. Cary followed me. Ulysses waited at the door.

"I like your dog."

"He's old, but faithful. I'm afraid he doesn't get enough exercise either."

"Maybe I can walk him for you sometime," I offered. "I'd like to hunt for seashells on the beach here."

He nodded.

"What are you going to do this summer?" he asked.

"I don't know. I'm waiting for my mother to come back or call for me."

"Well, tell her hello when she calls you." He stepped back into the studio and closed the door.

I looked at Cary.

"I didn't know how to say anything or ask anything," I explained.

"It's all right. Let's go. I don't think he would have admitted anything anyway. Maybe he doesn't even know himself." We started back to the truck, Ulysses following us.

"I should have said something more, asked something specific," I moaned.

"Next time. Did you get any sort of feeling about him?" Cary asked as he backed out of the driveway and started us toward the road.

"I think so," I said. "It's hard and it's not fair," I cried. "Mommy has to tell me the truth. She must!" I said firmly. "There's no reason for her not to now."

We bumped along the sandy road. When I looked back, I saw Ulysses turn and trot back toward the jeep. He looked disappointed.

After Cary stopped at a garage to refill his truck tires with air, we headed home. We had just made the turn toward the house when we both saw the police car parked right behind Uncle Jacob's.

"What's this all about?" Cary wondered aloud. We pulled up beside the police car and got out slowly. Both of us noticed that the front door was still open. We glanced at each other and then hurried inside.

There were two policemen standing in the hallway, the taller one with his hat in his hands. Uncle Jacob was talking to them softly. They all turned as we stepped in, Uncle Jacob's face darker and firmer than I had ever seen it. We heard soft sobbing coming from the living room and looked in to see Aunt Sara seated on the settee, May at her side stroking her arm.

"What happened?" Cary asked.

"There's been an accident," Uncle Jacob said.

"Who?" Cary asked. Uncle Jacob looked at the two policemen and when he turned back, his eyes were on me. My heart stopped and started.

"Mommy?" I cried. He nodded. "What happened?"

"Officer Baker here came to tell us they received a call from police in . . . where was it?"

"Pomona, sir," the taller policeman said. "It's near Los Angeles," he explained.

"What happened? Is she all right?" My heart stopped.

"Tell her what you know," Uncle Jacob said to the policeman.

The officer turned to me. "There was an accident on the freeway out there, single car, car caught fire. The gentleman driving the car was thrown from the vehicle, but —"

"My mother?"

"Apparently she was trapped in the car. The man survived and is in the hospital. His name's —" He checked a note pad, "Marlin, Richard Marlin. He claims the woman who died in the car fire was Haille Ann Logan and told the police to call here. The car exploded and there wasn't much anyone could do."

"Mommy's . . . dead?"

The policeman looked at Uncle Jacob. Aunt Sara started to cry louder. Cary reached for my hand, but I pulled away. "Tell me!" I screamed. I had to have them say it.

"That's what they're saying," Uncle Jacob stated.

I shook my head. "She was having auditions. She was calling me."

The policeman turned to Uncle Jacob. "They want to know if you want the remains shipped here," he said.

"Call Olivia," Aunt Sara cried.

"Aye, we'll want that," Uncle Jacob replied.

"Stop it!" I screamed. "Stop all these lies!"

I put my hands over my ears and shook my head.

"Easy now," Uncle Jacob said holding out his hand. "You —"

"You're lying! Everyone just spins one lie after another!"

I looked at Cary.

He shook his head. "Melody," he said softly.

"It's not true," I begged him. I turned and ran out of the house.

"Jacob!" Aunt Sara screamed.

I nearly tripped on the steps, but I recovered my balance and went around the corner of the house. I ran as hard and as fast as I could. I needed to get away from them, away from the story, away from the policeman's eyes. When I reached the sand, I slipped and fell, catching myself with my hands and then shooting up and running harder, tears flying off my cheeks. My lungs were screaming, but I wouldn't stop. I ran up the hill and fell again, this time just lying there, sobbing.

Mommy wasn't going to call me. She wasn't going to send for me or return. I cried until my ribs ached and then I just stared out at the cranberry bog. I never heard Cary coming, but he was suddenly at my side.

"Mom's worried about you," he said and squatted. He put a blade of beach grass in his mouth. I gazed ahead, not hearing, not seeing, not feeling. "The police said they were going very fast and probably lost control. They rammed into a pole and the car turned over, spilling your mother's friend onto the road. Her door didn't open and the car rolled over and over and then just went up in flames. Nobody's lying."

I turned from him. Mommy had done a selfish thing by leaving me here and by keeping secrets, but I could never harden my heart against her enough to stop loving her. There were good times to remember, lots of soft moments. Sometimes, I would catch her looking at me with a gentle smile on her lips and I could almost hear her thinking how pleased she was with me. She had come to depend on me so much. If only I had been with them, I thought. I would have made them slow down.

"They're going to bring her back and put her in the Logan section of the cemetery," Cary said.

I spun on him, my eyes on fire. "When she was alive, they didn't want her within ten feet of them, but now that she's dead, they'll put her in the ground near them?"

He had no answer. He looked down.

"She should be sent back to Sewell and buried beside my father," I said. "It's where she belongs."

Cary shrugged. "Tell Grandma."

I thought a moment. "I will. Take me there right now."

"Right now?"

I stood up and so did he.

"Right now," I said and started down the hill. I was running on anger and disappointment. He caught up.

"I'll just go tell Dad," he said when we reached the house.

"Just drive us there, Cary. Don't go asking for permission for every breath you take."

He looked at me, then nodded. "Okay, let's go."

We got into the truck and he backed out of the driveway. As we pulled away from the house, I saw Uncle Jacob step out and look after us. The moment we drove up Grandma Olivia and Grandpa Samuel's driveway, I opened the door. Cary hadn't even brought the truck to a stop. He hit the brakes and I was out, rushing toward the front door.

Cary slammed his door and followed. I pushed the buzzer, waited a second, and pushed it again. Grandpa opened the door, his face somber.

"Melody," he said, surprise overcoming sadness quickly.

"Where's Grandma Olivia?" I demanded. There was no sense talking to him, I thought quickly. She makes all the decisions in this family. I rushed in past him.

"Just what's going on here?" she demanded. She was standing in the sitting room doorway.

"You heard about my mother, your niece?" I fired. She stiffened.

"Jacob just called."

"What a terrible thing," Grandpa said, coming up beside me.

"I don't want her buried here. I want her buried back in Sewell beside my daddy," I said. "It's where she belongs."

"Sewell?" Grandma looked at Grandpa and then at Cary. "She's my sister's daughter. She doesn't belong there. She belongs here."

"Where she hasn't been welcomed for years and years," I spit back at her. "How can you be such a hypocrite!"

Grandma Olivia's face lost whatever color it had and became a pale, mean moon, bent on destruction.

"I'm no hypocrite. I have never said one thing and done another. I have never lied and I have always been a woman who keeps her word and her promises. Your mother was my sister's child and belongs in our ground near my father's and my mother's graves. She doesn't belong in some strange place beside a man who married her for all the wrong reasons."

"That man is your son," I reminded her.

"*Was* my son," she reminded me. "I will not lay out money to send her remains there. She should be with her family."

"Why couldn't you feel that way when she was alive?"

"You know the answer to that question," she said. "You're overwrought, emotionally disturbed. All of us have been taken by surprise. None of us wanted to see such a tragedy, but it's happened. It began some time ago and has finally been brought to this horrible end. The least we could do for Haille's poor soul is put her remains where she has some familial company. You're too overwhelmed to discuss the matter." She turned away.

"I'll dig her up and bring her back to Sewell. Someday I will. I swear."

"When I'm dead and gone, you can do whatever you want, but I would hope that by then you would have grown up," she replied. "I'm sorry for your sorrow. Losing a mother is never easy, no matter how your mother has treated you, but we must go on and do what is right, the things that are good. Cary, see that she gets home." She left us.

I stood there for a few moments.

"She's right, my dear." Grandpa put his

arm around me. "She usually is. She's a remarkable woman."

"She's an ogre," I said. "The only thing that's remarkable is how you all let her get away with bullying you." I pulled away from him and marched out of the house.

Cary followed and we got back into the truck. "There's nothing we can do," he said. "We have no money, no authority —"

"I know. Let's go home." I lowered my head.

The house was deadly quiet upon our return. I went directly to my room and lay there, thinking, remembering, crying when I had built up some tears again. May came to my door to sign her regrets. I thanked her, but I didn't want to be consoled, even by her. I was still quite bitter and angry. Later, Aunt Sara sent May up with a tray of food. I couldn't eat anything, but I let her stay with me and tried to explain and describe Mommy to her when she asked me to tell her about her.

Signing the thoughts, checking the book to be sure I was making the right gestures, made me think more about the incidents and the descriptions. For the moment it occupied my mind and my sorrow lifted a bit. I was exhausted and fell asleep early, curled up on the bed, still in my clothes. Aunt Sara stopped by to put a blanket over me. Late in the night, I heard my door open softly and looked through my cloudy eyes to see Cary tiptoe in. He stood by the bed, gazing down at me for a few moments. Then he knelt down to kiss my cheek. I pretended to be in a dead sleep.

Morning light brought a moment of disbelief, a moment of hope. Perhaps it had all been a horrible nightmare after all. But here I was waking in my clothes. Reality would not be held back. I got undressed, showered, and changed. By the time I went downstairs, Cary and May had gone to school. The house was quiet. Even Aunt Sara was gone. I made myself some coffee and toast and then I sat on the porch. About a half hour later, I saw Aunt Sara coming down the street. She was nicely dressed.

"Good morning, dear. Have you had anything to eat?"

"Yes, Aunt Sara."

"I was just at church, praying for Haille."

"Thank you," I said. I felt guilty not getting up and going with her.

"You can go with me tomorrow, if you like. It's a horrible tragedy," she continued, "but I want you to know you have a home here forever, dear. We love you."

"Thank you, Aunt Sara."

"I stopped at Laura's grave on the way home," she said with a sigh, "and told her the sad news. She was such a crutch for me whenever there was bad news. Laura had a way of filling me with hope, her smile, her loving, gentle smile. You should go to her grave and pray. You'll be comforted."

"Maybe I will," I said. That pleased her.

"Come in whenever you want, talk whenever you want," she said. I nodded and she went into the house.

I was on the porch when Cary and May returned from school. May started running the moment she spotted me. We hugged and she signed stories about her day, showing me a paper with stars all over it.

When she went in to change, Cary sat on the steps and told me about school, how everyone had heard the news. "All your teachers send regards and told me to tell you not to worry about your exams. They'll provide make-ups."

"I'll take my exams on time," I said. "I don't need to make extra work for them."

"Are you sure?"

"Yes."

He thought a moment and then smiled. "I was really surprised by how many kids came over to me to ask about you this afternoon, once the news had spread. You're more popular than you think. I bet you could have run for senior class president and gotten elected, instead of that blowfish, Betty Hargate."

"Somehow, that doesn't seem too important right now."

"Yeah, I know." After a moment he said, "My father says the funeral will be Saturday.

Your mother's — your mother will be back here by then."

I turned away and then I got up.

"Where are you going?" he asked, concerned.

"Just for a walk on the beach."

"Want company?"

"Not right now," I said. I threw him a smile and walked away.

It seemed as if the terns were following me, circling overhead. Against the horizon, I saw a cargo ship heading south. The ocean was calming, the tide more gentle than I had ever seen it. I walked close enough so my bare feet would be washed by the tip of the waves. The cool water felt wonderful, like some magic balm.

One of my science teachers told me that scientists believe all life came from the ocean and that was why we were all fascinated by it, drawn to it. Somehow, the sound of the surf, the feel of the spray on my face, the sharp smell of the salt air in my nostrils, and the freshness of it filling my lungs was comforting. A thousand sympathy cards, a thousand mourners in church, dozens of sermons, and hours of organ music couldn't bring any more consolation than the cry of the terns and the sight of the seemingly endless blue water. It revived me and gave me the strength to do battle with my own sadness.

The funeral was two days later. The church service for Mommy's funeral was long and very impersonal. Of course the casket was closed. The minister barely mentioned her name. Because she was a member of the Logan family, the church was filled to capacity. Grandma Olivia, regal as ever, ran the service with a nod of her head, a turn of her eyes, the lifting of her hand. Cars were drawn up instantly and the procession moved on to the cemetery. There, beside Grandma Olivia's father and mother, my mother's remains were laid. The minister said his words and pressed my hands. I was in a fog most of the time, but when I turned away from the grave, I saw Kenneth Childs off to the side watching. He wore a dark blue sports jacket and a pair of slacks. He actually looked rather handsome. His father, the judge, had been at Grandma Olivia's side throughout the funeral.

Cary was as surprised as I was to see Kenneth attending, even if he stood apart from the party of mourners. He left before I could say anything to him.

I went back to school the following Monday to take my finals. All of my teachers were sympathetic, but I asked for no special treatment. Studying helped take my mind off the tragedy. Cary worked hard to prepare for his exams as well. The day after they ended, Cary, Aunt Sara, May, and even Uncle Jacob surprised me at breakfast.

It was my birthday. I had vaguely thought about it but between studying and taking exams and all the tragedy, the event didn't have any meaning or joy for me. Somehow, they remembered and there were presents waiting for me at the breakfast table. I opened May's first. It was a tape recorder. She explained how she picked it out by herself and paid for it with her own money. She said she wanted me to tape myself practicing on the fiddle and singing. I thought it was amazing that someone so young would think so selflessly of those around her. She was truly like a little angel. I kissed and hugged her.

Aunt Sara and Uncle Jacob had bought me two gifts. One was a gold dress watch and the other was a pretty white cotton sundress with pastel embroidery trim. The hem was at least five inches above the knee. I was quite surprised, but Aunt Sara explained she had asked the shop owner for something fashionable and then had convinced Uncle Jacob it was proper and nice and something Laura would have loved.

Cary whispered that he had my gift on the sailboat.

"Taking you sailing today is my first gift," he explained. After breakfast, that was exactly where we went. He made it all look easy, and in minutes we were riding the waves, both of us screaming at the spray and laughing at the fish we saw jumping out of the water. When we settled into a calm for a few moments, he handed me a small, gift-wrapped box. I opened it to find an I.D. bracelet. On each side of the inscription, Melody, was a musical note.

"Look on the back," he said and I turned it over.

May there always be wind in your sails.
Love, Cary

"This is beautiful, Cary. Thank you," I said and leaned over to give him a kiss on his cheek, but just as I did, he turned his head and my kiss fell on his lips. He smiled.

"Happy birthday, Melody," he said.

I sat back, stunned. I put on my I.D. bracelet and we continued our wonderful sail.

As we walked up from the beach later in the afternoon, I saw Cary squint and then I heard him say, "I'll be damned."

I gazed toward the house.

"What?"

"Kenneth Childs's jeep is in our driveway," he said. We glanced at each other and quickened our pace. When we reached the house, we hurried inside to find Kenneth sitting in the living room with Uncle Jacob and Aunt Sara.

"Well now, how was the sailing?" Uncle Jacob asked quickly.

"It was good, Dad," Cary said. We both looked at Kenneth, who sat with his legs crossed. He wore a light brown safari jacket and khaki pants with sneakers, no socks. "Well, you two know Kenneth Childs, apparently. You've visited him, I discover."

"Aye," Cary said. He nodded at Kenneth, who was concentrating on me. My heart was thumping.

"Hello," I said.

"I didn't know today was your birthday," he said. "Happy birthday."

"Thank you."

"Kenneth has come with a proposal. Seems you told him you weren't doing much this summer, Melody."

"I had plans, but they have changed."

Kenneth didn't smile. Instead, his eyes darkened.

"I've decided I need an assistant," he said, "to help with the slave work, do odd jobs around the house and the studio, take Ulysses for walks," he added with a smile. "Naturally, I would like someone who has an appreciation for art and understands a little about my needs."

"Oh," I said. I glanced at Uncle Jacob, who looked very satisfied with himself.

"It's a trip to get out to my place, I know. But I get up early every morning to do my

530

shopping. Beat the tourists," he added looking at Uncle Jacob, who nodded. "I could swing by and pick you up. Of course, I would see to it that you were brought home."

"Well?" Uncle Jacob said.

"I guess . . ." I looked at Cary, who looked even more amazed than I felt. "Sure," I said. "I'd like that."

"Okay. Jacob and I have settled on a salary we both feel is fair," Kenneth said.

"I think you should discuss that with me," I blurted.

Uncle Jacob lost his self-satisfied expression and Kenneth smiled.

"Absolutely. I was thinking of a hundred a week. And food of course," he said. "Is that fair?"

"Yes, it is," I said not really knowing if it was or not, but happy I had taken control of my life.

"Then, it's settled. You can start right after the last day of school. Oh," he said standing, "you can bring your fiddle along. Ulysses likes music."

He started out, Uncle Jacob following. Cary and I gazed at each other with surprise again and then I looked at Aunt Sara who seemed confused as she stared at me. It was as if she had discovered I wasn't the person she had thought I was. It gave me a chill. I tried smiling at her. She smiled back, and then I offered to help with dinner. But it was

531

to be a special dinner because of my birthday: she wanted to do it all herself.

We had lobster and shrimp, wonderful home fries and mixed vegetables, Portuguese bread and a chocolate birthday cake. May helped blow out the candles and sang along with everyone else. I thanked them all. Even Uncle Jacob looked calmer, softer. How complex and confused all the people in my life now had become, I thought.

Cary pleaded with me to play the fiddle and finally I gave in. I brought it down and played for them. Afterwards I went outside for a walk with Cary. The stars blazed above, barely a wisp of a cloud to block their majestic beauty.

"Why do you think Kenneth's done this?" I asked him.

"It's probably the easiest way he knows to get to know you and to eventually tell you the truth," Cary said. "I'll come by as much as I can to see if everything's all right."

"You don't have to worry so much about me."

"Of course I do," he said. He smiled. "I see you wore Laura's scarf tonight. That's nice."

"Somehow, because of all that's happened, I feel closer to her than ever," I said.

He smiled softly and reached for my hand. Then he turned me toward the ocean. We stood there, listening to the surf. In the roar both of us heard voices, his different from mine, of course. And then we walked back to the house under a downpour of starlight.

Epilogue

Who I Am

The auditorium was filled to capacity. People even stood in the rear. Mrs. Topper said it was the biggest variety show they had ever had. I knew that many people had come to see and hear me play. The principal, Mr. Webster, revealed that when he came around to wish us all good luck.

"I knew a fiddle would attract interest," he said, but I understood many people hadn't come to hear the music so much as to see Olivia Logan's new granddaughter.

Everyone in the family attended, even Uncle Jacob. None of the students, except for the ones who had been at our rehearsal, had ever heard me play. Some of the girls came to laugh. I know the three witches from *Macbeth* had. They found themselves front-row seats. Behind them sat Adam Jackson with his friends and girl friends surrounding him, all woven together with giggles of ridicule.

Most of the other students in the show

sang or played guitar. One student played "Carnival of Venice" on the trumpet. It was a performance that brought the house down. Two girls performed part of a scene from *The Taming of the Shrew*, and a boy juggled eggs. When one splattered at his feet, the audience roared and cheered. He was embarrassed, but he continued to do his act until they stopped laughing and applauded.

After so much talent, I felt even more nervous. When it came to my performance, I waited in the wings while Mrs. Topper introduced me as the newest student. There was polite applause when I walked out onto the stage. I could feel all eyes fixed on my every movement. I was wearing the new dress Aunt Sara and Uncle Jacob had bought me. I also wore my identification bracelet, as well as what had once been Laura's charm bracelet.

I don't know what made me want to do this after so much sadness. I could easily have been excused, but I felt Papa George especially would have been proud to see me on the stage. My fingers trembled so badly when I started, however, that I hit a sour note. Those waiting for me to fail roared and clapped. I stopped, took a deep breath, and looked beyond the audience. I looked back through time and saw Papa George on his patio, his pipe in his mouth. I saw Mama

Arlene sitting on the lounge and then I heard Daddy shout, "Wait for me!"

I turned on the stage as if he were running from our trailer to Papa George and Mama Arlene's, and when he sat down, I lifted the bow.

The audience grew quiet. I began to play "Beautiful Dreamer" and closed my eyes to sing. When I did, I saw my Daddy's smiling face. He had loved me so much. Perhaps he never told me the truth because he had come to believe I really was his daughter, or perhaps he didn't want me to ever love him less.

I could never love him less.

The music and my singing continued. Papa George was smiling, Mama Arlene beamed.

Somewhere behind me, Mommy was chattering, complaining that, as usual, we hadn't waited for her.

Daddy told her to stop chewing on her lip and hurry over. I was about to begin another one. She joined him, and for a moment we were a family again, untouched by lies and deceits, without jealousies and fears. Our smiles glowed, love was in our eyes, and I wished only that this moment could go on forever.

I played harder to keep it so.

I was singing too — my voice had never been as strong, never so filled with hope. I was so into my own performance, I had nearly finished before I realized the entire audience had joined with me, even the students who had come to mock me.

Cary was beaming. Aunt Sara was smiling broadly and Uncle Jacob was nodding as if he had seen something special. Even May, who had experienced so much less, clapped and shouted my name. Grandma Olivia looked pensive and Grandpa Samuel was shaking his head and laughing.

Way in the rear, I thought I saw Kenneth Childs standing by the door. Before the deafening applause ended, he had disappeared.

But he would be there that first morning as he had promised.

I waited for him on the porch. The morning sun wasn't very old or high and the air was still quite cool. Cary had already gone to the boat with Uncle Jacob. May was still asleep and Aunt Sara was cleaning up after breakfast, humming to herself, pausing occasionally as if she heard Laura's voice, and then nodding and smiling and going on as usual.

His jeep made the turn toward the house. A long time ago, perhaps, my mother waited like this for him. That was before the great lies began and, like some monster, took over all our lives for a long time.

This was the beginning of the end of that, I thought. This was the beginning of truth.

Lies had brought me here, but I would stomp them out. There was a reason for all this then.

Kenneth Childs knew it too. He was coming to get me because in his heart, he had seen and heard a similar voice. The voice that had said, "Tell her. Let her know who she is."

We hope you have enjoyed this Large Print book. Other G.K. Hall & Co. or Chivers Press Large Print books are available at your library or directly from the publishers.

For more information about current and upcoming titles, please call or write, without obligation, to:

G.K. Hall & Co.
P.O. Box 159
Thorndike, Maine 04986
USA
Tel. (800) 223-2336

OR

Chivers Press Limited
Windsor Bridge Road
Bath BA2 3AX
England
Tel. (0225) 335336

All our Large Print titles are designed for easy reading, and all our books are made to last.